LOSING LOVE

What Will Be - Book Two

Laura Ashley Gallagher

First published in 2021

ISBN: 978-1-3999-0556-5

Visit www.lauraashleygallagher.com to read more about Laura Ashley and her upcoming releases. You can sign up for her e-newsletters so that you're always first to hear about her new releases, updates and exclusives. You can also find her on Facebook, Instagram, and Tiktok.

DEDICATION

For my mother,
Thank you for showing me that the love between a mother and daughter is
forever and for always.

PART ONE

Lost

PROLOGUE

"Hey, baby. I'm guessing you're getting ready, which is why you left your man to go straight to voicemail. I'm joking. I can't wait to see you. Sorry, I'm running a little late. I got caught up at practice with Garry. I'll be at your house in fifteen minutes. Missed you this week. The movie starts at eight, so we have time to grab something to eat first. There's a jerk in a car in front of me, swerving everywhere. What the hell is he doing? I think he might be drunk, so I better hang up. Love you. Oh, before I go. I totally forgot to tell you…"

ONE

Six Years Ago - Then

I had everything I wanted.

I had him, and our life was on the right path.

Until it wasn't anymore.

Why him? Why did it have to be him?

I asked myself that so often; it felt like my chest was going to explode.

What did I expect?

For weeks, I sat there watching him wither away. I was the definition of helpless.

His muscular frame had shrunk, the sparkle in his brown eyes diminished, and his once-booming voice was weak. What was most worrying—he had no eagerness for life. Not anymore. He left his fight in the car that night, or it flew from his body and through the windscreen just like his head.

I swallowed back the bile in my throat.

But I could get him back. He was in there somewhere. I refused to lose hope when I searched his face and couldn't find the man who used to hold me with so much heat I could melt.

We'd work hard and get everything back because together, we could conquer anything. I needed him to get healthy again. The hope would return to his eyes, I'm sure of it.

Only three weeks before, I thought I'd lost him. He was so badly injured, his face was unrecognizable, and it took me hours to accept it was him.

When I noticed I missed his phone call, I checked my voicemail, and at once knew something was wrong. Every nerve in my body stung with an icy chill, and my legs were running out the door before I could even comprehend what I was doing.

Five minutes away from my house, the ambulance was already on the scene, dragging his lifeless body onto a stretcher. I never felt fear like it, as if all the heat left my body, and my blood had turned to water. I screamed when they forced me back, kicking and screaming as a firefighter yanked me around the waist. They had to cut him from the car and wouldn't allow anyone to ride with him to the hospital. I didn't want him to die alone.

I hadn't told him I loved him that day.

After his surgery, he laid in the intensive care unit in an induced coma. No one gave much hope for his outcome. And if he did wake, doctors weren't sure in what state.

A week later, his tubes were removed, and they brought him round. My body functioned on fear and anticipation. Fear won in the end when he woke with voiceless screams.

After, he laid there, staring into the abyss with his mind in torment. He remembered nothing about that night. From what police gathered, he was correct about the drunk driver. The man in front had steered onto the other side of the road, driving directly into a passing truck, and Nick's car was hit with the brunt force of both vehicles. It was a miracle he made it out alive.

I smoothed my hand over his forehead and adjusted his oxygen tube.

"Do you need anything?" I whispered.

He said nothing and simply nodded. His eyes never left the white tiles of the ceiling. Waves of frustration, anger, and helplessness washed over his gaze all at once. He was twenty years old. He loved sports, hiking, and swimming. But he couldn't walk anymore. They said he would, but he would have to learn again, and he'd never get his full strength back.

Most of the time, he dipped in and out of consciousness. Tiredness overrode everything else his body commanded of him. Each time, before he dozed off, he murmured, "Mandy, I forgot to tell you something." As if sleep brought him back to the moment before the crash. His last words to me before he welcomed blackness.

It plagued me, gnawing slowly in the back of my mind. But he never remembered when he woke.

His neck cracked painfully as he turned his head. Pale eyes locked with mine, and he enchanted me completely. When he looked at me, life left only the two of us, and everything in the room faded away. The thought of no longer having him pained me deeply and battered my body from the inside out.

"What is it?" he asked, noticing how I was looking at him. His words cut short as each painful breath escaped from his chapped lips.

I shook my head. "Nothing," I replied softly.

I didn't want to tell him my life would be unbearable without him. I wanted to grab him by the arms and shake him. Beg him not to give up. I wanted him to fight for himself. For me. For us.

His lifeless body clung to the hospital bed so much I thought I might be able to peel him off. He was so weak, blinking came as a struggle, and he was so different from the Nick he once was.

He fought so hard to come through it. But he seemed too tired to go on hoping everything would work out okay.

His lack of hope scared me the most.

"I wish I could make you happy again," he mumbled, rubbing his thumb across the flesh of my palm.

His lips trembled, and I fixed the blanket, but I didn't think he was cold.

Inhaling deeply, I wiped the strands of hair from my face with my free hand.

"You always make me happy. Every day," I said as I kissed his hand. "You are everything to me. Don't you dare think otherwise."

The way he looked at me made my heart tighten and misty tears burned my eyes.

Was I asking too much by expecting him to continue fighting this horrible battle? I wasn't stupid. I could see his fight sourly turning into a struggle.

With that, there was a light tap on the door, and I quickly brushed away the tears threatening to fall.

"Am I interrupting?" His mother's slim figure stood against the door frame.

I admired her so much. Even then, when her son was sick, she dressed so elegantly. I'm sure it was for Nick's sake. She didn't want him to know how hard it was for her. Unfortunately, the dark circles around her eyes betrayed her efforts.

"Of course not, Kate," I answered.

Stepping into the room, her heels clicked against the tiles. She kissed her son and sat on the edge of the bed.

"You can go home, babe. You've been here all day."

I checked my watch, surprised at how fast the time had gone. My time at the hospital usually passed at a snail's pace.

I tried to object, but a yawn cracked through my cheeks and my eyes watered.

"Go home," he warned, squeezing my hand. "Get some sleep."

"Nick, I'm fine."

But I knew he wouldn't give up.

"Mandy, I love you but go home. Please."

"Are you sure?" I asked, swallowing the fearful lump growing in my throat. I hated leaving him. Anything could happen.

Though I needed a shower.

He raised his hand and tucked my hair behind my ear. "I'm sure babe. I'll see you tomorrow."

Standing from the chair, I could feel my legs throbbing as the blood rushed through my veins. I leaned over and kissed him, hugging his mother before heading for the door.

"I love you," he called after me.

I winked, tapping on the door frame. "I love you too."

It took all my power not to fall asleep at the wheel. I parked in front of my house, almost bumping into the back of my mother's car. I was beyond relieved when my father opened the door before I could root through my bag for my keys.

"Hey sweetheart," he chimed with a bright smile.

I love my dad, but I couldn't find the energy to talk to him. I could hardly keep my eyes from closing.

"Hey Dad," is all I managed. Any conversation with my father would have to wait. All I wanted was a hot shower and my bed.

But even the shower could wait until morning.

I almost drifted off to sleep in my struggle upstairs.

"Ouch," I groaned with a loud thud, snapping out of my daze after my toe clipped the edge of the top step and I plunged to my knees.

"Ugh. Why am I so clumsy?"

In my bedroom, I kicked off my shoes and flopped belly first on the bed.

The streetlight from outside shone on my face, reflecting on my skin. It was then, as the streetlights dimmed, I heard light knocks on the door.

I didn't bother to move. "Come in."

My bed dipped when my older brother, Matt, sat on the edge. He took some time off from college for a few weeks to be with me while dealing with Nick. My mother worried I wouldn't open up to anyone but my brother. She was right. I talked to Matt about everything. But with this, I couldn't. I preferred to deal with things myself, in my own way, and that meant keeping things inside until I got home at night. Then I'd cry until I tired myself out.

Matt was good to me, though. He never pushed me to talk. He often sat with me until my tears dried, or I went to sleep without saying a word.

My brother knew me better than I knew myself, which is why I loved him so much.

He was about to switch on my bedroom lamp when I caught his hand.

"Don't you dare. You'll be wearing the lampshade," I warned him, but he only smiled at me. Even in the darkness, I saw his smile turn sorrowful. He was going to ask about Nick.

"He's fine." I yawned before he said anything.

"I was going to ask how *you* are?"

"Tired," I retorted.

"Sorry, sis." He attempted to stand, but I pressed down on his thigh.

I needed to stop being such a bitch.

"It's okay. I'm doing fine."

He scrubbed a hand over his face. "I'm worried about you. You're spending every minute at the hospital. You love him. I know, but it can't be good for you. You'll get sick because you're not eating or sleeping."

I wanted to remind him I was about to sleep until he came in, but I bit the inside of my cheek.

"I'm fine."

"No, you're not, Mandy. And Nick hates seeing you wear yourself

9

out. Just ease off on yourself. If not for me, for Nick."

But I wanted to do things for him. He was almost stolen from me.

"I'm doing it to make him happy. I was so close to losing him. And losing him means I lose everything, Matt."

"I know." He smoothed the curls of my caramel hair. "But Nick needs you and only you. He appreciates everything you do, but he only wants you." He stayed silent for a long second. "Do me a favour. Go back to college on Monday. You haven't been there since the accident. Occupy yourself with something other than the hospital."

I knew he was right. If I wanted to get into my final year of university with Nick, I would have to focus more on my assignments.

The thoughts of going back there made my blood run cold. Eyes of sympathy and pity would follow me everywhere. I didn't want their stupid pity. I wanted a normal life. I wanted to go back in time and tell him not to get in his car that night. We didn't need to go on a date, but I insisted we spend more time together.

Guilt rose inside me, and tears stung my eyes.

"Fine. I'll go back. But I swear, if one person looks at me like my world is about to fall apart, I will not be responsible for my actions."

He chuckles. "We will stand by you in the courtroom."

"You better. Now, can I please get some sleep?"

The light from outside disappeared as he closed my curtains.

"Night, sis," I heard him say. He sounded miles away. I already succumbed to a darkness of my own—my sleep.

TWO

Then

Returning to university was the nightmare I thought it would be. Glares from across the hall and pitiful glances as I walked through the corridors. The campus was big, but not big enough for the anonymity I needed.

The student union organized a candlelight vigil the night after the accident. I appreciated the sentiment, and I also hated it. Why was everyone acting like he was dead?

Some looked disgusted as I glanced around the halls, and I knew what they were thinking. They wanted to know why I wasn't at the hospital, nursing my ill boyfriend back to health. But nothing they were thinking was as bad as what was in my head. I punished myself every minute I was there because I should have been with him. But if I wanted him to have hope, then I needed to have some too. I needed to show him that life would be normal when he got home. We could do it together.

The only people to treat me with a semblance of normality were my close friends. I gave them a stiff warning before they walked with me to class.

"Don't even think about it. I know you think I'm the biggest bitch to walk the planet, but I'm here against my will."

Their eyes narrowed in confusion.

"We don't think you're a bitch, Mandy. We're proud of you," my friend Claire assured, pursing her red glossed lips.

"We think it's great you're here. You were spending too much time at the hospital. Nick was sick of looking at your face," Garry said, rubbing my hand and tugging at me to walk with them.

"Gee, thanks."

I attempted to turn back on my way, but they dragged me along.

"Guys, I can't stand this. I should go home."

"You don't have a hope, Mandy Parker. I'm not opposed to throwing you over my shoulder. We'll be by your side the entire way." Garry smirked ruefully.

It was times like that I wished I was a loner with no friends; someone nobody knew. Getting attention was fine with me, providing it was for the right reasons. Sympathy has always been my worst nightmare. The tilt of people's heads as they spoke to me like I brought a puppy to class.

I grunted loudly for extra measure, but I knew all of this was for Nick. He deserved this, and so much more.

Inhaling a calming breath, I focused on keeping my eyes trained on the ground. If I couldn't see the sympathy, it wasn't there.

Claire caught my hand before I had the chance to walk further. I raised my head to meet her eyes. Deep blue orbs glazing and the small dent on her chin wobbled. She was holding back tears, and I hated it. I reached out, stroking my palms along her upper arms in my best attempt to bring her heat and comfort. My friends felt this as much as I did. We'd been together since we were four.

"He's going to be fine," I reassured her, wishing my voice sounded more confident.

She swallowed, biting on her red lip. "I know," she choked.

"And I'll be fine, too. I have Garry with me today."

Claire studied social care, while Garry and I both had ambitions of becoming teachers. None of our classes crossed paths and I could see it scared her to leave me alone. Or maybe she was the one afraid to be alone. I pulled her into a tight hug, holding her against me as her shoulders rattled.

"I love you. I know it's hard, but we will get through this. Before we know it, Nick will walk these corridors with us again."

I was making promises I didn't know I could keep, but she needed it. And to be honest, I did too. Because I didn't know where Nick would be the next day, let alone in a year. Would he walk again? If he couldn't, how would he cope?

All I knew: there were many bridges to cross.

She leaned away from me, wiping the fresh moisture from her cheeks before hugging Garry.

"Look after her," I heard her whisper before she ran her fingers through her long, mocha-coloured hair and turned to walk to her class.

My eyes followed her, and I wished I could have run after her and brought her with me. Maybe she'd enjoy teaching.

Garry threw a hand across my shoulder, gently kissing my temple. "Ready?"

"No. But let's get this over with." I shrugged, wrapping my hand around his waist.

I was grateful for his support because my legs felt weak. We needed each other. Nick was his best friend, and he was with him ten minutes before the accident.

"Garry?" I said, looking up at him. I had to ask because I needed the jumbled thoughts to settle. It shouldn't have bothered me, but it did. "Do you know what Nick needed to tell me? Did he say anything to you at practice before he left?"

His eyes roamed around the halls, searching in his mind for an answer before he lifted his shoulders and his mouth turned down. "Sorry. He said nothing to me. I'm sure he'll tell you."

"Maybe."

I kept my eyes on the floor, tracing the pattern of the red tiles all the way to our early education class.

Sitting in our usual spot in the middle row, I scribbled aimlessly on my notepad as our professor, Teresa Morgan, entered the large hall. The lecture theatre was full of close to two hundred pupils and she still found me. When her gaze landed on me, she halted at the door, like an invisible barrier prevented her from walking inside. It would seem I had that effect on people.

I'd only attended two weeks of college since the term started in August. It was the end of September now, and somehow, the entire campus knew who I was. I was the girlfriend of the guy who was almost killed by a drunk driver.

Teresa continued her walk to her desk, and her inexperienced eyes sagged with sadness.

Breathe.

Frustration bubbled all the way to my fingertips.

She had been my lecturer since starting college a year ago. She was great, and I liked her instantly. But she was looking at me through half-lidded eyes, and I didn't want to snap at her. She was in her early thirties at most, with rainbow hair and a smart suit. She was a complete contradiction, and I loved it. But she looked at me like I was the older one. Somehow, my experience over the last weeks had brought me maturity. Or maybe the bags under my eyes made me appear older.

I gritted my teeth and reminded myself to purchase eye cream.

"Good morning," Teresa began with a shaky voice, all the while keeping her eyes on me. Her lips moved in slow motion. Something about a chapter on child psychology in our textbooks. Garry nudged me, prompting me to follow. And I did, opening the book like it weighed a tonne.

Everything felt too normal, and it was suffocating. The world kept spinning while I was stuck somewhere in the middle, unable to find the right time to jump off and join everyone else. I wanted to. I think I did. But I couldn't jump off without Nick, and I refused to leave him behind because he was my world. Since the first time he nervously moved in to kiss me when I was fourteen, I was his, and he was mine.

Darting my eyes between my books and the grains of wood on my table, I sensed our lecturer's concerned look penetrate me.

Please, go away.

I heard her ramblings, but only as muffled sounds. My ears zoned in and out, but nothing went through.

"Mandy? Honey, are you okay?" She was close to me. Too close. I shivered, feeling her whisper blow through my hair.

When I dragged my eyes away from the table to see Teresa standing over me, her back was slightly hunched, trying to hide our conversation. It didn't matter. The entire class was looking our way.

"Of course," I answered quickly, fumbling to pick up my pen. "I'm taking notes now."

"You don't have to. Sit and rest."

I understood the place she was coming from, but I didn't want or need her pity. Maybe Teresa wanted to support me the only way she knew how, but I didn't want it. I didn't want anything from anyone.

I wanted Nick here.

I wanted him back.

Garry must have noticed my unease, and he gripped my hand on my lap. I pulled away sharply. Not even his touch could calm me.

"I appreciate your support, but I don't need it." I raised my voice slightly and watched as bodies shifted in their seats.

They could look. I didn't care anymore.

"We know, Mandy. We know it's hard," Teresa added, tilting her head.

Sweet Christ. I didn't bring a puppy.

My chest was going to cave in, squeezing what air I had in my lungs. I stood and spread my palms against the long desk.

"No, I really don't think you know how it feels. With all due respect, do you know how it feels to sit by a hospital bed and watch the person you love wither away before your eyes?" My voice was getting louder.

I tried to check myself, but it was too late. Emotions were boiling over.

I turned, facing those sitting behind me so they could get an excellent view of this breakdown, too. "Don't you dare look at me as if you know what I am going through: as if my life is falling apart. And yes, maybe it is, but it's not for any of you to tell me, and I don't need you to remind me." Hot tears burned the corners of my eyes, threatening to spill over. "I can't handle any of you looking at me like this. He's not dead," I shouted, hardly recognizing my own voice. I didn't expect the loud gasp that escaped me with the realization of my words. I'd never been so blunt about the accident.

I almost lost him.

Fear stiffened my body, every limb becoming rigid. My breathing quickened, and the room began to spin. My incoherent mumbles became muffled as sobs burst through my shoulders. I only noticed my hands trembling when I placed them over my mouth.

"Sit down, Mandy. You're going to faint." Garry pushed me down onto the chair. I obeyed without protest.

The speaker on the wall crackled to life and the secretary's voice boomed. "Can Mandy Parker come to the reception in the Main Hall?"

I stared at the brown box on the wall. The words slowly registered. Me?

I'm Mandy Parker.

Shit.

"Mandy?" Garry cupped my face in his hands, his warmth bringing me back. "Do you want me to go with you?"

15

I shook my head, my mind on autopilot. Then, as if I'd become robotic, I stood on shaky legs. Without saying another word, I walked down the steps of the hall and out the door.

What the hell did they need me for?

My pace quickened as my heart thumped heavy beats against my chest.

I almost passed the office when I saw Matt through the corner of my eye and all feeling dropped to the pit of my stomach.

"Matt, what are you doing…" I trailed off, knowing exactly why he was there. "Oh, God." I held my shaking hand to my mouth.

"I was in the area and it was faster if I came and got you myself. We need to get you to the hospital. I'm sorry, sweetheart, but Nick has taken a turn."

I had already left the room and was heading towards the door, running down the hall as fast as my legs could carry me. Matt grabbed my coat and tugged me backward, closer to his side.

"You're coming in my car. You're in no state to drive."

I didn't argue. I needed to get to the damn hospital.

What the hell happened?

"Don't you dare die. Don't you dare," I repeated, unsure if I was saying it out loud or in my head.

As we pulled in front of the entrance to Saint Andrew's hospital, the door was already open; my legs dangling from the seat, waiting for the truck to stop. I could hear the blood pound furiously behind my ears. My legs ached as I took the stairs two steps at a time, following the route which seemed second nature to me.

Nearing the end of the hallway, I saw his mother slouched uncomfortably over a green chair, her head in her hands and her husband's supportive palm on her shoulder.

Please be alive.

You better be alive.

"Mandy, love, there you are." Kate stood and wrapped her arms around my shoulders. She kept me in her embrace a little longer than needed, and I wondered if she was hiding something from me. "They're working on him."

Working on what?

I'd spoken with him on the phone two hours ago.

I didn't notice the tears running down my face until I saw the stain of my teardrops on Kate's blouse.

It was all happening too fast.

Medical staff rushed in and out of his room.

Then I saw him through an open slate on the blinds. His lifeless body hung limp.

There were so many tubes. Everywhere. All over his body, and his handsome face.

"Blood pressure is dropping," a nurse yelled, and I heard the distant slow beep of a monitor.

Doctor Farley spat out distinct orders. Words I would never understand.

"Blood pressure is still falling. What do you want to do?" the nurse asked anxiously, watching the monitor with wide eyes and a bouncing leg.

"I'll be damned if I'm giving up on him." The doctor leaned over and whispered something in Nick's ear.

"Come on, Nick. Come on. Please," Kate muttered at my side. Her hands were clasped so tightly together, I thought she'd break her fingers.

He can't hear you. What's the use?

I spotted an elderly woman standing outside the next room. Her eyes were rimmed with tears as she watched the scene unfold. With rosary beads entwined in her hands, I heard, "Hail Mary, full of grace. The lord is with thee…." She began the prayer slowly, pronouncing each word carefully as if his life depended on every syllable.

I hope it works.

I was numb. Empty. Like someone could reach back into my throat and find nothing in my chest.

Hollow.

I felt nothing.

I pinched myself to make sure it wasn't a nightmare.

I wasn't so lucky.

The corridor spun. The blood in my legs was icy, and my bones turned to jelly. I stumbled over my own two feet, but Matt caught me before I fell face-first onto the tiled floor.

"Whoa! Hang in there, sis," he breathed as I supported my weight against him.

"Blood pressure is coming back up," the same nurse bellowed, but the worry never left her small face.

I waited almost thirty minutes, shifting from one leg to another.

Then they cleared away their things and the nurses finally disappeared behind desks outside his room.

Doctor Farley huddled close to Nick's parents. "He is stable for now. We will keep a close watch on him, to be sure. He should wake up soon. He will be groggy, but he should know who you are and where he is."

They asked what happened, but I was already wandering into his room. Sitting in the chair I already spent so much time in, I took his hand and pressed it against my cheek.

"You are such a jerk. Do you know that? Was that your idea of a prank? Are you trying to give me a heart attack?" The tears flowed, hot and fast, and the sobs caught in my throat as I spoke. "God, Nick, don't you ever do that to me again. I should have never gone back there. I should have been here with you."

"There was nothing you could have done for him, Mandy," his mother's voice echoed from the other side of his bed. Her eyes were sore and blotchy. "They even told me to get out."

"I know, but I wish I could have been here. He must have been so scared."

"I know, honey, but he is stable now, and once they run some tests, we will know what happened. He wouldn't want you beating yourself up like this. He's going to wake up any minute, just you wait and see."

I wanted to believe her so much, but I couldn't find the power in myself to do it. What if he didn't wake up? Would this be my last time speaking to him?

As if sensing my unease, his mother said quietly, "He can hear you. You can speak to him."

I nodded slowly and turned back to him. Kate's shadow disappeared towards the door, leaving to give us some privacy.

"Hey, babe," I began, feeling a little stupid. He couldn't even talk back, and I laughed nervously because I knew he'd find this situation hysterical.

What was wrong with me?

I'd been friends with him since the age of four and dating for almost five years. Why couldn't I speak up? Why couldn't I say everything I needed him to hear?

Me and Nick were never people for leaving things unsaid. We told each other how we felt daily. We argued hard and loved harder. I had little to say he didn't already know. At least, I hoped he knew.

"See the big, bright, beautiful light you are looking at. Turn away. It's dangerous, Nick. You don't want to die, you big idiot. So, turn away from the light. It may not look ugly, but once you get past it, it's a whole different story. False advertising, if you ask me." I stopped, hearing him moan quietly.

"You always had a crappy sense of humour." He opened his eyes, his voice tight as if straining to speak. I let out a long breath of sheer relief and tears flooded my eyes, streaming along already soaked cheeks.

"You think I have a crappy sense of humour? You just played dead and think you're going to get away with it." I forced a light-hearted tone, but inside I was crumbling.

He chuckled gently, wincing from the pain it caused.

Before he could reply, his parents rushed in.

"Are you trying to kill this beautiful girl?" His father smiled, a dusting of tears threatening to spill over. "She was having palpitations outside."

Nick turned his head to me, his eyes narrowing. I waved off his father's comment.

"Take no notice," I whispered, leaning my head down to kiss him.

"I love you so much." It was the strongest I'd heard his voice in weeks, and I feared it. It didn't bring me relief, because he mustered the strength from somewhere for a reason.

"I love you too," I replied, putting my hand in his as I feathered his cheek with the other.

But when he closed his eyes again, they remained shut for seconds too long.

"Mandy," he croaked, and his voice caused my heart to constrict. "I forgot to tell you…"

"Nick?" I called as his eyes shut tighter, causing painful creases to line his forehead. But before I could say anymore, they shot open again, and it wasn't in response to his name. They were wide with fear. I watched them swirl back behind his eyelids.

"Nick! Nick!" I screamed, forcing his convulsing body down on the bed.

Doctor Farley sprinted through the door, already barking orders as he approached Nick's violent body. "Hang in there, kid."

I was still screaming, standing at the foot of the bed, my entire body trembling. He couldn't leave me.

19

Nick.

Please.

I was helpless.

Useless.

I couldn't do anything for him.

Closing my eyes, I heard only the chaotic noises filling the room. That was when I heard the beeping on the monitor slow to a pace I'd never heard before. A slowness that made my body drain of colour.

The doctor stared at me worryingly, fear gripping his small eyes. "Can someone get her the hell out of here?"

THREE

Then

"Please, Mandy. Sit down," Kate pleaded.

I was pacing back and forth outside the operating theatre for two hours.

"What the hell is taking them so long?"

Watching Nick have a seizure was something I prayed I would never have to watch again—with anyone. The images of his shaking body overwhelmed my mind, causing a violent headache to bang at my temples.

Doctor Farley approached through swinging doors, still in his scrubs, and removing the disposal hat from his head.

"Miss Parker," he acknowledged. "Mr. and Mrs. Sayres. Please sit down."

My face drained of its colour.

I could feel it.

I could feel the room suddenly becoming a little colder.

"We operated and closed the bleed," he began.

But I knew there was more to come. I could sense his terrified hesitation, see in his eyes that whatever he was about to say next would shatter us without care.

"The cause of Nick's seizures earlier was due to an internal bleed. We closed it, but Nick's heart failed during the procedure. We got it beating, but by the time we did, it was too late. The lack of oxygen to his brain…" he stalled, and I didn't give him the chance to continue.

I knew what he was going to say.

"He's brain dead?" I bit down on my lip to suffocate the threatening sobs.

"I'm sorry. We did everything we could." He lowered his head to the ground.

I expected the words, but it didn't mean I was prepared for them.

"Everything you could?" Kate began to shout in her state of hysteria. "If you had done everything you could, then my boy would be with us."

Her husband took her in his embrace and cradled her like a baby.

I sat in silence with my eyes cast to the ground. I wish I had the ability, but I couldn't cry. As it turned out, shock trumped tears.

Who knew?

"Mandy," the doctor started, facing me. "You should know: last week, Nick wanted to sign some papers." He inhaled deeply before continuing. As if he feared speaking. "When Nick came out of the coma, we knew he wasn't in the clear yet, but I did expect him to recover. He wasn't so positive, and he wanted to be prepared, should something like this happen. Which, unfortunately, it has. He wanted it to be your call—your choice to switch off the life support."

I'm sure the world had stopped spinning.

What the hell was he thinking?

I stared at him, my eyes wide, my expression becoming mad as I felt the space around me close in.

He was joking. He must be joking. This was some sort of sick prank.

"My choice?" My mind couldn't grasp the meaning. I couldn't shake the disbelief, and tension built around my temples. "What is he trying to do to me? Why is this my choice? I can't, I just…"

"It's okay, sweetheart." Kate grabbed my hand. "You can do it."

I turned to her, begging for answers to something I didn't understand.

How was I going to turn off everything that was keeping him alive?

"Did you know about this?" I asked.

How could they allow this to happen? They should have stopped him.

What a shitty decision, Nick.

"Yes, we knew. He's an adult and so are you. We had to respect his choices. And we never thought you'd have to do it. He knew this was going to be hard for you, so he wrote you a letter and gave it to me. He made me promise not to give it to you until something like this happened." Kate dipped her hand into her bag.

The pain tugging at my ribcage was unbearable and I gasped.

I gasped for air.

For understanding.

For Nick to come back.

I gasped because I couldn't stand it.

I accepted it with shaky hands, tears soaking through the paper, and the darkness spreading through the sheet reflected the pain rushing through my body.

"I need some time," I whispered. It was an automatic response because this was so fucked up, I didn't know what else to say.

"Can we see him?" Kate asked.

"Of course. Come with me."

They followed the doctor, but I remained seated. They needed time alone with him.

"Mandy? Darling, are you coming?"

"You go ahead. I'll be there in a bit," I said as my voice broke, endless tears streaming down my face.

She smiled at me gratefully and disappeared around the white corridor.

I knew I had a big decision to make. A decision with only one option.

Air.

I needed air.

Outside, the light mist of rain felt refreshing on my face.

I loved the rain. Everything about it soothed me; the smell, the feel, the noises it made as it pelted against my window at night.

However, right then, it did little to soothe my breaking heart.

***

It was harder than I thought it would be. I expected him to look— I don't know—himself. But he didn't. The circles etching his eyes were pale and dark all at once.

I sat there, watching as his chest moved evenly up and down.

Up and down.

Up and down.

Sometimes, I could hear the huskiness of his throat scratch through the air.

I sat there for four hours.

For four hours I argued with myself.

For four hours I begged him to wake up.

Four hours to realize, he never would.

The machines were doing all the work. I had come to terms with it.

Tears stung my eyes and threatened to spill over, but I wiped them away before they had a chance.

There was a hushed chatter outside.

I didn't release my grip on his hand. I couldn't let go.

Not yet.

The choice I had to make gave me motion sickness. My head swayed back and forth. I wanted to keep him. I wanted to hold his hand and have meaningless conversations about which takeout we preferred. And steal one more kiss. Just one more where he held me and wrapped his arms around my waist like he could shield me from the world.

Instead, the reality of everything persistently knocked, and I couldn't hold it back much longer. I wasn't sure I knew the person lying motionless in the bed. It wasn't Nick. It looked like him, but he wasn't there. He was an empty shell of who he used to be.

I slipped my hand into my pocket and removed the brown envelope.

"Time to face it," I muttered to myself, willing my throat not to close.

My hands trembled as I unfolded the letter. The tears that threatened to spill over crept down my face when I saw his handwriting on the faded blue lines.

To Mandy,

If you are reading this, it means one thing - a machine is keeping me alive.

I'm so sorry I did this to you, but I wanted you to know it's okay to let me go. I want you to move on and find a life without me.

Mandy Parker, I loved no one the way I loved you. I survived this long because of you.

You're beautiful and you're going to find someone who is going to make you happy. When you do, he will be the luckiest guy in the world. You are going to have

24

lots of kids and when they make a friendship as we did, tell them to keep it.

I'm sorry I never got to stand at the top of an aisle and watch you walk towards me. Just remember, I will be there when you do. I will watch with the biggest smile on my face, seeing the most beautiful brown eyes shine with happiness. The happiness you so rightfully deserve.

Don't hesitate in turning off the machine. I'm not there anymore. It's not me.

Let me go, sweetheart.

I love you, Mandy.

Always have, always will,

Nick.

He wanted me to do this.

He needed me to do it, and I had to be brave.

There was distant crying from the corridor. They looked blurry through the waves of tears I imagined were floating in my eyes. I simply dipped my chin, and it told them all they needed to know. I heard them walk into the room, but I refused to look at them. I wanted to be with him for a moment longer.

Really be with him.

Standing, I leaned over to kiss his forehead, and for the last time, I nuzzled my cheek against his.

He was warm.

So warm.

"I love you," I whispered.

I crawled into his arms and rested my head on his chest.

His heartbeat sounded strong, and I wanted so badly to believe it could stay like that. I cuddled closer in his arms for a little longer until I finally built enough courage to look towards the doctor.

"You can do it now."

My hand hovered above his chest as my vision blurred with tears. If we were in a Disney movie, they'd bring him back to life.

With a heavy intake of breath, I tried to block out the clicks of switches and tubes detaching.

I held my breath.

Up and down.

Up and down.

Up. And. Down.

Up.

And.

Down.
Then, nothing.
Everything that told me he was alive—disappeared.

FOUR

Now

I flick through the black folder and sort through my school schedule for the weeks to come. It's coming towards the end of the year and I have a school tour to organize.

I'm still not sure if I'm excited about the experience the kids will have or dreading the absolute chaos that comes with bringing twenty-five children out of the classroom. I'm expecting mayhem and nothing less.

Which reminds me, I need to tell the parents the kids can bring treats, but not to overindulge. It's going to be an exhausting day without overly excited children crashing in unison from the sugar buzz.

Slipping my folder into my black leather bag, I sit back and sip my fresh coffee.

Every Monday after school, I meet Garry at the aptly named Old Book Store. Tucked neatly in the back is a quaint coffee shop with tables scattered throughout the store. It allows the experience of delving into your favourite book while enjoying amazing coffee and the most amazing cakes. Though from outside, you may expect a dark room filled with dusty old books, it's quite the opposite. The space brings comfort and envelopes all those who enter, hugging them close, and inviting them to step inside a fictional world as they do so. Books line high, towering over me in rows on bookshelves.

I watch as both workers busy themselves, although not in any panic, skimming through the pages as they place books on shelves.

"Sorry, I'm late." Garry rushes to take the seat opposite me. "A parent wanted to speak with me."

He drops his laptop bag from his shoulder and onto the carpet.

"The dreaded unscheduled parent-teacher meeting?"

He rolls his eyes in understanding.

"Mrs. Mahony," he answers. His eyes are wide and then sink, exhausted.

I blow out a long breath. I understand the exact feeling. I have the youngest of the Mahony girls in my class, and Garry has the eldest. Sweet girls. Intelligent and funny children. But Mrs. Mahony has visions of them becoming solicitors or neurosurgeons and wonders why her precious angels are not top of the class—as they rightly should be, of course. And any whiff of a minor struggle must be the teachers' fault. The girls excel in most things if I'm being honest, but like any other child, they are learning, and have to get over the odd hiccup here and there. They're eleven and eight, respectively. They want to be pop stars and influencers. It might change. Probably so. But why not let them be children? It doesn't last for long.

I started teaching at Grand Ridge Academy in my first year out of college, four years ago. The school was looking for substitute teachers, and when both me and Garry applied, we got the jobs within two weeks of each other. After one year, we were both offered permanent positions and celebrated with loads of beer, and a bottle of tequila.

I've come to realize over the years, Garry is my constant. The one element that stuck, held my hand, wiped tears, and laughed with me. And we did so much of the latter. None of this is romantic, of course. It never even crossed my mind. We have a brother and sister relationship that sometimes I think he needs more than I do.

After college, we both moved into a small apartment in Penrith Town centre. It's a large beach town that bustles as if it's a city, and we took advantage of the nightlife. We enjoyed that time in our lives. When hangovers were for the weak, and we could still go to school and teach a class of screaming children for the day, albeit poorly. We may have only been twenty-five, but those nights had slowly dissipated and for the better.

I found a small bungalow on the outskirts of Penrith, just ten

28

minutes from the school. I argued if we stayed tied at the hip as we seemed, Garry would never find someone to accept he lived with another woman. And who could blame them?

But I was wrong. He found that someone in Sally. She accepted me as if I was a member of her family, and we've become close friends. She's never jealous of my and Garry's friendship or that we work together. I love seeing him so happy because he deserves it more than I can tell him.

I'm pretty sure there was a promise made to Nick in the past to look out for me, and he certainly hasn't failed him.

"Sally wants to know if you want to come over this weekend?"

I blink, realizing I've been in a daze.

"She's going to ask Claire too. Are you up for it?"

I grimace slightly but smile. "You know Claire still has the constitution of a fish? She can be dangerous with wine."

We both let out a laugh.

"Can you blame her? With her job, I think I'd hit the bottle every night."

I agree, nodding my head with a hum.

"I'm not doing anything else, so why not?" I give in, not sure if I'm making the right decision. I swore after the last time I would never put a drop of alcohol to my lips. I always enjoyed our girls' nights with wine flowing as often as the chatter, but I never seem to learn from the throbbing of my hangovers the following morning.

"And where will you be? Not in the middle of us, I assume?"

"Hardly," he scoffs, taking a mouthful of coffee. "Bachelor party," he explains, and I'm not sure if his expression is defeat or dread.

"We're getting old, honey," I sigh. "When your friends are getting married, you know it's time to get a move on." I eye him, bowing my head. I aim this remark at him, but I can't help feeling a little lost in the moment.

It's been over six years since Nick died, and I still have no desire to meet someone else. I'm not sure if it's because I'm holding on to a love I can't have, or a past no one could possibly accept. Maybe both, but I know I'm not ready. Someday, I hope.

"Yeah, you know you're getting old when you've spent your weekend looking at rings." His announcement is so nonchalant I almost miss it. I choke as the coffee gets stuck in my throat on the way down.

"Garry, you better not be messing with me?" My eyes are wide now, and the stinging I feel is a prickle of tears.

"I'm not." His smile etches up proudly.

"Oh, Garry." I leap from my chair and straight into his arms. I cup his excited face with my palms, placing a chaste kiss on his cheek. "I'm so happy for you."

"Thank you." He squeezes me a little tighter for a long second.

"When? When are you doing it? Does she know?" Too many questions need answering, and if honest with myself, I need this distraction in my life.

The nightmares have started again, as they usually do on nights with empty company and only my memories to keep my mind occupied. I shake my head as if I can physically remove the thoughts. This is Garry's moment, and I don't want to be selfish.

"In two weeks. It's our two-year anniversary, and we had planned to go away for the weekend, anyway. She has no idea, I hope. I'm so nervous, Mandy." He sits down again, wiping his palms along his black slacks, and he suddenly becomes the awkward teenager I remember him being. He brushes his fingers through his flaxen hair and removes his glasses to rub his fingers over the bridge of his nose.

"Relax. She loves you. There's nothing to be nervous about."

I suddenly find myself playing with the locket Nick gave me for our anniversary when I was eighteen. I remember how he placed it around my neck and promised the next piece of jewelry would be an engagement ring. Now it's the sign of a promise never fulfilled.

For so long, I was angry at him. I was angry at him for dying and leaving me behind to deal with so much grief, I was drowning in it. I was so mad he made me turn off those machines. I'm not as angry anymore, but why does it still have to hurt so much?

I bite my lip to distract my mind from running through the horrific memories I've replayed too many times and focus on Garry's excitement.

"I know, and I love her, too. It's just not my thing, this whole ceremony around an engagement."

"Ah, break out the romantic Garry. It's only for one day and she'll appreciate it."

He clasps his hands together, leaning happily into his chair. He seems content. As if floating on air.

He turns back to me, his gaze serious. "How are the nightmares?"

"Not now." I wave my hand in dismissal. "You have just told me the best news ever and you want to talk about my nightmares?"

I should know better because he can read me like a book. Garry has seen it, the effect it takes on my body, day in and day out, particularly at certain times of the year. He was there to wake me when my screams didn't. They aren't as frequent anymore, not in recent years, and I'm grateful for that much. But when they do come, they are nasty and cruel.

"It's one of those things." I shrug at him.

He merely smiles, but it doesn't reach his eyes, and he doesn't press me any longer.

"So," he starts, "I have a guy I want to set you up with. We met through Sally. He's a friend of her brother's. He has his own business, his own house, and doesn't sweat profusely."

I cringe, thinking back to the last blind date I let Garry and Sally set me up on. Garry met him through his football club and although the guy was attractive, built like something from Greek legend, and had brilliant success, we had zero in common. And the guy got so nervous he sweated into his soup. I learned more about protein and how rest days were as important for your muscles as exercise, I can't remember if we actually spoke about anything else. I excused myself at the end of the dinner, citing a headache as my reason for leaving so abruptly. But he made me gag, and I really had a headache from the numbing conversation.

"No thank you," I refuse, frantically nodding my head. "Maybe another time."

He winks at me with a wave of understanding.

"Of course," he agrees, his mouth turning down. "Another time."

I've always been a terrible liar.

FIVE

"Do you want me to walk you to your car?" Garry offers as we exit the bookshop, leaving the warmth and smell of books behind.

"Thanks, but I have to pick up some puppets from the toy shop."

He looks down at me, cocking his eyebrow in question.

"We are putting on a puppet show in a few weeks," I explain.

He chuckles under his breath. "Okay, Miss Honey." He kisses my cheek and hugs me quickly before saying goodbye.

I don't oppose the nickname. Miss Honey from Matilda has always been a favourite character of mine and if I resemble her in my teaching, then I can do so much worse. I've met a few Ms Trunchbull's in my time, though. That's for certain.

I make a quick stop at Poppets Toy Store, the elderly owner knowing exactly what I need. He also guesses I'm a schoolteacher before I even mention it.

Am I so stereotypical?

Earlier, I parked my car two blocks away. But by the look of the angry grey clouds threatening thunder, I quicken my pace, hoping I'll make it back before I get soaked. I clutch the brown paper bag closer to my chest and curse myself for not paying for a plastic one. But I've been teaching the kids about the planet lately and the plastic in the oceans. I couldn't be a hypocrite.

A single drop falls like a brick on top of my head, and I shudder as another one slips down the back of my blouse. As if that single drop is the key to open a gateway to a violent downpour, bitterly cold drops fall like bullets from above and saturate the material covering my shoulders. I let out an involuntary screech and curse once again when I get to the road on Main Street and the red hand on the opposite side signals for me to stay exactly where I am. Cars drive past, one after another, and I pray to whatever heavens to let me cross the damn road before the rest of me becomes sodden.

It was unusually mild earlier, and I slipped off my jacket to leave it in the car.

I shiver, holding the brown bag even tighter as if my arms can somehow keep the paper from falling apart.

Then, as if the gods themselves have answered my prayers, the rain stops falling on me and a shadow appears at my side. I immediately flinch and step quickly aside, the heat from another body startling my icy cold skin. My foot fumbles over the other and I see myself tumbling, as if in slow motion. But before I can hit the ground, a firm grip clutches my upper arm, putting me swiftly back on my two feet.

I look up through wide eyes, my dripping hair sticking to my face, and my heart beats madly.

"Thank you," I finally let out in a gasp, glancing upon warm eyes and an apologetic beam.

"I'm sorry. I didn't mean to frighten you." He gestures towards a large black umbrella covering us both from the elements. "These lights can be a nightmare."

Not sure what to say, I gnaw at my lower lip between my teeth. "Thank you," I repeat; it being the only thing I can vocalize.

I'm grateful to the stranger with the piercing blue eyes. And when I smile in response, his shoulders release his tension. "I'm really clumsy. I appreciate the umbrella," I point up, crushing the now mushy brown paper bag tighter to my chest.

The cars come to a slow stop and the green flashing hand allows us to walk to the other side of the street. All the while, he covers me, protecting me from the downpour.

"Again, thank you." I glance towards him, stepping away, wanting to get quickly to my car, and more than slightly embarrassed by my appearance.

"Wait," he calls out.

I turn hastily, sure I've splashed him with raindrops from my hair. I lean my body back, realizing I almost came too close to the mysterious stranger's face.

"Take the umbrella." He offers me the handle. "I'm parked right here. I don't need it."

As his hand reaches out, I notice the silver cuff links and my eyes wander to his shoulders. Broad, strong, and dressed head to toe in a navy suit.

"But your suit?" I question, eyeing him for a moment too long. It looks too expensive to be ruined by a storm.

"Honestly, this thing makes it out of the closet maybe twice a year, and I really am parked close. Please, take this. It will be my good deed for the day."

I appreciate he has picked me for a choice of good karma, but I blush under wet cheeks, realizing he probably sees me as more of a charity case. Standing there with wet hair falling around my shoulders, sodden brown paper clinging to my fingertips, and a blouse so drenched it's probably see-through.

"Thank you," I say again, unsure now if I have other words in my vocabulary as I reach over and take the umbrella.

"You better get going before it gets any worse?"

As if it could.

I smile again, hoping he will see how grateful I am, and I turn on my heels, running a few steps, careful not to fall as I don't have any free hands to catch myself. I stop, turning my head over my shoulder. I want to get the stranger's name and replace his umbrella, if possible. But he's already running in the other direction and turning right onto a different street.

His car wasn't so close after all.

SIX

On Friday afternoon, after the school bell rings, I tidy up the last of the stray objects from the classroom. I straighten books and hang the last of the colourful paintings on the wall. I key the door as I'm leaving, slipping the dangling metal into my handbag.

"Thank Christ it's Friday." Garry comes strolling from his classroom across the hall.

"Amen," I concur, rolling my neck to rid myself of tension.

"Give me a minute, and I'll walk to the car with you. I'm waiting for someone."

"Who are you waiting for?"

He walks to my side. "A friend of mine. He's meeting with Brenda. He has the contract for the school renovation over the summer. Actually," he starts but stops himself, letting out a slow breath as he runs his fingers through his hair.

I know that look.

"Spit it out."

He flinches away from me. "He's the guy I wanted to set you up with."

My mouth opens wide, and my gasp echoes in the empty halls.

"Garry Miller, you're an absolute moron." I use his full name for extra effect.

"Relax. He has no idea who you are. We never told him who he was going on the date with." He raises his hands in surrender.

"Okay, I'm leaving now. This is so awkward," I moan, feeling my fingers twitch along the strap of my handbag.

"Just wait. It's the bachelor party tonight and I'm running over the times with him. We'll leave then, and you won't even have to speak a word."

I swallow hard, exhaling dramatically before rolling my eyes.

"You're a pain in my ass."

"I don't doubt it. It's my favourite habit." He nudges me with his elbow, leaning his head back with laughter. "Anyway, here he comes."

As the door opens to the principal's office, Brenda steps out first, shaking the man's hand and bidding farewells.

"Alex," Garry calls, walking towards the office.

I lower my eyes to the ground, shuffling my feet forward.

I'm going to kill Garry if this guy knows who I am. After all, I said no to our date.

Coming closer, I notice the man's steel cap boots and muscular legs covered by black cargo pants.

"Alex, this is Mandy," I hear Garry say before I lift my gaze higher up the man's body, eyeing how the khaki t-shirt clings to his muscular chest for a little longer than necessary.

As my head tilts to look up at him, his chestnut brown hair seems oddly familiar. And then my eyes land on his. Piercing blue and staring right at me with his mouth ajar.

"Oh," I let out, involuntarily screeching, pressing my hand over my mouth to stop any more sounds.

"It's you," he says, smirking.

I nod my head, my mouth gaping. "It's you," I repeat his words because I've lost my own.

"You look dryer." He lets out a light chuckle. "It's lovely to meet you." His smile is gentle and warm like before. "Officially," he adds.

I almost choke. He looks the same, but different all at once. The face is the same. Not the choice of clothing. No longer is the crisp suit. Instead, he wears work pants covered in dried paint and what I think is plaster.

"Can someone tell me what's going on?" Garry's finger moves between us.

I open my mouth to say something, but I'm more than a little shocked.

"Just a great coincidence, Garry." He dips his chin, his eyes glancing over at me. "I gave Mandy," he says my name slowly as if asking permission to say it. Somehow, hearing him say it seems too friendly. "I gave Mandy an umbrella in town the other day."

Garry is more dumbstruck than I am. "Shit. That is a coincidence."

I'm sure Garry's glowering at me, but I can't take my eyes away from the man with the intense sapphire eyes.

"Anyway," Garry continues, shaking his head. "What time is everything starting tonight?"

The two men start a brief conversation as I stand there, still unsure of what just happened, running my eyes between them both.

"It was great to meet you properly, Mandy." The man reaches out his hand.

The man?

Christ, I can't think of his name.

Shit.

His fingers easily wrap around mine, and I shake his hand firmly. "You too…" I search my mind but come up empty. His face is too distracting.

"Alex," he finishes for me, still smirking.

That's his name.

How embarrassing.

The men say their goodbyes, agreeing to see each other later this evening.

As we make our way outside, I feel Garry glaring at me from the corner of my eye.

"What?" I clap.

"That was a crazy coincidence."

I nod, unable to find words.

"And Alex was flirting with you and you were gawking at him like a deer in headlights."

"Oh God, Garry. Don't tell me that." I cringe, feeling a rush of blood to my face. I throw my hands over my cheeks.

"You're out of practice, that's all." He wraps a supportive arm around my shoulder.

"I was never in practice," I squeal, my shoulders falling. "I don't flirt. Nick and I were fourteen when we got together. The extent of my flirting was offering to make the microwave popcorn."

I see him purse his lips, fighting back laughter.

"It's okay. You can try again tonight. He's coming to my house with

Sally's brother for a beer before we go out."

My face falls. I can almost feel it hit the floor.

"I don't want to flirt with anyone," I say as I open the door to my car.

"You sure?" Garry chuckles. "Because I don't think I have ever seen you gawk at a man before."

"I… I didn't. I need to go, Garry," I stutter, embarrassed and slightly hot.

"See you later." He winks at me with suspicious eyes.

I start my car, wondering why the hell my hands are suddenly trembling.

SEVEN

I bite nervously down on my lip before knocking on the door to Garry and Sally's house. I stopped to pick up a bottle of wine on my way, but with my nerves getting the better of me, I thought two bottles would be more appropriate. If I don't drink them both, Claire will.

I grip both cold bottles under my arm, brushing down imaginary wrinkles from my blouse. For a reason I am yet to understand, I spent extra time preparing my outfit. Usually, on a girl's night, the cab driver is lucky to see me in something that doesn't resemble pajamas. But tonight, I am wearing my red cuffed blouse, black jeans, and boots and have even gone to the effort of freshening my make-up.

The door flies open, Claire leaning into her hip on the other side, sipping from her wine glass. The smile spreading across her face is playfully evil, and her eyes scrunch into a line.

"Well, hello Mandy Parker. You look edible." Claire chuckles, throwing her free arm around my shoulders.

I close my eyes and sigh.

Am I that obvious?

"Hey." I kiss her cheek. "Thank you. I made the effort for you tonight," I lie, laughing along, and dying inside.

"Me? Sure, it was."

I glare into Claire's ocean blue eyes, her long hair swaying almost to her elbows, and her arm falls to her side.

"Garry told you?" I moan, rolling my eyes.

"Of course, I told her," Garry interrupts, leaping down the stairs towards us, and taking the bottles from me.

"Musketeers don't keep secrets," Claire reminds me, slapping my ass as we follow Garry into the kitchen.

He smiles over a generous glass of wine and hands it to me across the kitchen island. He opens a bottle of beer and sits with us.

"Where's Sally?" I query, looking around for any sign of her.

"She'll be down soon. She's in the shower."

I look towards Claire, and she's still eyeing me suspiciously. "How come you are here so early?"

She shrugs her narrow shoulders, waving her hand. "I didn't get out of work until almost seven, and I didn't have the energy to go home and change. It was a tough day. This wine is needed." She leans over the counter, staring into her liquid.

"How is work?"

Claire's finding it difficult lately. Given our history, and with her social care degree, Claire works with children. Unlike Garry and I, where we are lucky enough to see mostly the good parts, and children turn up to school happy. Claire doesn't always get to see that in the foster care system. It's taking its toll and from the limited information she can give her friends, I understand exactly why. Some of Claire's stories are horrifying, filled with neglect and abuse. She's become attached to her kids on more than one occasion, and she can't handle the situations when the children go back to their abusive parents. They claim and for a short time show, they've changed, only for the kids to go back into the system within months.

"It is what it is." Claire shrugs as Sally comes jogging into the kitchen in her sweatpants, swinging her towel from her wet hair.

"Ladies, the party has arrived. Babe, get your woman some wine." She points towards Garry, shimmying her way towards us before wrapping Claire and me in a group hug.

Sally gives me the once-over with her eyes but doesn't say anything. She takes the wineglass from Garry and positions herself on the high stool opposite.

"Mandy," she begins, "I hear you got acquainted with Alex." She sniggers into her glass.

Oh, for the love of God.

"I met the guy twice," I remind them, feeling uncomfortable with the line of questioning.

"Yeah, but we also heard about how you bumped into him. Have you ever heard of fate?"

I must admit, it was a major coincidence, but we lived in a beach town. It could have happened to anyone, couldn't it?

"Alex is a great guy," Sally goes on. "He's been friends with my brother since college. He built my parent's new house."

I shake my head slowly, unsure if I should ask for more. I don't want to seem too eager and put myself in the line of more embarrassing questions.

Without a chance for a second thought, the doorbell erupts our conversation.

"Speak of the devil," Garry says as he gets up to answer the door.

I put my wineglass back on the counter. My hands begin to tremble, and I feel my skin get clammy. I'm not accustomed to this reaction to the opposite sex. I'm not blind. I can appreciate a gorgeous man when I see one, but the ability to interact with one is a different story.

And I can sense him. Before I hear the boom of his voice or see his powerful presence standing at the door frame, I know he's there. A tingle creeps down the back of my neck. Claire glances at me again, winking supportively.

"Good evening, ladies." Alex steps into the kitchen, looking fresh in his charcoal slacks and white shirt.

Claire stands to shake his hand, and I notice how, without an ounce of shame, her eyes wander over his tall stature.

It isn't until Claire sits back down and Garry hands Alex a beer that our eyes find each other. He takes a step closer, and the smell of his heavenly cologne fills my senses. I suddenly feel a little lightheaded.

"Mandy." He motions closer. I put out my hand, but he doesn't take it, and a shiver claws at my lower back when his lips press against my cheek. "It's lovely to see you again." He winks with a soft smile.

I stutter for a moment; my tongue tangled in my mouth. "You too." I let out a breath.

As if time has suddenly caught up with us both, we look around the kitchen to three pairs of eyes gawking at us.

"We'll head out to the back garden," Garry finally interrupts the silence, leading Alex to the decking to enjoy the last of the evening sun.

The breath I've longed for finally fills my lungs, and I slump back on the stool. I'm not sure what that was, but it made my tummy feel funny and my head is spinning.

"Christ," I let out.

Claire and Sally look at me, mystified.

"What the hell was that?" Claire's eyes are wide, and her voice is a harsh whisper.

"Jesus, Mandy, whatever type of tension that was, you could cut through it with a knife," Sally bursts in.

I don't know what to say, and I can't lie. I felt it. A spark of some kind, pinching at my skin.

How cliché.

"I have goosebumps. It suddenly got awful hot in here." Claire fans the collar of her shirt.

"Can we talk about something else? He's right outside," I warn, darting my eyes towards the garden.

After an hour, the men are putting on their coats to leave. Sally stands to walk Garry to the door and say goodbye, and Claire has made her first wine-fuelled trip to the bathroom. Her timing is impeccable.

My eyes lower to the ground, his charge filling the kitchen, leaving me stuck for words.

"Mandy?" Alex says, his eyebrow cocked. When I look at him, he grins, and my chest feels like it has flipped. "I hope I see you again soon."

I swallow dryly, finding a new interest in my nail polish. But the words leaving my mouth are almost involuntary. "Me too."

He smiles in response, nodding slowly.

"Goodbye, Mandy. Enjoy your night."

"You too," I whisper before he turns to leave.

When he's gone, I feel a blush creep across my cheeks, but whenever there is heat, the cold always comes along to kill it. A pain stabs below my chest and I stiffen. I'm selfish and feel an overwhelming sense of betrayal. Somehow, my heart remains attached to a memory from over six years ago.

I hadn't noticed Claire coming back and I close my eyes when she pulls me into a hug, not saying anything for a long moment.

"I was outside and saw whatever was going on there. He likes you."

I pull away, wiping dry eyes in fear tears will come. Claire places a finger under my chin, tilting my face up to meet hers.

"Sweet girl," she says, "You can't keep waiting for a ghost."

EIGHT

"Congratulations, you two," I squeal behind a bouquet and a bottle of champagne.

I pop my head around to see Garry and Sally standing at their front door, radiating pure happiness and love.

Sally does something resembling a skip and a jump into my arms, almost squashing the fresh flowers. Garry comes to my rescue, taking the flowers from me before kissing my cheek.

"Thank you," he mouths, and I wrap my arms around Sally's shoulders.

"Oh, Mandy, I think I'm still in shock. I had no idea." Her eyes bubble pure mischief when she lies.

She's known for weeks what was going on. She did everything in her power to get me and Claire to admit to it just weeks before when I went to their house for drinks. The same night Alex kissed my cheek. The same night something came alive in my chest.

Both me and Claire kept mum on the subject, eyeing each other, wondering how the hell she had figured it out. But in all honesty, Garry is pretty transparent. He once stole a packet of chewing gum from our local shop when we were eight and went back thirty minutes later to admit what he had done; offering back a half-eaten packet of chewing gum and even the one he had in his mouth. He is honest to a fault.

All the same, I'm sure it doesn't take from what Sally must be feeling.

"Tell me everything. Come on." I nod down the hall towards the kitchen.

The details of their proposal sounded beautiful, and although Garry bottled doing it at the restaurant and instead chose to do it in the comfort of their hotel room, I can tell none of it bothered Sally.

As she potters upstairs to gather what she has of wedding plans, Garry waves my empty coffee cup in front of my face.

"Refill?"

"No, thanks. I should get going soon. I have homework to correct."

"Sally's parents are throwing us an engagement party this weekend."

"Nice." My eyes lift. We all need a night out. "Where?"

"Geo's."

"The new place?"

"Money isn't an object in her family, and she's their only daughter. They want to celebrate," he explains, crossing his arms. "And," he continues, a cheeky smile playing on his lips.

"Yes, Garry?"

"There might be a certain bachelor in attendance."

I hope he doesn't notice my cheeks flush, and the rush of heat in my tummy surprises me.

"And?" I shake my head as if the thought of Alex being at the party doesn't bother me.

And why would it?

But goddamn it, it bothers me to no end. It bothers me too much. Every inch of my skin tingles, and I'm already planning my outfit in my head. Something sexy but not slutty. Elegant but not too refined.

What is happening to me?

My heart is racing deep in my chest. If this is how a mention of him makes me react, I want to tell Garry I can't make the party.

"Don't give me that." He huffs. "I saw the way you two were around each other. All nervous and sexual tension."

"Oh, stop it, Garry." I raise my palms to my cheeks, hiding the furious blush. "I wouldn't know sexual tension if it hit me in the face."

"Bullshit," he hits back. "You may be practically a virgin again, but you're not dead, Mandy."

My mouth drops open. I'm not sure whether to laugh or cry. He's right, of course.

"You know who else is not dead? Alex. And he looks at you like he hasn't eaten in weeks and you're the best meal ever served."

44

"Garry," I gasp.

"It's true. What's holding you back, Mandy? It's been over six years. You can't hold on to Nick forever."

The mention of his name drops me straight back to reality, and my heart twists. I know I can't hold on to Nick forever, and truthfully, bit by bit, I'm letting go. I just can't get far enough to be comfortable feeling things for another man. I know it's stupid, and no one would judge me if I did, but my emotions are too caught up in him, my mind too clouded in his memory.

Wouldn't it be unfair to bring someone into that? What if I got so far into a relationship and realized, I can't go any further? I don't want to string anyone along.

And what about when I have to tell someone about my past after Nick. Would they run or think of me differently?

I know without actually being in a relationship, I will never have those questions answered, but the mere thoughts of it makes me ill.

"I miss him, Garry. It's been six years and I can't stop missing him."

The corner of his mouth edges up into an understanding smile.

"I know. Me too. And Mandy, you will never stop missing him. But your heart is big enough for another person."

"I know. It's nerves, I guess. I don't even think I'd know what to do."

His eyes widen, and I can tell he is smothering a laugh.

"It's a bit like riding a bike," he chuckles. "Mandy, as your best friend and a red-blooded male, I can tell you, you have nothing to be nervous about. You're beautiful and sexy and if it's Alex you want to try something with, he's an awesome guy. Take things slow. He won't expect you to just hop into bed with him, and if he does, I'll kick the shit out of him."

I furrow my brow, staring at him. Garry wouldn't hurt a fly, and I'm pretty sure Alex would knock him over if he blew him a kiss.

He ignores my glare and continues, "And you don't have to blurt out everything. Get to know him."

I shrug. "Maybe. I suppose it won't hurt to try."

"That's my girl." He smiles proudly.

Sally comes skipping into the kitchen, her arms struggling to wrap around a large purple folder. She sets it on the countertop with a thud. Garry looks at me and shrugs. There's something oddly smug about his smile. He's so in love.

"Christ, Sally. You've been engaged for forty-eight hours." I giggle as the rush of air from the folder hitting the counter blows my hair.

"I know, Mandy. But I've been preparing my entire life."

"Fair enough." I rub my palms together. "Show me everything."

Two hours we take to go through the details of a wedding that has yet to have a date set. Sally has planned every detail. Down to the colour of her invitations.

My eyes are burning as I sit back in my car. I never want to see another seating plan again.

As I rest my head back, my phone buzzes in my handbag.

"Hey, Mom."

"Hey, honey. Have you heard from your brother? I can't get through to him and I'm worried."

I roll my eyes.

"When was the last time you heard from him?"

"Two days ago."

Can she hear herself? She seems genuinely exasperated on the other end, worrying about her grown-ass man-child.

"I spoke with him this morning, Mom. He's fine. He needs some time with his wife. He took time off work for a reason."

"I know, but I can't help but worry about him."

"They'll get through it."

Matt and his wife, Suzie, have been trying for a baby for three years, and their first attempt at IVF failed. I try to be there for him as much as I can, but I can't help feeling guilty when he looks at me.

It'll happen for them. I'm sure of it, and my brother is going to be an amazing father.

"How are you, sweetie?"

"I'm fine. I'm leaving Garry's house. I wanted to call to congratulate Sally myself," I explain.

"I am so happy for him. Someday, you will give me a wedding to go to."

I don't hide the snort and moan.

"Someday," I agree. "I need to go, Mom. I have piles of work to get through. I love you."

"I love you too, honey. And please, if you do speak to your brother, tell him to call me."

Once my mother hangs up, I start the car, dialing my brother's number. It rings through the car speaker.

"Hey, sis." He sounds tired.

I don't even bother to say hello.

"Can you call Mom? She is about to send a search party out for you."

I lied to my mother about speaking to him this morning. I haven't heard from my brother in over a week and honestly, I was starting to worry too.

He says nothing, but I can almost hear the roll of his head.

"Sure."

"Why haven't you been taking her calls?"

"I'm really busy, Mandy," he says through a yawn.

"You answered me?"

"Yes, because I enjoy talking to you."

"Thanks. But you need to call her. You know how she gets."

"Okay," he settles. "Sorry I haven't called. I'm sorting through some stuff."

God, that breaks my heart. I wish I could reach through the phone and hug him.

"How are you and Suzie?" My voice cracks because hearing him in so much pain causes tears to sting my eyes.

There's a pause, and then I hear him clear his throat. "I just want to be there for my wife, but she's shutting me out. When the IVF didn't work, something in her shut down. We're going to try again, but it's draining everything. Our bank accounts and our relationship included."

I wish I knew what to say. I wish I had the answers. And I wish Suzie didn't hate me for things I can't change. She doesn't speak to me without a snap in her voice. It wasn't always this way.

"She loves you, Matt. All you can do is be there for her. And I'm here anytime you need me. I'm a good listener."

"Thanks. Dinner next week?"

He means for the two of us. I don't ask if Suzie will join us anymore.

"I'd love to."

"How have you been? All okay?" His concern is understandable but unwarranted.

It's coming close to the time of year when my heart aches so much it could break, and I know my brother's pain is as palpable.

"Everything is fine." I try to keep control in my tone.

Everything isn't fine. It has been six years. I've learned how to

47

control the pain and the tears that naturally fall with each memory, but I still feel every blow clawing at me until my skin is raw.

"I don't want to keep you too long. I just wanted to let you know that Mom wants to speak to you."

"Okay, sis. I love you."

"I love you too. Give Suzie my love and keep me updated on everything."

He agrees before ending the call.

I can't wait for the day one of these phone calls ends with me knowing I'm going to be an aunt.

Nick crawls into my mind, and I remember the emptiness after he died. The overwhelming loss crowded everything in my life. I imagine it's something similar for Suzie.

I put the radio on to drown out my racing thoughts, but I find myself humming and processing all at once.

Funny how this time, when I think of Nick, something else gets mixed up in there, too. Images of a tall, strong, gorgeous man. Thoughts of seeing him again and what I can say to not stumble over my own words. How I will act and how I will look at him.

Involuntarily, I lick my lips, sighing to myself. This rush of new feelings is foreign and scary.

Maybe I can do it. Maybe I can try. He may turn me down, and I can deal with it. But I have nothing to lose in trying.

NINE

Saturday evening and I'm pacing in my kitchen. My double doors are open wide into my back garden, allowing the warm breeze to creep in. The cold shower soothed my skin only momentarily. Wrapped in a towel, my skin is becoming sticky again.

I sit on the stool at my breakfast counter, only to stand again and pace some more.

I'm too nervous and on edge about what this evening could bring.

Why am I acting this way for a man I have hardly spoken to?

Christ, I feel itchy.

Another cold shower.

I've practically sanitized my entire body at this stage, but thinking about Alex makes me warm and pleasantly uncomfortable. I need to wash it off.

Again.

All week I've thought about him and the conversation I had with Garry. It's time for me to at least try something with someone. Why not the hot guy with the smoldering smile and piercing blue eyes?

I turn the temperature lower and squeal as it rushes down my back.

My mind is in torment, torn somewhere between not wanting to betray Nick and his memory, and not being able to help what Alex makes me feel. And I wonder what Nick would think? What would his opinion be? Not of the whole situation, but of Alex. Would he approve?

I like to think he would. After all, he was friends with Garry, and he hasn't warned me off.

Garry—the matchmaker.

I close my eyes and feel my chest tighten. He is going to be right in the middle of this with his happy little fiancé, stirring the love potion.

My best friend is both a blessing and a curse to me right now.

"Come on, Mandy. Big girl pants time," I murmur to myself, switching off the shower and once again wrapping myself in the towel.

My doorbell rings, and I catch myself before I slip on the tiles.

I hurry, drying my feet before clipping my damp hair off my face.

It can't be Claire. Not yet. It's only 4 p.m.

Garry asked me to collect his suit from the dry cleaners earlier because he and Sally were getting an engagement photo shoot before the party. I didn't even know that was a thing, and I'm sure Garry cringed the entire way through, but I happily obliged. He must be here to collect it.

"Give me a sec, Garry," I shout towards my front door before running into my bedroom to grab my robe. I take my hair down from the clip, sure if I left it there, I would never get the kink out of my hair. And I'm not sure if Alex likes kinky hair.

I blush, a heat unfurling below my ribs.

Maybe he likes other kinky things.

"Move along, Mandy," I utter.

I rush to the door, swinging it back.

"Your suit is in the…" My mouth flies open, and my gasp is loud. It's the loudest thing I've ever heard. "Alex?"

"Hey." His broad shoulders lift with a light laugh.

"What? Am… How?" I stutter, unsure if I've swallowed my tongue. "What are you doing here? How do you even know where I live?" I sound more forceful than I'd like, but I can't help it. I've been sweating over this man all day and he shows up at my door, out of nowhere.

"Garry called." His brow creases, and he looks as mystified as I feel.

"No, he didn't." I shake my head.

Please ground, open up and swallow me.

I should have held off on the cold shower because this situation calls for one.

We both stand there, staring, each as confused as the other, and now obviously embarrassed. And I've become acutely aware my silk robe is showing off a little more of myself than I like.

50

"Mandy, I'm sorry. I thought you knew I was coming. Garry got held up and asked if I could pop by to pick up his suit. He said he called. I didn't mean to frighten you."

That asshole.

I'm going to string him up and have his guts for supper.

But then I remember my phone sitting in my bedroom. Charging.

I swallow, trying to hide my mortification, and place a gentle smile on my lips.

"You didn't frighten me, Alex. You just weren't who I was expecting." I let out a light laugh. "Please, come in."

He doesn't move. He purses his lips, his eyes traveling along my body, all the way to my toes and back up again. His eyes become darker, roaming over me under thick lashes. I pull my robe tighter, trying to hide behind the light material.

It's no use. He can still see the outline of my body pretty well.

Something for my shopping list: a longer robe.

"You sure?" He raises his eyebrows, smirking, and rubbing his fingers along his jaw.

I want to reach out and touch the very spot.

Why do my legs feel like jelly?

One look.

That's all it takes, and my breathing comes faster.

"Sure. Just let me get changed so I don't flash a guest in my house."

I close my eyes and take a long breath. I need to make light of this messed-up situation or I'll crawl into bed for the night and die of shame.

I gesture towards the kitchen, and the corner of his mouth edges up. I'm sure he doesn't mean to be, but sweet heavens, he is sexy.

He nods, taking a step forward. "Thank you."

Once at the doorway, he passes me, and his arm grazes along my robe, gently rubbing against the skin beneath. His touch is as soft as the satin I'm wearing, but it burns as if he is branding the skin below my breasts. For a moment, his eyes connect with mine. And as he looks down at me, I know he feels it too. Whatever *it* is.

I'm definitely going to need another shower.

My eyes dance over his skin, the movement of his throat as he swallows, his broad chest rising and falling with each shallow breath, and I'm small beneath his roasting gaze. Blinking, I break our connection, and when he continues through the hall, I think I hear him mumble a curse. But maybe I'm hearing things now.

"Give me a minute while I change."

I'm about to take off to my bedroom, but he stops me in my tracks. "Mandy. Wait."

When I look over at him again, his eyes are glossy. His stare could be lava as it sizzles its way over every inch of my skin. And if I've ever seen hunger in a man's eyes, then this is it.

"I'm going to grab Garry's suit and head back. I don't want to interrupt you, and I'm sure Garry is going to need this."

He removes the hanger from the door, tossing it over his back, and letting it swing from his fingers.

My heart sinks to my stomach, and I recognize the gut-wrenching feeling. It's disappointment. But what can I say? I'm standing here, half-naked, in a satin robe. Maybe I've turned him off somehow. He might think I'm presumptuous.

God, I hope not. If he only knew the truth, he'd think I was a nun.

I lower my head, staring at my pink-painted toes before looking back at him, focusing on his chest.

"Mandy?" he questions, and my eyes meet his again. "Why is it, every time I meet you, you're dripping wet?" A smile plays along his lips.

Ground, please, please open up and swallow me.

"Because I was born with a knack for walking into the most embarrassing of situations."

We both laugh, and a nervousness fills the air between us.

"I'm looking forward to seeing you tonight, Mandy." His tone is serious and his voice coats over me like warm honey. He walks to the front door. "You should wear the robe." He winks and gives me one last breathtaking smirk before he closes the door, leaving me ready to melt into a pool of liquid at my feet.

I stare after him, unable to take control of my legs and walk away.

I want him to come back.

I want to kiss him so badly my lips are burning.

I spin on my heels and mutter, "Time for another shower."

TEN

It's 7:30, and I'm sitting patiently on my bed, fully dressed, staring at Claire as she applies the finishing touches to her make-up.

"You look gorgeous. Now, will you hurry," I complain, sipping on my cocktail.

There's still an hour to go to the party, but Claire is applying her makeup like she's the guest of honour.

"What's the rush? You have a cocktail in your hand. That's everything you need. And we have lots of time before it kicks off."

I exhale loudly, rolling my eyes. It isn't Claire's fault. My encounter with Alex earlier has left me a bit shaken and knowing I will see him again isn't helping matters.

He told me he's looking forward to seeing me. I'm not too sure how good my defences will be if he looks at me with the same hunger as he did today.

My mind flashes back to the moment when he was looking down at me from over his shoulder, his arm still pressed against my silk robe. I tingle, every nerve in my body coming alive.

He felt it, too. I could see it by the way he looked at me. But he didn't do anything, and I don't know what to take from it. He seems like a confident man who gets what he wants. So why, if he felt what I did, did he not act on it?

Maybe I'm reading too much into things. After all, I didn't act on it either and I could have. But I feared my robe would be little defence to his touch.

I've been out of the dating scene for far too long.

I've never really been in it, to begin with.

"Are you going to tell me why you're flustered today?"

In the mirror's reflection, I see Claire's eyes boring through me. Even with her lids squinting as she applies her mascara, I can tell my friend is suspicious.

She knows there's something wrong. She knew from the moment she stepped inside the house earlier. But I didn't give her a chance to ask before I pulled her into the kitchen and placed a cocktail in her hand.

"I'll explain later when I get my thoughts together," I said.

I cross my legs, pulling at an imaginary thread in my dress.

"Alex was here."

Claire jerks and pokes herself in the eye with her mascara stick. "Fuck. Ouch. It stings like a bitch."

I jump from the bed, handing her a tissue from the box on my dresser. "Take these."

She looks up at me from her good eye, her other watering as she places the tissue under it.

"I'm fine. Now go back to the part where you said Alex was here. Did something happen?" She's out of breath from excitement.

"God, no," I scoff. "Nothing like that. Garry asked him to collect his suit. But I had no idea he was calling and was standing there, wet, and in nothing but a robe."

My face blushes furiously again. Just the thought makes me shiver.

Claire's lips turn down, and I can tell she's suppressing a laugh. "Great thinking from Garry."

I roll my eyes.

"Is this why you're in such a state? He called by to collect a suit. Sweetie, I know it's been a long time, but if this is what's getting you so heated, then you're in bigger need than I thought."

I take a deep breath, unsure of how to explain what happened between us. He was at my house for all of two minutes. How could I explain what he made me feel in those two minutes? Claire will think I'm crazy and delusional.

Unable to find the right words to make her understand, I shake my head.

54

"Ugh." I throw my head back. "I don't know how to explain it, Claire. He wasn't even here for long, but something happened. Nothing physical, but I felt it." I swirl the straw around in my drink. "Sorry, I'm not explaining this very well."

My shoulders slump. The weight of today and all the confusion it brings, bearing too much.

"I mean, it's crazy, right? Please tell me I'm mad because I hardly even know the guy. I've met him a handful of times, and even then, we shared nothing more than a few words. I have no idea how he makes me feel like this or act this way. It's not me, Claire. I don't recognize this nervous ball of energy I've turned into."

When I look up again, her hands have fallen to her lap and her eyes are wide. At least one of her eyes is wide. The other looks involuntarily shut.

"You really like him." She appears shocked by her own statement. "I knew there was something there. Even with one bad eye, I can see it." She snorts through a giggle, patting the tissue under her eyelid. "But I didn't realize how much you liked him. To be honest, it has been so long, I was getting worried you would never let another person in."

Me too.

I never expected this rush of feelings, as if my body was slowly waking from a deep sleep.

Claire stands, takes her cocktail in her hand, and sits next to me on the bed. We both turn to look at each other, smiling, friends sharing a single moment we should have shared multiple times throughout the years. Claire has offloaded her stories throughout college and her dating life, but I never related to the bubbling of emotions when she met someone new. I only ever had it for Nick, and although I supported my friend, I never understood how she did it over and over again. But this is a first for me, and I suddenly feel shy. Child-like almost.

"And don't be nervous. He's going to lose his mind when he sees you in this dress." Claire smiles, rubbing a supportive hand over the powder pink material of my knee-length, flowing dress. "Can I say one more thing?" She asks, staring down into her drink.

"Sure," I say, feeling a little apprehensive by her change of tone.

"Of all the men you could have your pick of. I'm glad it's Alex because he is so bloody gorgeous." She fake cries, patting the tissue along her cheeks.

"I know." I join in before we clink our glasses. "Cheers."

***

An hour later and we're both entering *Geo's*—the swankiest new place in town. Two men open the door, allowing me and Claire to step inside. The large function room is bright, yet warm all at once. Luxurious golds caress every surface, and large tables scatter elegantly around the room with candelabras and fresh flower centrepieces. Servers don't busy themselves as they stroll around with hors d'oeuvres and champagne. Instead, they are calmly moving from person to person, heads held high in the air.

If this is the engagement party, the wedding is going to be a Hollywood affair.

My eyes land on Garry. His hand rests on Sally's back as they chat to a group of guests. The pint glass of beer he holds seems oddly out of place in somewhere so upmarket.

Claire leans in towards me. "How uncomfortable do you think he is?"

"Oh, he looks painfully itchy."

We giggle as we make our way down the steps and into the open hall. I say a silent thank you when I don't trip.

Tonight, I'm wearing heels. Me and heels always end up tangled around each other after I fall with the grace of a baby elephant. But not tonight. I've strapped myself extra tight into these bad boys.

Claire reaches out and grabs two glasses of champagne from a server, handing one to me. We sway to the soft music played by a jazz band. It's a far cry from the sweaty nightclubs we used to spend our nights in.

I don't think my usual dress and ankle boots would fit in here. Instead, my soft-pink velvet dress falls to my knees, and the sweetheart neckline sweeps across my chest, exposing my shoulders. I feel good in my skin, and I embrace it because it isn't a regular occurrence. And apart from the strange tingle in the pit of my stomach, I am comfortable. Or maybe it's the effect of a few sips of champagne and a body heated in anticipation.

Garry spots us from across the room, his head bobbing above a sea of guests, and he does a silly dance as he approaches us. He throws his

56

eyes exaggeratedly as if to say, *'have you seen this place?'*

I've been trying to get a reservation here for months. Sally's family is wealthier than I thought, considering they've reserved the entire restaurant.

"Ladies, you both look ravishing." He takes us both into a hug.

"As do you." I wink, adjusting his crooked tie.

"You're marrying well, Garry," Claire gushes, her eyes wandering around the room.

"And she also happens to be absolutely gorgeous." He sighs, looking back at Sally, who is still speaking to a huddle of people.

She's a social butterfly and looks stunning in a red, one-shoulder cocktail dress.

I look at Claire, both of our noses scrunching up with a wide smile. He's adorable when he speaks about Sally. The man is infatuated, and it's so beautiful to watch.

For a little while, Garry escorts us around the room, introducing us to his soon-to-be in-laws and family friends. My mouth is dry from speaking and my cheeks twitch from smiling. Garry is an only child, and apart from his parents, we are all the family he has, and I hope we are making a good impression. He's got close friends, but the three of us have been together through everything. We may not share blood, but we're family.

"When Caleb finally decides he wants to marry my ass, I want to have my engagement party here." Claire takes another sip from her empty glass.

"You've been dating for a few months. I like this one. Don't scare him," I plead.

Claire had a habit of falling for the stereotypical bad guy. She punished herself repeatedly, swearing they would change. They never did, and it always ended with her heart in tatters. Caleb is a police officer in the next town over, and he's a sweetheart. They're good together. He treats her like the queen she is, and I know she loves him. But hell will freeze over the day she gushes about him.

"Yeah," she drawls, "I got a good one." I don't ruin it by teasing her. It's the nicest thing I've ever heard her say about him. "Looking for someone?" She eyes me, her amusement obvious in her tone.

Childishly, I stick out my tongue. I must have been scanning the room.

I need a drink, and not to drench my sandpaper tongue, but because my shoulders suddenly knot, noting I still haven't seen Alex. And the volume of disappointment balls in my chest. Maybe he couldn't make it.

I know feeling this way is ridiculous, but dammit, I can't help it.

After Garry provides us both with a refill of our drinks, we make our way onto the spacious balcony and seat ourselves in the cushioned chairs. Even the balcony is fancy, with mosaic marble tiles on both the floor and railing.

I appreciate the fresh air on my skin. It eases the burning in my lungs, and the twinkle of the town lights is calming.

I'll see Alex again. Tonight, I get to be with my friends and enjoy a celebration. God knows we have been through our fair share of bad times. So, there are no better people to embrace a celebration and know exactly how precious it is.

"We're so happy for you, Garry," Claire says, patting his knee.

"I'm glad you two are here with me." His soft smile turns sorrowful, and we all glance towards the empty chair at our table.

"I was thinking about him last night," Garry continues. "Sally and I were going over details. Most of which went completely over my head, but she started talking about bridesmaids and groomsmen." He looks down at his beer. "Nick would have been my best man if he was here."

A painful lump forms in my throat. How handsome he would have been in a suit.

"Probably planning a crazy bachelor party." Claire giggles.

"He would be so happy for you, Garry. Most things in life, I try to imagine what Nick would think and what his opinion would be, but I know, he would be so proud of you."

Garry does that thing men sometimes do when they cry and try to hide it. He coughs, clearing his throat, and runs his hand roughly over his face.

It's nice to think of Nick in such a way, to imagine what he would do if he were with us. It's sad and painful, but there is something beautiful about letting him live on in our memories.

As they stand to go back inside, I excuse myself to stay. I need a moment. Talking about Nick always takes a minute to process. They understand, as they always do.

Family, you see.

I lean my arms over the metal railing, enjoying the warm breeze of the summer evening. It isn't quite dark yet, but the town lights gleam and flicker, and I can still see the horizon. The last of the sunlight dances on the ocean far away.

For a long second, when I close my eyes and focus hard enough, I can smell him, and the warmth reminds me of him, caressing over me with comfort.

I hear the door open onto the balcony, and I shut my eyes harder, clinging onto the feeling, afraid because it is slipping away.

Nick is slipping away.

"There you are."

His voice.

It takes only his voice, and Nick's imaginary warmth is replaced by his very real one.

I expected when I saw him again to go back to the nervous-wreck I was today, but only calm washes over me, as if his voice has brought me relief, I didn't know I needed. As if his voice alone can wrap around me and mend whatever is broken.

When I turn around, I see his eyes visibly widen, and I can't help the smile curving on my lips.

"Mandy, you look…" He stops, shaking his head. "Stunning," he finishes.

"Thank you."

I want to tell him how gorgeous he looks in his navy slacks and how his broad shoulders fill out his white dress shirt perfectly. And with the sleeves rolled up to his elbows, I imagine his arms wrapped around my waist, but I bite my tongue with hopes I don't embarrass myself further today.

He slowly runs a hand through his hair, his posture straightening to stand tall again like it will grant him back his composure.

"And I thought the robe would be difficult to beat," he teases, strolling to my side.

I visibly cringe, shuddering.

"Mind if I join you?" He gestures towards the railing.

"Of course not," I answer, hoping I don't sound too eager.

"We seem to bump into each other quite a lot, and I know very little about you. Mind if I ask some questions?" He raises an eyebrow, looking down at me with those irresistible eyes of his.

Breathe, Mandy.

"Do you interview all company you keep?"

"Only the ones I'd like to get to know."

His voice is playful, but I'm sure my heart has stopped beating.

"Okay, but only if I get to do the same?"

He leans his elbows back on the railing, crossing his legs at the ankle. "Well, it wouldn't be any fun doing it on my own."

I'm not sure if he meant it to sound so flirty, but it did something strange to my stomach, like a ball of heat unwinding and rushing down my thighs. I like flirty Alex. He's fun and Christ, this man is the sexiest thing I've ever set eyes on.

"I'll go first." He crosses his arms over his chest, and his eyes roll left to right, brooding. "What made you choose to teach?" he finally asks.

I ponder telling him the genuine answer. It's true, I love children and have wanted to be a teacher since I was just a kid myself, but my past makes me search the faces of the children in my classroom.

But I know better than to tell him that. He'll jump over the balcony to get away. So, I stick to the original story.

"I was the kid who always wanted to be a teacher when they grew up." I shrug. It doesn't sound very interesting, but it's the bones of it.

"There has to be more." His eyes narrow on me, and my train of thought passes me by again.

Am I that easy to read?

"Surely, if you've wanted to teach since you were young, it's a passion?"

I exhale, thankful this is his line of questioning.

"It is," I agree. "There's something amazing about getting a group of kids at the start of the school year and seeing how much they progress. I'm in a privileged position, and I get to nurture their talents and build their confidence. They trust me with their lives, as do their parents. And I love each one of them. They drive me around the bend sometimes, but they say the funniest things. And when they're not sticking crayons up their nose, they're quite enjoyable to be around."

He laughs then. And his laugh makes my knees buckle as if caressing them with hot chocolate. It pours over me in waves. I hold on to the railing, needing something to steady myself.

"That's more what I was looking for."

"Me next." I tilt my head, disappointed I said anything because he stops laughing.

I never want him to stop laughing.

He nods in silent agreement.

"Same question. Sally said you built her parents' house. What made you choose construction?"

"My father." He doesn't have to think about his answer. "My father has been in the construction business his entire life and started out on his own when I was a teenager. It was a small business, but successful. I went to university. I met Sally's brother there. And I got my master's in architecture."

My eyes broaden. I wasn't expecting the last part.

"I'd always loved design, but when it came to it, I also loved building as much. So, after getting a job as an architect and getting some savings together, I propositioned my father about expanding his business and doing it together. I loved architecture, but I wanted to get down and dirty too."

Alex, down and dirty. I like the image too much.

Focus, Mandy.

"I wanted to build what I designed," he continues. "Five years ago, we started Hale Construction, and it worked out."

I wait for him to say more. To tell me how successful the company has been because although I know little about construction—actually, I know nothing. I managed to hang my picture frames. I know enough to know Hale Construction is no longer a small family business. I've seen their logo displayed on most construction sites in town and far outside it.

But he says no more. He doesn't boast or try to impress me with how successful he has been in his business endeavours. He's humble.

I like that.

I like Alex.

I like Alex and the way he is looking at me.

I like Alex, and the way he is looking at me, and how his eyes narrow.

Shit.

I haven't said anything. I'm gawking at him.

Again.

"Do you enjoy working with your dad?"

It's a pathetic recovery, but I have to say something before he thinks I'm mute.

"The extra question is going to cost you." He smirks and I liquify.

What is he doing to me?

"Just answer the question." I want to know what I'll have to pay for that question with.

A kiss?

I hope so.

I will gladly change all my currency to kisses from here on out.

I lean back on the railing next to him, but I stand too close because my skin burns when it touches his.

Focus.

And breathe.

Don't forget to breathe.

He looks down at me, and I feel meek again. Like he can scoop me up.

I raise my brow and nudge him, hoping it will give him the hint to answer my question.

I really want to know. I want to hear his answer almost as much as I want to kiss him.

"My father stepped back from the business after my mother died. He likes to check in now and then to make sure I'm not running it into the ground, but he's enjoying retirement. After she died, he could never recover the passion to go back full time."

Why did I have to ask? I'm an idiot.

"I'm sorry. I didn't mean to pry."

"We agreed to answer questions, Mandy," he reminds me, comforting me with a simple smile.

I'm okay again.

"Quickfire round." He stands up straight, winking at me, and rubbing his palms together like he's about to win a jackpot.

He's completely oblivious to what that wink did to my balance and my head coats in a fog.

Jesus Christ, Alex. What are you made of?

"Favourite colour?" he starts.

"Purple."

"Mine's navy."

"That's boring." I scrunch my nose.

"Don't judge. What age were you when you had your first kiss?"

I ignore the lump in my throat and answer despite it. "Fourteen. You?"

"Twelve. Again, don't judge. Hormones hit me early."

I don't judge. I imagine he's always been devilishly handsome.

"A time of year you hate the most. Christmas? Halloween?"

I want to say the day I gave everything away, but I don't.

"My birthday. I hate my birthday. Too much fuss over another ordinary day."

"Do you have an issue with getting older? Are you secretly an old woman in a really hot body?"

I blush again.

Damn you, Alex.

"No." I nudge him playfully. "I turn twenty-six on May fourth."

Without even hesitating he says, "May the fourth be with you."

"And also with you," I answer just as fast.

We both break into a laugh, snapping the tension I felt about where these questions could go.

"You're beautiful, Mandy." He has stopped laughing and is staring at me. His eyes are serious, and nothing about what he said is a cheesy chat-up line.

In my best effort to break his gaze and to take back the breath he has stolen from me, I avert my eyes.

"When's your birthday?"

He hesitates, looking at his feet briefly.

"Thirty years old on April twelfth."

I smile, but then something gnaws at me.

Today is April twelfth.

"Alex," I gasp. "Why didn't you say something? Happy Birthday."

"Because I hate birthdays too. But thank you because I'm liking this one more than most."

I hope it's because he's with me. I hope I'm making this birthday a better one for him.

I tilt my head in the door's direction. "Come on. Let me buy you a drink for your birthday."

I circle to walk back inside, but warm fingers wrap gently around my wrist.

When I turn back, he is no longer leaning against the balcony railing. He's so close I can feel his breath sweep across my face.

"It's not a drink I want."

My neck is craning up to look at him, my throat exposed, and I'm sure he can see me swallowing back my nerves.

"Mandy, will you come with me?"

My face falls, my eyes narrowing, and all hopes drop to the pit of my stomach. If he thinks he came here tonight to get birthday bumps, then he chose the wrong woman. Maybe the silk robe gave him the wrong impression after all.

He shakes his head, his shoulders collapsing with a deep breath. "I'm sorry. It came out wrong. Can I show you something? It's in this building."

My hopes rise back up to my chest from my stomach.

"It doesn't involve a no-pants-dance, does it?"

"A no-pants-dance? You're weird." But he laughs, still shaking his head.

"Thank you. I think it's my favourite quality about myself."

"I think it's becoming my favourite too." He laces his fingers with mine, tugging me along behind him.

When we step back inside, I wonder how long we've been out on the balcony because the entire room has transformed. The tables are in the same position, but the lights are dim, and coloured spotlights move and shine down on what is now a dance floor. The band no longer plays easy listening music but party hits. The space is now a club, and it's like all the sweaty nightclubs I remember, but the people are better dressed and their sweat smells like Chanel and Armani.

I don't see Garry or Claire as Alex guides me through the crowd, his hand on the small of my back, and the spot burns like his hand is going to melt through it. He keeps it there until we pass through the swinging double doors into a busy, hot kitchen.

"Good evening everyone. Never mind us," Alex says, intertwining his fingers with mine.

"Good evening, Mr. Hale." Someone chirps from across a counter, but I can't see their face behind a pot of steam.

How the hell do they know who he is?

"This way." He pulls me closer, rounding out into a corridor.

We stop at the end, and he presses the button for the elevator.

"Where are we going?" I question, genuinely curious.

"You'll see." He smiles at me, his thumb rubbing along the flesh of my palm.

When the elevator doors open, we step inside, and the space seems large.

Until it doesn't anymore.

The doors shut, and the space rapidly gets so much smaller. It's too small for the bubbling of feelings pounding inside my chest.

I don't dare look at him. He'll see it. He'll see my want for him. He'll see how much I'm aching for him to touch more than my hand. I can tell he is staring at me, but I don't move, and I thank the gods I inherited my stubbornness from my mother.

"You ready?" He asks as the doors open again.

I think my heart has stopped. I simply nod because if I speak, I fear I will say something stupid.

We walk to the end of another corridor, and he pushes down on the handle to open the emergency exit. Immediately, a soft breeze creeps across my skin, causing goosebumps to play along my arms. When my eyes adjust, I can't help the sharp intake of breath, and something resembling a shriek.

"Alex." His name comes out in a loud whisper.

I'm walking into the most enchanted garden. Flowers adorn every hard surface. It makes the grey concrete of the rooftop appear soft and magical. Flowers are everywhere I turn, and I spin around slowly to appreciate it. They hang down over the walls, overflowing in baskets, and some grow so much they spill up into the night sky, obscuring the lights of the town. The whole top floor is decorated with archways of roses, walls of pansies, and pots of wildflowers.

Someone has spent a lot of time, love, and effort on making this rooftop how it is.

It's so beautiful.

He laces his fingers with mine again, bringing me back to him. For a moment, I forget where I am. He guides me towards the railing at the edge.

"Oh my God!" I thought the view from the balcony was pretty, but this is breathtaking. "It's amazing." I take slow steps towards the railing, drinking in the surrounding sights.

He wants me to see all of this. He wants to share this with me, and I don't know why.

"Do you always bring strangers up here to show them this?" I beam up at him. I don't care. I only care he has brought me.

He rubs his thumb over my knuckles. "No. I used to come here a lot."

"Used to?"

He takes a deep breath and turns to look at me. In his eyes, I can see pain and angst, as if it's hard for him to say the words.

"My mother planted these flowers. I was born in this building. It was an apartment complex, and it was my parents' first home when they married. It went up for sale about a year before my mother died and my father bought it. He wanted her to have this rooftop again. He loved her so much, he bought the entire building for a rooftop."

My heart swells because he has given me a sneak peek into another side of Alex, and it makes my heart hurt. But his pain makes my hand twitch. I don't want him to hurt. I want to wipe it away. I want to touch him until he doesn't hurt anymore.

So, I do.

"Thank you for coming here with me." He looks down at me as I press my palm to his chest, and his entire frame stiffens beneath my touch.

"Thank you for taking me here."

I can't take my eyes off him.

"I think I like birthdays now," he says.

"Me too," I whisper.

I breathe in sharply as he raises his hand and feathers his fingers along my cheek. He's staring at me with so much intensity I think my chest is going to crack. Then his fingers travel from my cheek to under my chin and he tilts my face up, so I am looking straight at him. I'm sure the pounding I can hear is my heart, but I don't care, and I don't want him to stop.

Ever.

"I think I want to kiss you, Mandy."

His face comes closer, and heat spreads from his touch, making my head spin.

I say nothing. I edge my mouth up a little higher, hoping I can pull him closer. His other hand comes up to hold the side of my head as his mouth meets mine. He stills there, our lips barely touching. But the brush of his lips has an effect so powerful I think I will crumble right here on the rooftop. He pulls away, and I hear him take a long breath. I can't open my eyes. I'm stuck in one spot and I never want to leave it. I never want his hands to leave my face. And before I have a chance to open my eyes again, his mouth covers mine.

As we move together, my breath hitches and a groan comes from deep in his throat. He kisses me harder. As if the slight pant of my breath makes him lose any control. I give back everything he is giving. And he is giving me so much. I feel everything, our desire, want, and need, wrapped up in one kiss. My arms drape around his neck because

I need his support to steady myself. Soft movements and gentle caresses swallow our moans.

"Mandy," he breathes against my mouth, both our chests heaving frantic gasps. "I don't think I'll ever want to stop kissing you." He brushes his thumb over my swollen lips.

One kiss.

One kiss changes everything.

I blink, fearing tears will come before whispering, "Then don't stop."

ELEVEN

I sit at my desk in my classroom on Wednesday afternoon. The kids are content with the colouring sheets I provided, chattering amongst themselves.

I've knocked my head in ways to stop thinking about Alex and that rooftop, but he consumes my every move now. With the touch of his lips against mine, he sunk into me, digging deep until my stomach filled with heat.

Goddamn that man and his arms. Those arms wrapped around me so tight they lifted me off the ground to bring my mouth closer to his. I shiver, remembering how his hands wandered over my body. Frenzied. Everywhere and nowhere all at once.

We went our separate ways that night. My lips were swollen, and my hair wasn't in the perfect position I put it in before going to the restaurant.

I didn't sleep because I was giddy as a teenage girl who had been kissed for the first time. I stared up at the ceiling, unable to focus on anything else as Claire snored happily in a drunken slumber next to me.

When I slept, it was restless and when I woke to a text message, my heart felt like it had flipped.

Alex: I know they say you should wait three days to contact a lady after you've kissed them, but to hell with that rule. When

can I see you again?

I quietly squealed, turning over and clenching the phone to my chest.

Maybe he couldn't sleep either?

The thought made my cheeks flush.

I waited until the afternoon to reply, not wanting to seem too desperate. But my fingers twitched all morning.

Me: I don't go out on school nights. Too much of a good girl. But I'm free next weekend.

I put my phone on the kitchen counter, but it rang before I could go back to reading the newspaper. Seeing his name, I went into full panic mode. I hadn't planned on actually speaking to him.

I couldn't not answer. I texted him less than a minute ago. And it's not as if his tongue wasn't back my throat twelve hours before. But I didn't speak to him much when we did that.

Claire came strolling into the kitchen, fresh out of the shower. "Answer the damn phone."

"It's Alex," I whispered as if he could hear me.

Claire's eyes narrowed, looking around as if expecting an explanation I couldn't give.

"And? Answer him." She waved her hands frantically. "I'll be in the bedroom getting ready. I have to get back soon anyway," Claire said, before walking away.

I filled my lungs.

"Hey," I answered, hoping I sounded cool and not like I was seconds away from hyperventilating.

"So, how much of a good girl are you exactly?" His voice was thick and husky and my legs immediately went to jelly.

I sat back in my chair. His greeting surprised me. I didn't mean for my text to come across as flirty.

Damn it, Mandy.

First the robe and now the innuendo text message. I really needed to start checking myself.

"Sunday to Thursday, I'm the best."

Shit. Everything I said to this man made me think of all the things he could do to me on Friday and Saturday.

"So last night was a glimpse into the not-so-good-Mandy?"

"Maybe." I twirled my fingers in a loose curl, stopping myself almost immediately.

What had I turned into?

"Today is Sunday, which means you have to be good. I hope you don't mind me being forward here, Mandy, but I can't wait another week to see you."

Thank Christ. I wasn't sure I could wait that long, either.

"Late lunch?"

I smiled, unable to stop my hands from trembling. "I'd love to."

An hour later, after Claire helped me pick out a red sundress and I stopped hyperventilating, the doorbell rang. Though I tied my hair back in a ponytail, some pieces still fell around my face. It wasn't summer yet but it was still warm and the humidity was a nightmare.

I calmed myself and shook my hands of their tremble.

I didn't think it was normal to get so nervous. How could one man make my insides turn so hot I couldn't think straight?

I opened back the door, and at the sight of him, I knew the feelings I had the night before were far from fleeting. I almost forgot how gorgeous he was. All strong, tanned, blue eyes I thought I could see through, and short dark hair but long enough to be beautifully messy. I remembered running my fingers through it so easily when he wrapped his arms around my waist. And those arms. Surely, it's illegal for him to have such a powerful effect with just his arms.

Everything about him was hard ridges, and I imagined even harder under those clothes.

Woah! Since when did I start thinking of him naked?

I needed a drink.

Of him.

It was intense.

Too intense, too quickly, and I needed to get a grip.

"Hi." I smiled, stepping out so I could close the door.

He was tall. My heels made it a little easier to look at him at the party. I craned my neck back as he stepped closer, looking down at me with one of those breathtaking smiles. It was even sexier when I knew it was all for me.

He cupped his hand around the back of my neck. I thought he was going to kiss me, but he didn't. Instead, he placed his lips against my forehead. My shoulders relaxed and my head spun. He smelled so good.

"You look beautiful."

I blushed like a little girl. "Thank you."

He took my hand in his and we walked towards the car.

"I hope you don't mind, but I brought someone along."

Okay. That was a little weird.

He chuckled at my reaction as he opened the door for me to get in his car. When I did, I got a wet tongue and fur along my cheek. Heavy panting came from the back seat.

"Bandit," Alex scolded, getting in on the driver's side.

I turned in my seat, seeing the happiest fur-ball.

Alex flashed me a cautious smile. "God, I hope you like dogs."

I couldn't help smiling so wide my face hurt. "Are you kidding? I love dogs." I wanted my own, but there was a time I couldn't look after myself.

Turning in my seat and up on my knees so I could lean over to the back. "Hey, boy. You are so gorgeous. Yes, you are," I cooed, giving him a good rub. His tail wagged against the leather seats. "What is he? There's definitely a German Shepherd in there."

"His mother was a German Shepherd. Not sure what the dad was. He ran the minute he knew she was pregnant."

"Asshole," I hissed, laughing again as the dog tried to lick my face. *Not today, buddy. This makeup took too long.*

"Sorry, I had to take him with me. He got neutered last week, and he's needy. If I left without him, he'd howl the house down." Alex reached his hand back to pet his head. "Poor bastard."

I bit my lip to stop the laugh. "Well, at least now he can't be a dead-beat dad like his father."

"Silver lining, eh." He patted the dog's head again. "Sit, Bandit," Alex said sternly. "Leave her alone." The dog let out a small whine but did as he was told.

I turned back on my seat and strapped the belt across me. My heart stopped when Alex leaned over and kissed me. Soft and quick, but sweet heavens. My chest exploded.

By the time he started the car, I was trying to figure out how to get the stupid grin off my face.

He brought me for lunch, and we sat outside so Bandit could join us.

We sat under the canopy, out of the sun. The restaurant was old school, and it made me warm with nostalgia.

"I've never been here before. It reminds me of our family restaurant back home."

I looked around at the tables with the blue and white striped tablecloths. The opened blue shutters were exactly like my dad had done at home and I loved the small-town feel. I hadn't been home in so long, and it made me miss it.

He raised his eyebrows when I looked back at him. "Your family has a restaurant?"

I smiled. "Yeah. My grandfather opened it when he was in his twenties, and then my dad took over, and now my older brother. My dad still works there but my brother is the head chef, and it will be his someday."

"You didn't want to get into the family business?"

I shook my head. "God, no. I paid my penance. I worked there throughout school and college and when I say, I was the worst waitress they've ever had, I'm not exaggerating. It turns out, you can't teach someone not to be clumsy."

But my cheeks warm when I remember all the nights I locked up on my own, and Nick would come so I wouldn't be alone. We lived with our parents, so it was the only place we had to ourselves.

Why did he always crawl back into my mind when I didn't want him there? I never wanted to forget him. I loved him too much. But I was trying to move on, and for once, I liked it. His memory in these situations made me feel like a boulder lodged in my chest, and I carried his weight on my shoulders. I wasn't betraying him. I knew that, but I hate when it felt like I was. I couldn't leave his memory in the past. He walked with me and I clung to him like a safety net and any excuse to stay closed off. I wanted to let go. I really did. And I knew if I didn't, I would stay cold forever. But I had control over that. Around Alex, I was thawing. I couldn't fight what he made me feel, and it scared me more than anything.

I was losing control.

I would need to tell Alex about Nick. I would need to tell him about everything, but it was our first proper date. I had time.

"Mandy." His warm hands rested on mine from across the table.

Why the hell was I shaking?

I looked up at him, hoping he couldn't see it. If he did, he didn't mention it and I appreciated that much.

He smiled and rubbed his thumb across my knuckles like he was waking me up and bringing me back.

"I said no to a date with you." I had no idea why those were the words I chose to say. My cheeks felt like I was sitting too close to a fire. "I'm sorry. I don't know why I said that."

His brow furrowed, and I held a little tighter to his hand because I feared he would get up and leave. But he didn't.

Amazing.

He shook his head, shrugged, and smiled at me again. "I know."

I pushed back a little, but he leaned closer. Garry promised he wouldn't say anything. Maybe it was Sally.

"Who told you?"

"You did. Just now."

Oh.

His fingers brushed across my knuckles again, and he seemed totally oblivious to the tingling I was feeling beneath his touch.

"Sally told me I would go on a date with a friend of Garry's. When I saw you at the school that day and at his house, I assumed." He dipped his chin, hiding his eyes. "Honestly, I said no too."

He did?

"I hate blind dates." He explained, almost shuddering.

I blew out a breath and laughed. "Me too," I said, remembering the last one I went on. It still made me cringe. "But you still asked me out today. Why?"

He released my hands and sat back in his chair. He stayed silent for a long moment as his eyes scanned my face. "Because then I saw you."

My breathing became shallow, and I wished I could look away, but his eyes pinned me to my seat.

"I'm a determined man."

In other words, he got what he wanted, and he wanted me.

My legs clenched, and I shifted in my seat.

And I don't even think I hid it well. It was so long since I was in the company of another man in that way, and none of them in those six years made my heart hammer in my chest with a simple look.

Alex did that.

Alex made everything in my body louder until it was screaming at me.

I didn't notice when the server came to take my order. I did notice how her eyes roamed over Alex and she stuttered her words.

Same, girl. Same.

I can't remember what I ordered or if I finished it because I was too busy talking, listening, staring, and doubled over laughing. I never knew someone could make me laugh so hard until I got hiccups. I was a child the last time it happened.

He reached over once to brush a strand of hair away from my face and I think I stopped breathing.

When we finished, he asked if I wanted to take a stroll on the beach. As it turned out, it was exactly where his house was, and it was beautiful, sprawling, and warm. Just like him.

I froze like an idiot when I walked inside. I don't know why. Maybe it was the scent of betrayal I couldn't avoid. He noticed but didn't press me and told me I would have lots of opportunities for a tour. Instead, he took my hand, guided me through the hall, into his open-plan kitchen, and out through the large sliding doors, onto his porch, where steps led straight onto the sand.

I'd been to that beach countless times, but being there with Alex and how he wrapped his arms around my shoulders as we strolled brought me a peace I thought I could never achieve.

He stopped me every few paces because we couldn't keep our hands or our lips off each other. We talked about everything and nothing. And I couldn't help but notice when his eyes landed on my lips, his jaw tightened, and he always shifted his position.

He told me about his family. He was the youngest of three and had an older brother and sister. He told me how he loved being the crazy uncle to his nieces and nephews. When he talked about the kids, I saw the boyish sparkle in his eyes. It differed from how he looked at me. When his eyes met mine, there was nothing boyish about it.

I told him about my family, but my throat closed when it came to mentioning anything else. My family, I could talk about. The family I failed to create and make a life with, I couldn't quite get the words out to explain that.

In time.

I asked him more about his business, and although he was reluctant, some projects he told me about sounded incredible. His passion burned in his eyes. His hands, strong stature, and tanned skin told me enough to know he wasn't just any boss. He wasn't sitting in an office somewhere, throwing out orders. He worked and worked hard with his employees. He had some extensive projects coming up that he recently signed contracts on, which explained the suit on the first day I met him.

I preferred what he wore to lunch. His navy button-down shirt rolled up to the elbows, gave me a chance to admire his build. The shirt gave me a clear outline of his broad shoulders, and this time, I didn't stop myself from reaching out and touching him when he spoke.

When it was getting dark, he drove me home and walked me to my door.

"So, you didn't follow the three-day rule by texting me. What are the rules for saying goodbye on a date?" I asked, smirking up at him.

His eyes grew brighter, breathing a chuckle. "I'm a gentleman, Mandy," he said, before resting his lips carefully against mine.

Don't be a gentleman, Alex.

My head grew light, and my trembling hands betrayed how cool I was trying to play it off. I wanted him to kiss me like he did the night before, but something about how delicately his lips moved with mine made my head spin as much.

As he pulled away, both of us breathless from a simple kiss, he swept my ponytail back from my shoulders.

"Goodnight, Mandy."

I swallowed, hoping when I spoke, my voice sounded stronger than I felt. "Goodnight, Alex."

It didn't.

As I put the key in my front door, he walked away.

"Mandy," he called, turning around. He was walking back, stalking towards me. I pressed my palms flat against the door, sure I would melt into it. "Like I said earlier, to hell with rules."

His lips crushed against mine, and when his hands went to my hair, it felt like my chest exploded. He leaned into me, forcing me back against the door, and his kiss was fast but steady, his tongue exploring mine, and his arms caging me in on either side.

"I'm starting to think you're going to make me break all the rules," he murmured against my lips.

Please break all the rules, Alex. Every one of them.

"Goodnight." He winked, walking away again.

But I couldn't speak. Instead, I unlocked my door and slipped inside.

That was three days ago, and although I've spent little time with him, I missed him.

"Woah. Look at that." Toby, the boy sitting at the front of the class, points towards the window, and everyone's gaze follows.

A truck is driving through the entrance of the school with enormous stacks of wood strapped and secured to the back. Two smaller trucks follow close behind. They carry on, passing the window, and continuing towards the back of the school. I assume they are beginning work on the extension and getting a start before the summer break.

Instantly and without permission, my heart pounds, and my stomach swarms with butterflies.

Is Alex with them?

But I squash those thoughts. He has bigger projects to work on.

An hour later and the children's colouring sheets are hanging on the wall and I've finished reading *The Gruffalo*. The children's excitement at seeing an enormous truck in their school quickly died down.

"Everyone can pack away their things. The lunch bell is going to ring any second," I announce.

I have the words out of my mouth and the bell in the corridors sounds to life, vibrating throughout the classroom. They grab their lunch boxes and run past me like a herd of elephants.

Yawning, I feel tiredness wash over me. I'm not sleeping great, and some strong coffee is in order to get me through the next few hours. But as I reach out to close the door again, my eyes avert to something towering over the children. They run around him, and he steps in and out of their way. I can't help myself. My eyes immediately drink in his amused expression, his shoulders tensing as if he can somehow make himself smaller, not to impede the children. How does he look so gorgeous in a khaki t-shirt and open red flannel shirt? And those faded blue jeans hang just right on his hips.

The hallway empties and his head comes up again, his eyes meeting mine. A faint smile threatens the corner of his mouth, but something else shoots across his face. Something that makes the hair on the back of my neck stand and my breath escape in tiny gasps.

"Miss Parker." He tilts his head politely as if he has transported us to the 1950s. I can tell he is restraining himself because I'm at work, but he's standing a little too close to be just a friend.

"Mr. Hale," I greet back, matching his tone. "Come in." I point my head towards the classroom.

His faint hint of a smile breaks into a wide one. He steps towards the door, but his physique is too big for us both, and he presses against me, his eyes wandering over my body. I swallow, hoping he doesn't notice how heavy I'm breathing, and my shoulders square. A light layer of dirt and perspiration covers his body, probably from offloading whatever was on the truck. But I love the ruggedness of him. His chocolate brown hair is rustled, and the sharp line of his jaw is tense, the muscles twitching.

"They didn't make teachers like you in my day." He raises an eyebrow, still studying me. "If they did, I wouldn't have bunked off so much."

I manage a breath for a small laugh as I slap his arm to move him into the classroom. He leans down, kissing me on the cheek, and the smell of sawdust, the remnants of whatever mint shower gel he washed with this morning, and the distinct scent that is Alex wash through my senses. He moves away from me, stepping inside before I close the door. The room feels smaller now he has stepped into it.

"You strike me as someone too disciplined to skip school?" I finally say, remembering I can speak.

He shrugs, his mischievous eyes locking with mine. "It's good to rebel sometimes."

Rebellious Alex.

I like the sound of that.

I walk to my desk and lean back on the edge, putting my hands on either side.

"Is that right?" I ask.

He stuffs his hands into his pockets, his feet shifting in his chunky boots. "Yes, Ma'am." His eyes leave mine to wander around the classroom.

I cross my arms over my chest, his expression amusing me far too much. "Lucky for me, I don't have to worry about eight-year-olds bunking off school."

"No," he says slowly, turning around. He blows out a loud breath. "It's far too colourful here. I can already tell you're a pretty fun teacher."

That makes my heart swell in my chest.

"You really love your job, huh?"

"Yes," I answer.

"I can tell. You look content here. Which, somehow, makes you even more beautiful. And it's killing me not to kiss you right now." His tone is even. Still swaying back and forth.

Why can't he kiss me?

I want to tell him to drop the chivalrous act and take me. Like I am his. He didn't have a problem with it before. But his eyes divert towards the window. I forgot about the kids outside, and when I look, three little girls are peering through the glass, excited to see who the stranger is in their classroom with their beloved Miss Parker. When they see me looking at them, they scatter away, giggling.

They will have never-ending questions after lunch.

"Sorry about that," I breathe.

I'm sorrier we aren't somewhere private, where I can kiss him without prying eyes.

"I didn't realize building work was getting started so soon." I need to change the subject because my lips are burning, and my fingers are tingling with the want to touch him. He's too far away.

"I have a team starting on Monday. We were dropping off supplies."

I bite down on my lip to smother the smile. "And they needed you?"

"No," he replies, his voice strong and honest. "I used the excuse to come and see you, Miss Parker."

Has he called me Mandy since stepping into my classroom?

"You know you can call me by my actual name here? I'm not *your* teacher."

He throws his head back, moaning and laughing at once. "Don't ruin it."

My mouth parts and a blush rushes to my cheeks. This man is fantasizing about me. The thought makes me blush for another reason.

"Like I said," he starts, "I didn't have teachers like you when I was at school. And I most definitely didn't have the same thoughts running through my head for any of them as I do for you right now."

I sit back on my desk, crossing my legs. My jeans suddenly feel too tight on my skin.

I'm already having a hard time getting through the day without his words making me flustered.

"I wanted to stop by quickly to see you, but I think I should go." He shakes his head, as if it's hard for him to say. I know what he's feeling. I want to run into his arms, but I need him to leave. At least I think that's what I need. "Being here, standing so damn far away, and not being able to touch you is driving me crazy," he says through gritted teeth, never breaking the blank expression on his face. He combs a hand through his hair, frustrated.

Yeah, me too.

He sighs, his shoulders falling. "Break a rule for me?"

My eyes narrow on him.

Since when do I have rules?

"I know it's Wednesday, and it's a good-girl-day, but break the damn rule and come to dinner with me tonight?"

I'm not sure if he's asking. If he is, he doesn't need to ask twice.

"Okay," I agree, relief washing over me because I don't have to wait so long to see him again.

"Really?" He seems surprised I cracked so easily.

I smile, playing with my lip between my teeth. I push off the desk, walk to the window and twist the bar to close the blinds, blocking out little eyes.

"Alex," I whisper, stepping towards him. I know now I'm not the only one to feel whatever it is between us. I wrap my arms around his neck, and he brings me closer, his hands firmly on my hips.

I repeat what he said to me on Sunday, "You make me want to break all the rules."

TWELVE

"Ladies first." Alex opens the gate to my front garden.

I roll my eyes, always making a joke of his old-fashioned charm.

For weeks, this is how it has been between us. Dates in and out of the house, kissing me goodnight at the door, sometimes going inside. We're getting to know each other and getting to know each other's bodies without ever going the full way.

I want to, more than I can ever tell him, but I close off every time.

The man has the patience of a saint, and I know, eventually, he will want to know why. But I feel no pressure from him. I only feel it from myself.

Anytime I go to his house at the beach, I never go upstairs, and although he doesn't question me on it, he must be wondering. Who gets nervous going upstairs in their boyfriend's house? It's pathetic.

And why, of all things in a relationship, is sex the deal breaker for me?

It's been so long since I even let somebody touch me. I know at least some part of it is because of Nick. But buried deep down, I know sex is a big step in a relationship. A step that will open a floodgate I shut a long time ago. Complications come with sex. You give yourself to the other person and the person deserves to know your past.

Somehow, and I don't know why, but tonight is different. I was unusually quiet during dinner and my chest was heavy. I need to open up to him. He deserves that much. Alex is making me feel things I haven't felt in a long time. His touch has thawed out parts of me I was sure would stay cold forever. He brings warmth and passion. And a simple look from him makes me feel like I'm the only other person in the world.

He makes me feel that.

Alex makes me feel.

Alex makes me want to claw back any reservations and give myself to him completely. But there are steps that need to be taken first. For both our sakes.

"Will you come in?" I can't meet his eyes, and the back of my throat stings.

"Of course," he breathes.

He knows me well enough now to know something is off. He hasn't asked, but sometimes he squeezes my hand a little tighter or pulls me closer to his body.

He slips off my coat from my shoulders, hanging it on the hook in my hallway.

"Drink?" I ask.

I don't look, but I know he's staring at me.

"No, but I'd like you to look at me."

I close my eyes, fighting back the tears, and pray he doesn't ask again. This is going to be hard enough.

"Mandy, look at me," he presses.

I square my shoulders, raising my chin to look up at him. I see a brief flash of panic cross his face before his eyes soften and a small smile creeps across his lips. He leans into me, kissing the top of my head as he takes a deep breath. I could stay this way for the rest of the night. I'm happy never moving, with his arms around my shoulders, keeping me together.

"Want to talk about it?" His voice is muffled against my hair.

"Yes," I sigh. "But let me change first." I back away from him, squeezing his hand before I leave for my room.

I make my way around my bedroom, switching on my lamps and closing my curtains. I hear Alex doing the same in the living room, and then the sway of soft music filters under my door.

What is he going to think? He doesn't strike me as the type of person who will have an issue with my past, but how would I know? We've been dating for eight weeks. Sex is my deal-breaker. For now, at least. What's his?

81

I slip off my black heels and tie my hair back, reaching for the zip at the top of my dress. It goes halfway down before it gets stuck. I yank it. Then yank it again.

"You have got to be kidding me?" I mutter, frustrated.

My arm begins to cramp from the awkward position and sweat breaks out across my brow. My head falls between my shoulders, defeated.

"Alex," I call.

"Uh, huh?"

I hear his footsteps coming down the hall. I called for him, yet he still knocked before opening the door.

Always the gentleman

He smirks, his eyes playing over my face. I'm sure I look crazy.

"I need help." I frown, putting my lower lip over my top one. "I'm stuck." I turn around, showing him the zipper.

He chuckles, his eyes growing bright as he steps inside the room. His heat at my back makes my stomach do somersaults, and my skin zings with anticipation.

"Baby," he says, pressing his lips to my neck. My head falls back on his chest. "If there's anything I am going to be good at, it's getting you out of a dress."

I huff, pushing my back against him. "Open the damn dress," I order, not stopping the giggle. "And don't rip it," I warn, knowing his hands can cause damage to delicate material.

"Spoilt sport."

Carefully, he pulls the zipper back up, closing me in before slowly–painfully slowly–unzipping it. I feel the air hit each inch of my skin as he makes his way downwards, and I shiver as his fingers graze my bare skin. I gulp dryly, my chest rising and falling as he stiffens at my back. The dress slips off my shoulders, and I catch it at my breasts, holding it in place. I don't want to lead him on, but I also don't want him to stop touching me.

I don't know what I want anymore.

"Alex," I breathe, turning around to face him.

He runs his hands over my shoulders and down my arms.

"I know." And nothing but understanding shows in his gaze. "I'll be outside."

I wait until he's far enough to expel the breath I am holding, and a single tear falls from the corner of my eye.

I didn't mean to fall for him so quickly, but my heart twists painfully, suffocating me, and depriving me of air. That's not how it always feels. That's how it is when the fear of losing him creeps to the forefront of my mind.

I change quickly into my sleep shorts and t-shirt and make my way to the living room. He's sitting on the couch, leaning forward, his elbows on his thighs and his head in his hands. When he hears me, his head shoots up, and he replaces the worry in his eyes with a reassuring smile. He catches himself before his eyes reach my legs. Rarely, but sometimes even Alex fails in his attempts at being a gentleman. He's a man after all and sometimes those needs take over.

He doesn't question me when I take the chair opposite him. I want the comfort of him close, but we need the space. His touch makes me forget things.

"Okay," I say, and curl my legs under my body.

"Mandy, you're killing me," he blurts.

I cross my arms over my chest as I sit back.

Strap yourself in, sweetheart. You're in for a wild ride.

"I'm sorry. I need to tell you some things."

His hands ball into fists and then release again, his knuckles turning momentarily white. He's not angry. He's out of his mind with worry. Sometimes, I think Alex would prefer if he could fold me up and carry me around with him every day. He's a fixer and fiercely protective of those he cares about. It's one reason I'm falling so hard, and why I'm petrified of saying what I'm about to say.

"I gathered that much." He half-smiles, his elbows still resting on his thighs, but his shoulders are tense.

"Let me get this out. Don't stop me, and you can tell me all your thoughts at the end. But if you stop me, I'll lose all courage." I try to smile when I say, "Ignore any tears."

His brows furrow and he pinches the bridge of his nose.

I need to get a move on before I give him a heart attack.

He nods, eager for me to keep going.

"I never expected for this to get so intense so quickly. And it's not a bad thing," I quickly correct, afraid he thinks this is his fault. It isn't about him. Not really. "And if we are moving how I think we are, you deserve to know the person you are doing it with." I inhale deeply, filling my lungs with some well-needed oxygen.

"As you already know, I've been friends with Garry and Claire since we were kids. We went to school together. But it wasn't always the three of us."

"Nick?" He nods, saying his name like he once knew him.

My eyes widen and my heart pounds at the mention of his name. It was oddly uncomfortable when Alex said it.

"I don't know his story, but Garry mentioned him," he explains.

Oh. My shoulders relax back into the chair again.

"Yes. But when I was fourteen, we became a little more than friends."

I'm expecting him to say something, but he doesn't. He stares at me attentively. I look down at my t-shirt, playing with a loose thread while I continue. "He was my first kiss. He was my first *everything*," I say slowly, blushing, and becoming suddenly shy. "We went to the same university and because it was local, we all stayed at home while studying. I was nineteen, and it was our second year of college. I remember it was a hectic week for us both, so we didn't see each other for a couple of days. We planned to go on a date that weekend. Dinner and a movie." I shrug, remembering how simple it was and how easy we were. "He was running a little late, and he called to let me know. I didn't pick up, and I still can't remember what I was doing that was so important I couldn't pick up the phone." Tears overflow and tickle my cheeks as they lull and then splash onto my hand. I wipe them, but it's no use, more fall in their place. I need to get this part of the story out before I tell him the rest. I need him to understand.

He shifts in his seat, and I know it's because he hates seeing me upset, but I asked him not to interrupt. The air around me turns cold and I wrap my arms around myself.

"I checked the voicemail after he called. He told me he was on his way, and we had time to grab a bite to eat first. But then everything changed. He mentioned the car ahead was swerving on the road. He assumed they were drunk, so he told me he loved me and said he had to go." I try to shake the memories from my head because the next part of the voicemail still haunts me. "Then he said he forgot to tell me something. And that's when I heard a scream and then lots of banging and moaning. Then there was nothing. The voicemail was still running, but it was silent, and that silence was the loudest thing I've ever heard." I blow out a breath in my best attempts to calm the trembling of my body. "He survived the initial crash, and there was hope again. But all that time, he was slowly bleeding internally. It was something so small that everyone missed it. They couldn't restore the oxygen to the brain in time." I rub my palms down my arms to get heat in my body. "He wrote a letter that week. I'm not sure if deep down he knew what was going to happen or if he was being cautious, but he made me his next of kin, so I decided to switch off his life support." I don't look at Alex. I can't bear it.

"It's a strange type of guilt to end someone's life when all that is left is a body. I should have fought harder for him. I wish every day I had, and I've carried him with me for over six years."

I stand, going to the sofa and sitting close to him, feeling like he needs me as much as I need him. He needs to know it's difficult to speak about, but I'm okay. I reach out, tangling my fingers in his.

"Alex, I'm telling you this, because Nick is the only other person I've ever been with. I've tried to date once or twice, but it never got past me running away from dinner. I've never slept with anyone else. I've never even kissed somebody else. Nick has been with me for so long, I can't get past feeling like I'm betraying him. And I want you so badly, but I want to be sure I'm ready." I squeeze his hand. The tears flowing from my eyes come for a different reason. They are sorrowful tears for Nick but mixed in there now is Alex, and everything he makes me feel.

I bring my eyes up to meet him, hoping he can see how much this means to me. "I've never felt anything for anyone else. Until you."

His eyes become wild, and his breathing is as heavy as mine, matching every shallow breath.

"I just need a little time. I don't want to scare you every time I get nervous. I'm a little scared of what it will open me up to. So many times, I've wanted to tell you to stay. Stay here with me for a night, like a normal couple, but too afraid to tell you why nothing can happen beyond that. So, I understand if you can't wait. You shouldn't have to hang around for me." I'm rambling, but I can't stop talking. I'm sitting here with a man who is giving me everything and I am giving him every excuse to walk away.

"Are you done?" he finally speaks, interrupting my word vomit.

I nod while wiping my cheeks with the back of my hand.

"Mandy, I won't pretend like I know what it was like for you. I wasn't there. I didn't know, Nick. But I don't think he'd want you living your life with this guilt. Guilt you have no reason to feel." He curls his fingers under my chin, so my eyes meet his again. "None of what happened was your fault." He brushes his thumb across my jaw.

It doesn't feel that way.

"I'm not what you want." Maybe he doesn't know it yet, but it's true.

His body stiffens, and he curses under his breath. "No." He shakes his head, and my heart fills with tiny shards of ice. "You're more than what I want. You're what I need."

A sting prickles the back of my throat, and when I close my eyes, more tears fall down my sticky cheeks. His reaction isn't what I expected, and at that moment, I fall into him a little deeper. Cautiously holding onto the hope, he can accept more.

As if reading my mind, he says, "Is that what you're worried about? You're worried I'll leave?"

I nod, unable to take my eyes away from him.

"You think I'll get scared because you once loved somebody so much it took you six years to meet someone else? You think I'll run because the person you chose was me?" He rubs the tears away from my face with his thumb. "Mandy, none of it makes me want to run away. Never. I don't know how it's possible, but you're suddenly more amazing than you were ten minutes ago. You're strong, and you're-"

"Alex." I stop him, closing my eyes.

There's more.

There's so much more.

I have to say it.

I need to get it out.

Goddammit, just say it.

As I open my mouth, his lips press against mine, swallowing the words I need to say. And just like that, they slip away, melting into him until they disappear.

"Come here," he murmurs against me, his voice commanding as he lifts me and puts me across his lap. "I'm not here to get you into bed, Mandy. And I'm not a caveman. I can share a bed with you without needing to have sex. Couples do it all the time." He laughs, breaking the tension, and the sound swirls in my stomach like a warm drink.

I wipe my face again, laughing with him through sniffles, and lie my head on his shoulder as he rubs his hand up and down the outside of my thigh. His touch brings me the relief I have craved all day.

"I won't lie, you're sexy as hell, but I'm a grown man. I can control myself." He moves his hands to either side of my head, forcing me to look at him. "I'm not going anywhere. You take the lead, and I will follow."

Tonight, this is enough. The rest must be told, but I want to hold on to him a little while longer.

So, later, when he kissed me to leave, I grabbed the inside of his elbow. Everything in my body knew I would crumble if he walked out the door.

"Stay." I'm not sure where the strength in my voice came from, but he simply smiled through a long breath, his shoulders relaxing as if he was waiting for the word all night.

He undressed, climbed into bed next to me, and pulled me closer. My head rested on his chest and I fell asleep to the thumps of his heart. The only heartbeat I had fallen asleep listening to in six years, and each beat carved away at what barriers I had left.

***

The clouds are black like coal and the ocean looks murky. The sand below my feet feels unstable, and the wind has a bitter edge that cuts right through me. A single, ice-cold raindrop falls onto my lips, distracting me from the concentration I have on the movement of the ghostly clouds.

"Who is he?"

I jerk a little before twisting my head towards the familiar voice. His black hair is perfect; his brown eyes are lustrous but the stern lines on his forehead show he isn't pleased. He looks hurt and disappointed.

I want him to know that I, too, am not pleased.

"Where the hell have you been?" I snap, anger boiling in my throat.

"I asked you a question, Mandy?"

"And I asked you one, Nick?" But he remains silent.

He's also very stubborn. We won't get anywhere shouting at each other, so I give in, as I always do.

"Who's who?" I question, knowing exactly who he's talking about. I want to buy myself time.

How am I going to explain this?

"Oh, come on, Mandy. He's sleeping in your bed. If you still don't know who he is, I'd say you have changed from the girl I once knew."

I'm a little hurt by that.

"How dare you? You think because you show up every time you

87

feel like it, you get to dictate who I am. Screw you, Nick. It's none of your business who is in my bed."

Ugh, he makes my blood boil sometimes. Who the hell does he think he is?

"You're right. It is none of my business. But it's a simple question."

"In your *'I mean business'* type of voice," I defend.

"I'm dead, love. How much business could I mean?"

He shines a breathtaking smile at me and that's it. I've melted.

"Damn you," I curse, not able to keep the grin edging on my lips. "His name is-"

"Alex," he answers before I can.

My eyes narrow as I stare at him.

"I know who he is. I wanted to make sure of the look in your eyes when you thought about him."

"What look?" I sound terrified, like he has caught me cheating. But I can't cheat on a dead guy, can I?

"The way you used to look at me."

My heart crushes to a thousand pieces and tears mist my eyes.

"I'm glad you are moving on. I want to see you happy again."

Something inside pains at my chest.

"You know it would be a lot easier to move on if you stopped turning up in my dreams like this."

"You keep me here."

"But I can't control what I dream."

"Neither can I. I'm not going anywhere until you let me go."

I smile then. "Never it is. Not until you tell me what it was you wanted to say before the accident."

I always ask and I always get the same reply. Silence.

He chuckles under his breath before turning his head where he becomes fixated on something. His eyes gleam with pride, longing, and what kills me most—disappointment.

"Beautiful."

I follow his gaze across the sand. There's a patter of little feet in front of the crashing waves and small footprints make a path in the sand. Short black hair blows lazily in the wind, falling against perfect porcelain skin.

My heart stops.

So tiny. Fragile. Beautiful.

My pulse quickens and tears fall from my eyes. I turn to look at

Nick, and I've never seen two people look so alike. My breath catches in my throat at the picture of truth running towards me.

He looks back at me and blood is pouring from the open gash on his forehead. He's pale and his eyes are dull.

Not again.

He runs a bloodied finger across my collarbone.

Lightning flashes in the distance.

"Regrets?" he asks, and a sob makes my throat tighten.

"Don't go," I beg.

"I was never here. Regrets?" he asks again.

Why is he doing this?

I cast my eyes down to my fingers as they clutch at the sand, but I can't get a grip and the grains seep between my fingers.

I swallow before answering, "Every day."

***

"Mandy! Baby, wake up."

My body shakes a little until my eyelids become like repelling magnets, flying open to a concerned look that penetrates through my skin. He releases his tight grip from my wrists to wipe away the tears cascading down my cheeks.

"It's okay," he assures me, lifting me onto his lap, and rocking me back and forth. "It was only a dream." His words become muffled as he kisses the top of my head.

It's only then, as I adjust to my surroundings and come back to reality, I hear my sobs. Controlling my breathing, I tilt my head to look at him.

It's far from the first time I've dreamt of Nick. It's also not the first time he's been my nightmare.

My throat burns and my fingers are cramping like I had them balled in a fist for too long. "I'm so sorry."

He pulls my head back on his chest and lays down, his arms keeping my body molded to his side. "Don't do that. Don't be sorry. Try to get some sleep."

I never sleep after my nightmares. I always get up, no matter the time. But tonight, I do.

When I wake, it's morning and I'm exactly where I was when I fell asleep—safe and wrapped tightly in his arms, like he's trying to make

89

the rest of the world disappear.

Gently, I creep away from him and tiptoe out of bed.

He'll be awake soon, so I make a cup of coffee and sit on my picnic bench in my back garden.

If he decides he wants to sneak out and leave, I will understand, but I can't watch him do it.

I should've told him about the nightmares before he came to bed. I probably scared him half to death.

I stretch and enjoy the feel of the sun on my neck. I always feel so stiff after those dreams, but not today. Alex held me like he could glue back all my shattered pieces.

"There you are."

He appears in the doorway bare-chested with his jeans hanging low on his narrow hips. Did he rush to get dressed?

Surely, I shouldn't be this flustered in the morning. But I've never had a half-naked man walk around my house, and definitely not one as gorgeous as Alex. He really pulls off the sleepy bed head.

"I thought you did a runner on me." He strolls to my side and kisses the top of my head. "Are you feeling okay?"

I shift in my seat and stare down at my coffee as he sits on the other side of the bench.

"Embarrassed. You should be the one doing the running."

He rolls his eyes and his mouth sets into a hard line.

I know. I'll need to get it through my thick skull, Alex isn't like me. He doesn't run.

"I'm right here."

I was never here.

Nick's words make bile rise in my throat.

"I should've told you about the nightmares. It rarely happens, but apparently, they look worse than what they are," I lie. He already knows who the dream was about. Garry told me I scream Nick's name when they get bad. "I guess talking about everything last night triggered something. I'm sorry."

He blows out a loud breath and runs a frustrated hand over his face. "I don't care that you have nightmares and stop saying sorry. I care because they hurt you. You were in pain last night. Now, I never want to leave you alone at night, so if it happens again, I can do what I did last night. It probably doesn't help, but I needed to stop the pain in your eyes."

A single tear tickles my cheek.

"It helped. I usually don't go back to sleep. I did last night."

"Have you ever talked to anyone about them?"

This is not something I want to talk about. "I did, but the dreams always came back. He was in my life for so long." I shift in my seat, feeling a little awkward.

"Don't feel like you can't talk about it around me, Mandy. Everyone has a past, and he is a big part of yours. He was your boyfriend and your best friend."

He gets it.

He really gets it.

"Yeah," I breathe, more than surprised. Or maybe it's relief. I'm not a complete basket case after all.

His shoulders relax and so do mine, and I sit back, trying to hide how emotional I want to be.

He comes to my side, crouching down. "No more talk of me running anywhere. I'm here. I promise. I'm not going anywhere."

I needed to hear that.

He presses his forehead against mine, lingering there for a long moment.

"Are you up to going for some breakfast?"

My eyes light up and I can't help but smile. I love how he can take my heavy and make it lighter.

Alex fixes.

I tilt my head and kiss him.

"Pancakes?" I laugh gently against his mouth.

"If it keeps the smile on your face, you can have pancakes every day of the week."

Then his head dips to my stomach, and before I know it, he's slinging my arm over his head and standing with me on his shoulder.

I laugh so hard it hurts.

"Alex, please let me down," I squeal. "What are you doing?"

He strides through the kitchen and towards my bedroom, but I can hardly see anything from tears of laughter streaming down my face. I jerk, playfully fighting him when his palm comes down on my ass.

"Before pancakes, I'm taking you back to bed so we can make out like gross teenagers."

He's distracting me, and it's exactly what I need.

He wants to protect me from my demons. But it breaks my heart because I realize, my demons are in my past and with the only other man I've ever loved.

THIRTEEN

"Bandit," I shout, rushing from my room and seeing him molesting my new sofa cushion. I grab it and put it back. "I thought you got fixed."

I swear, this dog would hump anything in sight.

No shame.

I rub my hand through his fur and his tail wags with excitement.

"Want some breakfast?" His tongue hangs out of his mouth and he jumps up, his paws almost reaching my shoulders. I don't know where Alex is going to put him when he's fully grown. He's like a bear.

Alex has been away on a business trip for four days and I felt each minute he was gone. Though Bandit didn't give me much time to dwell on it. If I don't walk him twice a day, he finds ways to tire himself out by tearing the rubbish apart, finding socks to chew on, or by humping absolutely everything. Including my neighbours' dog.

That was a disaster. I almost broke my back trying to pull a seventy-pound fur-ball off a dalmatian, while explaining to their owner, Bandit was neutered so there was no chance of puppies. My neighbour laughed and went on to explain, his dalmatian was also male, so there were definitely no puppies.

But I needed company when Alex wasn't here.

He kept his word. There's rarely a night we don't spend together. I haven't had a nightmare in weeks, but I think it's mostly to do with knowing I share a bed with a man whose shoulders fill a doorway.

Even the slightest disturbance and all I do is reach out and he's there. The bed felt empty and too big without him.

I can't believe how much has changed in such a short time. I always enjoyed having the bed to myself, but not anymore. For four nights, I distracted myself around the house until it exhausted me enough to not notice he wasn't there. Maybe the novelty of him will wear off, and I'll soon be kicking him out for snoring. But somehow, I doubt I'll ever want him to leave.

I can gradually feel myself opening up—mind, heart, and body.

When we first met, I wanted to take things slowly. I wanted to be confident of how I felt. But I knew sooner than I thought I would, and with him, I stayed away from the darkness.

I give Bandit his food and as I tidy away the plates from the dishwasher, the distinctive sound of his car pulls into my driveway. I can't help the smile and rush of blood to my cheeks. He's early. Why am I not surprised?

I open the front door as he pulls a brown bag of groceries from the back seat, shutting the car door with his foot. I devour the sight of him, my eyes roaming up his navy slacks, the sleeves of his white button-down rolled up to the elbows with the top button opened at his neck. But it's his face that makes my heart thump harder. His full lips relax as those piercing blue eyes find mine.

How does someone look this good so early in the morning?

"Hey, you." I lean against the door frame as he walks towards me.

"Good morning, gorgeous. You're a sight for sore eyes." He winks.

That I have undressed him with my eyes, has not fazed him in the slightest.

Bandit zooms past me and runs circles around Alex's feet. That's the thing with dogs—they have no sense of time. He thought Alex up and left him here with me—the woman who doesn't allow him to hump things.

Alex clicks his tongue against the roof of his mouth and pats his thigh. "Come on, boy." He lifts the paper bag before pulling me towards him with his free hand and presses a hard kiss to my lips. "I'm cooking breakfast."

I giggle as he slaps my ass on the way back into the house. "Well, good morning to you too."

God, I missed him.

He places the groceries on the countertop, ridding himself of his tie before unpacking the bag.

"Pancakes," he informs me.

Because pancakes make me smile.

He likes to keep to his word, and he's worried about how my nights were when he was gone.

I stand behind him and wrap my arms around his torso. My fingers tingle at the feel of his toned muscle beneath his shirt.

"Good trip?" I ask.

He turns his head over his shoulder and kisses the top of my head. "As good as it could go. Went to meetings. Worked on new designs. Went to dinners. Went to more meetings."

I roll my eyes and press my lips against his shoulders. "All work and no play makes Alex a dull boy."

He merely glances at me and smirks.

I peel myself away from him and stand at his side. "Do you always dress like this to cook breakfast for a woman?"

It's the second time I've seen him in a suit and the effect is no less than before. He commands attention without speaking a word, filling a space with his presence.

"Not just any woman," he corrects.

I chew my lip between my teeth, curious.

"Spit it out, baby. And stop biting your lip."

How does he do that: know what I'm thinking and doing without even looking at me?

I shift on my feet. "Have you cooked breakfast in many women's kitchens?" I've never asked him about his previous relationships. I've been too distracted by him to think of it.

From the corner of his eye, he looks at me, an amused smirk pulling at his mouth. "Are you asking how many women I've slept with, Mandy?"

My face is hot. "Not really. Not sure I want to know the answer." I laugh nervously. "But you know about my extensive dating history. Or lack of. What about you? Any hidden wives I should know about?"

He barks a laugh and rolls his eyes. "No wife. No ex-wife, either. I've had girlfriends. If that's what you're asking. One of those got serious enough to think about marriage and kids."

Oh. That was serious.

"What happened?"

He shrugs and turns to face me, leaning his hip on the counter. "Me and Rachel met when I was still in university. After I started working for the firm, we moved in together. And then life got busy. I began branching out with Hale Construction, and she was starting a career in law. We were busy, and when we finally found the time to be with each other, we realized the same spark wasn't there. It was mutual, and we remained friends."

Straight forward. Simple. No complications.

But how friendly was friendly exactly?

A laugh, deep and low, vibrates from his chest. "You're hot when you're jealous."

My mouth falls open, exasperated. "I am not jealous."

I am. I just don't have any right to be.

I slap my palm against his arm, but his bicep is too hard, and I hurt myself. I blow at the sting tingling my fingers, but I hardly notice because my lungs are having a hard time finding air when he stands closer. My stomach flips, and I'm surprised I haven't gotten used to this yet.

"So, why the suit?" I ask, distracting myself.

"I had an early morning meeting."

"Straight from the flight? On a Saturday?" I raise my brow.

That doesn't seem fair. Or maybe I've become too accustomed to my Monday to Friday teaching schedule.

"Business is business." He removes a large bowl from the cupboard.

Alex is all things rough and ready, but watching him in such a domestic setting, preparing pancakes in a suit, makes a fire pool at my core. He's at ease, and completely at home in my home.

He tips flour into the bowl. The powder creates a cloud and speckles his shirt. He cracks in two eggs before continuing.

"I've wanted a new architect for a while. It's becoming too much for just me. And I have better ways to spend my time now." He kisses the tip of my nose and I press my lips together to stop the grin. "I had to convince the best in the business to leave his firm and come work with me. He's leaving for a month to finish up on his last project so he could only meet me at six this morning. Hence the suit."

"Who is it?"

"Ian."

My eyes widen. "Your friend Ian? Sally's brother? You wore a suit to convince your best friend to work with you?"

He turns to face me, looking at me like I'm crazy. "Mandy, for five years I've been trying to get that asshole to come work for me. He says no every time."

"And did you win him over this time?"

Of course he did. Alex wins everyone over.

He returns to whisk the batter, pouring extra milk, and his brawny arms make simple work of it. "Yes, I did."

"What made him change his mind?"

He winks at me. "The suit."

I nudge him. "Cocky much? I guess money had nothing to do with it."

He shakes his head and cups his hand under my chin. "You have no faith in me. How could he say no to working with this face every day? And money may have had a tiny part to play."

I thought so.

I smile up at him. "Let me cook. You'll destroy the magic suit."

I catch his glare from the corner of his eye. Alex doesn't give a shit about the suit. He turns to me, kissing me again before putting his hands under my arms and lifting me onto the corner of the counter.

"Nonsense. I'm cooking you some breakfast. And then," he turns back to the bag of flour, "You and I, are going to watch movies all day." He runs two fingers down either side of my cheeks. I take a moment to realize what he's doing.

"Alex," I squeal, laughter vibrating through my chest as the flour falls from my face.

"And after movies, it looks like you are going to war, soldier." He chuckles, standing between my legs, gripping my hips, and pulling me closer.

My laughter trails off as his hands find the bare skin of my back, and his fingers slide below the waistband of my jeans. His bright eyes become suddenly dark, and my lungs scream for more air because he pulled what was left in the room. I lick my lips, wishing I could taste him instead, and every inch of my skin tingles when his look roams from my eyes to my lips. I straighten, wrapping my legs tightly around his back, my core pressing hard against him. I swallow dryly, boldness washing over me when his hands leave my back and explore every curve. He dips his chin, his eyes meeting mine again as his thumb brushes across my lower lip.

"Kiss me," I breathe, not caring if it sounds like I'm begging, and neither does he.

He grabs the back of my neck, pulling me into him. When his tongue meets mine, we move together, surrounded by searing heat. My moans greet the groan in his chest, and my fingers grip onto his shoulders for support, digging my nails into the material of his shirt. It doesn't matter if I'm already sitting. Every muscle in my body has become liquid, going lax against him, and it feels like I could become one with the counter below me. I fist at his shirt, pulling it free from inside his trousers, and my fingers dance along the hardness of his torso, my body screaming for more of him.

As my nails scratch at his chest, his kiss devours me completely, like we're starved of each other's taste, and needing everything the other will give. I don't know how much that is yet, but I know I don't want this to stop.

And as if karma herself has heard my thoughts, the buzz of his phone ringing sounds from behind him. I pull away, leaning my forehead against his, breathless, and silently cursing whoever interrupted us.

I close my eyes, disappointment lodging low in my stomach because I wanted to see where that look got me.

He takes a glimpse at it, and I can't help but notice how his eyes light up.

"I'm sorry. I have to take this."

I tap my palm against his chest, shaking my head and smiling.

He taps the screen and holds the phone up. Video call.

"Hey, pretty girl."

I hear a small huff and then, "Mama won't let me wear her lipstick to summer camp."

This must be his niece. I know he's close to her.

Alex looks to me for the answer, like this is a conversation he hadn't prepared for this morning, and I can't help but laugh at his helpless expression.

"Ava, it's eight in the morning. Listen to your mama. Where is she?" he asks.

"I don't know. She told me to call you."

Alex tilts his head. "Did she now?"

From where I'm standing, I get a brief look at Ava's small face. Her hair is tied back, and she's holding lipstick between her fingers.

I purse my lips because I could burst into laughter at any second.

"No lipstick. You're six. You can wear it when you're thirty."

Six?

My chest tightens and I let my mind wander to another little girl. Maybe she would have liked to wear my lipstick.

Casting my eyes back to the screen, I ignore the burn in my throat.

"Uncle Alex, where are you?"

Six-year-olds and their questions.

"I'm at a friend's house, Ava."

"Is it Mandy?"

I'm smiling so big my cheeks are aching.

She's feisty and seeing him speak to her means I get to see a different side to him. And damn it if it doesn't make me warm all the way to my fingertips.

"Yes," he drawls.

"Can I say hi?"

He glances at me like he's afraid I'm about to run for the hills.

When he doesn't answer, she says, "Is Mandy my aunt now?"

I swear the colour drains from his face. He needs rescuing.

Without a second thought, I grab the phone from his hand. I clear my throat. "Hey, Ava. I'm Mandy." I wave at the screen.

I can see a blush creep across her cheekbones as she swipes a black-coloured strand away from her face.

"Hi." She's suddenly shy and her voice is small.

I dart my eyes back to Alex and I don't know if the look in his eyes is fear or if he's gone a little mushy.

I set the phone on the counter and lean down on my elbows, resting my chin on my palm.

"So, what lipstick did you want to wear?"

She holds up the crimson stick.

Sweet heavens.

"I like the colour, but I think it might be a bit much for summer camp. And you don't need lipstick. You're already so pretty."

And she is. Big brown eyes covered with thick lashes and the cutest pout.

She sighs and puckers her lips. "That's what Uncle Alex tells me."

I nod and smile. "You should listen to him. Let me tell you something my mom taught me when I wanted to wear makeup." I pinch my cheeks between my fingers. "If you do this a couple of times, it makes your cheeks all rosy, and then you won't need anything else."

Alex grunts at my side. "Jesus Christ, she will have her cheeks ripped off."

I wave my hand at him to shut him up.

When I look back, she's already doing it.

"See. Beautiful."

She smiles a big, toothy grin. "Thanks, Mandy."

"No problem. Do you want to talk to Alex again?"

"No thanks," she says and the phone drops from her hand. I'm looking at a ceiling when I hear her shout, "Mama, look at my cheeks."

Hand on my hips, I turn back to Alex, quite proud of how I handled that. "Crisis averted. She's a cutie."

"She breaks my heart. She's six going on sixteen and she has the attitude to prove it."

"It's nice you're so close to your family. She obviously adores you."

There's affection in his eyes, and it warms my blood.

"We're all close, but when my mother died, Lydia took on the mother role. I was twenty, but she still felt like she could boss me around. Then Ava came into our lives and there wasn't a dad in the picture, so I wanted to make sure she at least had some kind of father figure. Can't say I'm doing a good job at it, but she has me wrapped around her little finger."

I can see that.

"It looks like you're doing a great job from here."

His eyes turn dark, and the atmosphere around us doesn't seem so playful anymore. He leans in closer, pulling at the waistband of my jeans so I'm pressed against him. "You're sexy as sin, woman."

I want to keep talking. I want to know more. I want to know everything, but his hands are suggesting something else.

Conversation over.

I press my palm against his chest. "Oh, really?"

He nuzzles his face in the crook of my neck and kisses the skin along my collarbone.

Don't stop.

But his phone buzzes again and this time he doesn't hide his frustration. "For fuck's sake."

It's not the ring tone for a video call. I assume it's not Ava.

"Ignore it," he groans, his voice unrecognisable.

I want to. I want to tell him to throw the phone far away and get back to kissing me, but I know better.

100

"It could be important. Business never stops, remember?" I smile reassuringly, kissing him once more before releasing him.

Reluctantly, he pulls away from me, and I immediately regret telling him to take the call. My body feels empty in his absence.

His lips edge up apologetically as he brings the phone to his ear. "This better be important," he snaps, making his way to the back garden.

I continue where he left off, making the pancakes, heating a pan, and pouring a scoop of batter in. Every so often, my eyes dart to the window. His face is animated with what I think is frustration, and he is waving his hand in the air. Whatever the phone call is about, he isn't happy. I hope he doesn't have to leave. I want more of what I got on the counter.

Long minutes later, as I finish putting the pancakes and bacon on plates, he walks back inside. He switches off the phone and tosses it on the table. His shoulders tense, and his feelings are clear on his face. Glancing at the food, he huffs and throws his head back.

"It's fine," I say, already knowing he's about to apologize. "I enjoy cooking pancakes." I stretch on my tiptoes to kiss his chin. "Everything okay?"

"It's nothing that couldn't have waited until Monday. Some of those men still need me to hold their hand."

"Sit," I order, pulling out a chair. "You're grumpy when you're hungry."

"Thank you." He smiles, giving in to my demands. "These look better than my pancakes, anyway."

I bite the inside of my cheek to stop my giggle, knowing the comment is an extra blow to his ego.

He gets stuck in when I take my seat, his mood lifting with every bite. "My mom used to make pancakes every Saturday when we were kids."

The titbit of information about his mother and an insight into his childhood makes my face stretch with a grin.

"Even as adults, we always went to my parents' house on a Saturday morning for pancakes. Some families do Sunday dinners. We had Saturday morning breakfast." His eyes are soft as he replays the memory. I reach across to stroke his hand with my thumb. "We don't do it as much as we should since she died. None of us can make pancakes like she used to, but these are the best I've had since hers."

He takes my hand in his and kisses my palm.

"It's love," I blurt, and both of our eyes widen at my declaration. My cheeks blush furiously. I need to sew my mouth shut. "The secret ingredient in the pancakes," I quickly explain, but he's looking at me like I make no sense because I don't. "My mother used to always say, the secret ingredient to the best pancakes is love. They have to be made with love."

His lips purse painfully before his shoulders erupt in waves of laughter. I quickly follow, his amusement easing the tension, but I still burn with embarrassment.

"I really need to start explaining myself better," I moan, covering my face with my hands.

Getting up from his seat, he crouches in front of me, forcing my hands away, and taking them in his. The look in his eyes makes me instantly relax.

"It's definitely love." He smiles, his voice strong and reassuring, and the way he says it makes my heart jump in my chest. I don't know if we're still talking about pancakes. "Your mother is a smart woman. I'm looking forward to meeting her." Before taking his seat again, he places his lips over the back of my hand. Eyes covered by thick lashes closing momentarily.

"Speaking of my mother, and while I'm out here blurting things out. Would you like to meet my parents? It's their thirtieth wedding anniversary in three weeks, and they asked if you would come to the party they are having at our restaurant?"

His head rolls back, another grunt escaping him, before roughly running his hands over his face. This man is a ball of frustration today. Am I scaring him that much?

"I'm sorry, Mandy, I can't. I can't tell you how much I want to, but I can't."

That's a lot of *can't*.

My heart sinks, and I'm sure it's visible in my expression.

"Baby, I'm sorry. That's what the phone call was about. The latest build: the apartment complex has proven to be more difficult than originally planned. A shipment from overseas has been delayed since last week, so now to catch up with the deadline I must put men on different shifts over twenty-four hours. The call earlier was from my colleague, Andrew. He was having trouble getting the permits, but I got it sorted. I'm so sorry." He seems genuinely disappointed, like the thought of letting me down pains him.

"Alex, you will have plenty of opportunities to meet my parents. I understand." I get up to sit across his lap, wrapping my arms around his neck. "Best to enjoy today then, because it sounds like you are going to be a busy man."

He cups the side of my face with his hand, bringing it closer to his.

"Mandy, you are overflowing with the secret ingredient." He covers his mouth over mine, both of us gasping against each other.

Love.

It's definitely love.

FOURTEEN

Something happened to me this morning. Something strange and uncomfortable and I didn't like it.

I woke up and felt needy.

I've woken from my sleep because of loneliness on more than one occasion, but I was never needy.

I chastise myself and try to convince myself it's juvenile, but it's not. Deep down, I know he's my gravity, and he pulls me towards him always. His atmosphere breaks away all the dark clouds.

Over the years before Alex, I grew accustomed to the cold and loneliness. It became my constant companion. I was living in this murky underworld where everything appeared bland, and my heart always threatened to cave in.

Then he came along.

He eases the pain, like a drug I can't get enough of because, without him, I begin to slip back under. It might not be healthy, but it's too late. I'm addicted.

I'm addicted to him.

I'm addicted to his touch and the way he looks at me.

I've lost my damn mind.

This is why I'm pulling onto a dirt road and passing the sign for Hale Construction. I continue until I reach the site and bounce around on my seat as my car screeches against gravel, throwing dust clouds in the air.

It's the weekend, but Alex is working every minute he can. The deadline for his project is approaching quickly. With delayed shipments and clients driving Alex within an inch of insanity, everyone works around the clock. Including the boss.

I hate admitting how much, but I miss him. The feeling pains me, digging at me somewhere below my ribcage until I feel bruised.

He shared my bed last night, but I haven't seen him properly in a week. He was late at work, and I already exhausted myself with sleep that would not come. So, when he called before midnight, I tiredly made my way to the door. He wrapped me in his arms, kissing me deeply, the scent that is uniquely Alex filling my senses, and I allowed myself to melt into him. No words, just heated kisses before I pulled away. His shoulders were tense and straining under the material of his flannel shirt, his eyes rimmed red, and dirt smeared across his face.

"I put fresh towels in the bathroom." I knew he wouldn't relax into sleep until he washed the day off.

He didn't say a word. The right side of his mouth rose before he took me, claiming me with his tongue.

I returned to bed as I heard the water run in the shower. Five minutes later, he crawled in beside me, his intense heat at my back as he pulled me towards him, our bodies fitting perfectly together, and he encased me against his strong chest.

"Seeing you at the end of a tough day will always make it worth it, Mandy." His voice was tired and lazy. "Goodnight, baby."

"Goodnight," I whispered, interlocking my fingers with his at my chest.

Neither of us needed to say it, but we both knew why he was there. We slept better when we were together. Within minutes, his breathing fell even at my neck, and then I welcomed a deep sleep of my own.

I woke to cold sheets, an empty bed, and an even emptier heart.

I don't know what I'm expecting from showing up to see him unannounced, but I need to. I may be crazy, but I'm enjoying insanity.

I step out from my car and my eyes take in the ten-storey luxury apartment complex that wasn't there three months ago. The site bustles, busy workers everywhere, and the loud sounds of heavy machinery drown out their voices.

I glance around, hoping I can set eyes on him, but nothing familiar catches my attention. I know he'll be close to killing me for walking through the building site without a hard hat, but he's worth it. And I enjoy the thought of him trying to be mad at me.

I walk deeper into the site, and I regret wearing my knee-length sundress and sandals. There's still no sign of Alex.

"Excuse me," I interrupt a man whistling a tune as he gets on with his work. "I'm looking for Alex."

He takes me in, his eyes roaming from my head to my toes. I really should have worn something a little more practical.

"We've got a few of those around here. Got a last name for me?"

I shake my head, feeling foolish and completely out of place. "Sorry. Yes. Alex Hale."

His mouth purses before edging into a knowing smile. "You're here for the boss-man. He's in the office." He turns, pointing to the far side of the site at a temporary prefabricated building.

"Thank you." I smile appreciatively before moving away.

"Good luck, love," he calls after me. "He's in a foul mood."

That wipes the smile right off my face. Swallowing hard to suppress my nerves, I wave another thanks before walking towards the office.

It isn't until I get closer I hear the boom of a roar. The voice I know. The tone of said voice is completely foreign. Alex always has a strong vibration when he speaks. His voice is deep and always reminds me of whiskey over ice. But I've never, in the short time I've known him, heard him raise his voice. Even slightly.

"Bullshit, Dominic. The shipment was your responsibility. You fucked up. And Aiden, wipe the stupid look off your face. You fucked up just as much. You both better get your shit together, and if I see one of you slacking again, you can walk off this site, and don't come back. I've got enough to deal with besides having to hold your hands."

Some muffled words follow and then I watch two grown men walk out of the office looking more like children after a humiliating spanking. One thing's for sure: he's most definitely angry.

My shoulders square and more than once in ten seconds, I deliberate turning around and leaving. Maybe I'm the last person he wants to see. But as much as I fear interrupting his day at work, in his voice there was more stress than anger, and I want more than anything to soothe away the stress.

I lean against the door frame, drinking him in before putting a break to whatever torment he's in. I could soon be in the firing line of his rage, but I don't care.

His back is to me as he leans against his desk, and his muscles strain

106

against the material of his white t-shirt. The veins along his tanned arms protrude as he grips the edge of the table, and his head has fallen between his shoulders.

I tap my knuckles lightly against the door. "Why so serious, Mr. Hale?"

For a split second, his fingers clutch tighter around the edge of his desk before recognition hits. He spins around, and his eyes lock with mine.

And boom.

This is why I am here.

This is why I am needy, because with a single look my way, everything else disappears.

A tingling sensation prickles along my spine, causing me to stand up straight as he drinks in every inch of me. I feel it. I feel the slow pull of his eyes down my body and back up, landing on my breasts before his eyes fasten on mine again.

But dammit, apart from the obvious lust, and how he's undressing me with a stare, I don't know what he's thinking.

He lets out a loud breath. His shoulders visibly relax as his fingers stretch out from the fists he has balled them into.

"Exactly what I needed." Ever so slowly, his lips lift into a gentle smile, and I'm mush again, about to pool to liquid right here in his office.

Nervously, I shift from one foot to the other.

"Hey," I breathe.

The look in his eyes has stolen my voice, and the heat is suffocating. I bunch my hair in my hand, remove it from over my shoulders, and allow it to fall down my back. I wish I'd tied it up because my curls feel too heavy. But I don't think the heat from the sun is the only thing making me hot, and my skin becomes clammy.

Alex sees his opportunity and takes it. As Alex always does. He's in front of me in a second, with his lips tracing along the skin of my collarbone, traveling leisurely up my neck, below my ear, and across my face.

"And here I was, thinking you were angry." My laugh is futile, and my breathing comes heavier.

I close my eyes, fully aware of the busy work going on right behind me, but he doesn't appear bothered.

As his lips reach mine, they smother my moan, and he wraps his arm tightly around my back, bringing me closer. He pulls me inside the office, not once removing his lips from mine when he slams the door and backs me up against it. Finally, away from prying eyes.

"Oh, believe me, Mandy. I am angry." He rasps, and it makes my knees lock.

His arm cages me in above my head, palm flat against the door, while his other arm is keeping my body close to his. His fingers run roughly along my shoulder, pushing my bag to the ground.

That reminds me. I have breakfast.

"I brought you some…" I swallow, blinking as his hand cups my breast.

Alex is staring down at me, his eyes like lava, nothing playful, and all serious.

"I brought you some food."

Both our breathing frantic, crazed heartbeats pounding at our chest, and almost molding into one.

This should scare me, shouldn't it? This should make me want to run away. But it doesn't. It makes me want to say yes to everything his wild eyes are suggesting.

"Thank you, baby, but I'm only hungry for you right now. And if you walk through my site again without a hard hat and in this dress, I'll put you over my knee," he warns with the hint of a smirk before his lips come crashing against me again.

I'll never survive this man.

His tongue is hot and needy, swallowing every moan and breath between us. I feel his knee nudge between my legs, cautiously separating me, giving him space to move closer. He does so slowly, keeping his eyes locked with mine for a reaction he doesn't like.

To hell with the cautious approach.

I move my legs for him, separating myself around him, and for the first time, instead of freezing, I wrap my arms around his neck and pull him back to me.

We both lose it then. Our need is nothing short of animalistic.

In one movement, his hot hands push my dress up around my waist, his fingers gripping tightly to my thighs before lifting me high against him. I lock my ankles around his back, and his hands need little effort to hold me in place. He nips along my chest, pulling at my dress to expose my breast, taking it in his mouth, sucking, teasing with his tongue.

And oh. My. God.

If heaven is a place, it's Alex's mouth.

"Alex," I gasp, throwing my head back against the door.

I want more.

So. Much. More.

He can have me right here against the door. Although, I'm afraid the door won't stand a chance. His mouth is so feverish, his hands everywhere, and my hips rock against him.

But his kisses become slower, and his mouth gentler as he moves along my jawline, pulling the top of my dress back up.

No.

Don't do that.

He presses his forehead against mine. I'm so hot now, I'm sure if I could radiate the heat, I'd burn the entire construction site down.

"You're so fucking beautiful." His voice is still soaked in his left-over need.

He holds me in place with one arm as his other hand comes to my face, brushing away the waves of wild hair that have fallen around my cheeks. I pull my lower lip between my teeth, but his eyes lower to it before he tugs my lip free with his thumb and places a gentle kiss on the swollen skin.

His eyes find mine again, and I feel a part of my heart explode. The part I closed off for so long, I was afraid I would never find it again. Alex has opened it with the force of an atomic bomb. He has thawed out the frozen parts of me, while the rest of me continues to fall. I am falling so fast and so hard; I could never catch up. Not even if I wanted to.

I don't want him to stop and remove me from being wrapped around his body. His consideration of what I want, or what I wanted, makes that part of my heart melt even faster. I'm glad I can help ease his tension. But maybe now I've created a different type of tension for him.

He kisses me once more before lowering me down and steadying me with his hands on my shoulders. I look up at him gratefully because my legs are like jelly and I have a deep ache between them. He does his best to be a gentleman, fixing my straps, tucking my hair off my shoulders, but I take over and smooth out the wrinkles of my dress.

Still fixing the material, I say, "I'm sorry. I know you're busy. I just really wanted to see you." I feel shy, like he didn't have me pinned to the wall with my breast in his mouth thirty seconds ago.

His finger presses gently under my chin, bringing my face up to look up at him. "Thank you for coming. You're a breath of fresh air and exactly what I needed." He kisses the tip of my nose before bending over to pick up the bag he flung from my arm. "Now, what have you brought me? I'm starved."

I'm sure he's being polite. He's probably too busy to even think of eating in the middle of the morning, but I won't apologize for it. He needs to eat.

When have I become a suburban housewife from the forties?

"I could get used to this," he says, unpacking the food from the bag.

I laugh. "Don't."

I did what I needed. I've given him his food, and I got to see him. I shouldn't take up more of his busy day. I throw my thumb over my shoulder. "I should probably get going."

He's having none of it. "Sit." He gestures to the seat on the other side of his desk. "I didn't want you to come here to bring me food and so I could molest you against the door."

A blush creeps up my neck to my cheeks.

"Mandy, sit your ass down and have breakfast with me."

"I already ate."

What the hell is wrong with me?

I don't want to leave. Why am I acting like I want to run a thousand miles in the opposite direction?

He winks at me, and my shoulders relax. I think I have a thing for Alex's wink, and he knows it. His effect is intoxicating.

"Then stay and keep me company while I eat."

I shake my head, unsure why I make things so complicated. "Of course."

I eye him as I take my seat. He glances back and forth as he removes the food from the bag, and I run my hand over the goosebumps dancing along my arm.

I'm not sure what just happened between us, but it left me aching for breath, and I'm unable to fill my lungs with adequate oxygen.

I cross my legs at the knees, leaning my elbow against the arm of the chair.

"So, this is how the other half lives?" I look around his office. Nothing extraordinary. Four walls, a desk, two chairs, and a large board with pinned blueprints. His desk is riddled with papers, what looks like a broken measuring tape, and a hard hat. The latter makes my legs clench, remembering what he said he would do to me if I didn't wear one next time.

He takes his seat, and I enjoy how his eyes close briefly as he takes the first bite of food. He mumbles something incoherent and points to the meal with his fork in a way that tells me it's good.

My mother is right: a way to a man's heart is through his belly.

He swallows, washing it down with his coffee before leaning back in his chair. He waves his fork around the open space.

"Not exactly luxury. This is the first thing I've eaten here in weeks that doesn't have dust as a side dressing."

I stand and go to the building designs pinned to the whiteboard. "Is the poor big man afraid of a little dust?" I mock.

He doesn't laugh at my joke, but amusement flickers in his eyes, and I think he might really put me over his knee now.

I trace my fingers over the drawings. Every detail is laid out to perfection. Each apartment with precise measurements. I suppose it's how architecture works, but I can hardly teach my eight-year-old's math.

I avert my eyes to the tall building outside and I'm mesmerized by how these drawings can convert to an actual real-life apartment complex. And all of it straight from his mind to the page, and then bricks.

"This is amazing, Alex."

He pushes the food aside, brings his laptop closer, and opens it.

"Come here." He leans against his seat and pats his thigh.

I sit across his lap, wrapping an arm around his neck as he holds me with one hand. The other is typing and opening a program on his computer. "I want you to see this."

For fifteen minutes, he walks me through a virtual tour of the complex. All the way up to the rooftop heated pool. I don't have the slightest idea what he is talking about, but the way his eyes light up, enthusiasm dripping with every syllable, he keeps me interested.

Alex is a complete and utter nerd. An extremely talented, charismatic, and dripping in sex appeal type of nerd. The nerd I think I can never live without now because he has burrowed himself so deep in my heart, I've lost him in there somewhere. And every day he takes up a little more space until I am consumed and possessed by him, wholly and without hesitation. With every stroke of his palm along the outside of my bare thigh, I relax deeper into him. His arms have become the most comfortable place to be, and not being in them brings back the coldness.

When he finishes, he looks at me, the eagerness in his eyes quickly diminishing and unifying with the fire I recognize all too well now. It's the fire I'm always drawn to because Alex brings heat wherever he goes. He's my furnace, and he banishes away demons in his wake. Demons he doesn't know I fight with every day. Those demons retreat from battle when I'm in his presence. But I'm not a fool, and I won't be lured into a false sense of security. Those same demons have plagued me for as long as I can remember, and although they may have temporarily retreated, I'm nowhere close to winning the war.

With a deep breath, I gather those demons and once again push them to the back of my mind.

Not today.

I run a gentle finger across his jawline, watching how it tenses under my pressure before placing breathy kisses over the points I've touched. Feeling him hard beneath me, pressing against my thighs, I continue the delicious journey of his face with my lips and tongue. I finally land on his mouth and tenderly take his bottom lip between my teeth. His groan is something deep in his chest. Pulling away, I lean my forehead against his.

"I should go," I whisper against his mouth.

He stills with even breaths and I can tell it leaves him as tortured as it does me.

Cupping the side of my face, he rubs his thumb along the base of my throat. "I'll come over tonight. Don't wait up. I hate waking you. Hide a key somewhere outside and let me know."

On instinct and without a second thought, I say, "Take my spare one." I stop myself, backing away from him, and my eyes scan over his features for any signs of fear. The words came out so easily and I realize all of this may be too soon for him. It felt natural, but it doesn't mean the feeling was mutual.

His mouth eases into a slow smile. "It's about time," he scoffs through a light laugh, slapping my ass playfully. "You've had mine in your purse since last week."

My eyes narrow.

What?

Taking advantage of my silence, he continues, "I wanted to be sure, if there was ever a night, you were up late constructing buildings and you wanted to come home to me, then you could."

I'm sure my face is so skewed it's painful.

"Why didn't you say anything?"

"I'm surprised you didn't find it."

How had I not noticed it? But he probably put it into the side of my purse I never use. It still looks brand new on that side.

He pinches the bridge of his nose as if gathering his thoughts and how to vocalize them in a way that won't have me welcoming back the demons. He reaches for my hand, interlocking our fingers, before bringing his gaze back to mine.

Playful Alex disappears again.

"Because, Mandy, I realized very early into this, I am ready for everything. All of it. You make me want to not second guess anything and go headfirst. But I want to make myself clear. I'll never be one hundred percent ready until you are. It will always be your lead."

And I wonder why I'm needy when he goes around saying things that go straight through my chest.

There he goes, consuming me a little more than he did before.

FIFTEEN

"It's such a pity Alex couldn't make it. I really wanted to meet him."

My mother busies herself with cleaning already spotless countertops.

"He wants to meet you too, Mom, but he's a busy man. I'm sure you'll get another opportunity to meet him. If you promise not to scare him, I can bring him for dinner sometime."

I want him here too, but he can't be everywhere, and as much as I want to introduce Alex to my family, I'm not sure I'm ready. I have so much to tell him first.

My family will love him. But meeting each other's families is a big step, and one I never had to make before.

Everything is new. Everything appears complicated when it isn't.

Alex isn't complicated.

Alex is perfect.

I swallow, breaking through my daze. That man is fast becoming my every thought.

"Honey, I wouldn't be the one to scare him. That's your father and brother's job." She nods towards the next room, where the sounds of a football game and shouting fill the air.

I roll my eyes but smile.

"Claire tells me he's a dish." My mother darts her gaze towards me, looking away again to hide the smirk, and my face gets hot.

Claire, the traitor. It's times like these I wished my friends weren't treated more like my siblings.

"Nobody describes people as being a 'dish' anymore, Mom." I take a sip of my coffee. "But he's definitely a dish."

We both laugh, and my face flushes even more. She turns to look at me. Tea towel in one hand, the other on her hip, and her smile fades away.

"I've never seen you like this before, Mandy." She walks to me, placing a gentle kiss on my head. "Seeing you so happy is the best anniversary gift. I like Alex already if this is how he makes my girl feel."

I can almost see some worry lift from her shoulders.

"I am happy, Mom," I agree, hugging her around her waist.

Sometimes, I just needed a hug from my mother.

She takes a seat with me at the table, placing her hand in mine. The worry comes back to her shoulders. "Have you told him?"

"No. Not yet." I take another long breath. "I never expected to feel this way about someone. And with him, it was so instant and intense. If I'm honest, it scares me." I look down at my lap. "But I will tell him. He's going on a business trip this week and I'll tell him after. It's been four months. I can't keep it from him any longer. He knows about Nick, but my throat closes every time I try to tell him the rest."

My mother moves the hair away from my face.

"He knows when I'm finding something difficult to talk about, and he always tells me to do it in my own time. Sometimes, I wish he'd demand I tell him," I explain, taking a steadying breath. "It's not his fault, and I know I need to tell him before we go any deeper into this."

Who would've thought I'd be someone who needed less space?

My mother flashes a reassuring smile, patting my hand and prompting me to continue.

"I have that fear again, Mom."

"What fear, sweetie?"

I bite the inside of my cheek and look up to stop the tears threatening to fall. "The fear of losing someone else."

"Oh, Mandy," my mother says as she takes me in her arms again. She pulls back after a minute, taking my face in her hands. "Everyone has a past. If Alex is as amazing as I hear, he will understand that."

We both smile at each other, tears floating in our eyes as understanding flickers between us. It's an understanding that never needs to be spoken.

"Okay," I say, shaking my head as I stand. "Not today. Today we are celebrating you and Dad, and the life sentence you are both serving. And I need to get to the store." I hug my mother again, and this time I kiss the top of her head. "Thanks, Mom."

"Anytime." I feel her eyes on me as I leave the kitchen.

"Call me if we need anything?" I shout out before leaving.

As I close the front door behind me, my eyes catch sight of a tall figure strolling up the driveway. He stops, a grin playing on his lips, and every nerve in my body instantly tingles like it always does when he's near.

"There's my gorgeous girl."

I've still not blinked, and the shock has stolen my breath.

"Alex, what are you doing here?" I finally say, but the sight of him makes me smile with relief, and instinctively, as if I am no longer in control of my body, I go straight into his arms.

"I was an idiot," he says, kissing me before running his hands down my bare arms. I sigh and feel my legs need extra support. "I shouldn't have told you I couldn't make it. I complicated my own plans when I shouldn't have."

Alex isn't complicated.

Alex makes life simple again.

"But aren't you busy with a deadline? Don't you need to be at the site in the morning?"

His features turn down, serious when he says, "I'll never be too busy for you. I booked into a hotel tonight. I can leave in the morning. It's going to be an early start, anyway. An extra hour or two to drive back won't kill me."

"Thank you," I breathe, his gesture knocking me sideways. I hang my arms around his neck, grateful he is here. "But how do you know where my parents-"

"Garry," we both answer before I can even finish asking.

"My friends are really going behind my back lately," I mutter to myself, lowering my head. I can't wipe the stupid, joyful look off my face. "I have to go to the store to pick up some anniversary banners for the party later. Will you come with me?"

"Try to stop me."

But my stomach knots into something painful. "Before we go. I think it might be time to introduce you to my family."

He continues to smirk at me, stealing all my air in the process, as if meeting my parents doesn't faze him. I appreciate his confidence and

I hope it will rub off on me because I'm sweating.

I take his hand, but before I can move, he pulls me back.

"I have to do this before we go in there because if they see me doing what I'm about to do to their daughter, it may affect their opinion."

I don't have a chance to react before his mouth comes down to meet mine. Soft and slow, his tongue plays against my mouth. And I forget where I am. I can't remember who we are about to meet or why I was so nervous a moment ago. His fingers wrap delicately around my neck, holding me steady, and his kiss becomes harder. Both of us want more than we can grant in the driveway.

His palm slides over my shoulders, down my arm, and skims the side of my breast. With my moan, he bites gently on my lower lip.

"You're becoming impossible to stay away from," he breathes against my mouth, while his hand goes lower on the back of my dress.

Don't.

Stop.

Going.

Lower.

"I hope that's Alex because if it's not, you're in trouble, sis," a voice sounds from the front door.

My eyelids burst open. Alex is looking directly at me, but his confidence never falters as he stares at me, his desire flickering in his deep blue eyes.

And did he just wink at me?

Maybe less confidence is sometimes good.

Alex steps aside, turning me around with him as he places a hand on my lower back.

"No trouble needed. I'm Alex." He nods, a smile gracing his gorgeous lips, and he reaches out his hand to Matt.

Please don't hit him.

My body relaxes when Matt takes his hand, and they both grip each other a little too firmly.

"It would have been better to see you when you weren't feeling up my sister, but it's still good to meet you." Matt smiles back begrudgingly.

I glare at him. He needs to stop eyeballing Alex.

I click my tongue against the roof of my mouth, rolling my eyes, and hope it will give Matt the message to stop with the protective brother nonsense. I'm not seventeen anymore.

117

Matt dips his head. "Don't worry about it. People have caught me in worse situations."

Both Alex and Matt laugh then, easing the tension between them. I let out the breath I don't know I'm holding, and I relax against Alex's side.

"Come in. My parents will be happy you're here."

And they are. My mother almost throws her back out, her mouth parted as she eyes him from his head to his toes. My father looks at her, blinking and amused by her lack of discretion when Alex enters the room.

"You realize we're married thirty years today," he says, but she doesn't answer him and merely shrugs. She's too busy looking.

Even in my family home, his presence fills the space. Tall and strong, his piercing blue eyes attentive to everyone and everywhere, including the hidden glances to my legs only I notice. His face gives nothing away, but the tightening of his jaw as he watches me walk around the kitchen, making coffees, tells me exactly what's on his mind.

The men quickly fall into chatting about the football game and Alex's construction business. Never boasting, but he's impressive all the same. He has that effect on people.

My mother hints she wants to add a little extension to the back of the house.

It's the first anyone's heard of it.

They're happy he's in their home. They're more impressed at how happy he makes me.

When we leave, he is leaving, having been already welcomed by them. He shakes my father and Matt's hand and when my mother puts out hers; he takes it but places a quick peck on her cheek, and her entire face burns.

He also has that effect on people.

"It was great to meet you all. I'll see you later. And happy anniversary," he says, before leaving. "I'll wait in the car. We'll take mine," he tells me at the door.

When my parents have gone back inside, Matt looks down at me, and a rueful smile plays across his mouth. "The driveway, Mandy? Really?"

"Shut up." I slap his arm. "When Suzie used to stay here, you were always sneaking into her room."

"That was different."

"How?" I huff, crossing my arms over my chest.

"You're my sister."

Will he ever see me as anything but a little girl needing his protection?

"Just get your ass to the restaurant and make sure everything is going smoothly."

On our drive to the store, Alex reaches over and places his hand on the bare skin above my knee where my dress has shifted up. Neither of us said much when we got in the car. We didn't need to. Meeting my parents went well, and I thanked him with the kiss I placed on his lips before we left.

I relax because he's by my side again. Alex always makes the gaping hole in my chest feel a little less vast.

Every so often, his fingers graze my inner thigh, and my breath catches in my throat, but he always keeps his thumb respectively across my knee.

Has he any idea what he is doing to me?

I can't tell from the even expression on his face. His attention is always on the road ahead. But then a smirk plays along the corner of his mouth. It disappears as fast as it appeared, and he purses his mouth to hide it.

He knows exactly what he's doing.

Two can play that game.

Without even glancing in his direction, I reach over to place my hand on his thigh, matching his movements. Then my fingers dance along the material of his trousers as a bare brush on his skin.

No reaction.

Nothing.

His face is blank, but his grip tightens on my leg ever so slightly. Then my fingers edge higher and higher. With every inch, I press my palm harder against him.

His eyes become wide, and he sucks in a breath.

Bingo.

He looks over at me, his eyes in a frenzy, all fire and amber dancing at the corner of his blue pools. I observe my hand working its way up his leg.

"Eyes on the road, Mr. Hale." My voice is breathy as I look up at him again before biting into the flesh of my lower lip.

His hand leaves my knee to grip both hands on the steering wheel.

My fingers tease higher, and something grumbles in his chest. My legs clench, tightening with every heavy breath crossing his lips.

Roughly, he grabs my hand, immediately turning gentler as he brings my fingers to his lips. He glances from the road to my hand, his lips kissing the tip of each finger, branding the skin with his mouth.

"Don't threaten me, Mandy." His voice is thick and drenched in something primal. "I won't think twice about pulling this car over." I can't take my eyes off him as each of my fingers opens, and he smooths his lips to my palm. "And we don't want that."

He gives me back my hand, placing it on my lap.

I throw my head back against the seat, swallowing hard. I suddenly feel parched.

"We don't?" I question.

I don't think I'd protest if he pulled over.

He shakes his head, blinking over the fire in his eyes, and releases a long breath.

"You could be the woman who kills me, Mandy."

I open the window a crack, allowing the air to cool my clammy skin. I rest my head back again and close my eyes.

"Not if you kill me first."

***

Later that night, as the music plays around us, everyone is a little merry from alcohol and comfortable in the family restaurant, me and Claire slip into our seats. Our feet ache, exhausted from dancing, and a gulp of wine does little to extinguish the burn in my lungs.

Alex has company with Garry at the bar, but looking at him now, with the group of men from my family, he walked straight in and became one of them. They laugh and joke as if he's always been there. It makes me happier than I ever knew I could be. He doesn't have to pretend.

Every so often, he came to my side, kissing me, asking if I needed another drink. He's my designated driver tonight.

Despite the company, his eyes wandered to me on the dance floor, and from the glances I threw his way, he hadn't taken his eyes off me. He's still watching me now as I take my seat.

"Are you staring at him because of all the wine you have drunk or does the man intoxicate you?" Claire nudges me, bringing my attention back to her.

She's right. I've drunk more than I should have, and my head is spinning. But it's Alex who makes me lightheaded. His eyes find mine one more time, and he smirks with a wink before getting back to the conversation he's having with the other men.

As I sit back and put the wineglass to my lips, I suddenly feel my mouth pool with saliva.

No more wine tonight.

I blink, trying to make the haze over my eyes go away, and it takes so much effort.

Nope.

This is how I see things now.

I turn to Claire, feeling like the room is moving in slow motion.

"I think I need to get home. I'm exhausted and I don't want to puke."

She throws her head back and laughs. "Lightweight."

Standing, I grip the table to steady myself. I don't have to look. I can already feel my mother's eyes boring a hole through me from the opposite table.

I point a finger at her. "Before you say it. I know I'm drunk. I'm going home. I love you." I blow her a kiss, but I think it comes from my nose, and everyone laughs at me.

I don't get drunk very often, so I'm sure they are looking at me like a zoo animal.

I inhale a steadying breath, hoping my legs will work, and walk in a straight line. I get a few steps away from Alex and reach out for him. He notices me just as I sway.

"Whoa." He rushes to my side, putting a hand around my waist and planting me straight again.

Why do I always stumble around him?

I swallow again and fight hard not to get sick. He's too beautiful to vomit on.

"Need me to take you home?"

"Yes, sir," I say, putting my fingers to my head in a mock salute.

"You didn't look drunk when you were dancing." He puts his lips closer to my ear. "You looked sexy as hell."

My eyes roll in my head, and I hold back a whimper as his breath sweeps across my neck.

This man will be the death of me, I'm sure of it.

"That's because," I look up at him, "everything stands still when I move my head."

"You're so weird," he chuckles, holding me tighter. "Come on. I'll grab your things."

I follow him, taking his hand while waving to everyone on my way out and blowing more nose kisses in the air. The party is busy enough for people not to notice as I stumble.

"I'm sorry," I start as he helps me into the car and straps the safety belt across my chest. Even that simple touch causes my stomach to tighten. "I don't drink often."

He kisses my nose. A real one this time. Not an air kiss.

I laugh to myself.

He moves the hair that has fallen onto my face. "You have nothing to be sorry for. Although, your headache in the morning might disagree." He scrunches his nose up and places a chaste kiss on my forehead.

I moan something inaudible, but I think I'm singing.

I crack open the window on the drive home, thankful for the cool breeze as it smooths across my skin. It clears the fog and eases the waves crashing in my stomach. I look over at him. His eyes are going from the road to me and back again.

"What are you thinking?" I turn around on the seat, putting my legs up and letting them fall to my side. I want to look at him. He's beautiful.

His lids crease over his eyes. He's probably surprised I can put a coherent sentence together.

"You don't want to know," he says, glancing at me from the corner of his eye while running his fingers over his hair. It has grown a little since I first met him, and it makes all his features darker. Not his eyes, though. They are brighter than the sun, and when I look at them for too long, they blind me.

I giggle at myself.

Again.

He frowns, the indent of a line across his brow.

I say something before he thinks I'm crazy. "I do want to know. That's why I asked."

He inhales a deep breath, blowing out again harshly. The car comes to a stop at traffic lights, but he doesn't look at me.

"You take up everything." His head falls between his shoulders briefly, like he has to gather himself before coming back up.

I take up everything.

What the hell does that mean?

I feel my heart drop to the pit of my stomach. Am I a total embarrassment when I'm drunk?

I close my eyes, bracing myself with an invisible barrier because I'm not sure what comes next.

His fingers tap against the steering wheel. "You're right next to me, and it's you. You're all I can think of. I'm thinking of how I'm going to hate leaving you tonight. I'm thinking about how your body moved when you danced and how I constantly have to stop myself from putting my hands all over you. I'm thinking of how it almost killed me to be so respectful all night when all I wanted to do was take you into a corner somewhere and be very disrespectful. I'm thinking, even when you're drunk, you're the most amazing thing I've ever set eyes on." He laughs under his breath, and as if he has been fighting to keep those in all night, his posture relaxes. "I'm wondering what the hell I was doing when you weren't in my life."

My eyes go wide, and the rush of blood causes my heart to pound behind my ears. My head stops spinning, and my tongue is like sandpaper against the roof of my mouth. I don't know what I expected him to say, but it wasn't that.

I don't feel so drunk anymore. His words have sobered me. But he still hasn't looked my way, even when the lights go green, and he drives again.

Take them back, Alex.

Take back every word.

I still have so much to tell you.

"Alex?" My voice breaks, getting wedged in my throat.

His eyes are soft when he finally looks over at me, smiling. "I'm admitting this now because you won't remember in the morning."

He doesn't mean that. He's protecting himself. I see it because I do it too.

And is he crazy?

I'll never forget.

The moment those words left his mouth, they burned through my ears and were branded into my memories.

I moisten my lips with my tongue, my fingers beating rhythms against my thigh, and the overwhelming full feeling in my chest makes my body tingle.

"Take me back to the hotel with you." My voice hardly makes a sound, but in the car's silence, I hear it like I've screamed the words.

His jaw tightens painfully, grounding his teeth. A firm hand crosses my chest, bracing me as he brings the car to an abrupt stop.

"Jesus Christ, Mandy. I didn't say those things to get you into bed."

But I want to.

"Is that what you think?"

No. That's not what I think. I know he's serious because his thoughts reflect mine, but I don't say that because I'm still catching my breath from the shock of the car stopping and the crazed look in his eyes.

I've hurt him.

Come back to me, Alex.

I reach my hand over, placing it in his hair, and we both relax into each other.

"I'm sorry," I whisper, and his eyes warm again. "I know it's not what you meant because I feel it too. But I meant it when I said I want to go back to the hotel with you."

My entire body aches for him.

I need him to touch me.

I need his strength around me.

I need to know he is mine before I ruin everything.

His lips curve ever so slightly, but it doesn't reach his eyes. And as he closes them, he leans over, pressing himself against me.

"As much as I hate saying this, I can't take you back with me. When I take you to bed, I don't want you to wake up the next morning and regret it."

"Alex, I could never regret anything with you."

He shuts his eyes harder, causing his face to tighten.

I'm making this more difficult for us, but I don't care.

"Then, I don't want you doing something you might not be ready for. And I can't stand wondering if you are. Not tonight."

I throw my head back, away from him, letting my temper get the better of me.

He's right. Of course he is. I'm drunk, and it's not how I want it. But goddamn this man and his patience. And it doesn't help when he makes fun of my frustration, chuckling as he starts the car again. I cross my arms, staring out into the blackness. I'm sulking like a petulant child, but I want something, and he won't give it to me, and now I want to scream.

"What are you thinking?" He takes my hand in his, forcing me to release the tension across my chest, and kisses the sensitive skin of my wrist.

It's not fair.

But he doesn't mean it in any other way than to soothe me. I just can't cool my body from the uncomfortable heat.

"I hate when you're such a gentleman."

He sneers at me but laughs and his shoulders shake.

Alex and I have a lot in common. He's grumpy when he's hungry, and what I've learned within the last five minutes is I get grumpy when I'm turned on. They're both a kind of hunger, and we can appease only one in this car.

A painful knot ties in my stomach when we pull up outside my family home. I don't want him to leave. But I need him to. We both do.

I don't understand how two people can need to be so close to each other, but need so much distance to cool off.

He helps me out, walking by my side with his hand around my waist before taking my keys and unlocking the front door.

I lean against the porch, and his seductive grin zings around my skin. But the fire in his eyes betrays the playfulness of his smile. With a simple kiss to my tender lips, he holds softly for a moment before pulling away again.

I want more.

I want it all.

I know now, gentlemen are assholes, and chivalry is all smoke and mirrors.

"Goodnight, gorgeous."

I veer my eyes to the ground, unable to find words that will keep him here.

"Goodnight."

Reluctantly, I push off the wall and turn to walk inside.

No. He's not done.

His touch scorches my skin, grabbing the inside of my elbow, and spinning me back around.

He holds my face between his thumb and index finger, stroking the skin along my jawline. It's soft enough not to hurt but rough enough to make my legs go lax.

He comes closer. "And, Mandy," he says, running his other hand between the dip of my cleavage, "When you come to my bed, I won't be such a gentleman."

Okay, maybe they're not *all* assholes.

SIXTEEN

I wake with mascara gluing my lashes together, knotted hair, a mouth that tastes like I haven't brushed my teeth in three weeks, and an unmerciful banging at my temples.

What have I done to myself?

Before I can even stretch, a blinding light assaults my eyes, burning my retina to a crisp.

"Rise and shine," my mom chirps, in only a way she can. It's the most annoying sound I've ever heard.

I open one eye, afraid the other is still repairing itself.

"Jesus Christ, Mom. Don't do that. I think I might be dying."

I feel the side of the bed press down as she sits.

"You don't drink enough."

Most mothers scold you for getting too drunk. My mother told me I don't do it enough.

"Huh?" I moan, rubbing my temples and licking my lips with a dry tongue.

"What I mean is: you don't do it often enough. Not get drunk, have fun."

I have fun.

Sometimes.

"This is why." I swirl a finger around my face. "This is torture." I groan as I pull myself up on my elbows. "Did you have a good night?"

"It was so lovely."

She crosses her arms and leans back, like she is searching for answers to her unasked questions.

"What?"

"I didn't think I would see you here this morning. I thought you might have wanted to stay with Alex."

Images of his car stopping, and me asking to go back to the hotel, flash before my eyes. I feel hot and it's not from the hangover.

Oh, sweet heavens, I begged for sex.

I make a mental note to call him before I leave to check if we're still dating.

I toss my legs over the bed, ignoring the pounding in my head so my mother doesn't see me flustered. "I told you I was staying here."

"I know," she drawls. "But when your boyfriend shows up, and you leave with him, you usually stay with them for..." she stops, and I silently beg she doesn't finish the sentence. "You know—sex."

"Stop talking, Mom."

I stumble into the bathroom and begin brushing my teeth with too much toothpaste. I have to get this taste out of my mouth. And I'm not talking about sex with my mother.

"Did you two have an argument?"

I roll my eyes and brush my teeth again. "No," I mumble.

"How come you're here and not there?"

She is far too invested in my sex life.

I spit, and rinse my mouth, feeling reasonably better. A shower should fix me completely.

"He had to work, Mom."

"And?"

She turns around on the bed, facing me. Her eyes narrow on me, and it's only now I see the glossiness around her green orbs. She's hungover too, but she's hiding it better.

"You *are* having sex, Mandy?" she asks slowly, edging closer.

Why? Why me?

"Mom, I am not having this conversation with you. Don't worry yourself about my sex life. Focus on your own."

She tuts and stands to help me make the bed. "Actually, your father and I-"

"Don't you dare finish the sentence. I'm sick enough."

I swallow the bile in my throat.

She fluffs the pillows and sighs. "You've seen the man you're with, haven't you?"

"Do you want to have sex with him?"

Her eyes widen, and her face flushes a furious red, but when she doesn't answer, I can't help but burst into laughter.

I shake my head. "Unbelievable." Before she can ask any more questions, I ramble, "There's nothing wrong with our sexual appetite. I just haven't taken a bite yet."

Now I'm as red as my pajama bottoms. Crimson.

"Why?" Her voice is casual, like I'm the daughter who calls her every week to discuss my sex life. My mother could hardly bring herself to tell me the facts of life. Instead, she threw a book at me and told me to ask questions when I finished reading.

I take a calming breath and again swallow the saliva pooling in my mouth.

"Mom, I love you. But I don't feel comfortable discussing this with you. You don't need to worry. Everything is fine. Alex makes me happy. And I'm sure we will have sex in the near future."

"Good," she clips, before coming to kiss me on the forehead. "Now, have a shower, because the tide wouldn't take you out the way you smell right now."

My mouth gapes open and it remains that way as she saunters out of my room.

After my shower, I feel refreshed, with only a lingering banging behind my eyes.

I check my phone to see a text from Alex. My heart skips a beat.

Alex: Good morning, beautiful. How's the hangover?
Me: Miserable. Do you still want to date me?
Alex: What the hell?
Me: I vaguely remember I embarrassed myself beyond belief last night.

I don't vaguely remember anything. Unfortunately, I vividly remember everything.

While in the shower, it all came back to me in waves. I almost put my head through the shower door when I remembered he told me how he felt, and I asked if I could go back to his hotel room. And then I recalled how he caught my face in his hands before he left, and my body pooled at my feet.

My dating etiquette is in the dumpster and my mind in the gutter.

Alex: You're embarrassed?
Me: Of course I am.
Alex: You want the truth?

No.

Me: Yes.
Alex: I haven't been able to stop thinking about you. And none of my thoughts are appropriate.

Sweet Jesus.
I smile so much my face hurts.

Me: You want the truth?
Alex: Always.
Me: I haven't been able to stop thinking about you either. And my thoughts are so much dirtier than yours.

He doesn't reply.
See, my dating etiquette is in the dumpster.
After what I'm sure is the longest minute of my life, the bubbles pop up on my screen.
Nothing.
A bead of sweat breaks out on my brow and I muster the courage to text him again.

Me: Alex? Are you sure you still want to date me?

At the same time, his text comes through.

Alex: Do you know how hard it is for me not to leave the site right now and go and get you?

I don't doubt him either.

Alex: And yes, Mandy. I still want to date you.

Me: Can I come over tonight? We can get Chinese food. I think it's the only thing that will cure me.

I'm lying. I already feel fine. I just want to ball up in his arms.

Alex: You know you don't need to ask. I'll pick it up on my way home.
Me: I'll be the one with all the dirty thoughts curled up on your sofa.
Alex: Mandy?
Me: Yes?
Alex: I meant every word last night.

My heart inflates in my chest.

Me: I know. Me too.
Alex: Fuck.

I giggle at his last message but don't reply. It's true. I wouldn't have regretted if we had sex last night, but I love him even more for thinking of me first.

Whoa.

Love?

I do. I love him, and it scares me so much I want to climb back under the covers.

***

Dad cooked eggs and bacon for breakfast, which cures the remaining headache.

"Matt." I hiss as he crunches too loudly on his colourful cereal. "Stop breathing." But then I smile because he's here this morning and not at home with his wife. She wasn't at the party either. He told me she was sick, but I called bullshit on that. She's going through the motions. I get it. They need their time.

He grunts at me but continues. "What's wrong, sis? Did Alex not feel you up again last night?"

I choke, as does my dad.

"Oh, they're not having sex," Mom adds from behind her

131

newspaper.

I've entered an alternative universe. There's no other explanation for this conversation and why sex is on the tip of everyone's tongue this morning. And at the breakfast table, of all places.

My father glares at them both, but they ignore him.

"You could have fooled me." Matt barks a laugh, taking another spoonful of cereal. "Seriously, sis, go get laid. What has it been, seven years?"

"Matt," my father warns, booming across the kitchen.

"Seven years?" My mother looks simply horrified.

See, this is why we don't discuss sex because she is looking at me like I've sprouted horns.

"But it's seven years since…" she trails off, her face becoming pale. "Oh," is all she says when she realizes.

Great, now my mother is going to worry about me more than she already does.

I look at my father, whose expression mirrors mine—like he wants the ground to open up.

"Dad, please cover your ears," I grit.

He does as I ask.

I look at Mom and Matt. "Will you two shut up about my sex life? It's ridiculous. And who cares if I'm having sex. I'm happy." I look at my mother. "And no, I haven't had sex with anyone since Nick. And no, you don't have to worry about me. I don't have some sort of sexual dysfunction." I think. "Have you two ever heard of taking it slow? We've been together for four months, not four years."

"And you." I turn to Matt and point my finger. "When I tell you things as my brother, it doesn't mean you get to blurt them out to anyone. This is my life, Matt. It wasn't your secret to tell."

I'm not sure if it even is a secret. But surrounded by my family, it feels like one.

I'm surprised to feel the back of my throat prickle, and tears sting my eyes. Though I'm pretty sure I'm too dehydrated to cry.

Matt's face immediately softens. He jumps up and throws his arms around my shoulders. "Shit, Mandy. I'm sorry. I wasn't thinking."

I know he didn't mean it. He's my brother. We know everything about each other, and we take our secrets seriously.

"I know," I sniff, wiping dry eyes. "It's fine. I'm hungover and sensitive."

He kisses the top of my head in a wordless apology.

My father has taken his hands away from his ears and is glancing between us. "Have you all finished?" he grounds out. "Can we get back to eating breakfast? And please, stop talking about jiggy-jiggy time."

Matt and I pin our eyes on each other and burst out with laughter.

"Jiggy-jiggy?" I choke, trying to catch my breath. "Come on, Dad. You can do better than that."

He barks a laugh, winks at me, and gets back to his breakfast. I know he doesn't call it that. He did it to lighten the mood for me. I smile and make a mental note to hug him extra tight before I leave.

***

"Oh, Mandy." My mother comes running after me as I open my car door.

I swear, I'll cry if she mentions sex.

"Letters." She reaches out her hand filled with envelopes. "These came for you."

"Thanks. It's probably alumni stuff from the university." I stuff them into my bag.

She kisses my cheek. "Safe drive home, sweetie."

I don't know why I feel the need to tell her this, but it might ease some of her worries. "I'm in love with him, Mom."

She tilts her head, one side of her face lifting in a soft smile before she squeezes my arm. "I know, honey. I'm your mother. I see these things." Of course she does. "And I can also see when a man is in love with my daughter. He looks at you—I don't know—it gave me goosebumps yesterday."

It's not just me then.

My mom blows a long breath. "You need to tell him, sweetie."

I swallow back my fear. "I know. I will."

But not tonight.

Tonight, I want to be just me.

One last time.

SEVENTEEN

6 Years Ago - Then

"Mandy, I think you should go to the doctor. You don't look well. You're so depressed, you've started throwing up everything you eat," Mom warned while clearing the plates after breakfast.

Matt scowled and rested a reassuring hand on my shoulder. "Ease off. Her boyfriend just died."

"I know. But I still think she needs to see a doctor. I don't mean for tablets. Maybe she could suggest someone for her to speak to," she continued as she loaded the plates into the dishwasher.

"Please, Ruth," my father pleaded. "Leave her alone."

"But I'm worried about her. I mean, look at her. She looks like a zombie. She's all skin and bone. Surely you agree with me. She is walking around in a daze and it's killing me to watch her. Nick wouldn't want it either."

My head shot up at the mention of his name.

"She barely talks. I mean, any sign of communication would be good, but she doesn't even give us that."

I closed my eyes in a desperate attempt to block out her voice and rubbed my fingers over my temples. I suddenly had a headache coming on.

"She hasn't cried since the day of his funeral. It's been over a month. It can't be right."

I cried. Though she didn't see it.

"I'm sitting right here, Mom. Stop talking about me as if I'm invisible. I'm fine, and I don't need anyone to talk to."

"Mandy, listen to me. You're ill. You're making yourself physically sick from this. You're not sleeping. You haven't touched your breakfast and when you do, it comes back up. Your friends are calling you all week. You don't even get out of bed to tell them you don't want to speak to them."

My father gripped my hand, sending me shock waves of support. He understood how overbearing my mother was. How the man survived with her constant nattering for so long baffled me.

"So?"

"Fine." I huffed, pushing out the chair to stand. I couldn't handle sitting there as my mother went off on another rant about how I needed help. "If I go today, will you be happy?"

Her smile seemed forced when she said, "Yes."

She mumbled something else under her breath, but I already left the kitchen.

I got it. I was a mess. She was worried.

But I was submerged in something. I didn't know what it was, but it was cold. It was murky and desolate, and my chest felt empty. Nick took up so much space there, it felt hollow without him.

I was sinking. Lying on my back, allowing the darkness to surround me. Like the feeling when you're in water and all the sounds disappear. I was hanging on by a thread. My head bobbed on the surface, but I was being pushed under and I didn't have the energy to fight anymore.

I was tired.

"Are you okay? I know she can be tough sometimes," Matt asked as I threw myself on my bed.

"I will be when Mom gets off my case. She knows I hate doctors. They usually involve needles." I sighed, cuddling my arms around my pillow.

"Do you want me to call and make an appointment for you?"

He was doing everything he could for me. I saw how he looked at me. It hurt him too; to watch me unravel.

"I'll do it. But you can come with me if you'd like. For moral support."

135

He smiled at me gratefully.

"You make the appointment and if there's time, we'll go for a walk in the park first."

Instantly, the tension released from my muscles.

"Thank you," I breathed, lowering my eyes. It was exactly what I needed.

An hour later, we were walking through the enormous gates of West Harbour Gardens. As usual, it was breathtaking. I loved coming to the park in Autumn. It was my favourite season. The grass still felt soft beneath my feet, and a layer of red, yellow, and brown leaves dusted the path.

We strolled along the open pathway, listening to the wind whistling through the branches as our feet swept the leaves away. We stopped to enjoy the view of the river to our right and I leaned against the metal railing.

"I'm proud of you, Mandy." He rubbed his palms together, gathering heat. "The way you're handling everything." He draped his arm around my shoulder, bringing me closer. "Just don't cover whatever pain you're feeling for the sake of other people."

He was wrong. I wasn't handling anything.

"It's difficult to explain. I want to talk about him. I do. But everyone wants to talk about his death, or how he was right before he died. I want to remember him as he was before any of that. I want to remember the way he smiled without pain and how he cursed when he did something silly. I want to talk about the way he loved, and how, even though he was sick, he took care of me. He made me whole."

I wanted to remember and forget all at once because remembering brought so much agony.

"You can talk about him like that with me." He squeezed my arm and kissed the top of my head. "It's hard to watch you when someone mentions his name. You hold yourself like you're about to break."

I flinched. I tried my best to keep my pain to myself. I couldn't even do that right.

"I want you to know; I'm proud of you for trying because that's all anyone can ask. Never feel rushed into moving on."

I smiled, but it faltered. Would the empty feeling always be with me?

"You're the best big brother." I pecked him on the cheek and circled my arms tightly around his waist.

"Don't tell anyone. I have a reputation to keep," he joked, pushing me playfully.

"I've been thinking," I started, linking my arm in his as we walked again. "I think it's about time we meet this girlfriend of yours."

His head snapped so fast he almost broke it.

I may have been buried in grief, but I knew when Matt was up to something.

I tilted my head. "Oh, come on, Matt. Walking out of the room when your phone rings. The stupid grin on your face when you get a text message. I can read you like a book."

"I'll never have any secrets from you, will I?"

"A-ha, so you do. Come on. Tell me everything. What is she like? What is her name? When do I get to meet her?" I rolled out every question, knowing it would annoy him. He was my big brother, and he protected me for long enough. It was my turn to be the protector.

"Calm down. You're hyperventilating." His eyes danced around the harbour before resting on a small boat. "Her name is Suzie." His grin when he said her name didn't go unnoticed. "And she's amazing. You'll get to meet her at Christmas. I want to see how she gets on with Mom's scare tactics."

Christmas?

Wow. It was serious.

He appeared flustered, in the best possible way.

My brother was giddy with this girl. I never witnessed him acting that way. I was elated, but something didn't feel right. He never kept things from me.

My chest ached. Did he think he couldn't speak to me? I closed off from everyone, but I never wanted to close myself off from Matt.

"Why are you only telling me this now?" I questioned.

"Did you honestly think I was going to go on and on about my girlfriend when you lost Nick?"

"I'm sorry," I mumbled, swallowing back the burn in my throat.

"For what?"

"For not being there."

He stopped walking and held me by my shoulders. His stare was so intense, I looked away.

"Don't you dare. Mandy, you can't blame yourself because you're mourning." I recoiled under the weight of his words. "Please don't. I can't bear it."

"Okay," I whispered, feeling tears sting my eyes.

I felt the need to apologize for my reaction but thought better of it. Instead, I linked my arm with his again and tugged him along.

"I can't wait to meet her. I can tell her all your secrets," I teased, eager to lighten the mood between us.

His smile didn't reach his eyes, but he was happy, I knew.

We sat on a bench and watched people walk by, enjoying our silence and the cool air.

"I'm thinking about going back to college on Monday."

I didn't look at him, but I could tell he was smiling.

"That's great news."

"If I want to graduate next year, I think I should go back."

I didn't want to. The thought alone was crippling, but I couldn't stay in my bedroom forever. Eventually, I would need to rebuild something resembling a life. It would never be the same, but maybe I could gather some shattered pieces and glue them together.

Later, when we arrived at the clinic, my fingers twitched and my shoulders squared, as if ready for an attack.

I wanted to be anywhere but there. I wanted the numbness back to soothe my aching body.

I didn't have pain—so to speak. Not pain at the point of moving. This pain ran deeper. This agony was so raw, so tender, it was as if every nerve in my body was exposed.

Doctors couldn't treat that pain.

Inside the clinic, it somehow seemed warm and cold all at once.

And familiar.

Too familiar.

The smell was too clean and fresh. I knew better, but for a minute I was back there, in the room with Nick.

I shuddered and shook my head, willing the thoughts away.

Matt checked me in with the receptionist and we took our seats in the waiting room.

Resting my head back on the chair, I closed my eyes. The blue carpet rustled beneath my feet, and I was back in the room again. My hand balled into a fist and I dug my nails into the flesh of my palm to distract myself. I didn't want to cry.

The slow beep of the monitor replayed in my head. And the moment I made it stop.

The moment he stopped breathing.

The moment I killed the person I loved with my whole heart.

"Hi Mandy," Doctor Roberts said softly, startling me out of my reverie.

I opened my eyes slowly, relief washing over me. I wasn't in that room anymore. I was here. In the doctor's surgery. "Are you ready?"

"Sure." I willed a smile to my face.

The doctor's office was small but dazzling. Lights beamed down like something from a spaceship. I squinted over the momentary pain in the back of my eyes. On the other side of the desk, the doctor shuffled papers around until she finally found what she was looking for.

"I understand you've been getting sick, finding it hard to keep down food, not sleeping, and, according to your mother, extremely depressed?"

My mother called. There was no end to the lengths the woman would go to.

My huff filled the small space. "I'm assuming you were speaking to my mother."

"She called before you arrived."

Of course she did.

"It's not as bad as she made it sound. I'm tired," I mumbled.

"You can talk to me, Mandy. It's what I am here for. I'm aware of your current circumstances."

Nick's death was a circumstance?

How cold.

He wasn't a circumstance.

To me, he was everything.

I lowered my eyes to the blue carpet at my feet, unsure of what to say.

"If it helps, I understand. My husband passed away two years ago."

I gulped and jabbed a finger in my chest to ease the knot building there.

"I'm sorry," I stuttered.

Bonding over a shared pain is a strange type of respite. You pass your grief along and into the hands of someone else because, in sharing, the weight becomes less of a burden.

"Thank you. I want you to know, you're not alone in this. Grief is natural. It has a process, and we must go through it."

Tears flowed endlessly down my face. This lady struck something in the centre of my agony. Somehow, I'd thought I wasn't worthy to feel my grief. I was young and people looked at me differently for that reason. As if my loss wasn't the same. If he had died when we were five or ten years older, I'd have more of a right to grieve.

But what those people didn't realize or see, is that me and Nick weren't some teenage crush or puppy love. We were *it* for each other. Each other's missing piece.

I wiped tears roughly with the back of my hand before speaking. "Some days I wake wishing I hadn't, and those are on the nights I can sleep. I walk into a room full of people and feel empty without his touch, or a brief smile to let me know he's there. It feels like half of me isn't here anymore."

Doctor Roberts took my hand from across the desk. "I won't lie to you and say it gets easier and the pain eases. It will always be there. But in time, you will find ways to cope with it. I know it feels like the day will never come, but eventually, you will start to feel a little normal. Bit by bit. Day by day."

"How did he die?" I asked quietly, trying to avoid the thumping of my heart. Through my sobs, I take a tissue from the box on the desk.

"He was sick for a long time." Doctor Roberts sat back in her chair. I guessed she answered the question so often, she no longer flinched saying it. In time, maybe I could do the same.

Maybe.

We both remained silent for a moment. It wasn't an awkward silence. It allowed us an insight and understanding of each other's pain.

"Could you hop up here for a moment?" The doctor patted the white leather.

"Will there be needles involved?"

"I'm afraid so. I will do a full check-up, and I might prescribe you something light for nausea so your mother actually believes you were here." She smiled as I rolled my eyes.

Even underneath my jeans, I felt the coldness of the leather and a sudden shiver crept along down my spine. She pressed the stethoscope to my chest, checked my ears and throat, and pressed warm fingers firmly along my lower abdomen. I chose to ignore the narrowing of her eyes as she did the latter.

"I'm going to need a urine sample."

I nodded in agreement. Anything to get out of sticking needles in my veins. But my relief was short-lived. When I returned from the restroom, the doctor took my urine sample for tests, instructed me to take a seat again, and to roll up my sleeve.

"Turn the other way if you like."

I did.

"All done." The doctor patted my arm as she placed a tiny bandage where the needle pricked the skin. "While I have your urine sample, is there any chance you could be pregnant?"

I almost choked and my entire body flushed of any colour. The question was so unexpected.

"I'd like to do a pregnancy test but there isn't any need if you're a virgin."

How had this soft lady gone from being so kind and reassuring to so abrupt? The sudden change in personality was giving me whiplash.

"Apologies for the sensitive questions, but I have to ask."

Frantically, I shook my head, still reeling from embarrassment. "I'm not pregnant but I'm also not a virgin." My eyes found the floor, and my face burned.

"To cover all the bases then."

She pulled clean gloves over her long fingers and got to work.

"With respect, Nick died over a month ago. It was at least three weeks before the accident anything happened between us. We were both busy working this summer." Nick and I rarely kept our hands off each other, but those weeks before he died, we struggled to make time to speak on the phone. And we were always safe. "I'd have noticed by now."

A sudden ache gnawed at my neck. As if a penny dropped somewhere.

Holy shit.

I couldn't remember my last period. I frantically searched through my memories.

How the hell had I missed it?

Noticing my unease, the doctor interrupted my inner turmoil. "Let's not get ahead of ourselves. I'll do the test and you will know for certain."

Never.

I couldn't possibly be pregnant. I never even entertained the thought.

My mind flashed to the unused box of tampons sitting in my bathroom.

Nausea. The dizziness. The missed periods.

Sweet Lord, how did I not put all of it together?

But I had, and surely it was just grief. Stress can do that to your body.

Before I started hyperventilating, I took a calming breath, sitting back in the chair. I was overreacting.

"It will just be a minute," the doctor assured me, removing her glasses and letting them rest around her neck. "Is there anything else you would like to discuss while you are here?"

This woman had a stick dipped in my urine to check if I was pregnant, and to fill the three-minute gap she wanted to discuss things?

Instead of saying that, I nodded.

"Mandy?"

"Huh?"

Had I blacked out or did I ignore the last few minutes? When I looked back up, the doctor was standing at her counter, stick in her hand.

She didn't have to say it. Her face said enough.

My hand instinctively shot over my mouth, trapping the air my lungs were burning for.

I stood but immediately sat back down, unsure of where to go or how to move. I lost all function of my motor skills.

"I don't understand."

I must have been wailing because I heard the door swing open and Matt was on his knees, pulling me into his chest.

"What the hell is happening? I could hear you screaming from down the hall."

I rocked against him. At least I thought I was rocking. Maybe my head was spinning. He pulled away from me, removing the hair from my face.

"Doctor, what is it?" He was panicking, so I took a deep breath, gathering myself as best I could.

"Sit down, Matt." My voice sounded strangely stoic.

"Mandy, you're scaring the shit out of me." His jaw was so tense I thought it would crack.

I couldn't hold back. What was the point?

"I'm pregnant."

In all our years of being siblings, I never saw Matt turn a shade of green until then. He looked ill.

There was nothing in my head distracting enough. Just blankness. I was sitting there, numb, and pregnant with a dead man's child.

I was angry at myself for having missed all the signs and furious at Nick for having left. How could he have left me like this?

The fury towards him built, bubbling beneath the surface. He gave up. On me. On our child. It was his decision to have me switch off life support.

His choice.

Thinking back on the events of the weeks gone by, I gritted my teeth and burning tears slipped down my cheeks.

I was shocked, of course. But I was more than that.

I was furious.

I wasn't sure how long we'd been sitting there in silence when the doctor's voice interrupted.

"Mandy, there are options."

She pulled some tissues from a box and passed them to me. With trembling hands, I took them but didn't wipe my eyes. I needed to feel and no amount of aloe vera tissues were going to fix it.

I hadn't thought that far ahead yet, so I asked, "What options?"

"There's termination."

"No," I answered quickly, feeling uneasy.

"Mandy?" Matt cut in, obviously anxious.

He didn't understand my reasoning.

"Matt, this isn't about a termination. I'm so angry at him right now. Not because I'm pregnant. It takes two to tango. But because he isn't here. I may think of him as the biggest asshole right now. But he was my asshole." The sob that escaped me came from deep within my chest. Further, if possible. If pain had a sound, then that was it.

"Mandy, there is still a lot we need to figure out. Dates for a start. Maybe then, we can discuss other options," Doctor Roberts continued speaking, but the ringing in my ears was too loud and the room was becoming too small.

I needed to get out of there. The walls were closing in. I stood, swiftly pushing the chair away from the table.

"This is a massive shock. I can suggest someone for you to speak to."

I only wanted one person to speak to, and he wasn't there.

Ignoring her advice, I turned to Matt. "I want to go home," I whispered, feeling like my throat was closing in.

He said something to the doctor, but I didn't hear it. I didn't hear anything. Even as he wrapped me in his arms and walked me out of the building. Even when he sat me in the car and drove away.

I couldn't do this without Nick.

So, when the pain became too much, and I was suffocating. When I was sure I was dying. At that moment, in the car, as my body shook, I felt it happening. Like a switch. The only way I could protect myself. Everything else fell away, and I welcomed the darkness and the cold because there, I didn't fight against my suffering.

Numbness became my constant companion.

EIGHTEEN

Now

Alex returned home earlier with Chinese food and after I ate my weight in noodles, any awkwardness I thought I would feel seeing him again disappeared the minute he walked in the door and I threw myself into his arms.

He made me feel safe to say things I otherwise wouldn't. Even if it was begging for sex while I was drunk. He made me feel.

I wanted him.

All of him.

But for now, I simply want to be with him, curled up in his arms as we watch the waves lap in on the shore. The sun is still shining, but the breeze has turned chilly and the clouds in the distance look almost black. I know we don't have long here, sitting in the sand with my back pressed against his chest.

"I love it here," I say, resting my hands on his as they drape around my shoulders.

"I'm glad." He kisses my temple.

We've been sitting here in comfortable silence for what seems like hours. There isn't any need for words when you're this happy in someone's arms. Yet, something has shifted. Alex's lack of words weighs heavily on me and I don't know why.

"I hope my family didn't scare you too much last night."

I feel a light chuckle vibrate at my back. "No. Your family is great."

"Are you suddenly realizing I can't handle my alcohol and want to run miles away?" I say playfully, but inside, I freeze over.

He nuzzles his nose into my neck before kissing the sensitive spot under my ear. "Stop. Saying. That." He places his lips on my skin with every word. "You had fun and I'm not running anywhere."

I relax back into him, but something is still off.

I shift around in his arms until I'm facing him. Straddling his muscular thighs, I rest my hands on his shoulders.

"I give up. You're killing me. Something's off. What is it?"

He leans one hand back on the sand and tucks my blowing hair behind my ear with the other. His eyes cast downwards, and his features grow dark. The grey clouds overhead are prowling closer and I know I don't have long before the storm comes, and my opportunity will be lost.

"Is everything okay at work?" I ask, grasping at any reason he's acting this way.

He shakes his head as he cups my cheeks with his palm. "Everything is fine."

I sigh, my shoulders slouching. "Alex, if it's something you don't want to talk about, just say. I'll drop it."

But it doesn't appear that way. Whatever words he's playing with in his head seem like they are suffocating him and on the tip of his tongue.

A soft smile curls at the corner of his mouth as his gaze darts over every inch of my face. And suddenly the familiar heat zings through my veins. He takes a deep breath and I edge closer, like he's pulling me to him.

"I really meant every word last night."

"I know," I say quietly, repeating what I said in the text messages this morning.

He says nothing for a long minute. His eyes are lost in his thoughts somewhere.

"Alex-"

"I'm in love with you, Mandy."

Now it's my turn to take a deep breath.

Six words and the entire universe settles on one spot. All the crazy thoughts of my past, present, and future come to a halt and I get lost in his dark blue eyes.

Everything is right in my small world. Even if it is momentarily. I'll take it and hold it tight; it won't get away.

I love you too, Alex.

I love you.

I love you.

I love you.

But the words won't come out of my mouth.

Open your damn mouth.

"Alex, I-"

He cuts me off, putting his hand behind my neck and bringing my mouth to his. Everything about him is wanting, almost possessive, and dripping in love.

God, there's so much love.

I feel it with every movement of his mouth against mine, and I can't help but whimper as I rock into him. He grows hard against my core and I throw my head back as his mouth takes my neck and his fingers rub against the peak of my breasts. I want him so badly it's almost painful.

His hands grab my hips, pulling me down onto him, and the friction is almost too much. Melting into his strength, I dig my nails into the muscles of his biceps, hardly hearing the clap of thunder above our heads because my heart is beating like crazy.

And oh, fuck, that's cold.

What the hell?

My eyes go wide, and when I look up, I can hardly keep my eyes open. The rain is so heavy. I can't help it. A deep laugh rolls in my belly as the heavy drops wash over us. When I look back at Alex, his eyes narrow and he must think I've gone mad, but then his lips twist up and I forget my wet clothes sticking to my skin. I'm wearing a coat, but the rain is slipping down the back, and it makes me shiver.

When he begins to laugh, too, I kiss him because I can.

He's mine, and I am his.

Completely.

Our kiss is wet, but his mouth is warm, and I never want to leave. My hand balls around his sweater and my fingers dance lower until they're pulling at the waistband of his jeans.

"Baby." He's gasping, and I'm glad the rain is hiding my tears. Hearing him say he loved me pulled at something I buried deep. "I need to get you inside."

I swallow and nod in agreement.

"The beach is no place for this. Sand gets everywhere."

I stop, my shoes dangling from my hands.

"You've had sex here before?" I shout because the rain is pelting on the ocean so loud, I can't hear myself think.

He stops walking and turns back. In two breaths, I'm over his shoulder and his big hand is groping my ass.

"My sweet, perverted, Mandy. I never said anything about sex. I need to get you inside because you're soaked."

Yes.

Yes, I am.

I blush because he's right and my mind went to all the dirty places again.

"Asshole." My arms are dangling down his back, so I take the opportunity and grope him, too.

"Pervert," he retorts, laughing.

There isn't a point in fighting him. He'll insist on carrying me back to the house, and I'm getting quite fond of how he enjoys throwing me over things.

He only puts me down when we reach the house.

We scatter up the steps, toes flicking sand and shaking off our wet coats. I giggle and bump against him. The sudden burst through the clouds and wetness on my skin feels refreshing and my cheeks tingle. The ocean sounds angry against the shore, and the rain pelting against it proves unsuccessful in its efforts to chastise it.

I press my chin towards my shoulder, feeling his heat against my back as we both hang up our raincoats. My eyes meet his, and I swear I feel an electric current rush to my fingertips. He lowers his lips to my bare shoulder, keeping them there for a moment before rubbing his finger over the marked skin.

"You're soaked," he says, coating a finger over a drop on my brow. "Just like the first time I saw you." He turns serious, his voice like velvet.

I turn my body to meet him, looking up at him, both of us remembering the day in Penrith Town Centre.

Gazing at him, I feel a shiver creep ever so slowly down along my spine, rounding at my abdomen and swirling inside. Somehow, I don't think it's from the rain. He feathers his index finger along the curves of my face; along my brows, over my eyelids, across my flushed cheeks, and he places a gentle thumb over the sensitive skin of my lower lip.

"You're beautiful, baby."

I suck in the air between us, hoping it will bring him closer to my lips. Instead, he places his mouth on the top of my head, breathing in my scent.

"You need to get out of those clothes. We should change. I'll get the fire going."

It's August, but it has been unseasonably cold this week.

I'm not sure what to say. I'm happy to remain planted here, dripping wet, and his eyes locked with mine. Surely his heat will dry me, anyway. But I freeze momentarily.

What's wrong with me? I was all but dry-humping him five minutes ago.

And it dawns on me. I've never stayed in Alex's house. I've come here on dates, but I've always left, or he stayed with me at my house. It's been four months and I've never even seen his bedroom.

It feels like I'm close to a line here, and any minute I'm about to cross it.

Sensing my unease, he squeezes my hand. "The weather is too bad to drive. We can get you into something dry and wait for it to pass. I can take you home then."

"No." I nod slowly, surprising myself. "I'd like to stay the night with you."

I'm sure my eyes must be wild, and I probably look in a state. But the storm is down for the night, and although it's only seven in the evening and should be still bright, it's getting dark.

With that, a lightning bolt flashes far out at sea and the spark of light through the doors gives me the briefest glimpse of his bright blue eyes, his tight jawline, and how the dampness hangs on his t-shirt, contouring his biceps.

In truth, I don't want to go home. I don't want to leave the comfort of his side.

He kisses me lightly again, and his voice is a whisper when he says, "Now, let's get you out of those wet clothes."

He tangles his fingers with mine, leads me through the house and up the staircase. I pray, for once, I won't be clumsy and clip my toe on a step. But he's careful with me, as if leading me on a path I cannot see.

He brings me to the large bedroom, letting go of the grasp on my hand as he goes to his wardrobe to find some clothes. I pause, drinking in the sight of the large windows looking out at the ocean and his bed standing against the wall, dressed in white covers and all too inviting.

My heart plays uneven beats against my chest and my toes curl in on the soft grey carpet. Apart from Nick, I've never been in another man's bedroom. And although for most women of my age, stepping into the bedroom of the person you're in love with would bring great excitement, I feel something different. He stays in my bed, but I've never even stepped inside his room. We never discussed it, and he never said if it bothers him. Maybe it's a comfort and security thing on my part.

My cheeks blush hot, and I brush my palms against my wet top. Of course, my belly aches in the best way possible, but a sudden pain knocks me back. The pain tastes of betrayal and something forbidden.

Nick's bedroom was no secret. Before we dated, we spent most of our days there as friends and when we went a step further, our minds and bodies were young, innocent, squirming around in a nervous giggle.

Alex's bedroom is none of those things and I imagine nothing about it would bring the innocence I remember, but more of a meeting of lovers, entangled with each other and knowing exactly what they are doing.

Will I be any different to the wriggling teenager I once was with the only other man I've ever been with?

I suddenly feel nervy and twist my finger around the material of my hanging shirt.

"Mandy?"

Looking up at him from out of my daze, he's standing there with clothes hanging from either hand. He's worried. I can see it in the creases on his forehead as he studies me.

As if reading my thoughts, in two strides, he takes me in his arms and brushes his lips against my ear. "Oh God, I hope you don't think I brought you up here for any other reason than to make sure you get dry. You can change in the spare bedroom if you'd like? There will be no pressure, Mandy. I hope you know that. I take the lead from you."

I breathe in his scent at his neck and bury my head against his shoulder.

"I know. Thank you," I mutter, unsure if he can hear me over another clap of thunder.

Given my previous reservations, it surprises me to feel disappointed I may have to leave for the spare bedroom. I suppress the hunger I feel for him and squeeze him a little tighter into my body. I can still feel his heat through our wet and cold clothes.

"I'd like to change here."

He nods, kissing me quickly on the cheek.

"I better get a fire going," he says, pulling his sodden t-shirt over his chest and tossing it into a basket.

I like how his chest muscles move with the action, and I flush. He smirks, catching my embarrassment.

"I hope those are okay." He points towards the clothes laid out on the bed. "Everything I have will be far too big for you, but hopefully you can tie those pants tighter. Grab another sweater if you're cold."

"You mean you don't have the clothes of other women here I can have?" I joke.

He sneers at me and shakes his head. "Just you, baby."

My heart flutters.

I glance towards the t-shirt and check bottoms and thank him by delicately placing my lips on his.

When he disappears downstairs, I draw the strings as tight as I can, tie them in a bow at my navel, and pull the large t-shirt over my head. In the spacious bathroom with matching his and her sinks, I splash some water on my hot skin and brush my fingers through my curls. He didn't leave me, but I feel unexpectedly lonely without him. I've grown accustomed to his heat, and without it, my skin prickles icily.

I grab my clothes quickly to place them by the fire to dry. As I put them in front of the burning logs, Alex is already entering the living room with a tray of food. My stomach rumbles, reminding me of my other hunger.

"This is lovely," I mumble, taking a bite of the bread as he turns on some hushed music from a speaker. I sway happily and take a sip of wine he poured for me.

I'm comfortable, and I don't think I've ever been this content.

After, he wraps me snuggly in his arms, laying on the couch, and we both fit perfectly together, as if two pieces of a jigsaw. He grazes his fingers along my arm. Enjoying the silence between us, we listen only to the sound of our steady breathing and the fire blazing strongly. He rubs his face against my hair, leaving chaste kisses along my head. I melt into him, and he tenses as I raise my leg along his thighs and

151

rest it across his lower abdomen. He stiffens more but eases again as he repositions himself.

"I could stay like this forever." I pull him tighter, exhaling.

His palm presses against my lower back, holding me here. "Me too." He chuckles gently then. "But I won't lie. Every time you move against me, it drives me a little crazy."

A furious blush spreads across my cheeks and I lower my eyes. I may be naïve in the art of lovemaking, but I'm a woman, and I know exactly what I'm doing with my body.

Tease.

I smile to myself.

Alex tucks a finger under my chin and tilts my face to meet his gaze. Fiercely, he leans in and kisses me with so much fire my lips burn with passion as he leaves them.

My eyes grow heavy and heat from the fire washes over my body before I give in to my sleep.

***

I wake with a start, my breathing frantic, and I desperately fight away the heavy fleece blanket covering me. I can't have been asleep long as the fire is still throwing sparks and glowing a dark amber. My shoulders slump when I realize I'm alone. I wanted to reach out for him, to feel his warmth and his touch.

I'm unsure of the details of this nightmare. All I know is I need him. The yearning quickly sets through my body in ripples and tears dust my cheeks. I brush them away with the back of my hand and pull the blankets aside. My breathing escapes in heavy pants and I can't calm my pulse. This isn't some fleeting thought, because I knew from the moment I met him. It's much more than a simple attraction. We've become entwined with each other before ever sharing a bed. We share a gravitational pull I can't quite understand.

I catch sight of his strong silhouette, sitting up straight on the sun lounger outside, protected from the storm under the shelter. My fingers pull at the oversized sweater and I know if I don't go to him now, I will lose all confidence and regret it.

Before sliding the double door open, I take a moment to study him. He seems lost in thought, staring out at the black ocean. The only light is coming from the moon, highlighting one side of his face. His hair is rustled, and he brushes his fingers over his eyes.

When I can't stand there any longer without touching him, I pull back the door. The cool breeze and light mist blowing onto the porch do little to extinguish my heat. He looks over at me, a smile edging on one side of his face.

Christ, that face is so handsome, and my legs suddenly go weak.

"Hey, gorgeous. I hope I didn't wake you?"

I shake my head, and he sighs with relief.

"Come here." He taps his knee, beckoning me forward.

I don't move. I think my feet have become one with the floor.

"What are you doing out here?" I ask.

His lips set in a hard line as he looks away momentarily. He seems a little embarrassed.

"Alex?"

He blows out a long breath. "I needed to cool off. As much as I wanted to keep you in my arms forever, you're hard to sleep with in such a small space."

The knot that forms in my chest feels hard, and I look away. Every inch of skin on my body flushes, and I'm grateful it's dark.

"I'm sorry. Was I thrashing around again?"

As if realizing his mistake, he shakes his head. "Mandy, you were as still as a statue. That's not what I meant. Honestly," he begins, rubbing his hand down his dark jeans, "You turn me on something crazy, so I thought some air would be better than torturing myself."

The blush in my cheeks is furious now, but for a different reason. And that's when I see it: the ravenousness of need reflecting on his blue orbs like the moon dancing its light on the ocean. And I recognize it. It devours every cell in my body.

My legs move towards him before I can register what I'm doing. He parts his knees so I can stand between them and he rubs his hands down the small of my back and along the back of my thighs. Allowing myself to enjoy his touch, I close my eyes for a moment. My heart is pounding, and my chest feels tight.

"Mandy?"

I look down at him but say nothing. Instead, I gently press my hand on his shoulder and push him back. I climb on top of him, my knees on either side of his hips, straddling him, and I bring my face close to his. Something's changed, and he knows it. He's panting now too, our breathing a frantic union across each other's faces. I press my lips closer, and ever so softly pressure my mouth over his. They move together, a bare brush of skin at first, and as my pulse quickens, so does my kiss. It's greedy, aching, and helpless.

I break away, breathless, and I can't help but smile at the shocked expression on his face. But his eyes are dark, and his features become serious.

"What is it?" He's searching over me as he brushes my hair away from my face and over my shoulders.

We lock eyes on each other, and our gasps of breath and frenzied heartbeats drown out the sounds of the storm.

Shocked that I've not yet lost all courage, I'm spurred on by my newfound confidence.

"Alex, I want you to take me inside."

His eyes widen, and his mouth parts slightly, but enough for me to notice his surprise. I don't want to be taken inside, out of the cool air, and away from the elements of the storm. That's not the reason.

With a wild huff, his hands find their way into my hair, his thumb stroking the base of my throat, and he pulls me into a kiss of pure infatuation.

"Mandy?" he groans; the sound coming from deep within his chest.

I know he's about to question if I'm sure, but I cut him off.

"You told me to take the lead here. I'm giving it back because I'm in love with you too, and I'm asking you to take me inside." My voice is soft but assertive, and when I say it, all doubt shifts, leaving my body until all that's left is me and Alex.

He needs no more ques. In one push off his feet, he is standing with my legs still wrapped around his waist. He brings me inside and sets me back down on the rug in front of the fire. The only sounds are our breathing and the crackling of the flames. His lips leave mine briefly, only to lift the t-shirt over my arms. His kisses follow an invisible trail across my cheeks, down my neck, and my breath lodges in my throat when his mouth delicately grazes across my breasts.

He has taken the lead now, and I've never felt so safe.

His mouth continues down my body, and my head falls back when he hovers above the waistband of my pants. He looks up at me, his eyes asking permission, and I nod, allowing him to slip the bottoms down between my legs. Despite the heat from the fire, goosebumps play over my naked body, and his fingers caress all of it, across every curve, his mouth on every part of my skin. When he comes back up to

154

meet me, his lips move slowly, like he could break me. He's careful and thoughtful through every stroke of his hands, down my back, up to my arms, and across my collarbone. Breaking away, he looks down at me, and his eyes roam from my head to my toes.

"Every inch of you is beautiful." His voice is gruff and a painful throb aches at my core.

But I become acutely aware I'm the only one standing here with no clothes on, and instinctively my arms cross over my body. Nobody has looked at me like this since Nick. But Nick looked at me through the eyes of a nervous boy. There is nothing boyish or nervous about Alex. He isn't merely glancing at me. He's staring. Drinking me in. His eyes are all wild and hungry, like he will never get enough. And with a warm confidence, he grabs my arms and puts them back to my side.

"Don't do that, baby," he says, furrowing his eyes.

Whatever I've done, he doesn't like it.

"Do what?" My voice is hardly audible.

"Hide yourself from me. I could look at you forever."

I don't have time to blush. His words send a heat all the way to my fingertips, and my hands fist at his shirt. In one swift movement, it's off and discarded, with his bottoms quickly following.

The man is the most gorgeous thing I've ever set eyes on, and the light from the fire only enhances the raw hunger in his eyes. The flickering flames dance over his biceps, contouring every hardness beneath his skin. With soft kisses, my mouth eases all tension across his jawline. I want to kiss him everywhere, but he doesn't give me time. With a loud breath, his hands are in my hair on either side of my face.

"Jesus Christ, Mandy," he blows out, his mouth coming quickly. It's soft, but the pressure of his tongue against mine explains a need words never can. Our hands become frantic, grabbing flesh, fingers in each other's hair, suffocating each other's moans, swallowing the sounds with every kiss.

And when he picks me up again, his solid chest pressing against me, he does so only to lay me down on the rug beneath us. I don't care it's here. I need him. I need every touch and every kiss.

He stills above me. Concern flashes beneath hooded lids.

"You need to be sure, baby."

"I am. I've never been so sure about anything." My voice comes in panting breaths.

And in one slow turn of his hips, he has claimed me, filling me completely. My head falls back, fingers digging into the threads of the rug, my back arching beneath him, bringing our bodies even closer.

His mouth etches up into a slow smile, and the craving in his eyes comes back tenfold. As if I've starved him for too long. He pushes into me again, slow and delicious, with a pressure that has me moaning with every movement. His mouth presses against mine, stifling the cries of his name.

With every flick of his hips, my body warms. My heat spiralling upwards, curling and caressing every part of me. His hands are manic and betraying how careful he is with every thrust. My hips circle around him, needing more, needing all of him.

With every kiss, I fall deeper into him. Every movement and he carves himself a little deeper into my heart. He becomes part of every nerve in my body.

With our legs entwined with each other, I raise my thigh, gliding it along the side of his body, and grind deeper. He grabs it, keeping it there, and his fingers scorch my skin.

As he plays kisses along my neck, heat possesses my core, rolling down my legs. My eyes shut tight, and my nails claw into his back.

"Open your eyes, baby," he whispers roughly, staring down at me with so much love, I've never felt so full. "I want you to look at me."

This is where I expect to feel self-conscious and shy, but I feel none of those things. I feel safe and protected. I feel like I will never get enough of Alex. And most of all, I feel loved.

We match each moan, every feverish grasp of fingers along each other's bodies. Exploring, needing, possessing each other completely. Each movement comes faster and harder.

"Alex," I gasp, my eyes widening as the heat swirls inside.

My legs tighten around his back as his arms cage around the curve of my waist, pulling me towards him.

My entire body quivers. Then we both tense and my cries echo around me. Each rhythm of his hips taking me higher and higher.

"Christ, Mandy," he groans as his mouth comes to meet mine, drowning out my screams as we both shudder.

And for the first time in so long, I find myself in the arms of a man I've lost myself to.

***

I wake to panting and a wet tongue along my cheek.

Alex is definitely more skilled at kissing.

I open one eye, peering up at the happy ball of fur lying beside me.

"Good morning, Bandit." I rub his head and he's calm again, resting his head on his paws.

I stretch, feeling the tight muscles of my body screaming. I'm stiff and aching in the best way possible.

At some stage, we made it to bed, and we continued where we'd left off downstairs. It was getting bright before we fell asleep. I'm not sure if it was punishment or a reward for making him wait. I'm not complaining. The man's body isn't something to just admire. He knows exactly how to use it, too.

Alex pulled me close to his chest, and I fell asleep that way, tucked into his warmth, my hand on his solid chest, feeling the thumps of his erratic heartbeat until it evened.

But now, all I can feel is tousled sheets and an empty space where he slept.

"Where is he, boy? Is he gone for his run?"

His head perks up, and he lets out a small whine before he goes back to rest. I swear this dog can understand me.

It's only eight in the morning. I got little sleep, but I feel more rested than I have in years. Well, apart from the aches. But it only reminds me of everything Alex made me feel last night. I never felt safer, more protected, and cherished.

With Alex not there, I clean myself up. I look exactly how I thought I would—like someone who stayed up all night having sex. My hair is knotted, my lips are swollen, and my cheeks are rosy, but there are also subtle changes only I would notice. My shoulders have lost their tension, and there's a comfort in my skin I haven't felt before. Maybe it's the effects of an all-night sexathon or this is what it feels like to be loved.

Only months ago, I didn't want to meet anyone. I wasn't trying, and I didn't know if I could ever date, let alone love someone else. Then Alex walked into my life and turned everything I thought I knew upside down. He was patient, and he waited. He treasured, and he loved until I was ready. How could I not fall in love with him?

I tie my hair back loosely and take a quick shower to freshen up. I dry myself off and wrap myself in a towel. Bandit has disappeared again. I hear him running down the stairs. I grab a clean t-shirt from Alex's wardrobe before dropping the towel.

"I could get used to this." His voice startles me, and I jerk around. Although I'm standing here naked, my eyes rake over his body. His shorts hang low on his narrow hips and his navy t-shirt sticks to every hard ridge. And suddenly, my body forgets I've been up half the night making love to this man, and a throb erupts between my legs. When my eyes land on his face, he's doing the same to me. His heated stare pulls up my body, causing a heavy heat to swirl low in my stomach. Feeling shy, I quickly fumble to get my arms through the t-shirt.

"Oh, no you don't." His voice is almost a growl and his eyes are dark.

I swallow back nerves when he strides towards me, grabbing the material from my hand and tossing it aside. My stomach flips and my panting betrays how shy I was feeling a moment ago.

"Good morning," I whisper.

The corner of his mouth curls up into a grin, and I swear my heart stops.

"Good morning. How are you feeling?"

A blush creeps up my cheeks, but I don't look away. "Good. Tired but good."

He smirks and leans down. I think he's going to kiss me, but he grabs the back of my thighs and scoops me up around his hips.

"Alex," I squeal, throwing my head back with laughter. "I just showered."

"Well, it looks like you're about to get dirty again, and then you can come shower with me."

He lays me down on the bed and kisses me quickly before his mouth lowers to my neck.

"But I was going to cook breakfast," I protest.

He lifts his head to look at me and arches his eyebrow in question. He knows me too well.

"Okay. Okay," I give in. "I lied. I wasn't even thinking of breakfast."

He laughs but continues his journey of my body with his mouth.

"Alex," I moan as he kisses my breasts. My back arches, and sparks of heat jolt downward between my legs.

Breakfast is the last thing on my mind, and I would gladly never eat again if he stayed here with his mouth on me.

I gasp as his tongue flicks the sensitive skin of my inner thigh.

And right before he takes me in his mouth, his eyes flick to mine and there's so much heat I could combust. A low groan comes from the back of his throat and a smirk plays on his lips.

Christ. This man.

I throw my head back.

Breakfast in bed it is then.

NINETEEN

I've tortured myself this week, opening my mouth to say words that wouldn't come out. And he's noticing the distance in me.

Nick and I were friends since we were kids. Trust came naturally. We built our foundation on playdates since we were four.

I didn't have that starting point with Alex, but we laid our foundation anyway and steadily worked our way to the next level.

Tonight, I promise myself.

He needs to know.

My past is mine. It will always be with me, and I've come to terms with it. I will wear it forever with pride because even though the bigger memories are bad ones, there are hundreds more amazing memories that outweigh and crush all that is bad. I don't regret getting pregnant. It taught me how to love unconditionally and opened my eyes to a new world.

But no matter what, or how hard I try not to feel ashamed of myself, sometimes it creeps in. I can't deny the battering my heart takes every time I remember the emptiness I felt. So, I'll live every moment with the pain, because I need to. Without the anguish, I don't have the wonderful memories, and they are worth the torment. I hope I can make him understand that, too.

"You're cooking dinner, huh?" His voice brings me back.

I smile, choosing to ignore how my stomach clenches painfully. "Yep."

I called him while at the store to let him know I'm cooking this evening. I even bought a new dress. I don't know why. Maybe my brain thinks dressing nice will convince him I'm not the horrible person I believe I am.

"I'm happy you got a dress, but how easy is it to remove?"

My cheeks burn because I haven't figured out how to stop doing that.

It's very easy to take off, but I don't tell him that.

"You're such a man."

He hums. "Yes, I am. A man who can't get any work done because all he can do is think about you. Naked. In my bed."

I press my lips together to keep from smiling. I don't know why. Nobody is paying any attention to me. Regardless, my cheeks dimple anyway.

"Get back to work and stop annoying me so I can shop to feed your massive appetite," I tease as I roll a shopping cart around the store. We've been on the phone for two minutes and I've already heard his name called four times.

"Where are you?"

He's stalling, and my heart does a flip.

"Nico's," I answer.

"Isn't that a vegan store?" He sounds concerned. God forbid someone doesn't give him meat for dinner.

"I hope not. I've been buying beef burgers here for years." It's true. They're the best. The store has a vegan section if that counts.

He booms with laughter. "If we need anything, I can pick it up on the way home."

Home.

Not *his* home.

Just home.

It sounds like ecstasy rolling off his tongue.

"It's okay," I say as I throw some salad in the cart. "Carl has me covered."

I hear him smack his lips together. "Carl, huh? Competition?"

"Maybe. It depends how good the steaks are." I'm sure he's trying to figure out what the hell I'm talking about. "He's the butcher," I explain.

"I can't compete with Carl, his good steaks, and have you seen a butcher's hands?"

I bite my lip to hold back the laughter. He really should get back to work instead of procrastinating with me on the phone. But I won't complain. It's the most I've talked to him all week. The building site is ten minutes from the store, but he's busy, and I don't want to be the girlfriend who shows up at work. I did it once, and I got more sneers than hellos.

"Mmm," I moan. "I hadn't noticed, but maybe I will now."

"Really? I think someone will have something to say about that."

The moisture of my tongue wets my lips as I slide it across the skin. This man's voice alone has turned me on in the middle of buying groceries.

"No." I shake my head, even though he can't see me. There's an edge to my voice, and I have no clue where it has come from. "I prefer the hands of a certain builder." He stays silent, so I take the opportunity. If he turns me on here, it's only fair I repay the favour. "Especially when I think of him putting his hands right between my…"

"Mandy Parker, finish that sentence. I dare you. I'll come to the store, put you over my shoulder, and carry you out of there." His tone is all roughness, and hard, just as I imagine he is.

I swallow back the word I was going to say, because a throb erupts right in that very spot. I've stopped, and I don't know how long I have been standing here, not moving, with my legs clenched. He's threatening to put me over a lot of things lately, and I'm not opposed to the idea.

The thought fills me with boldness. It's new, and I like it. And he should know. I can never refuse a dare.

Silly Alex. I'm going to call your bluff.

Before I even have time to think about it, my mouth opens, and the words spill out. "Right between my legs."

There's a groan at the other end. "Jesus Christ, Mandy." And the line goes dead.

I stare at it for a long minute before slipping it back into my bag.

I win.

I'm rarely so forward with Alex, but maybe it's time I should be. Satisfaction courses through my veins as I continue to the back of the store to get some steaks. I get vegan garlic butter on my way.

Twenty minutes later, and I'm loading the groceries into the trunk of my car. I wasn't carried out of the store over anyone's shoulder, and I haven't heard a peep from Alex. I'm tempted to call him back so I can gloat, but I think better of it. I've won. He'll know better than to threaten me next time.

I lean in, fixing a bag that has fallen over when I feel the tight grip of two firm hands at either side of my waist. My body jerks back, but he holds me tight. I'd scream, but I know exactly who it is. A millisecond before he came up behind me, I could sense him, and goosebumps pricked my skin.

"Now, tell me. Where is it exactly you wanted my hands?"

His voice coats over me, and my legs go slack as my back presses against him.

Silly, Mandy.

"Is it here?" he whispers as his lips graze my ear and his fingers move delicately across my collarbone. He moves to my breast, kneading the flesh in his hand. "Or here."

I don't know if it's from the fright, or how his touch is making my body sing, but my breathing is audible and hitches with every low moan. I'm grateful I parked so far away, and my car is backed up against the parking lot wall. I glance around to check nobody's watching. There are cars everywhere, but they're empty, and those going to the store are too far away.

"There's nobody here." He nips at the sensitive skin below my ear and soothingly runs his tongue over it. I shiver despite the sun baking on my shoulders. He fists my hair before letting it flow over my shoulder, and I watch as the caramel locks bounce past the curves of my breast, hiding his fingers beneath it.

"I warned you, baby." His tongue flicks and kisses along my shoulder, and I throw my head back on his chest. His hand smooths over my dress and goes lower on my stomach before his fingers dance along my pelvis, and I can feel him shifting my dress up in a ball. I can't move, because it's not until this moment, I realize how badly I've wanted him buried there. He drops my dress around his arms, but his palm is already sliding along my inner thigh. "So where was it you wanted my hands?" he repeats, squeezing my skin with the rough pads of his fingers.

Sweet heavens, if the man can build an entire complex with these hands, Lord only knows what he can do to me in a parking lot. My core tightens as my chest fills with air. My mouth is dry, but it's the only part of me that is.

"You need to tell me, Mandy."

He's handing me the lead again. He needs my permission.

I chew my lip between my teeth before bringing my hand down to cover his. I clasp our fingers together, and even in the chaos of all of this, he finds a moment to be gentle by massaging his thumb across my knuckles. His lips press against my temple, and I can feel the heavy movements of his chest against my back. I guide his hand until his palm is pressing against my centre, and I whimper at the simple touch.

"Fuck." He curses through gritted teeth, his lips still against my temple. His fingers slip to the side, burying themselves under my satin underwear. I think I cry out his name, but I can't hear anything over the pounding in my ears. He must be able to hear my heart.

At first, his fingers are light, brushing against me, with every flick a growl in my ear, and a buck of my hips. His tempo quickens as my lungs become greedy for air. His finger slides down, and slowly, he thrusts it inside me.

"You have no idea how bad I've wanted to do this."

My response is a moan because I don't have words anymore. I lose them with every push of his finger inside me, and when he adds a second, my knees buckle, and I almost wail.

"Alex," I gasp, but just as quickly, his other palm covers my mouth, dulling the shrieks of my whines. I bite down on his fingers as he goes faster. He wedges his knee between my legs, separating them further. His palm motions in circles, and I feel the pressure building. Like I have too much heat in my stomach. My hips rock faster, and hotness unfurls between my legs.

"Watching you is the sexiest thing I've ever seen."

And the chaos of the world around me drowns out. I don't hear people with shopping carts in the distance. I don't hear the chatter of voices. All I hear is Alex's breath and kisses on my neck, and I can almost feel his heart pounding between my shoulder blades.

When my back curves, I press against him, and when I feel he is hard against my lower back, I come undone. My legs shake, and my body convulses in his arms. The scream of his name is muffled against his hand. I grip his hips behind me and dig my nails in for extra support.

As I come back to the world around me, my moans die down to heavy breaths, and my body feels weak.

He removes his hand from over my mouth and moves my head to look up at him, and I realize it's the first time I've looked him in the eye since he left this morning. I blush, but I'm positive he can't see it because I'm already all a flush.

"How am I supposed to get any work done when all I will think about is that for the rest of the day?"

I'm not sure, because I don't think I even know how to get out of this parking lot.

I want to tell him not to go back to work, to come home with me and take me to his bed, but I haven't found my vocabulary yet.

"I will be twenty minutes late for dinner tonight. I had to see a woman about her behaviour, and she's put me behind schedule." He lowers his lips to mine, but he doesn't kiss me like I want him to. It's soft, but quick, and my head spins when he pulls away. "You look beautiful by the way." He eyes my yellow sundress.

"Thank you," I murmur, and it could be for the compliment or the orgasm. I don't know yet.

He chuckles lightly, before kissing me once more, and walking away, leaving me wondering what the hell just happened, and who I think I am for provoking him.

I slip into my car, wordless and still trembling.

I lost.

Although no matter the outcome of that situation, I was always bound to win.

TWENTY

It's 10 p.m. and Carl's steaks have been in the bin for over an hour, after sitting on the kitchen table, cold and uneaten. The candles have burned out. My anxiety is threatening to kill me, and I'm pacing every inch of the kitchen.

He's late. Not like the twenty minutes, he'd told me he'd be, but *I-am-going-to-kill-him* late.

No phone call or voicemail with an explanation. Not even a text message.

There are phone numbers on the fridge. Some names I recognize. Frank is one foreman, and I know some of the guys go for drinks after work on Fridays, but Alex rarely goes with them. And he would've told me if he wouldn't be home.

Fuck it. I have to do something.

He better have the world's best excuse, and he better be in one piece, but when I see headlights from a car pulling up outside, I put my phone back down. There's no sound of keys in the door, and when the doorbell rings, my heart falls into my stomach. Why isn't he walking through the door right now?

I can't help the sounds of a voicemail listened to too late replaying in my ears.

Bandit barks, startling me into moving.

I wanted to kill Alex thirty seconds ago, but now I'm praying he's okay.

I dash to the front of the house, picking up pieces of my nervous system on my way. When I pull back the door, I swear I'm going to be sick. The man I was about to call is standing in front of me, with Alex leaning against him, his arm lazily around Frank's shoulders, and doing little to support his own head, let alone his body weight.

What happened?

"Hiya, love." Frank smiles at me sympathetically before rolling his eyes in Alex's direction.

I rush to his other side, throwing his other arm around me for support, and we both pull him into the house. My eyes are roaming over his body for any injuries, but all I find is the smell of beer and whiskey.

I'm going to kill him again.

"What happened?" I ask, trying to look at Frank from across Alex's body. Why does the bastard have to be so big? I'm breathless, and I'm pretty sure, even in his state, Alex would have better luck in supporting me.

Frank shoots me a knowing glance. "Let's get him to bed and I can tell you everything."

I nod because I don't have air to form words. I eye the staircase and curse him for making it so big. We will never get him up those stairs. Frank is a well-built man, but he's no match for Alex.

"We'll put him in the spare bedroom down the hall." I pant.

Alex raises his head to look at me. Beads of sweat are forming on his brow and when his eyes meet mine, they're half closed but rimmed red. What has he done to himself? He frowns and shakes his head.

"I'm sorry, baby," he slurs, and his legs stumble.

I grip him tighter to me. "It's okay. We got you."

I push open the door to the spare bedroom with my foot, and when we sit him on the edge, he topples straight on his back with a groan. His entire world must be spinning around him.

I grab his hand and pull him back up. "No, you don't. I've got to get these clothes off you. Or your shoes at least, and you need to drink some water."

He slouches over, grabbing me by the waist before he buries his head against my stomach. A lethargic laugh vibrates against my skin. "Oh, you're going to undress me?"

I roll my eyes before smiling my apology at Frank, but he merely chuckles with amusement.

I bend down between his knees and take his face in my hands, doing my best to keep him upright. My Alex is in there somewhere, behind the glossy eyes, and flushed cheeks, but more than anything I can see his pain. I hate it. There was none of this in his eyes when he was with me earlier. What happened in a matter of hours?

"I'm going to get you some painkillers. Do you think you can stay awake for two minutes until I get back?"

He shakes his head in agreement, before rubbing both his palms along his face. His eyes are a little clearer when they meet mine again. "You're the most beautiful thing I've ever seen." I don't know if I imagine his eyes welling up. He's a sentimental drunk.

I kiss his forehead. "Oh, I'm in trouble. Alcohol doesn't diminish your charm. Just stay put for a minute."

Frank squeezes his shoulder. "Goodnight, big man."

I go with Frank to walk him out. When I look back, Alex is cursing under his breath, his fists balled up, and anger rising out of him like steam.

When we get far enough I'm sure he won't hear, I turn to Frank. "What happened to him?"

He stuffs his hands in his pockets, and I have a feeling he's as perplexed as I am. "No idea, love. He left the site today for a bit and when he came back, he was like a bull in a China shop."

That must be when he left me. After he had his fingers in my underwear.

He was angry about that?

It didn't appear that way today. The logical part of me says it must be something else, while my heart crushes into tiny pieces.

"Some of the guys go for drinks on Friday evenings after work. Alex rarely comes, but today he did. At the most, he grabs some food and leaves. He's a workaholic. I've never seen the guy drunk, and he's a big guy. It takes a lot of drink to get him in that state. He was drinking like the bar was about to run out of stock. I'm on early shifts at the site over the weekend, so I told him I'd bring him home. I drove him home in his car, and Jimmy followed behind. He's outside waiting, so I better go." He throws his thumb over his shoulder.

"Thanks, Frank. I appreciate it."

He laughs under his breath, shifting back to his feet. "No problem, love. Go easy on him."

I wanted to strangle him before. Five minutes ago, I wanted to walk out and let him deal with this mess himself. But something clawing at my chest wouldn't let me. This isn't Alex. There's more.

When I go back to him, he's sitting up, but light snores echo around the room.

"Alex," I shout, and he jerks awake, mumbling incoherent sentences. "Take these." I pop two painkillers in his hand and give him a glass of water. He doesn't argue.

When he's done, I set it down on the bedside locker before pulling his shirt over his chest and tugging off his boots. He's a stupid drunk, and apparently, I'm the best thing that ever happened in his life.

Charmer.

"In you get." I pull back the blankets and cover him when he lies down. I kiss his cheek, grimacing. God, he stinks, but he's still absolutely gorgeous.

I will have to stay awake and keep an eye on him because depending on his excuse for this, I may have to kill him myself. I don't want him dying from intoxication first.

As he rests his head back, his eyes are already closed, and his muttering is slowly switching to light groans. I run my fingers through his hair. "What's going on in there, huh?"

As I try to step away, he grabs my hand, whispering, "I don't deserve you, Mandy."

Pain.

That's all I see.

I press my lips against his palm. "Get some rest." We can talk in the morning.

He's snoring by the time I change into my pajamas and grab a book from his bookcase. I curl up on the chair in the corner of the room, relaxing a little more with every page I turn. I won't sleep tonight. He won't choke to death on my watch. I stay this way for hours, watching his muscular chest rise and fall with even breaths. I want to climb into his mind and see his dreams. I want to know what caused him to get in such a state because this wasn't a purposeful thing. I like to think I know that much about him.

I must have dozed off into a light sleep because when I look at my watch, it's morning. 7 a.m. I got two hours of sleep, which is more than I expected. I stretch, easing the tightness in my muscles when I realize I'm not where I was when I fell asleep, and neither is Alex. The bed is empty. No sign of him when I sit up and look around. No clothes on

169

the floor. No half-drunk glass of water on the bedside table.

My legs feel like lead as I drag them out of the bedroom and down the hall towards the kitchen. His back is to me, absent eyes staring out the window. He looks fresher than I expected. Showered and dressed.

"There's coffee in the pot," he says, not turning around to look at me.

Is he serious?

"I'm sorry I missed dinner last night. I should have called."

He grabs keys from the counter. He can think again if he thinks he's leaving.

I go to his side, press my hand on his and take the keys.

"Mandy, I have a business trip tomorrow. I need to get stuff done today."

No eye-contact.

He's giving me no clue of what's going on in his mind.

I shake my head, frustration boiling. "Yeah, I don't really give a shit. What the hell happened last night?"

"I apologized for dinner."

"You think this is about some uneaten steaks? I don't care about dinner. I care about you." I reach up and force his face down to look at me. "Frank said your mood changed when you went back to the site yesterday. That was after you met me. Have I done something?"

His eyes widen and he puts his coffee cup on the counter. "God, no. It's never you."

Relief washes over me, but it's quickly replaced with a pounding heart and clammy hands.

"I'm going to need a little more here."

He huffs and walks to the other side of the kitchen, resting fists on the counter. I go to him and squeeze his shoulder. He flinches and brushes me off, and I can't ignore it when my heart crushes a little. I fight the sting behind my eyes.

"My sister, Lydia, she's sick." He laughs without humour, anger flaming behind his blue pools. "Scratch that. She's been sick for months. She's dying."

I gasp, holding a hand over my mouth. He never said a word.

"Stage four pancreatic cancer. She was told at her appointment yesterday that treatments weren't working. And suddenly, a countdown has begun somewhere. Six months apparently."

I realize now why the look in his eyes is so familiar. He's fighting with himself, and the agony. He's trying to stay afloat.

"I am so sorry." I don't have other words, and I hate it because I remember how I hated hearing that after Nick.

Sorry for what exactly?

I understand a little now. I'm sorry I can't heal what broke him yesterday. I can't soothe his hurt. And by the look in his eyes, it seems he won't let me.

"Mandy, can you leave?"

Instinctively, I step back, quickly steadying myself, and close my eyes like a shield, like I can stop his words from hurting.

I get it. I get his pain, but it hurts anyway.

"Don't push me away," I beg, clinging to his hands like it will change his mind. Something tormented washes over his gaze. He's balancing, and the slightest movement in either direction will tip him over the edge. Shoulders squared, heavy breathing, and balled fists. There's a battle going on within him.

"I can't have you here today. You need to leave. I need…" he stumbles over his words. "I need…"

"Time," I finish. He's going to break, and he's too proud to do it in front of me. "I know." Reaching up on tiptoes, I place a gentle kiss over his mouth, swallowing a cry when warm fingers graze the back of my neck. "I'll go," I whisper, falling back on my feet.

He doesn't say another word, even when I feel his gaze on me all the way to the door before I close it behind me and do as he asked.

***

It was midnight when I finally succumbed to my sleep, so I know it's late when I stir to a dip in the bed and a warm hand on my face.

"Mandy?" His voice vibrates against my hair.

My eyes flutter and adjust to the room, but it's so dark, and when I shift around, I only see the outline of him sitting on the edge of the bed. His hand is on my cheek, fingers massaging my scalp. He's close, and a tingle wakes my sleepy skin.

"Hey." My voice comes out in a quiet moan.

"Forgive me," he begs, and moisture burns my eyes. "I never meant to hurt you. Not you, Mandy. I never want to hurt you."

My heart twists. Did he think I wouldn't understand?

"I'm sorry, baby." The words escape in a tortured cry.

I squeeze his forearm, sitting up quickly. "It's okay."

"No, it's not. In the middle of everything, you were all I could think about. I wanted you with me and I told you to leave."

I remember shutting people out. Unlike Alex, it took me a long time to right my wrongs and see what I had done.

"Alex, we love each other, and you can't love without hurt sometimes." His forehead presses against mine. "When we stop trying not to hurt each other, we'll know there's a problem."

I massage the tension in his shoulders and his relieved exhale sets my chest on fire. He's in so much pain.

"Alex, I get it. I really do."

There's a groan in the back of his throat. "Better than most," he agrees. "I'm sorry I didn't see that."

In one fell swoop, I'm in his arms, laying across his lap. He positions himself, sitting up against the headboard. While he keeps a supportive arm around my back, I lace my fingers in his.

There's a long breath and then he starts, "We're a close family, but it's always been me and Lydia. For months, even with her treatment, she's had this crazy energy. 'No loose ends,' she said. She was drawing up a will. She was reaching out to people for Ava. I thought she was crazy because she was going to get better. She's my sister. In my head, there was no other option. And when we got the news yesterday her treatment wasn't working." His voice escapes in a low, tortured hum. I don't say anything and let him continue. "I can't fix this," he confesses so low, I almost miss it. "I got angry with her for giving up, but I can't blame her. I saw what treatments did to her." He scrubs a shaking hand over his face. "And Christ, little Ava."

"Hey." I climb off his lap and kneel so I can straddle him. It's dark, and only shadows dance around the room, but I need to look at him. He rests his hands on my waist. "Ava has you and the rest of your family. It will never replace her mother, and it will be hard, but cherish the moments you have. Don't waste them being angry, Alex. Talk to your sister because the things you don't say will haunt you." I swallow the lump in my throat, but it lodges in my chest, ever present.

His fingers squeeze my bare thighs under the material of his t-shirt I wore to bed. "I should have never let you leave today." He tips his head down and kisses my hand resting on his shoulder. "You wanted to talk to me over dinner last night. What was it?"

I bite my lip, hoping he doesn't catch the wobble in my voice. "It

172

doesn't matter. You have a business trip tomorrow. We'll talk when you get back."

"Mandy-"

"It doesn't matter right now," I insist.

"I'm sorry it's so late. I couldn't be anywhere without you tonight."

When he attempts to reach over and switch on the lamp, I stop him, catching his elbow in my palm.

"Don't." I sweep my hair over my shoulder and lean closer, feeling the hardness of his chest against my breasts, and there's suddenly not enough air in my lungs. "It's okay to stay in the dark for a while. Tomorrow, we can face it. Together. But not in here. In here, in this bedroom, it will always be just me and you."

His fingers come to the back of my neck, bringing me closer as his other hand cups the curve of my hip.

"I love you so fucking much."

"I know," I breathe, tears coming whether or not I like it.

His husky voice soars through my soul. "I need to feel you, Mandy."

Pulling away from him, I sit up straight on his lap, feeling him stiffen and strain in his jeans. The air in the room becomes hot, our breathing comes heavier, faster, and frantic as I pull at his belt and unbutton the waist.

Then slowly, because he needs to feel me. We need to feel each other, and not what happens on the outside. Not what happens when we leave this room tomorrow. I pull my t-shirt over my head, leaving myself exposed, but worshipped by the glaze in his eyes. He fists his sweater behind his neck and pulls it off. My mouth hovers over the hot, hard skin of his chest, peppering kisses over his pounding heart.

With both hands on either side of my face, he pulls me up, mouth so close I can taste him. And it's somewhere between a beg and an order when he growls, "Now, baby." His voice alone makes me whimper.

He leans forward, arms tight around my body, fingers sprawling across my back, and with a quick lift of my hips, he places me back down onto him with a snarl deep in the back of his throat. He fills me, consuming every inch of my body. And when he pumps into me, hard and controlled, I'm possessed by him, wholly and without a doubt.

Tonight, it's us.

No thinking, just feeling.

Skin to skin, I rock with him, and he presses his face into my chest.

Then his lips. Along my collarbone, my neck, my shoulders, my face, my lips. Anywhere he can. Hot and lingering, branding me all over with his touch. And after each brush of his lips, he murmurs a word that causes heat to swirl low in my stomach and root itself in my heart, branching out to devour every cell in my body. Because I know during all the days to come, in ice and in heat, inside this room and outside, in the light and in the darkness, it will always be true.

One word.

"Mine."

TWENTY-ONE

Alex: Flight landed. Want to meet my family someday?

That was an abrupt change of subject.

He's been away on a business trip for two days, but I know he's going straight to work from the flight. I'm okay with that. I need today to get my head together. I'm going to tell him everything this evening when he gets home.

Me: Glad you're home. I'd love to meet your family.
Alex: Good. We're going to dinner with them tonight. I love you.

Say what now.

If I could crawl through my phone to slap him, I would. This is not what I planned. He knows I want to talk to him tonight. Of all times, why tonight to meet his family?

Alex: I promise I tried to get out of it, but they insisted. It was Lydia's idea. I'm afraid if we don't go to them, they'll come to us. You'll understand when you meet them.

Sucker punch.

I haven't replied yet because I don't know what to say. I can't get out of this. He has met my family. It's the least I can do, but I thought I'd have time. And after the last night we spent together, I know this will mean so much to him. I take a deep breath, run a nervous hand through my hair, and sink into the chair. I don't know why I smile because he can't see me, but maybe I'm trying to convince myself all of this will work out.

Me: Great. Looking forward to it.
Alex: Do you need me to come home? Are you having a panic attack?

Even through text, he knows me.

Me: I'm fine. I promise. Nervous, but fine.
Alex: They'll love you as much as I do. Thank you. Now, do me a favour and come see me. I want to show you something.

He sends directions to my phone.

An hour later, I make a left onto a dirt road. It's brand new but dusty, and the bustle of construction vehicles tells me exactly why.

White and red brick two-storey houses line up on my right, with a large green area and a playground opposite. I slow down as the dust rolls off my tires and scatters around my windscreen.

That's when I see him, standing on the new pavement outside a house. My heart leaps as I watch him, chatting to the men at his side, and looking like a god in his white t-shirt, faded blue jeans, and hard hat.

I say a silent prayer my cheeks aren't flushed when I get out of the car.

The moment he sees me, his face lights up, and he rushes to my side, placing a firm kiss on my lips.

"I missed you." I beam up at him, catching my breath. I feel a little silly because we saw each other two days ago before he went on his business trip. But it's the truth. I missed him with a deep ache.

"You have no idea," he says as he places his arm around my waist, pressing me closer. "Come," he orders, setting a hard hat on my head. He wraps his fingers in mine and tugs me towards the house.

We enter through the front door, and the loud charge of a chainsaw cutting through a plank of wood fills the air. Large windows make the space bright, but it's empty, nearing the finishing stages before furnishings.

"Guys, you can finish this later. Give us a minute." His voice is polite, but the underlying authority makes my knees instantly go weak, and I grip his hand a little tighter.

The men give me a nod as they exit, leaving us alone.

"These houses are beautiful, Alex. I love how bright they are."

"Me too." He is grinning at me with hooded eyes, like he is about to have me for dinner.

I look down at my shoes, hoping he won't notice the want in my eyes.

He guides me around the house, showing me the spacious kitchen and the three bedrooms upstairs. These are lovely houses, but I'm still unsure what I'm doing here.

"Alex?" I finally find the courage to say.

He has let go of my hand to look out of the window. I don't blame him. His handy work is something to be appreciated, but I've never known him to be this way about his work. He always seems to have quiet confidence about what he designs and builds without the need to show off. I don't mind, not in the slightest, but why the change of heart?

I stand beside him, watching the vehicles. They're loud as they reverse, and men work but laugh together, and I imagine the kids that will eventually be in the playground across the street. They'll be happy and giggling.

I manage to suppress the knot in my chest.

"I've seen your work. Anything you design is beautiful, and you should be so proud. But why have you brought me here?" I suspect there's more to this than just showing me a house. "Unless you want us to make use of these houses before they're occupied?" I raise my eyebrows, flashing him a cheeky wink.

His thumb laces over my lower lip, tugging it free from the hold of my bite.

"Christ, Mandy, don't tempt me." And there is nothing playful in his tone. It's serious, deep, and primal. "You're awfully distracting." He laughs lightly, placing a soft kiss on my lips. "But that's not why I brought you here. You've heard of the Hope Foundation, right?"

My eyes narrow. Of course I've heard of them. Claire works with them a lot, and I've even volunteered at some charity events for the organization. They help kids in the foster care system, and those hoping for adoption. A lot of the kids are older. Unfortunately, families don't want an already grown eight-year-old, so they become trapped within the system, usually going from family to family.

"I know who they are."

"I got involved with them a few years ago and I've always wanted to do something. A lot of kids with the foundation are with families they love but because of illness, the families don't have the facilities or the money to care for them." He walks to the other side of the room, pacing a little as he goes in full flow. "I met a little boy when I first became involved who had an illness and he adored the family he was with and they loved him like their own, but he needed treatment and medical supplies in the house. He also needed a downstairs bedroom. And I remember thinking: is that all that is stopping this little boy from having a family? A downstairs bedroom and some medical supplies? So, I got my team together, and we renovated the house to suit their needs."

I'm sure my mouth is hanging open. I've seen how generous he can be with my own two eyes, but this is on another level.

"Alex, that's amazing."

"But then, I couldn't stop thinking about it." He ignores my previous statement. "That was one kid, and there are so many more like him. Surely, every child deserves a home and a family to love. I knew I couldn't help all of them. Each had different circumstances, but I could at least try to make a start."

I close my eyes to stop the dusting of tears from falling. His words are speaking to me more than he could ever know.

"I met with the foundation last year and I offered my services. I wanted to build houses with a community centre where a doctor could visit once a week, or where they could come and get supplies, and have somewhere the kids could play. Not all the kids have an illness, but all of them need a home, and the amazing people who love them need support. I hate talking about money because it sounds dirty and arrogant, but I've been blessed with a successful business and I could do this. It was something I could give back. So, I built twelve homes, customized to each family's needs."

I knew I loved Alex long before today, and even before we said it on the beach, but I don't think I could ever love him more than I do at this moment. Watching him, so enthusiastic, inspired, and hopeful.

He is *so* hopeful.

This man cares more than I ever knew someone could. And without the slightest consideration for my efforts to stop the tears, they fall anyway. My heart is swelling too much to contain them any longer.

He's staring at me. His eyes are begging for me to say something, but I can't stand still, and I don't have the words to describe how I'm feeling. Instead, I notice my feet moving. Slow at first, and then faster, until I leap into his arms. My legs wrap around his waist. My hard hat falls to the floor with a thud, but I hardly hear it as I lower my lips to his in a hungry kiss. I want him to know I love him, respect what he is doing and who he is, and hope he can feel how much I admire him, because soon he will know my story, and he will know what he is doing means something to me too. The low growl deep within his chest as he holds me tighter makes me deepen the kiss. Every emotion I've felt over the past few months pours out of me and into him until both of our breathing comes in desperate pants and our lungs scream for oxygen.

Slowly and reluctantly, I pull away, loving the feeling of his hungry blue eyes as they scan my face.

"Alex Hale," I say, smiling, "You are the most amazing man I have ever met, and I love you."

"I love you too, sweetheart. If I'd known this was the reaction I was going to get, I would have brought you here weeks ago."

We both laugh, frantic breaths sweeping across each other's faces. I shimmy myself down from his waist.

"Thank you for sharing this with me."

He has allowed me into a part of him that means so much and I'm grateful. It's time I pay him the same courtesy. My heart breaks with the real possibility I may lose him, but I can't keep it from him. This man deserves far better than secrets.

"Mandy Parker," he places the strands of hair back from my face, "I want to share everything with you. I'd like to have you involved in the next project and get your input."

Oh, Christ, this man will kill me with his words.

"Hey, don't cry." He smooths his fingers over my tears.

The knot in my chest is threatening to break into sobs, so before I embarrass myself any more, I turn away from him. He catches my arm, spinning me back around, and pulls me close to the warmth of his chest. After a long moment, allowing me to catch my breath and calm my breathing, he places his hand under my chin, tipping my face up to meet his.

"Never walk away from me with tears in your eyes, do you hear me?"

I nod my agreement, swallowing hard.

"Whatever it is, Mandy, you'll get there in your own time. You take the lead, remember?"

I know that. He handed me the reins long ago. I just don't know where I am leading us now.

Tonight, after dinner, I need to tell him everything.

TWENTY-TWO

I'm flying around Alex's house like a headless chicken. Panic and nerves course through my blood as I cling to the towel wrapped around my body and try not to sweat my makeup off. Tonight is the night I meet his family and I reopen old wounds.

"You need to relax." Alex stands at the door, an amused smile curling on his lips and looking unfairly gorgeous in his dark grey slacks and dress shirt. He was in sweatpants ten minutes ago.

"Relax?" I screech. "You sprung it on me this morning that I'm meeting your family tonight. How could I possibly relax?" I huff, blowing a strand of hair off my face.

He chuckles and crosses his legs at the ankle as he leans against the door. I glare at him because this is far from funny, but it only causes him to laugh more.

"It's only dinner and the first two dresses you had on were beautiful. What's the problem?"

"I want to make a good impression." My shoulders sag as I run my eyes over the outfits I have on the bed. I went home earlier to pick up clothes for this evening's dinner and now I regret not getting more. None of these seem appropriate.

He comes to my back and runs his hands down my bare arms. "They are going to love you no matter what you wear. You need to calm down. They don't bite." He pauses and I feel him shrug. "Okay, Charlotte can be a little nippy and Ava is six, but she's possessive." He chuckles again.

Asshole.

I can't shake the uneasiness in my stomach. Alex has done this before with other girls. Everything in this relationship is new to me, and my inexperience is getting the better of me.

"Here." He grabs a hanger with a red fitted knee-length dress. "Red is sexy as hell on you."

I blush when he lifts the dress and matching red lace underwear is lying beneath it.

"What can I say?" I look up at him. "I like to match."

"Jesus, Mandy."

He presses against my back and encloses his arms around my waist.

"No," I warn. "I've just done my makeup. And we need to go." But I can't help my heart from hammering in my chest as his hand slips under the towel and strokes my stomach.

"But I want to watch you put on the underwear," he rasps in my ear.

I shiver but turn around in his arms so I am looking up at him.

"I know, but if you wait a couple of hours, you can watch me take it off."

His eyes widen slightly and his mouth parts before he raises his hands in surrender, backing away and stepping out of the room.

He greets Bandit at the door, patting his thigh so the dog will follow him.

"I don't know what I am going to do with that woman of ours, Bandit," he says as I hear him going downstairs.

I have a few ideas.

I dress quickly and give myself a once-over in the mirror. I must hand it to him. He picked well with the dress. It hugs my curves but is modest enough to cover my cleavage and the cap sleeves are cute.

God, I hope they don't hate me.

I shake my hands at my sides to release some tension before slipping on my heels and going downstairs, holding extra tight to the railing. I find Alex sitting on the back porch, elbows on his thighs and eyes straight ahead.

"Alex."

He rolls his shoulders and stands up before looking at me. When he turns, he takes one step and stops. He inhales a deep breath. "God, you're beautiful." His face strains, his smile is tight, but his words are soft.

I go to him and put my palms on his cheek. "I love you."

His eyes land on a strand of my hair, and he tucks it behind my ear. "I love you, too." He kisses the top of my head. "Now, let me show you off."

When we enter the restaurant, he takes my hand, squeezing it when he notices I'm trembling and offers some reassurance with a smile. I walk along behind him, wondering if I can hide here for the night.

What is wrong with me? I meet people all the time. Why has this got me so worked up?

Before I can answer my thoughts, he stops and places his hand on the small of my back. Two people stare back at us. One with fire engine red hair, freckles spotted across her nose, and curves I could only dream of. And the other is—well—just like Alex, except his hair is fairer, his eyes are more on the hazel side, and his nose looks like someone has broken it before, but they're definitely brothers. I can't deny that. Around the same height, both with a sharp jawline, and shoulders made for lifting heavy things and their swooning women.

Jeez, that's a great gene pool.

"Owen. Charlotte. This is Mandy."

I compose myself before Charlotte catches me gawking at her husband.

"Hi," I say, a little louder than I expected.

Owen reaches out his hand and I take it. "It's great to meet you, Mandy. I've heard a lot about you. I've never seen this guy smile so much, which is a change."

"Shut it," Alex barks, but I push into his side playfully.

I make him smile, and it makes me giddy.

"It's lovely to meet you, Charlotte." I offer to shake her hand too and hope she doesn't actually bite it off, but she pulls me into one of the warmest hugs I've ever received.

"My goodness, he told me you were beautiful, but you really, really are. I haven't seen him this way about a girl since we were teenagers."

I blush as she holds my upper arms. I look at Alex and he lifts one shoulder. He's not even slightly embarrassed.

He pulls out my chair for me to sit. Owen informs us their father, sister, and Ava are on the way.

"I didn't realize you all knew each other so long."

"Oh yeah," Alex drawls. "Owen is only eleven months older than me, and Charlotte here has been climbing in our window since she was ten. We can't get rid of her now. She's married to one of us."

I don't know whether to laugh at the teasing, but when Owen's shoulders begin to shake, I can't help it. Charlotte slaps his thigh and throws a glare at Alex.

"Oh please, you love me." She takes a sip from her glass. "Honey, you'll get used to these two. When they're around each other, it's like they never matured past the age of fourteen."

I laugh and start feeling a little more comfortable in my skin.

Catching sight of something, Alex releases his grip on my hand, stands up, and his face lights up in the most beautiful grin.

"Incoming. Here comes the only person you really have to impress."

Before I can follow his gaze, a small body comes running into his arms.

"Uncle Alex," she squeals, burying her face in his neck. Long black curls cover the rest of her face.

Ah, Ava.

Seeing how bright his eyes have become makes my heart swell in my chest and I'm smiling so wide, I think my face will crack.

I stand.

"Ava, I would like you to meet Mandy."

When she raises her head, a pink blush tints her cheeks, and warm brown pools connect with mine. She's smiling, but I swear she looks me over, head to toe. I'm pretty sure I've become the woman trying to steal her uncle. Alex is looking at her with so much pride. I think I can see him melting right here in front of me.

"Mandy," he continues, "This is the other special lady in my life."

Ava's gaze darts from me to Alex and back again. Her entire face beams, perfect little white teeth as she giggles, and another blush speckles her face.

I know the feeling, kid.

"Hey, Ava." I smile my best teacher smile. "It's so lovely to meet you. In person," I finish.

"Hi." Her voice is almost a whisper.

Her arms clasp around Alex's neck. I bite my lip to stop the laugh from escaping and he rolls his eyes. He was right; she is a possessive little thing. I don't blame her.

"What age are you?" she asks. Her voice is small but packed with feistiness and I love her already.

"Ava," Alex scolds.

I flash him an amused smile and shake my head to let him know it's okay. I'm used to kids.

"I'm twenty-six," I answer.

She leans into Alex and whispers loud enough so I can hear, "I like her. She's pretty and her dress is cool."

Alex's shoulders shake with quiet laughter and he lowers Ava back down. "Glad to have your approval, kid."

An hour later, and I have no idea why I was so stressed out about this dinner. His family welcomed me, their hugs were warm, and I got to hear some of Alex's embarrassing childhood stories. It feels—I don't know—like family.

His father is a quiet man, involving himself only when he feels the need, but he appears happy. I think he likes to sit back and watch his family together.

Lydia is—well, stunning. Her frame is thinner than I imagine it once was, but it doesn't take from her beauty.

Every so often, Alex will take my hand or squeeze my thigh reassuringly.

At some stage, after the appetizers, Ava snuck onto his lap and he had eaten his dinner with one hand while warning Ava to eat hers or she couldn't get ice-cream for dessert. They both ignored Lydia's instructions for Ava to sit in her own seat. I think he was just as happy to have her in his arms.

It fascinated me. It's a side to Alex I've only seen glimpses of. It all comes so naturally to him. Eating dinner while engaging in conversation, all the while bouncing Ava on his knee and paying her the attention she wanted. From the outside, he looks like a loving father, and I'm realizing that's what he is. He never gets annoyed, even when she's squishing his face with her hands and asking him to say something, so he sounds funny. He's happy when she's happy.

Her brows pull together every time she catches him touching me, but she doesn't seem to hate me for it. She's clarified he's not just *My Alex*. I'm grateful she's willing to share him.

"Ava, why don't you go look at the fish tank and give your uncle a break," Lydia instructs from across the table.

"Mama," Ava whines, her arms dropping to her side.

Lydia raises her eyebrows and her eyes become darker. "Ava, don't start."

Her little face drops and I can't help feeling sorry for her. I'm pretty sure I feel the same when I leave his arms.

Alex wipes his mouth with the napkin. "I'll go with you, Ava."

Lydia rolls her eyes. "Alex, sit down."

As he walks away, he presses his hands on her shoulders and kisses the top of his sister's head. "I haven't gotten to spend a lot of time with her lately. Leave her be."

He kisses my cheek next, and the feeling of his lips lingers there as he walks away with Ava's hand in his.

Owen and Charlotte are deep in chatter with Tony, so Lydia shuffles her seat closer to mine. She's beautiful. With deep sapphire eyes, just like Alex. Her hair is fairer like Owen's, her sharp cheekbones flush now from the wine, and her eyes are glossy, but her shoulders are elegantly straight, and her smile is prideful when she turns to me from looking at her daughter.

"She has him wrapped around her finger, I'm afraid."

I lean my elbow on the back of my chair and look over at them. Alex is crouched, and Ava is giggling uncontrollably.

"It looks like he's more than willing to me. They're amazing together."

She smiles and I notice the discolouration in the corner of her eyes and when she flicks her hair over her shoulder, there are bruises on her hands. They look like puncture wounds. I flinch and I hate when she notices.

"Treatments have made my veins almost non-existent. I've become a pincushion." She laughs and holds out her hand as if showing me a diamond ring.

I blush, embarrassed she felt the need to explain. "I'm sorry. I didn't mean to make you uncomfortable."

She waves her hand. "Honey, please. It's impossible to make me uncomfortable. Doctors have seen more of my body than I have. I'm practically married to my oncologist."

I breathe a sigh of relief. She has the same knack as Alex for making me relax.

Her mouth turns down, and she studies me for a long minute. I want to say something or look away, but I can't.

"Since our mom passed away, I've mothered Alex. I'm ten years older and even though he was only starting college when she died, I still felt the need to be there. He stayed with me while attending university and when he started working at the architecture firm. He was there when I first brought Ava home from the hospital. He missed work nights out with his friends when I was so exhausted, I couldn't keep my eyes open, so he'd do the night feeds. Ava had colic and was always one for dramatics." She shrugs, smiling over at them. "He showed up late for dates because Ava puked on him right before he left, and he'd have to shower and change. She always came first." She looks back at me. "He's a good man," she breathes.

I'm not sure if this is a warning or if she is trying to scare me. She must notice my expression change because she takes my hand. "I'm sorry. I'm his big sister and I should give you the *what-are-your-intentions* speech, but I'm telling you all of this because I like you, Mandy, and you make my brother happy. He deserves you.

Don't cry. Oh, God, don't cry in front of this woman.

"My brother is absolutely crazy in love with you. You know that, right?"

I nod and bite on my lip so hard it throbs, but a choked sob escapes. Damn it.

"I ask that you be patient with him." She dabs the corner of her eye with her finger. "He didn't take my mother's death well, but we had each other. I won't be here for much longer and I'm so glad he has you."

Shit. I've lost it now. What is this woman doing to me?

I squeeze her hand. "I'll be here," I promise.

"Watch him like a hawk. He will distract himself to the point of exhaustion. He will work too hard."

He already works too hard. If he works anymore, he'll fall down.

"He distracts himself with Ava, and…" She smirks and her eyes glisten. "Now you."

My face gets hot, somersaults happening deep in my belly.

I love Alex, but Lydia is selling him to me all over again, and I want to get him home, because he is a good man, and he deserves the truth. He'll never have all of me until that happens.

"I'm fortunate enough to experience how amazing he is. He makes me happy. And I can see how great he is as a brother and an uncle."

"He really is," she agrees. "He supports me even when I make choices he doesn't agree with. When I decided I wanted to contact the agency and reach out to Ava's birth mother, he argued with me for weeks. He only sees things from our side."

My heart jumps into my throat and I swallow the fear-soaked lump
What did she just say?

"Excuse me? You said Ava's birth mother." I shift in my seat.

Her eyes narrow briefly, but she continues. "Yeah. When I got my diagnosis, I wanted to reach out because Ava doesn't have an actual father and I thought, maybe stupidly, the woman who gave her up was this amazing person. Which she is, but I hoped she'd want to get to know her. Just a little, so Ava would have a mother figure. It's silly, I know, but in my desperate mind, it made sense. She never replied to our letter. Alex said it was for the best and she made her choice. Maybe he's right."

I didn't hear half of what she said because the pounding in my chest is ringing in my ears. I slide my hand off the table and wipe it along my dress.

I gawk at her. "I still don't understand."

She laughs and shakes her head. "Why am I not surprised he didn't tell you? He never sees it as an issue. In his head, she's mine and only mine. Ava has always known, so I don't get the big deal, but Ava's adopted."

My blood runs cold, and it takes all my power not to slide off the seat. With tunnel vision, my eyes go to her—the little girl with black curls, the biggest brown eyes I have ever seen, and Jesus, those dimples. The world is spinning in slow motion, and I beg for it to stop.

I'm imagining it. Everything.

I'm hallucinating.

It must be a panic attack.

I didn't see the resemblance before. My brain is clinging to some distorted hope. Or maybe it's shock. Probably dread.

I don't see Alex anymore. I only see little Ava as she spins in circles. I feel a single tear leak from my eye because as much as my brain tries to rationalize this; it can't.

"Mandy." It's Lydia. I forgot she was here. "Are you okay? You've gone pale."

My mouth is dry. I think I'm shaking.

"When's Ava's…" I swallow again. Why is my mouth so fucking dry? "When's Ava's birthday?"

Not March fifth.

Please don't say March fifth.

Lydia's voice is small and sounds far away when she says, "March

fifth."
Fuck.
No.
No.
No.
My head turns back to Ava.
It can't be her.
It can't be because fuck it, it just can't.
She can't be my little girl.

PART TWO

Found

TWENTY-THREE

Then

It was 4.30 a.m. on a stormy morning on March fifth, when tiny wails filled the maternity ward.

My body was shaking. I could hardly breathe, and it felt like a truck hit me.

All the other voices in the room lulled in the background, and I vaguely remember my mother wiping sweat from my forehead with a washcloth.

None of it mattered but those tiny cries. And when they placed her straight on my chest, the rest of the world melted away.

"Congratulations Mommy. It's a girl," the midwife said, still cleaning the little one's face.

She was warm, and I swear, once I held her in my arms, she crawled straight through my chest and planted herself in my heart.

In an instant, she became my world, and the purest love rushed through my veins.

"Hey, baby girl," I whispered, pressing my lips against the black wisps of her hair.

Black hair like Nick. The hint of a dimple on her right cheek like me. Ten fingers, ten toes.

Perfect.

"I'm so proud of you, sweetheart," Mom cried, stroking a finger delicately over my baby's arm while kissing the top of my head. "You did it."

I didn't look at her because I couldn't take my eyes off the bundle in my arms.

"Chloe," I breathed, nuzzling my nose against her skin.

And she was mine.

***

"Sweetheart." My father's arm tightened around my shoulder. "You're falling asleep. You should rest."

I didn't want to rest. I wanted to look at her forever.

All night, I stayed that way. I didn't sleep. I fed her. I changed her. I held her close, and when she wasn't in my arms, I sat on the edge of the bed and stared at her all night in her crib. Even when the doctor came into the room to do a full medical check, I didn't take my eyes off her.

They didn't ask too many questions. Not the usual ones you'd ask a first-time mother bringing her baby home because I wasn't taking Chloe home with me.

They spared me the agony of needing to explain, and I was grateful.

I didn't bother to wipe the tears that fell.

The months of my pregnancy went by in a haze. But not this. I felt every moment. Every memory branded in my brain, forever to replay there.

Everyone got their chance to see her. Mine and Nick's family, and even my friends, but today, I needed to be alone. I didn't want people to crowd me and cloud my decisions.

And when there was a knock at my door, I looked up, and knew the minutes to come would crush me.

The doctors had cleared both me and Chloe to leave the hospital, but we couldn't leave together, and I thought I was going to die. My heart would surely stop.

I recognized the petite lady standing at the door. I hated her colourful clothes and everything she represented. I hated myself for my choices. But my baby girl deserved so much more.

Julie was the counsellor from the adoption agency. I'd met her on countless occasions, but that day, she didn't bring the usual reassurances. Honestly, I didn't want them.

My father pressed a firm kiss on my temple, patted my knee, and left.

I felt the bed dip before I looked up at her. Hair greying at the temples, kind grey eyes, and a smile I should have taken comfort from.

"How are you doing, Mandy?"

What a stupid question?

How was I doing?

I didn't want to open my mouth in fear I'd say something I didn't mean, so I merely nodded.

I averted my gaze back to the beautiful girl in her crib. Still and peaceful. Birds chirped outside the window, and the lightest breeze whistled through the trees. Out there, where she was, it was beautiful.

In here, with me in my head, it was grimy again. I thought happiness would break through, but it was muted, vague muffles making cracks in the dim.

"She's a cutie," Julie said quietly. Taking a deep breath, I felt her apprehensive stare burn a hole in my face. "You've yet to sign the final paperwork, Mandy. It's not too late."

I closed my eyes, rocking some comfort into my aching body, and gulped back the burning I felt. It was everywhere.

"I thought it might be different when I saw her," I started, my lids staying shut. "I've loved no one like I love her. But it's still so dark in here, and I can't bring her with me. Seeing her. Seeing how beautiful and amazing she is, I won't ruin that. She needs so much more. She deserves the world. And my world is broken."

Her warm hand squeezed my shoulder. I shivered.

"You have nothing to be ashamed of, Mandy. It's a brave thing you're doing."

Bullshit.

She told me that before. I believed it less that day.

"It's almost time."

Oh, God.

The selfish in me wanted to say no, because saying goodbye was agony.

Inhaling a deep breath, I shook my head, opened my eyes, and reminded myself who I was doing this for.

"Are they nice?"

194

Julie's laugh was sad, and her eyes filled with tears she wouldn't let fall. She was a professional, after all. This wasn't the first time she had to do this.

"They're amazing, and they're going to love your little girl."

Good enough.

"But you know I can't share any more information with you. I'm sorry."

I knew that.

"And you told them I won't bother them, but if they ever need me for anything, or if Chloe asks questions, they can reach out?"

Another sad smile.

"I even put it in the paperwork."

So, with shaking hands, and through blurry eyes, I signed the final paperwork. I've never hated writing my name so much.

"Can I have a minute with her before she goes?"

"Of course. You take the time you need."

For the next thirty minutes, I held her close to my chest and kissed every inch of her tiny face. I kissed each finger and each of her toes. I sang to her and told her how proud I was to be her mommy.

"Somewhere in this building, there are people waiting for you. And they are going to love you and take care of you. Little one, I'm sorry it wasn't me. But I will always love you. Always. Someday and I am going to hope that we do. We might find each other, and I can tell you everything. I love you so much."

TWENTY-FOUR

Now

"Mandy." The sound of my name knocks me out of my reverie. "Honey, you're shaking."

I am.

I can't stop, and my lungs are burning.

I mean, it can't be her.

It's Alex's niece.

This can't be the person I've tried to imagine for over six years.

It can't be.

I need to get out of here before Alex and Ava get back.

I could be wrong. Lydia said she sent a letter. I didn't get any letter. Shit.

My mind drifts back to my parents' anniversary party. My mother gave me letters when I was leaving. I never looked at them because they're always from the university.

Kneading my fingers over my chest, I plead for my heart to slow.

I push my chair back, stumbling in my heels before catching myself, and I plaster a smile on my face. Wiping the back of my hand across my forehead, I hope Lydia doesn't notice the beads of sweat breaking out there.

My blood has turned to acid, burning as it gushes through my body.

"I need to get some air." I swallow hard because if I don't, I'll be sick. Saliva pools in my mouth and I blink to stop the world from swaying.

Lydia is observing me like I'm about to lose my mind and create chaos in this restaurant.

Maybe I am.

"I'll go with you." She attempts to stand, but I dismiss her with a wave of my hand.

I think I've caught Alex's attention from the other side of the room, but I can't give him time to get to me. I need to make sense of this. And I don't want to look at that little girl and see everything I didn't see before.

Everything that seems obvious now.

"Honestly, I'll be fine. I need five minutes," I stutter, taking backward steps until I'm far enough to turn around. I don't dare look in Alex's direction, or at the little girl I'm acutely aware of now. I want to sprint, but I don't. Alex will be on his way to the table to see what the commotion is about. If I act naturally, he might give me a minute. That's all I need, to get into a cab and go home. I need to open those letters.

I'm in luck. As I leave the restaurant and begin my jog down Main Street, an elderly couple exit a cab.

"Wait," I shout, waving my hands.

This isn't the city. We don't get cabs on every corner.

I shoot an apologetic smile towards the elderly couple and slip into the back seat.

"Mandy!" Alex burst out of the restaurant. His voice is panicked and goes straight through my chest.

"Please, just go," I urge the driver, followed by the ramblings of my address.

I can't look at him. If I do, I'll crumble, and I don't have time for a mental breakdown.

I hear my name again, and before I close my eyes, I see him running towards me, but the driver has already driven away, past the restaurant, and away from the heartbreak I'm bound to face. He'll be after me, I'm sure of it. I only need a few minutes to know for sure.

But what if it's her? What do I say? What do I say to her? Will there even be a chance?

Every day I think about her. I torture myself because I deserve that much. But the questions never stopped stacking up. I wondered when she first rolled over. What her first word was? When did she start walking? What was her favourite part about school? Did she have a best friend? And every other question in between. But most of all, I wanted to know if she was happy. I only wanted to give her the best chance, and she never would have had it with me. Not then. Not in the nights that followed, after her birth, when I couldn't sit up long enough to brush my hair or have a shower.

I survived after Nick, but not after Chloe. After Chloe, I didn't live. I existed. I merely walked around the house and university campus, but with no life inside. In company, I smiled empty smiles, and cried dry tears, to show them I wasn't void of human emotion. Inside, it buried me alive. Day by day, dirt seeped through my blood until all I had inside was darkness.

Black.

Nothing.

That summer, I agreed to go on medication. They said it would help.

It didn't.

It made me sleep. I slept so much my nights blended with my days, and days into weeks, and it wasn't getting better when I woke up. My mom was so scared, she handed me my tablets herself so I wouldn't have access to too many. I'd like to say she was paranoid, but she wasn't. I wanted everything to end. I didn't want to open my eyes anymore until I realized if my little girl ever came looking for me, I wouldn't be there. I would have abandoned her all over again. I couldn't do that. Living with the pain was easier than losing the opportunity to see her again.

So, for years, I dragged myself through my days. Slowly, it got better. My lungs opened and I could breathe again, but never without pain. I needed the pain because I needed the reminder.

I'm still unsure what I was thinking after Nick's death. I wanted my little girl to have a better life. How I convinced myself it was okay not to be involved in that life; I still can't comprehend. I remember little of that time. There was a haze over the memories, as if I've put a barrier between them to protect myself. But there's always one memory I can still see so clearly. It could have happened yesterday. It was the moment I heard Chloe cry for the first time. Her high-pitched wails slowly subsided into tiny whimpers when they placed her in my arms. Her low grunts and even breathing relaxing as I pressed her body on my skin. For such a small person, she filled my arms and my heart more than I ever knew possible. I placed my lips on her warm cheek, breathing in her smell. And when I let her go, my arms were empty beyond anything I imagined. The space became cold, and my chest burned, knots churning low in my stomach. And the coldness has embedded itself there ever since.

I bounce my leg nervously and pick at my nail polish until the car comes to a halt at the curb outside my house. I fumble with money in my purse before tossing it in the driver's direction. I don't have time to count it. Alex is going to come storming through my door any minute.

My house is cold when I switch on the light inside. Maybe it's from all the time I spend with Alex in his house, or maybe it's from the chill that crawls up my back.

I drop my clutch, heart pounding so hard against my chest, I think it will bruise, and run to the kitchen. My handbag is hanging from the hook on the door.

It won't be in here. I'm overreacting. I see a little girl with black hair and brown eyes, and I jump to conclusions.

But a brown envelope sticks out amongst the white ones with the university's stamp. This one has a handwritten address, and my insides curdle. How did I miss this?

I skim my finger under the seal, ripping the paper. Inside there's a white sheet and another smaller brown envelope. When I remove it and unfold the sheet, my blood turns to water. My eyes run over the words, but I'm hardly reading them.

Dear Miss Parker,

We recently received a request from the adoptive parents of your child. As you requested to receive contact should the adoptive family wish, we have enclosed the letter for your consideration.

Please note, you do not have to do anything about this letter. If you decide to move forward, you can do so in a controlled manner through the adoption agency. If you have further questions, you can contact us directly.

The letter slips from my fingers, floating to the ground. I can't finish it because I already know what's in the other envelope, and before I

199

open it, a tear slides down my cheek, soaking the brown paper in my hands. The A4 page is covered in handwritten blue ink.

I've forgotten how to breathe.

To the amazing woman who made me a mother,

I hope this letter finds you in good health. My deepest apologies. I know it must be a shock to hear from me after so long. I do not mean to bring up memories, but I have wanted to do this for the longest time.

Our daughter,"

Those words.

Our daughter.

My sobs escape as my legs give way and I slide against the wall.

"Our daughter has just turned six, and she is the most beautiful little girl. She has always known about you and her story of how she became my daughter.

Unfortunately, I am unable to fill in the parts of your story, and she has begun to ask questions.

For various reasons, that would take too long to explain in one letter. I would like her to get to know the woman who brought her into this world.

Please know, I don't have any expectations, and I have not told my daughter anything about reaching out to you. I would like to meet you first.

I completely understand if I never hear from you. But if you feel ready, and are in the position to do so, I would love to meet you to discuss how our little girl can come to know you.

Again, I hope this letter hasn't shocked you too much, and if you feel this is not the time, then let me say one thing.

Thank you."

"Oh, God." The screams come instinctively, and my legs come up to meet my chest. I hear a voice in the distance, but I'm too busy focusing on the world crashing, collapsing around me until it squeezes my lungs so tight I don't have air.

"Mandy," a voice shouts, grabbing my face in warm hands. It's him. "Baby, you need to breathe. Can you do that for me?"

I don't move. I don't think I can anymore.

I rock and clench the paper between my fingers. In his arms, I'm numb now. He presses my face to his chest, hushing me with whispered words.

From the floor, I can see through my kitchen window and out onto the dusk sky. The sun setting feels fitting. The same is about to happen for me and Alex.

How did this happen?

And what can I say to convince him I didn't plan this?

I've met my little girl. It's what I've wished and dreamed about for six years, but I don't know her, and she doesn't know me. She's not mine. I gave up my right to say that.

It's the first time since I met Alex I feel anything other than love. I envy him. I'm jealous he's had my daughter all this time while I yearned for her. I'm angry because he wasted his days with me instead of filling hers.

I have no right to any of these feelings. I don't know their story. I don't know the circumstances. I don't know fucking anything, and it's killing me.

I need to scream.

The warmth of his fingers around my wrist brings me back. My eyes glaze over, but I look at him anyway. It doesn't matter what he sees now. Everything is going to change in a matter of minutes. The moment I begin to speak is the beginning of the end.

"Hey," he says softly, pressing his lips to my wet cheek. "Come back to me, baby." A crease forms on his forehead as his eyes narrow in on my me, and he tries to smile, but it falters. "You need to say something before I go out of my mind."

I look away, because like I said, it doesn't matter anymore. I'm about to break this man in more ways than I ever knew how. And it hurts. Like something sharp clawing at my chest, pinching the skin every time but delicate enough that I suffer each splice until I become raw. I'm all but bleeding out. It will come. I'm sure of it. I will lose him, and I deserve it.

But I could lose more than Alex.

Have I ruined my only chance with my daughter because I fell in love with a man I didn't know loved her too?

I'm about to find out.

My stomach churns with acid as I pull myself up. He helps. It's the dead of summer, but it's chilly, and I hug my arms around myself. He tries to guide me to sit on the stool, but I pull away. Instead, I walk straight to the cupboard to get myself a glass and pour some water. I take a sip before setting it back on the counter because my hands are trembling, and I rest my palms on the ledge to steady myself.

I swallow back the tears and try to put a barrier around my heart. I can feel it already.

Alex is slipping away.

I sense his heat at my back before his arms come around my waist. He holds me tight, and I wish we could stay this way forever. When all of this is out in the open, I don't know where we start in putting it back together.

This feels different from when we stood here months ago when I told him about Nick. That brought us closer, while this will tear us apart.

I push against him to put space between us. I don't deserve his comfort.

I fight the urge to fall to the floor and sob until the world around me disappears. The pain beneath my ribcage is suffocating, and I dig my fingers in, as if I can somehow pull it out. When I turn around, he's looking down at me, eyes narrowed, strain across his forehead, and I can almost see the pulse throbbing in his neck.

"This is one of those times when I ask you to let me say everything and don't interrupt, but I also understand if you need to."

He wraps his arms around my shoulders, pulling my neck so my face is pressing against his chest, but my arms stay limp at my sides.

It's coming—that ice wall forming around me, barricading me in, trapping me until everything is empty again. The way it always was.

The alternative is to let myself feel this, but if I do it, secure in his arms, it will shatter me because no matter how tightly he holds me, he will never put me back together.

"Christ, Mandy. You're shaking." His eyes penetrate me, but I'm sure my wall has gone high enough. He can't see the emotions swirling in my eyes.

"Don't love me or comfort me right now." I step out of his grasp. "You'll regret it."

"Mandy-"

"You never told me about Ava."

He did.

"I mean, I knew you two were close, but you're more like a father to her," I correct.

It's a strange thing to say, I know. He blinks a few times, and his breathing seems calculated.

"It's one of those things." He shrugs. "It can be strange unless you see it. I wanted to introduce her to you first, so you could see it with your own eyes. I'm not her father, but I'm more than her uncle. She comes to me on holidays and stays at my house some weekends. I would have introduced you sooner, but everything has been in chaos at work, and I haven't been able to spend as much time with her." He arches a brow in question. "Is she why you're acting like this?"

"Yes. But not for the reason you think," I say flatly. Remembering the two of them together, I can't prevent my voice from shaking. "She loves you, Alex. You're incredible with her." Before he can answer, I blurt, "Ava was adopted." He'll take it as a question. It wasn't.

He blows out a breath, a smile appearing at the corner of his mouth. "Jesus, how much did you and my sister talk? She doesn't discuss Ava's adoption with anyone but family."

I am family.

I don't say anything, and he's looking at me like I've sprouted extra arms.

"Mandy?"

"You've been looking for her birth mother."

"What's going on?" He glances around the room as if the walls can answer his questions.

I'm acting crazy. I know it. But I need to try to make sense of this.

When I don't respond, he continues, "Lydia wrote to the adoption agency months back, but we heard nothing. We assume she doesn't want to be found. I can't imagine what it's like to give a baby up and then have their adoptive parent come looking for you. We're not sure what her story is, but we wanted some answers for Ava. And with Lydia being sick, I suppose she is looking for someone who might give Ava guidance when she's gone."

My body is shaking so violently, my teeth are chattering. The blood in my veins runs cold, and the buzzing in my ears is deafening.

"Ava's birth name. Do you know it?"

Silence.

"It's Chloe, but I'm sure you already knew that."

His eyes become wide as he runs his fingers through his hair in frustration. "Nobody knows that."

He takes another step back.

And it's happening.

He is slipping further away from me. I can't reach out and touch him anymore.

"I wanted to tell you this when we got home tonight." I take a deep breath and swallow. I have to say it, and I don't know how, but it must come out.

"Okay," he drawls, trying to make sense of something he couldn't possibly get his head around.

"Chloe." I bite my lip. Fuck. "I mean, Ava. She's mine, Alex."

Another step back. "What are you talking about?"

I better get this out before he thinks I've lost my mind.

"After Nick died, I found out I was pregnant. I was nineteen, grieving, and out of my mind, but I loved her from the moment I felt her move." For the first time, I allow a tear to fall. It was Christmas morning. Before then, I felt the butterflies. It was like popcorn popping, but this was a full kick below my ribs and my belly waved. "I knew I couldn't do it. I wanted her to have everything I knew I couldn't give her. Or what I thought I couldn't give her. And when they placed her in my arms on March fifth, six years ago, she became my whole world, and she has remained that way ever since—from afar."

He takes a step towards me.

"She's mine, Alex," I repeat, stopping him in his tracks when I outstretch my arm and he sees the letter shaking between my fingers.

Only then, I see the weight of my words sink in like our paths on different worlds have collided, leaving us suspended in the air, unable to find our footing.

Still staring at me, he grabs the letter, and the longer his eyes scan over the page, the harder I fight for air.

"No. No," he echoes, and every time he says it, the word becomes more desperate. He doesn't want my words to be real. But they are. And now, I must deal with the crash. I must accept the consequences of my past, and all the words I chose not to say.

Come back to me, Alex.

"Is this some sort of sick fucking joke? Because it's not funny, Mandy."

I shake my head, feeling the tears spill from my chin. "No."

"This isn't real. You're not her mother. You're not the person we've been looking for." The muscles in his jaw tick before he turns away from me, only to spin back around. "You?"

"I had no idea. The letter went to my parents' house. I got it at the anniversary party but only opened it tonight. Lydia mentioned Ava was adopted and all the pieces fell into place. I never expected this."

He doesn't care, but I feel the need to explain before he cuts me out completely. I know, deep down, it won't work, but I need to try.

His eyes wander unblinking around the kitchen. Anywhere but on me.

"Alex, look at me." My voice wavers, so I swallow back the fear. "Alex, fucking look at me." My scream startles him long enough for me to continue, and I ignore his eyes as they bore through me like shards of glass. "I didn't know it was you. I promise. I thought I'd never see her again. I wanted her to be happy." I scrub a hand across my face before looking back at him. "I didn't know who I was falling in love with."

He glares at me like he has met a stranger—one he doesn't like.

"So, you'll leave them alone now—my sister and Ava?" And damn it if that doesn't break my heart.

I suck in a breath and hope I find more strength in my wobbly legs. "I can't."

"Why?"

"Because I can't, Alex. I've seen her now. I'm so sorry." I'll tell him I'm sorry until the day I take my last breath, but I don't think it will ever be enough. "Your sister said she is going to need me," I add.

Every feature on his face becomes wide, like my words have punched him. "Fuck you, Mandy. She needed you six years ago."

I close my eyes, absorbing what he just said. It hurts more than I ever knew words could, but I deserve every syllable, every letter, every angry inflection in his voice. I deserve it all because I can't deny what's true.

"I didn't know if we'd ever find Ava's birth mother, or if she ever wanted to be found. I sure as hell never wanted to find her, but for Ava's sake, I thought about what she'd be like. What her circumstances were." He barks a humourless laugh that sends a chill down my spine. "And she was in my bed all this time. I bet you got a kick out of that."

"I didn't know. I promise," I insist, my lips trembling.

He shrugs, his features suddenly awash with calm. "I guess I'll never know."

God, even I couldn't make sense of the coincidence. My knowledge of our situation isn't an hour old, but a lifetime wouldn't be enough to get my head around it.

"Fuck!" he roars and his voice echoes around the house, hitting me repeatedly. I jump, my body becoming stiff as his hands sweep over the table, causing my teaching folders and plates to crash to the floor. His fists lean against the table, his shoulders rounded and lifting with each harsh breath. I can't help my feet from moving towards him. For selfish reasons, I have to touch him. He flinches when I gently press my fingers to his back, but he doesn't push me away. Instead, a sigh escapes him.

He moves around slowly. My hand brushes across the tense muscles of his shoulder, then his bicep, until I can fist my fingers in his shirt at his chest.

When he curls his fingers under my chin, raising my head to look at him, I want to see his heat, his love, his understanding, but I see none of those things. His eyes flicker with unrelenting defiance, and when he glowers down at me, it doesn't bring the fervour I'm used to, but indifference that makes my blood go to acid.

"You will never take her, Mandy. Do you understand me?"

My hand falls from his chest, slapping against my thigh.

"I don't want to take her from your sister or you. I promise. I only want a chance to get to know her."

His hands come up to either side of my head as he presses his forehead against mine, and I would do anything to make the rest of the world disappear so I could stay this way, with his fingers in my hair and his lips grazing against mine. We stay like that for long minutes, but it's not long enough.

"I need to leave, Mandy."

"Please don't go, Alex," I whisper against his mouth, my fingers gripping tighter to his arms.

He presses his lips gently against my forehead. "Why did it have to be you?" he whispers.

Why did it have to be you, Alex?

And just like that, as he steps away, I can feel the final slip—like one last finger hanging on a ledge before letting go.

His absence is staggering, and when he opens the door, he gives one final pained look over his shoulder before stepping out and shutting it.

The emptiness takes hold. My knees buckle and I crumble to the floor.

TWENTY-FIVE

I feel his presence before I see him, but my breathing remains calm, and I don't feel the usual tingle on my skin.

"You found her." He attempts to reach out and touch me, but he hesitates and rests his hand back on the sand.

I shake my head and cross my arms to protect myself from the bitter breeze stinging my skin.

"I wasn't looking for her," I correct.

He huffs like it makes him angry. "You've been looking for her since the day she left your arms. You searched for her in crowds, in the children who entered your classroom, at every little girl with black hair like mine, or dark blonde curls like yours. You never stopped looking for her."

I turn so I can look at him, but not even Nick can bring me comfort. "I didn't look hard enough, and I should've never been in the position to look for her in the first place. She should have been with me." My voice breaks and my throat burns.

"You did what you thought was right. You gave her the best opportunities. That's love."

I stand, frustrated, and I aim my anger at him. If he hadn't left. If he stayed alive and spoke all the words he never said. Everything would be different.

"You should have stayed," I roar, my heart pounding in my chest, and resentment making my fingers ball into a fist.

He pushes onto his feet. "You made your choice, Mandy. She was ours. We made her with nothing but love, and you gave her to somebody else."

Sucking in a lung full of air, my mind races with thoughts I can't decipher, processing his words that hurt so much I feel myself bleeding. But he's right. Handing our baby girl over to somebody else to love was all on me.

Tears spill, but I refuse to wipe them. It's no use, more will fall in their place.

"I'm losing it again, Nick," I breathe.

He smiles the smile that makes everything feel okay. "You're not losing it."

He doesn't understand.

"I'm not talking about my mind. I'll keep it together this time, for her. It's love. I'm losing love all over again. Everywhere I turn, I lose it."

His shoulders sag and he stuffs his hands in his front pockets while taking a step toward me. "But you always find it again so easily, because you, Mandy Parker, are the easiest person to love." He takes my hand in his. "Do me a favour?" he asks.

I don't think I have it in me anymore, but I agree with a nod.

Pressing his cheek against mine, he whispers, "Fight. Fight for your little girl. Don't give up. And when you've won that fight, go ahead and fight for him." My heart stops. "Because you love him, Mandy. Fight for them both."

***

Sometimes there are snippets in life, brief moments of calm. Like after a storm, when the clouds clear and the smell of rain hangs in the air. The breeze is cooler and cleaner, and somewhere, there's a fresh start happening.

Sometimes that happens to people.

I'm not one of those people.

I was carried away by the storm. I watched the sunshine from a distance while my heart took a battering of thunder, my eyes cried the rain, and in my heart, I got brief lightning flashes of memories to torment my soul in spectacular outbursts.

I'm unsure how long I've been lying here, curled up on the bathroom floor. But it's the only place I found comfort in the dark.

When Garry and Claire burst into the bathroom, it's bright outside.

"Mandy," Claire cries, rushing to my side.

Garry pulls me up from my shoulders so my back is against the wall. He brushes his hand down my face as Claire tugs me into her arms. "We were so worried. We've been calling you all morning."

I don't know where my phone is.

"I'm sorry," I whisper, my voice sounding small and exhausted from crying all night. Then I realize they're here. "How do you know?" I glance between them both.

Garry's Adam's apple bounces in his throat as he swallows hard. "Alex called me."

God, my heart is twisting just hearing his name.

When life hurts, it's easier to go back to the familiar. To flip a switch and go back to being numb.

As if reading my thoughts, Claire pulls away from me, brushing tears from her eyes. "Don't go back there, sweetie. Please don't go back there."

A sob breaks through my chest. "I don't know how to stay away."

"Garry, will you come to help me make some tea?" Sally is standing at the door. She offers me a small smile. I try to smile back. "Give the girls a minute alone." She winks at him, and after he kisses the top of my head, he leaves and closes the door.

"What happened last night?" Claire asks, running her fingers through the strands of hair on my shoulders.

I shake my head and shrug. "The inevitable happened. When I thought of telling Alex about Chloe—I mean Ava—I knew he'd be surprised, but Jesus, I never saw this coming. You should have seen the way he looked at me. He hates me and I can't blame him for it."

"He doesn't hate you."

She's my friend and as a friend, it's the right thing to say, but she's wrong.

"He does. I've ruined everything. I don't know if I'll ever get to see her again." I bite down on my trembling lip to distract myself from the burn in my chest.

"But you got to see her, Mandy. After all these years of wishing, you got to see your little girl."

I always told my friends, seeing my baby, just once, would be enough.

"I lied, Claire."

She rubs my arm. "About what?"

"It's not enough."

It will never be enough. How could it? I've longed for the little girl with bouncing black curls for six years. I can't go back there again.

But I'm not her mother—not in the way she always needed and if her actual mother decides she doesn't want me involved in Ava's life, I will have to accept it. But in accepting that decision, I will have to welcome back the darkness. There isn't one without the other. They're perfect companions in misery.

"Let's get you into the shower. You can freshen up. We'll have some tea and try to figure some of this out."

I don't want tea. I want Ava and I want Alex's arms around me. And I'll never figure this out. I want to go back to lying on the cold floor until I can't feel anything again. But my friends don't need to worry about me any more than they are, so I oblige Claire, and she busies herself turning on the shower and getting fresh towels.

I wash quickly because I'm afraid my legs will give way and I'll crumble to the floor. I've never felt so zapped of everything—of emotions, energy, thoughts. There are so many thoughts, I don't have time to focus on one, and my head is fuzzy.

Everything is so fuzzy.

When I dress, I check my phone. Nothing back from the six voicemails and countless texts I sent Alex. He needs space. I get it.

I'm halfway through a now cold cup of tea when I realize there's chatter around me. Their laughs are forced, smiles sympathetic, and small talk too normal.

"Garry, you spoke to Alex?" I blurt, putting silence to their conversation.

"Mandy," he pleads, frowning across the table.

"You spoke to him, Garry," I persist, ignoring the tears coming again.

He takes a deep breath and glances at Sally, but she doesn't have the answers he is seeking.

"He called me this morning. He asked if it's true—if you had a child. I think hearing the same story from me made it real for him." He gulps, searching my face as if he doesn't know if he should say more. "He asked if we'd check on you. He said you'll need your friends."

He wasn't wrong and because I need to torture myself further, I ask, "How did he sound?" I wish he would answer my calls so I could hear his voice for myself.

"Don't do this to yourself."

"Please, Garry." I need to know.

He throws his eyes up and shakes his head. "I don't know, Mandy. Like you, I suppose. He's shocked."

I hate that he's hurting, and I can't be the one to comfort him. Instead, I'm causing the pain.

When my phone rings on the counter, my heart hammers so hard I think it will come right out of my chest. Even when it's not his name on the screen, I can't help but cling to a shred of hope.

"Hello?"

There's silence, a long breath, and then, "Mandy. Hi. It's Lydia Hale."

My fingers tighten around the phone and I grip the counter to steady myself.

"I hope you don't mind that I've called. I got your number from Alex."

My stomach becomes tight. "Of course not."

"Look," she starts, "I'm as lost as anyone else here, but I think we should talk. I mean, if that's what you want?"

"I do," I say quickly. I would take any opportunity to explain myself and to apologize. She deserves that much face-to-face.

"I was hoping we could meet up. Ava is here, and she knows nothing. I don't want to confuse things, and this isn't a chat we can have in a café or restaurant. Would you be willing to have me call to your house tomorrow afternoon?"

If she asked me to fly to the other side of the world, I would do it. Anything.

"You are more than welcome here. Thank you, Lydia. I don't know what to say."

"We can say whatever we need tomorrow."

By the time we say goodbye, a small beam of light breaks through the darkness.

211

TWENTY-SIX

I cried at least twenty-one of the last twenty-four hours. I cried for Ava, and the years I missed. I cried for Nick, and how vast his absence was again. I cried for Alex, and the hurt I've caused. I cried for Lydia, and the amount of anxiety she must have felt about meeting me: this strange woman who gave birth to her daughter. And I cried a little—okay, a lot—for myself. I wallowed in self-pity and I couldn't find the energy within to drag myself out of it. It's too heavy. It weighs me down until I'm drowning in it. But three hours ago, after my sixth cup of coffee throughout the night, I stood, dried my face, and cleaned.

I cleaned until my fingers blistered, and then I cleaned some more. I cleaned every surface, even the ones not visible, but I wanted the place spotless before Lydia called. My house wasn't dirty. I gave it a thorough clean just days ago, but it wasn't *my-child's-adoptive-mother-is-calling-and-I-need-to-make-a-good-impression* clean. Then, I realized the entire house smelled like bleach, so I cleaned it again with lemon spray, opened every window, and lit some scented candles only to blow them out again because they're a fire risk to six-year-olds. I didn't know what else to do with myself.

Once I finished, I showered, dressed, and made myself presentable. As presentable as I could be, with bags under my eyes the size of suitcases and a red nose from wiping it so often.

God, I'm a mess.

I didn't contact Alex again. I've taken his non-response as a hint to leave him alone. Alex isn't a man to let his pride get in the way and he doesn't hold back. If he wanted to talk to me, he would. For now, I'd have to hold on to hope, he'd someday decide to do that because if I didn't hope, I'd lose it all over again.

I've gone over the words I'd like to say in my head, but it's no use. I don't want this to be rehearsed. We've both waited for this moment. She deserves honest answers. But it also feels like I'm about to attend the most important job interview of my life.

I sit at the breakfast counter, ignoring how quiet my house is without Alex walking around, or coming up behind me to kiss the sensitive spot below my ear. I even miss Bandit's panting as he sniffs for food, or as he snores in the corner. I wish I had work to go to or something to distract myself. But there's still a week left of the summer break, so I'm left with my thoughts.

Wonderful.

My phone vibrates with a text from my mother.

Mom: I think Suzie might be pregnant.

What?

I gulp, the blood draining from my face.

Hello to you too, Mother.

Behind my shaking hands and stuttered breath, excitement rises in my chest. I can't call Mom to ask why she thinks that. Lydia will be here any minute. I haven't said anything to them about Ava. I can't get my head around it. I need more answers before I drop that bombshell.

And how do I explain to my parents I haven't gone cuckoo again, and I wasn't stalking Alex for over four months to get to my daughter? That's what anyone would think. Shit, I think that's what Alex thinks. They'll think I've conjured this up, and then they'll come and see if I need help, and everything will be a mess.

No, I need to sort this first.

Me: Really? That's amazing, but what makes you say that?
Mom: She's pale.

Jesus.

Me: That's her complexion.

Mom: It's not. She's pale, and she's smiling, and Matt seems back to himself. Has he said anything to you?

Leave it to my mother to come up with this conclusion because my brother is in a better place with his wife. Though, I must admit, things were bad between them. She could be onto something, or it could be nothing at all.

Me: He hasn't said anything. But give it time, Mom. If she is, we will know when they want to tell us. They've been through a lot. I can understand if they are cautious.

Mom: I hope she is. I saw the cutest baby clothes at the store earlier.

I roll my eyes.

Me: Step away from the baby clothes. You'll make things worse. Have patience. I need to go. I'll call you later. Love you.

Mom: Talk later. Let me know if Matt calls you. Love you.

I won't tell my mother if Matt calls me. She spreads the word faster than the news.

With the sound of a car approaching, my head spins so fast, my neck cracks. And I'd know the sound of that car if they threw it in with all the other cars in the world. Every time I hear it roll into my driveway, butterflies swarm in my stomach. But the butterflies today are full of anxiety.

What is he doing here? Has Lydia decided not to come?

I wipe my eyes before tears fall and dry my clammy hands against the legs of my jeans.

I can do this.

I can do this.

The engine cuts and I hear a door shut. I don't think I can face him today or all the words he wants to throw at me. I resist the urge to press on the knot in my chest, take a deep breath, fill myself with fake confidence, and approach the door as a figure appears on the other side of the glass. It isn't over six foot two, and there aren't broad shoulders or the outline of a stature I've become accustomed to.

I open back the door before she can knock, not caring if I look like a crazy woman. Today, I am a crazy woman. I feel every bit of one.

I met Lydia two days ago. I know what she looks like, but my eyes still widen, and my mouth parts like she is the last person I expected to see at my door. In a way, she is. She's the mother of the daughter I gave up for adoption, and although I knew she was calling today, something is only catching up in my brain now. This is the woman who raised my daughter when I couldn't. I never thought I would set eyes on either of them. And she's here. Standing at my door, in a beige mac, sleek dark blonde hair, and cheekbones that could cut through glass with elegance and class you only see with royalty.

This is the woman I must live up to.

I'm screwed.

Her mouth is tight, but she smiles, her lids hooded, and a misting of tears dust her lower lashes. While I am showing how much of a mess I've been in the last forty-eight hours, she doesn't. I'm sure she's been through as many emotions as I have, but somehow, she hides it with the grace of a ballerina.

"Hi," I breathe, becoming suddenly aware of who is still sitting in the car on the curb. I feel his stare without having to look in his direction.

She fiddles with the handles of her bag hanging from her arm. It's the only sign she's nervous. Her breathing is even, she isn't sweating like I am, and Jesus, does she have someone to do her makeup? It's perfect.

She nods, exhaling a shaky breath, and a tear falls down her cheek. "Hi, Mandy."

I really want to hug her. She looks like she needs a hug as badly as I do. But she might not be a huggy person.

Apparently, they exist.

She eases my worries when she reaches out both of her arms and embraces me. I can't hold it back. She's actually hugging me. This amazing woman has me wrapped in her arms, and a sob erupts onto her shoulder.

"Thank you," comes out in a strangled voice.

Thank you for everything. For hugging me. For being a mother when I couldn't. For the opportunity to speak to you. But I don't say any of that because my vocal cords are severed.

And when I open my eyes, I see him. Eyes I've lost myself in so many times, shoulders tight and hunched, fingers gripping the steering wheel so tight his knuckles are white. A part of me wishes it was him holding me right now. Those arms would wrap me up and put me back together. He'd try, at least.

Our eyes lock, and as I stand here, mending tiny shreds at a time while I cling to Lydia, the distance between me and Alex grows further. I'm fixing and shattering all at once. I'm two people, sliced down the middle. And God, I want to go to him. The urge is strong, and I'm suffocating. But the pull in the other direction has been building for over six years, and I won't ignore it. For anybody. There's a little girl somewhere, oblivious to this situation, who needs me to pump some strength into my backbone and build on what I didn't have before. She needs me, and it will always be her first.

And he knows it because betrayal and secrets aside, we share the same priority. It will always be Ava for us both. The difference between us: he doesn't see why I deserve the chance, but I'll prove it to him. I need to prove it to Ava, Lydia, and myself first.

We both pull away at the same time, and I avert my gaze back to Lydia. I scrub the back of my hand over my cheeks and notice the streaks of black mascara on my hand.

Great.

Lydia wipes her tears too, but she has a tissue ready and dabs below her eyes.

I stand back, making room for her to step inside. "Come in. Please." I smile again, the slightest weight lifting from my shoulders. She didn't strangle me within the first five minutes, which is a good sign.

She dips her head, like Alex does, and quietly says, "Thank you."

I give one last glance over her shoulder, but Alex isn't looking anymore, and I close the door.

"He's going to wait," she explains, hesitantly following me to the kitchen.

My eyes narrow, but I try to make a joke of it. "Does he think I'll kidnap you?"

Thankfully, she laughs.

"I can't drive with my medication."

You're an idiot, Mandy.

"It makes me groggy. I told him I would call him to pick me up, but he wants to wait."

In the case I really am crazy. I get it. She didn't say that, but I would

216

do the same.

I resist the urge to ask about Ava. It's probably too soon and opt for, "Would you like a drink? Tea, or coffee? Something stronger?" I grin nervously and immediately regret it.

She rubs her palm up and down my upper arm like my mother would do. "I'll have a tea, thank you, but if you want to throw in a shot of something stronger, I need it." She laughs and so do I because I need her to laugh more than I need the numbness alcohol would surely bring. I can tell from the glint in her eyes, she is joking, but my shoulders relax another inch.

She slips off her coat and hangs it over the back of the kitchen chair as I go about getting the tea ready.

No chitchat.

I try to make tea without the cups chattering together, or letting it spill out over the top from my hands shaking. I set milk and sugar on the table.

When I'm done, I take the seat next to hers at the top of the table and turn the chair to face her. I wipe my sweaty palm against my jeans again.

This is really happening, and I suddenly don't know what to say.

My eyes drift from my cup to her face, and then to the hand she has outstretched towards me.

What is she doing? Should I know?

"This is as strange a situation as I've ever known. If we are going to do this, we need to start afresh. I need you to act like you didn't meet me two days ago, or what happened. And as much as I hate saying this: for today, you need to forget about my brother. I know you love him because he loves you, and right now he is hurting and confused, but we need to focus on this, and only this."

I nod frantically. I can do that. For today, I can put everything else aside.

"I'm Lydia Hale. It's good to finally meet you."

My chest tightens, and I fight back tears from my sore eyes. We're starting again.

I take her hand, tightening my grip.

"I'm Mandy. I think you're amazing and I'll never be able to thank you enough."

Her head tilts to the side, but not in the pity way I hate so much.

"I think we both believe we owe one another more thanks than the other, but this isn't a competition, honey. You gave me the greatest gift anyone could give, and I accepted it with the most grateful heart. I'm not here to judge you, Mandy. People can't judge you for making a decision like that. I only want to fit the pieces of my daughter's story together. I want to hear *your* story."

Can I do that? Can I go back there again? But the only way to move forward is to face my past.

She moves her hand to brush my hair away from my face. She's so nurturing. "My God, you are still so young."

I breathe out a laugh and bite my lip. "I think I've aged ten years in two days."

She pats my hand again before letting go and adding milk to her tea. "You and me both."

I know she's only forty-four, but her eyes look younger, yet she carries herself like a woman much older.

She takes a sip of her tea and puts it back on the saucer before taking a deep breath. So do I. "Alex told me what he knows."

A guilty knot clenches in my lower stomach and I swallow the saliva pooling in my mouth.

"I understand Ava's birth father died before she was born."

I shake my head, wishing he could be here with me. "Car accident. He didn't know I was pregnant."

She grimaces and sits up straight again. "Do you have a photo of him? I can see the resemblance between you and Ava, but I'd love to see if she looks like her dad at all."

My heart is actually breaking. It has snapped in two.

During those moments, when I set eyes on Ava, all I saw was Nick. Once I put together who she was, it seemed like the most obvious thing in the world.

All him.

I inhale another steadying breath.

"I'll go get one."

She probably thinks it's strange I don't have any pictures of him around the house. I tried, but he's always too painful to look at because, in his features, I knew I'd see the little girl I gave away.

Two minutes later and I'm back in the kitchen with a photo album. She asked for one, but which one would I choose. Maybe I'm hoping she'll see some of our story in the stills of our faces when we were kids, all the way to the last picture we have together: a week before the accident.

She shows me a soft smile before sliding her hand down the cover of the booklet, and when she opens it, she takes her time going through each picture, a small gasp, a single tear, amazement, and curiosity shining in her eyes. I explain what is happening in each picture. From our first day at school together. To our awkward phase when we realized we had a crush on each other. Then when we first started dating; my unruly curls and his long lanky warms draped across my shoulders topped off with a braced smile. Then, as if by magic, he transformed into a tall, muscular young man, which I knew wasn't by magic at all, but by training hard at sports so he could get a scholarship to college—which he did. He just never got to use most of it.

She cried at a picture of our graduation and again at one of us kissing in front of the fountain at our university. She sobbed, even more, when I told her it was the last picture taken of him.

"You were both so in love."

I agree with a hum because I've lost my words.

We were infatuated.

"She is very much like him. I can't believe the similarities. Of course, he's her father, but I've never met anyone who shares her blood."

How crazy is that? To never have met someone who looked like your child. How tough would that have been for Ava growing up?

I can deal with the guilt later.

When I don't reply, her eyes narrow in on me, searching my face. "I never even asked if you want this. If this is too hard-"

"Every day," I cut in. "Every day I've wanted this." My throat burns again. "I wish I had a good reason for doing what I did. I wish I had more answers for you and Ava and even Alex, but I don't. I don't know what I was thinking back then. Looking back on it now, I can't make sense of it. I know I felt like I was doing the right thing for her because after Nick died, I couldn't look after myself. But then I couldn't understand how having empty arms hurt so much.

"I packed a maternity bag with baby clothes that came home unworn because all the baby books only told you what to pack for when you bring your baby home. My breasts ached, full of nourishment for a child I couldn't feed. And it was all too late. I couldn't go back, and even then, I don't know if I would. Most days, I couldn't open my eyes. I couldn't bear another day, and she deserved more than half a human. Yet now I look back and I don't recognize myself or the choices I made." I gulp back a sob, but it bubbles in my chest. "I forced smiles until it felt like I meant it. Eventually, some of them were real. I lived because there wasn't any other option for me. And in between, over time, there were bursts of happiness." Alex's face flashes when I close my eyes, and the look she gives me tells me she knows what I'm thinking. "But behind it all, she was there. I carried her with me just as I've carried Nick."

"That's a lot of weight to carry on your shoulders."

Sniffling, I look down at my lap and bite the inside of my cheek. "Lydia, I swear, I didn't know who Alex was when we met." I need her to know that.

Stoic, she simply replies, "I believe you."

Millions wouldn't.

"I wish I had more answers for you. At least, I wish I had some that made sense. I don't know what it was. I don't know what made me do it."

"Survival," she quickly says, taking both my hands in hers. My head jerks up, eyes wide, tears streaming like a river. "It was survival, Mandy. When our heart can't take any more trauma or hurt, this takes over." She points a finger at her temple. "The mind is so powerful, and it makes decisions so we can survive and because you needed to keep going. But sometimes, when we look back, we see those strong decisions that kept our heart beating as a weakness. Honey, you survived. So did your little girl."

Oh God, I've lost it again. My body is hurting and filling with some kind of strange relief all at once. She survived, and it's only because I don't want to embarrass Lydia, I don't get down on my knees and thank her.

"What was she like growing up until now?" It comes out in sobs and sniffs.

Lydia looks around for a moment before her eyes land back on mine and she squeezes my hands. "Would you like to talk about that with both me and her sometime?"

What? Really? Someone needs to wake me up if this is a dream because I'll never survive this if it's not real.

"I can meet her?"

She purses her lips together, thinking. "I can't promise anything. She's a clever little thing. She's always known she was a gift to me, but

220

I will need to explain this to her, and although she knows, she's still only six and it's a lot to take in. Ava didn't have a choice in this, and she won't have a choice in many things to come." Her eyes flicker with deep sorrow, and I know she's talking about her illness. God, this little girl has gone through so much. "She needs to have her say in this, and if she decides she doesn't want to meet you, then I'm afraid we will need to respect that."

It breaks my heart, but I get it.

I shake my head in agreement, still holding on to a little ray of hope.

"And Mandy, if that's what she wants, I will also have to ask you to stay away from Alex. If that's her choice, you can't be in her life in any shape or form."

I dry my face and nod again.

"I'll speak to her. Give us a little time to adjust and I will contact you whatever the decision."

See, job interview.

But a half-hour later, when Lydia leaves and Alex refuses to look in my direction, I sit on my bed and no tears fall for the first time. Slowly and painfully, all the broken pieces are finding their way back together. Maybe not in the same places they were before they shattered, but back together all the same.

TWENTY-SEVEN

Three days ago, I got a phone call that changed my life. Lydia called and asked if I would like to come and visit. It was a week after she came to my house and that week was the slowest of my life. Each minute dragged by. Time pulled at me from the inside out. I hardly slept or ate, and I spent my time mentally preparing myself for the call that said I am never to set eyes on Ava again. But it didn't happen, and now I'm here.

I never thought I'd see the day I'd be sitting in a beautiful garden, in a wicker chair under a canopy, waiting to meet my daughter for the first time in over six years.

I've met her only as her uncle's girlfriend. Now I'm meeting her as her biological mother.

I know she's a child, but will she see me as the woman who abandoned her? If so, I'll have to accept it. I'll do anything for the opportunity to get to know her.

I shift in my seat; the wicker creaking under me and fold my hands on my lap, only to release them again for a sip of water.

She was in her room when I arrived. Lydia already told her who I was. How confusing all of this must be for her.

I spent my morning practicing what I would say to her. How I would introduce myself and how I would stand.

How hard can it be? I'm a schoolteacher. I'm around children her age every day, but I've never done such simple things with my own daughter.

At the sight of the little girl bobbling down the steps towards me, I beg for the world to stop spinning, for my breathing to relax in my lungs, and my heart to steady.

I shoot up, my legs feeling like metal rods. I rub my hands, then stuff them in the back pockets of my jeans. I take them out again and cross them across my chest. I shift my weight from one foot to another and fight back the heavy tears by taking a deep breath and smiling.

Why does acting normal become impossible when you're trying to act normal?

I soak her in—how her chocolate eyes pinned on me as she swipes a stray curl from her face, and how she grips Lydia's hand as she shuffles a foot behind. There's no denying the bounce in her dark curls, the bright brown pools feathered with thick black eyelashes, and the fullness in her lips. If I could draw a blend of me and Nick, I wouldn't do this little girl justice. And he's there, in the way her honest eyes shine as she walks cautiously towards me. I've looked into those eyes before, and it strikes me how amazingly familiar yet completely foreign they are.

This situation is hard for my adult mind to comprehend. I can't imagine what she's thinking. Though, what I've learned as a teacher is to never underestimate the strength of a child and their ability to adjust.

I cough to clear my throat from the bubbling of emotions as they come to stand in front of me.

"Hi, Ava," I say, hoping my voice is kind and she will relax.

"Hi," she whispers, huddling closer under her mother's arm.

"It's lovely to meet you." I reach out my hand like a fool because I can't wrap my arms around her.

Her face breaks into a silly smile—like Nick used to do.

"I've met you with Uncle Alex." She giggles and the sound pumps through me and straight to my heart.

I drop my head. "Of course. I'm sorry."

I have no idea what to do and I should know, shouldn't I? A good mother would know what to do. I look at Lydia, but she only offers a reassuring smile and drops Ava's hand to take her seat at the table.

She's trusting me with this situation, and I take some confidence from that. She knows her daughter.

She's a good mother.

I crouch down so I'm eye-level with Ava and ignore the hammering in my chest and how clammy my hands are.

I reach for the gift bag at my feet. "I brought you something."

Her eyes light up and she leans closer to get a better look.

"It's lipstick," she squeals as I remove the small box from the bag.

"I know you like makeup and these are special ones for little girls. It's only a little colour and comes off easily," I say loudly so Lydia knows I haven't gotten her daughter something that will stain everything she wears.

She gasps, and her eyes are so big, they almost bulge. Then I witness the most beautiful thing I've ever seen or heard. Her shoulders shake, and her mouth opens wide as a loud, belly-deep laugh echoes around the garden. I don't think my heart has ever been so full.

Lydia and I join in because who wouldn't laugh with this kid. I'm not sure why she's laughing or what's so funny, but she's happy. Maybe she has a nervous laugh like me.

She runs towards me and when her body crashes into mine, she wraps her arms around my neck and rests her head on my shoulder. I try to hide how my laughter has changed to a choked sob, and I smother the reminder of how many of these hugs I've missed.

This is the first time in six long years I've held my baby girl and I cling to her like she will evaporate if I let go.

"Thank you, Mandy," she says as she pulls away, a blush tinting her cheeks, and an adorable shyness reappearing in her eyes. She looks at Lydia and back to me after her mama gives her a comforting thumbs up. "Mandy, would you like to play with me?"

Would I like to play with her?

God, I love her more than anything.

"I would love to. Thank you. I'll follow you in a minute."

She smiles before she skips away to her toys.

Standing, I brush away the tears I can't stop. I need to pull myself together—for Ava. I can bottle the tears until I'm home alone. This isn't the time to dwell. This is a time to appreciate the present and look forward.

"I'm sorry. The hug got me." I sniff and take another sip of water.

"When you get to know her better, you'll see she's her own person. Ava does what Ava wants to do. She wouldn't have done that if she was uncomfortable. You're doing great, Mandy."

Maybe it's Lydia's natural maternal instinct or how grateful I am to her, but I find encouragement in her kind eyes and soft smile. This can't be easy for her either.

"Thank you, Lydia."

She waves her hand dismissively. "Stop thanking me and go play with your daughter. It's long overdue and I'm happy you're here."

She doesn't have to tell me twice.

***

As the evening creeps in, my cheeks are sore from smiling, my legs are burning from running after Ava, and my hair is soaked from the water fight we had earlier.

I expected my first time meeting Ava to last an hour at most, but Lydia insisted I stay for lunch, and when Ava batted her lashes and said, "Please, Mandy." I went to mush.

Ava talked about Alex—a lot. She told me how he brings her to her favourite ice-cream parlour and when she stays at his house, she can stay up past her bedtime to watch movies. He really was her father figure. My throat burned when I thought about him, but I refused to let it show. Not today.

I'll never replace the memories of letting go of my baby girl, but now, I can think of how when she laughs so hard, her knees buckle, and she doesn't make a sound until she is gasping for air. She twirls a finger in her curls when she is concentrating and her nose scrunches when she's waiting for an answer to one of her thousand questions. I'd stay here answering questions forever if it meant I had her attention.

When it was time to leave, Ava hugged me again, and we both broke into laughter because we yawned at the same time.

It was a small yet magnificent moment.

"Mandy, before you leave," Lydia calls after me. "I forgot to give you this." Both her hands are outstretched, prompting me to take the folder in her hand. "It's a scrapbook. Little snapshots. I documented all her milestones, and there are pictures in there too. You wanted to know what she was like growing up. It's all in here."

I don't realize tears are falling until they splash against the folder.

She'll never know what this means to me.

Untangling my tongue, I pop the book under my arm and hug her with the other. "Thank you, Lydia."

"We'll see you next week?"

225

It isn't a question. Not to me.

Though it wasn't the first time I said goodbye to Ava. This time I knew it wasn't goodbye for good.

TWENTY-EIGHT

"It would be great if one of you could say something now?" I lick my lips and interlock my fingers on the table.

My father is the first to speak. "Her name is Ava?"

I nod, my lips curling slightly, and my eyes are wet. "She's amazing."

Matt is staring at me like I've told him I've found the Holy Grail and my mother's shoulders have begun to shake under her knit sweater. I came to visit so I could tell them about the last two weeks in person, and they've been staring at me like I'm only one crazy sentence away from needing a doctor.

"Mandy." Mom takes my hand. "Is everything okay? You understand what you're saying, sweetheart?"

I try hard not to roll my eyes.

"I'm fine, Mom. I know it's a shock. Believe me, it has taken me two weeks to realize it's real. But it is, and she's the most beautiful thing I've ever seen."

"You're being serious, aren't you?" Matt cuts in, wide-eyed, and chest heaving with each intake of breath. "I can tell."

"Oh my God," Mom shrills, her hands shaking beneath mine. "You've found her. You've really found her."

She found me, but I don't correct her.

My dad is lost in his thoughts somewhere. Pretty sure he's next to freak out.

"And you've seen her already. How is she? Who does she look like? Can we meet her?"

Woah.

"Hold your horses. This is going to take time, and everything will be on Ava's terms. She doesn't even know me yet. I'm sure you'll get to meet her soon, but not yet, Mom. I have something for you, though." I reach into my bag and take out the scrapbook Lydia made for me. Although it won't answer all their questions, it should satisfy their need to see her.

She's fine, she's amazing and beautiful, and she's having a wonderful childhood with her family.

And after everyone hugs and cries for what seems like forever, they go through each picture and documented milestone, examining it in fear they'll miss something.

"And this lady, Lydia, she's sick?" Dad asks, looking up briefly.

I shake my head and ignore the needles prickling my throat. "She's incredible, but she's refusing treatment. It will prolong her life, but she wants quality. She doesn't want Ava to see her wither from chemo."

"Poor baby girl," my mother mutters, flicking the page of the scrapbook. "Is there a father?"

Lydia mentioned this briefly at lunch, but I didn't want to pry.

"She was married. They had applied to adopt together, but they got divorced, so she went ahead with it herself."

I hadn't noticed, but Matt has switched chairs, and I jerk as his arm comes around my shoulder. He kisses the side of my head.

"Alex?" he whispers, rubbing his hand along my back.

I shake my head and frown. "Of all the people in the world, I fell in love with him. Had I never met him and came into her life not knowing him, I don't know if things would be different. Can't help but wonder, though." I shrug, using the tips of my fingers to dry the corner of my eyes.

He squeezes me tighter. "Sometimes, we need to make necessary sacrifices."

He knows it better than anyone. And I have my little girl. I shouldn't want anything more, but I'd be lying to myself and everyone else if I said I didn't miss him. He will always have the part of me he took when he walked away. He can keep it. I don't want anyone else to have it.

"I think she's sacrificed enough," my father grunts. There's an anger in his tone I haven't heard before. He's hurting for me. I'm his little

228

girl, and he hates when he can't protect me from something.

My mother pats his thigh. "Calm down, love."

His palm comes down hard on the table. When he stands, he runs a frustrated hand across his face. "It's not right. He made her happy, but she was missing her little girl. Her little girl makes her happy, but she's missing Alex. Why does she always have to go without?"

I swallow back the lump threatening to choke me and go to him, cupping his face in my hands. "I'm happy, Dad. I know he loved me, but this is beyond anyone's comprehension. She's enough. She will always be enough for me."

He grabs my arms and pulls me into a hug so tight I can hardly breathe. "You're a strong little thing, and I'm so proud of you."

The selfish part of me wants everything he wishes I had, too.

***

When I left, I visited Nick's parents. They were all the things my family was. Shocked, elated, not sure if I'd gone crazy, but when all else settled, the urge to meet her was first in their mind. I explained the situation, and they happily agreed to wait.

After, I drove to Nick's grave, put Ava's photo in some plastic, and tucked it inside a lantern. I run my finger along his picture and the engraving on the stone.

Nicholas Sayres
Aged 20
Loving son, brother, and friend

And father.

"She's like you," I whisper. "She has your smile and goofy sense of humour, and I bet she would have been a daddy's girl." She wouldn't have had a choice with Nick.

The pain of missing him never gets easier, but I've learned how to breathe through the knot in my chest. I'll always have a part of him with me now, in Ava.

"I wish you were here for this."

If I'm throwing out wishes, I wish he never left.

"I love you."

And as I stand, I ask of him the same thing I always do when I

229

come here. It doesn't change now she's back in my life. "Watch over our baby girl."

TWENTY-NINE

"Mandy, I'm stuck."

I swear that kid can project her voice across an ocean.

"She can't be stuck again." Lydia rolls her eyes and continues cleaning Ava's things back into her bag. "I think she does it on purpose, so you'll go get her."

That makes my heart swell. Her tiny little butt can get stuck in the toilet all it wants if that's the reason she does it.

When I go to her, she's already up, washing her hands, and batting her lashes as she admires herself in the mirror. As she should.

I cross my arms over my chest, my eyes narrowing, and I bite the inside of my cheek to stop myself from laughing at the faces she's pulling. "Hey, I thought you were stuck."

"Oh, I'm not anymore. I forgot Uncle Alex told me I was strong now because I'm six and I should be able to get my own butt up from the toilet."

I stifle a laugh. So, she does it to him too.

"You go, girl. You got this."

"I got this," she repeats, drying her hands and patting down her dress.

It's been two months since she came storming into my life and it's the happiest I've ever been. It happened fast, but we went where Ava brought us. She asked last week if she could come and visit me at home, and she's come twice since.

My house is nothing like hers. It's a hell of a lot smaller. I don't even have stairs, but each time, her nosy little face has found something she loves, and she seems happy here.

I hope she is.

To my disappointment, Alex didn't drive them. I haven't seen or heard from him since the day he dropped Lydia off, and the hole in my heart is nowhere near closing. I've contacted him in every way I knew how without getting anyone else involved. I've called, texts, and even emailed, and each time, I received radio silence in return. I even drunk dialed him one night, which still makes me cringe, but a girl has got to try.

He's done. I get it. Pity my heart won't take the hint.

My friends don't bring him up anymore because I cry each time, and then try to laugh it off like his name doesn't stab me. Ava talks about him all the time, but there's a numbing defensive mechanism that latches hold of all my features. I smile and nod because she adores him. If being honest, so do I.

I spent over six years in an empty bed, but now he's left it, it feels colder than it ever did back then.

I shake my head at the thoughts because if I don't, they slowly consume me, and I have everything I need in my life. We don't always get what we want. I'll count my blessings because for so long, I didn't have much of them.

"Sit down," I insist, hearing Lydia become out of breath. She's trying to tidy away Ava's dolls into her toy boxes. They're toy boxes I have for my house, and she shouldn't exert herself. "I can do all of this. Relax." I press my hands on her shoulders until she sits down. She obliges, smiling behind the pain. "You okay?" I ask, low enough so Ava won't hear as she colours a book on the table.

"Tired," she admits, a yawn stretching her cheeks. "This week has been tough. I've got a doctor's appointment next week. He should give me something."

I don't know what to say to her, or what to do, so instead, I tap my hand against her thigh, feeling the bones beneath my fingers. She's deteriorating, and I hope it doesn't show on my face. "If you need anything."

She leans back, resting her head on the chair, and closes her eyes. "I know that, honey. Thank you."

In the past two months, I've gained a friend in the woman my daughter calls Mama, and seeing her in pain aches at my chest. She's exactly who I think of when I hear 'Bad things happen to good people.' It's not fair. It's cruel.

"Are you sure you don't want me to drive you home?" I offer, gathering the last of Ava's toys.

"Uncle Alex is coming to pick us up," Ava chimes in, swaying on her chair.

I try to ignore how my breath hitches and my heart hammers in my chest.

It's been two months of nothing.

I haven't even seen his face.

Lydia leans forward and squeezes my shoulder. Her smile is sympathetic, and I look up to stop the moisture pooling in my eyes.

I need to get over this. This can't be the reaction I always have to him. I can't live my life longing and in agony every time I hear his name. This, I have to deal with first. Then, I can move on to physical interactions. One small step at a time. I'll get there.

"She's staying with him tonight. I'm going for acupuncture this evening and it's amazing how lying on a bed, doing nothing but getting poked with needles, is so exhausting."

I sigh a laugh and plaster another smile on my face.

When I hear the familiar sound of his engine, my brain stops working, and I almost open back the door and run to him, like I used to. But then I remember, I can't do it anymore. We're no longer those people.

I take a deep breath, count to three, and turn back around.

"Come on, little lady. Alex is waiting. Put your coat on. It's cold outside."

She wiggles from the chair and comes to me to slip her hands through the sleeves.

I can't help but eavesdrop when Lydia answers her phone. "Be out in a minute. She's putting on her coat... Uh-huh... All is good... No, it's fine. Mandy has everything packed in her bag and ready to go... Okay."

She ends the call and I smile when she catches me glancing her way.

I crouch down and wrap Ava in a hug, embracing her warm face against mine. "I'll see you in a couple of days."

"Ask what you wanted to ask, Ava." Lydia nudges her. "I've never known you to be shy."

She nods enthusiastically and slaps a wet kiss on my cheek. "Can you come with me when we go to pick out my Halloween costume?"

Oh, sweet heavens. I think every chamber of my heart swells. My daughter is asking me to go shopping for a Halloween costume with her.

I've won at life.

I will not cry.

I will not cry.

"I would love to, Ava. Thank you for asking me."

She shrugs, cool and casual, like it's not a big deal. Not even slightly aware, it's the most beautiful question anyone has ever asked. "You're welcome."

I open the door, still smiling so wide, I think my face will crack, but Alex has parked on the curb, hidden behind the hedging of my garden. I wish, for once, he'd allow me to look at him. I don't know what I expect to see, but not knowing is worse.

Lydia hugs me before taking Ava's hand. "Bye Mandy." She waves from the garden. "Love you."

What?

My throat has closed, and I'm definitely crying now.

Oh, baby girl, I love you, too.

I swallow and find encouragement that Lydia is also wiping tears. "I love you," I choke out in a strangled sob.

She waves back at me again. "I'll tell Uncle Alex you say hi."

What again?

But what do I tell her?

So, I stick my hands in my pockets, ignore the mortification clawing its way down my spine, and grin because he may hate me, but my daughter loves me

***

It's getting dark when my phone buzzes on the coffee table. I tried to watch a movie after Ava left, but I must have fallen asleep halfway through, and now it's deafening loud to my sleepy ears. I fumble for the remote, turn down the volume, and grab my phone.

Only I don't expect the name flashing at me.

Alex.

I don't think about it because something could be wrong.

"Hello?"

A small giggle erupts and then I hear, "Hi Mandy, I wanted to say goodnight."

My breathing calms and relief washes over me. She's melting my heart today.

"Hey, you. Does your uncle know you're calling people from his phone?"

"Uh, huh. He's right here with me. He's making me some warm cocoa before bed."

I can tell I'm on loudspeaker, and I hear Alex opening cupboards in the background. That alone causes my blood pressure to spike.

He's right there.

"Yummy. You're a lucky girl."

His voice comes closer. "Ava, say goodnight to Mandy. Your cocoa is almost ready, and you still have to call your mama."

Her lips smack together. "Goodnight, Mandy. Love you lots."

There it is again.

I swoon.

"Goodnight, sweetheart. I love you."

And then, before Ava ends the call, she demands, "Say goodnight to Mandy, Alex."

I'm shaking.

The phone is rattling in my hand.

I may be about to receive actual words from him.

There's a long pause, and I wait for what seems like forever. I'm about to tell her it's okay when I hear him clear his throat, and his low, gravelly voice murmurs, "Goodnight, Mandy."

I close my eyes and hang on to how he says my name, hating when it still makes my heart skip a beat.

"Goodnight, Alex."

THIRTY

Winter passed by in a blur. Ava made the cutest bumble bee for Halloween. Lydia was too weak to walk around the entire neighbourhood. She came to the first five houses and after she returned home; I took Ava trick or treating.

Christmas was amazing. My most beautiful memory of Christmas was when Ava kicked for the first time when I was pregnant. She outdid herself this year. I didn't get to see her on Christmas day, but Lydia invited me to Christmas Eve dinner, and after we exchanged gifts, laughed till our cheeks hurt, and a little blushed from the bottle of wine I shared with Lydia, Ava sat with her gifts and simply said, "Thanks, Mom."

No lie, I choked. Lydia slapped my back until I cleared my airways. But honestly, if I had died at that moment, I would have died happy.

It was a slip of her tongue at first. I see it with my students. But after, it was deliberate. So now, sometimes I'm Mandy, but mostly I'm Mommy Mandy, and I've never loved my name so much.

I spent Christmas Day and New Year with my family. Lydia took Ava away with the family for the holidays. We video called every night before she went to bed. I updated my family on how she was and showed them photos and videos I'd captured.

Over the months, she has asked about them. Her questions come in drips and drabs. If she asks, I answer, but only when she wants to talk about it. Sometimes, she even asks about Nick, and her face lights up when I tell her a story about him.

We're adjusting.

All of us.

I don't know how I got through this week. I counted down the hours until she was back, and I could see her again. I've tried to fill my days, but everything is meaningless until she's with me. I kept busy by preparing for the return to school after the holidays. I have every shade and shape of marker, new notebooks, and activity sheets organized until Easter.

I shopped, bought a new playhouse and a swing set for my garden. Garry helped me put it together.

I'm lying.

I watched Garry curse and sweat as he put it together.

I decorated the spare room. It's painted pink with princess stickers, and a tepee tent wrapped in fairy lights in the corner. For now, she can use it as her playroom. I've childproofed my entire house because she may be too old to stick her fingers in sockets, but I still catch mine in the cabinet doors, and it appears she has my clumsy nature.

"All done," she chimes, sitting back on the kitchen chair.

I blow on the wet nail polish and examine the red gloss applied to perfection. "Amazing. Thank you."

Lydia sets two cups of coffee at the table before sitting with us. "She paints mine all the time."

"Uncle Alex lets me do his too." She giggles.

I sense Lydia's eyes on my face, but I don't falter. The mention of his name still causes daggers to my chest, but I live with it. My only fear is the pain will be there forever.

"Mommy Mandy?" Ava bats her eyelashes like she is going to ask for a pony. I swear I'd give her one.

"Yes," I say slowly.

"Can I have a sleepover at your house?" I'm taken aback by the question. I expected to have her sleep over at some stage, but I didn't think she would want to so soon. I swallow to rid myself of the burn in my throat. I look straight at Lydia. After all, this isn't my call. She smiles, but I can see it is hurting her. How could it not? She rubs at her eyelids, and I can't help but notice how much darker they look in the last few weeks. The bruise-like bags under her eyes appear painful, and she has small wrinkles around her mouth now. She's still beautiful, but

I see how sick she is behind her blue pools. She looks exhausted.

She runs her hand over Ava's loose curls. "Sweetie, can you go play in the garden? Mommy Mandy and I will discuss this sleepover."

Ava nods enthusiastically before jumping from the chair, singing as she runs on the grass. She's screaming at her imaginary friend when I look back at Lydia.

"I'm sorry. I had no idea she was going to ask me that. She hasn't mentioned it before."

Lydia takes my hand in hers. "I did. She brought it up last week. I don't mind, Mandy. I came to terms with this a long time ago. I'm just so happy she is comfortable enough with you to ask and want to do it."

This woman is my hero. I can only wish to have half her strength. I owe her so much, and I'm afraid there's not enough time to repay her.

She wraps her hands around her cup as she continues, "If I'm honest, these new painkillers are wiping me out, and I could do with a sleep-in."

My mouth turns up into a small sympathetic smile. That's all I can give her—sympathy. And she deserves so much more. She deserves to have a longer life without suffering. But if all I can do is give her something as simple as a sleep-in, I am more than happy to do it. Even if it's also for selfish reasons.

"I'd love to have her sleep over. I can take her tonight if it suits?"

She relaxes into herself with a deep breath. Her shoulders are slimmer too, and her knuckles are protruding from the bluish skin.

"That would be amazing. Thank you, Mandy."

I think about my next offer before saying it. I don't want to step on any toes, but over the months Lydia has become a friend, and if I can't help a friend when they need it, I'm no use.

"If there's ever a time when you don't want Ava to leave but you need someone to watch her, I can always come here. I don't mind staying a night. I live an hour away. It's not a big deal."

Relief washes over her features. "Thank you, Mandy. I might take you up on the offer. But you deserve your own time with her too, and I'm glad she's staying with you tonight." She pats the back of my hand. "You didn't ask, but I want to tell you. You're doing amazing."

Now it's my turn to wipe my eyes. I don't deserve her praise, but it's still reassuring to hear it.

When she calls Ava back inside to tell her the good news, she twirls around, and hugs me so tight around my neck I can't breathe.

"Can we watch a movie?" She claps her hands and jumps on the spot.

"Of course."

"And ice-cream?"

"I have some cookie dough ice-cream."

Her eyes widen, and she shoots a toothless grin at me. "It's my favourite." I know because it's mine too. "And can I stay up until eleven?" She says that one in a whisper and leans into me, darting her eyes at Lydia. This kid is no good at being sneaky.

I poke her nose. "We both know your bedtime is ten at the weekends."

She rolls her eyes with that sassy attitude she has. "Fine."

As much as I want to give her everything she asks, it's not fair to Lydia. She has worked too hard for me to unravel everything because I feel guilty.

As Ava skips around the table with a skipping rope hanging from her hand, I hear the familiar sound of the front door. Lydia rushes to put her cup back down and her eyes go wild with panic.

"Mandy, I'm so sorry. I told him to call me before he came by."

I can't help feeling like my blood has thickened, and it's struggling to get around my body. I haven't been so close to him since the night he found out. We've danced around each other, making sure this exact moment never happens.

Fuck.

"Uncle Alex," Ava squeals, and she runs out of the kitchen. From down the hall, I hear him as he takes her in his arms.

"Hey, kid." His voice is light and playful, and all the good things come rushing back. His voice coats over me and I feel it all the way to my toes.

Jesus, I haven't even seen him yet.

Will he always have this effect on me?

"I'm staying with Mommy Mandy tonight."

Her admission makes my throat close, and his silence makes my blood go cold.

"Really?" he says tightly. "Good for you, sweetheart. Why don't you go play? I have to speak with your Mama and," he stops, and the quietness is deafening, "Mommy Mandy," he finishes.

239

Ava bounces back into the kitchen with a new toy in tow. She continues out into the garden, where she sits on her blanket and continues her tea party from earlier.

My body can sense him before I look his way. I know his eyes are on me, but when I find the courage to look back, his gaze averts to his sister. His shoulders square like he's about to walk through a wall. He stalks to the table and leans his palms flat against it.

"What the fuck is going on? She's staying over?"

Lydia purses her lips and rolls her eyes. "Don't be difficult, Alex. Sit down. And I told you to call."

"Since when do I need to call you before I come by?"

He's right. He should be able to walk through the front door anytime he likes, as he has always done.

She shoots him a look that says, 'things are a little different now and that reason is sitting at my kitchen table'. It's me. I'm the reason he needs to call, and I feel my face get hot. This shouldn't be the way things are, but it's not my place, so I press my lips together.

He ignores her. "And she's calling her Mommy. Have you lost your mind?" His voice is low but harsh and spills out of his mouth like venom. He's blatantly ignoring me like I'm part of the furniture.

It hurts.

No, it more than hurts.

It's torture. I need to look him in the eyes.

I need to see it for myself.

"Mandy is helping me out. I could do with the break, okay?"

He stands up straight, looking at her as if it's the most ridiculous thing he has ever heard. "I told you I will take her."

"Alex, you have her all the time. And you're working around the clock. I can't expect you to take more time off."

"Well, I do. I expect it," he retorts, running a frustrated hand over his face.

Lydia crosses her arms over her chest. The movement causes her to flinch. She previously mentioned it was almost time to take her pills. I go to the faucet to get her a glass of water and grab the container from the cupboard.

"Thank you," she whispers, smiling apologetically. I shake my head. It's not her fault I'm in this position. This is all me.

She turns back to Alex as she swallows the tablets, and his expression softens. He doesn't like seeing his sister in pain. Alex is a fixer. He restores things. Watching Lydia like this must cause him great torment.

"Alex," she says, wiping the moisture from her mouth. "It was Ava's idea. No one pressured her into anything. She asked. And Mandy *is* her mother."

"No, Lydia," he snaps in quiet disdain. "You're her mother."

That's like a knife straight to the chest.

I shouldn't be here. I can busy myself somewhere else. "I'm going to pack Ava's bag."

As I walk away, my shoulder brushes against him, and his fingers grab the inside of my elbow.

"Stay," he pleads, but anger is radiating from him. He drops his hand, as if touching me has burned him, and when I look up, all I see is the tension across his brow, and half-lidded eyes staring at the table.

His scent washes over me, and it takes all my power not to bury my face in the crook of his neck and inhale all that he is.

Please look at me, Alex.

I swallow dryly before taking a deep breath to calm my pulse. "This isn't about me."

He closes his eyes, his chest collapsing under the weight of his sigh. "This is all about you."

I nod in agreement because he's right. I've caused this. "Yes. But not this, Alex. This conversation doesn't involve me. Talk to your sister." And I walk away. I look back only once, and when I do, he has Lydia in his arms.

Fixing.

***

When I leave her room and come back downstairs with her backpack, Alex is in the hallway waiting for me. His hands are in his pockets, feet shifting beneath him, and eyes to the floor. He looks up, but not at me. His eyes are everywhere. Over me, through me, past me, but he never looks at me.

Goddammit, Alex, look at me.

"I'll pick Ava up from your house tomorrow. It's something we have to get used to," he says when I reach the last step.

He takes a pace backward when I stand in front of him. He can't even tolerate my presence. I chew the inside of my cheek because if I

241

don't, tears will come. My shoulders are beginning to shake with threatening sobs. I take a steadying breath, tapping my fingers against my thigh in rhythms to distract myself.

I want to reach out and touch him, comfort him, tell him I'm sorry by putting my mouth on his. But it's not my right anymore. Someone else will fill that space in Alex's life, and I can't help the bitterness rise in my throat.

I'll cross that bridge when we get to it.

"What time works for you?" he asks when I don't respond.

"Is four o'clock okay? I can make sure she eats before she leaves."

"Okay," he agrees, and his lack of words is slowly killing me.

Just once, I want his eyes to meet mine for more than a flicker. But he doesn't and turns to leave, leaving an empty space and ice-cold air in his absence.

He stops before reaching the door and turns his head over his shoulder.

"Mandy," he chokes, and tears come despite my efforts because the sound of my name rolling off his tongue brings back too many memories. It doesn't sound the same when he says my name now. Only traces of warmth linger around the letters.

He turns around and when his eyes meet mine, I can't move. I'm stuck in this spot.

He takes a step forward and I suck in air, but he breaks mid-stride, cursing under his breath. I quickly wipe the tears tickling my cheeks. His face flickers too many emotions at once, and none of them stays long enough to see the ones I remember.

"I know you're her mother. I shouldn't have said what I said in there. I'm glad Ava is happy. That's all I care about."

Message received.

And I can't hate him for it, because it makes my heart break with so much love for him. At least we share our priorities.

"Thank you," I whisper, but my voice breaks.

He looks like he's deliberating doing or saying something else, but he turns on his heels and leaves, taking a part of me with him.

THIRTY-ONE

"My mommy is having a baby." Kyle looks up at me with a gummy grin from the back of the classroom. All freckles and green eyes and excitement.

"Well, I think Kyle wins News of the Week. What do you think, class?"

The rest cheer and clap and continue to argue about whose brother or sister will be cuter.

There's something in the water in this town. At least five of the other mothers are pregnant and it's only February.

The classroom door swings open, and everyone's head turns. Marie, the secretary, scurries into the room and leans close to me, whispering, "Mandy, there's a call waiting for you in the office. She said her name is Lydia. It sounded rather urgent."

The blood drains from my upper body and pools at my feet. Marie must notice because she pats my back. "Go. I'll wait here with them while you're on the phone."

"Thank you. Kids, get out your copybooks, and draw me a picture of your favourite place." That should keep them occupied.

I practically sprint out of the classroom and down the hall. Lydia has never called me while I'm at work. I gave her the number for emergencies because I didn't check my phone during class time.

I try to fill my lungs before I answer. "Lydia?"

"Mandy, I'm sorry to call you like this." She sounds dreadful.

"It's fine. Are you okay?"

She catches her breath, and there's an obvious wheeze. She's struggling. "I'm not doing well today. I'm feeling a little weak and nauseous. Ava finishes school in just over an hour, and I don't think I'll manage the walk."

This must be bad. Ava's school is five minutes from Lydia's house. She usually walks the block to drop her off and collect her.

"Alex is out of town until tonight. My dad is getting over the flu, so I can't risk him being around, and I can't get in contact with Owen or Charlotte. I know you're at work, too, but-"

"I'll be there to pick her up on time," I cut in.

She sighs. "Thank you, Mandy."

"I need to get the substitute to watch my class and I'll go get her. Do you need me to get you anything?"

Her laugh is tight and causes her to cough. "Ice-cream."

I laugh too.

"My throat is on fire. Some ice-cream would be good."

"You got it. I'll see you soon. Try to get some rest."

"The door is unlocked. I'll call the school and let them know you're picking her up. You'll need your ID. I'm sorry this is so awkward."

"I'm a teacher, Lydia. We have the same policy here. I've got identification with me. Get some sleep. Crisis averted. Now, get off the phone or I'll be late," I say playfully.

"Yeah. Yeah. Now you sound like a teacher. Thanks, Mandy. See you soon."

I hang up, but the boulder resting on my shoulders feels heavier by the second. Lydia didn't sound good at all, but right now, I don't have time to dwell. I need to get my students sorted so I can leave.

Garry has a student teacher with him this week and I'm about to steal him.

Knocking on his door, I straighten up and rest my hands on my hips so he doesn't notice them trembling.

"What's up?" He pokes his head out. I gesture for him to come outside so the students won't hear.

"I need your student teacher."

His eyes narrow. "No fair. I was enjoying the rest." But his eyes finally catch up and he notices when I break out in a sweat. "What is it?"

244

"Lydia's sick. She needs me to pick up Ava."

"Shit. Of course. He's not qualified to be with them on his own though, so let me get my kids ready and I'll take both classes to the hall for some games for the last hour."

I have the best friends.

I wrap my arms around his neck and kiss his cheek. "I owe you, Garry."

"Go. I'll sort them."

He doesn't have to tell me twice. I rush to my class, grab my bag, and explain to Marie that Garry is taking over.

"It's an emergency. I have to go pick my daughter up from school."

Her face visibly drops. I forgot I hadn't told anybody at work.

"You have a daughter?"

Shit.

I'm not ashamed of my story. Not anymore, but I don't have the time.

"Oh, Marie. I'll explain. I promise. But I need to go. Ask Garry, he'll tell you all about it."

She's dumbfounded. Poor woman.

"Kids, behave. Mr. Miller will take you to the hall for some games." They cheer. "I have to leave, but Mr. Miller will tell me if anyone steps out of line. I'll see you all tomorrow."

"Bye Ms. Parker," they singsong in unison.

It's an hour to Ava's school. I can get there and pick up some ice-cream after.

On the way, my thoughts aren't how big of a moment this is: to pick up Ava from school, but my mind immediately goes to Lydia. I noticed since Christmas, the strength she once had was deteriorating both internally and externally. Her muscles were withering, and the ones she had cramped unmercifully. It caused her agony. She'd lost weight, and it was more than her body could handle. Her skin was dry because some days she couldn't keep water down. Alex and I did our best with Ava. Mostly, when we had her, we stayed in Lydia's house. We didn't cross paths much, but at least Lydia could be with Ava.

I hate thinking of it, and I curse myself when I do, but I know her body can't hold on much longer.

I don't want Ava to lose her mama and endure more loss. And I don't want Alex and his family to go through the pain of burying their sister and daughter. But selfishly, I don't want to lose a friend. Because she has become more than that. She's my mentor on this crazy journey. She loved and accepted me when she didn't have to. She opened her heart and her home to a strange woman and trusted I was there for the right reasons.

"Snap out of it, Mandy," I mutter to myself, shaking my head and wiping the tears streaming down my face. Ava can't see me like this.

I've made it with two minutes to spare, and when I park my car, classes are streaming outside into the schoolyard. My eyes catch her immediately. Messy curls floating around her face. I'm pretty sure Lydia ties her hair back going to school, but now her elastic hangs on for dear life on a few strands of hair, and the rest is in a tangle.

Poor thing has my hair.

I remove my identification from my purse and stand inside the school gate until she sees me. Her face lifts, eyes wide, and she immediately breaks into an awkward sprint as her bag bobs on her back.

"Mommy," she screams like a child possessed and runs straight into my arms.

"Hey, sweet girl. You ready to go?"

She nods enthusiastically, her beautiful smile never faltering.

"You must be Mandy?" A young woman around my age approaches and reaches out her hand. I shake it and pass her my ID.

"Nice to meet you."

"Ava's told us lots about you."

I look down at the child, who looks like she ran through a bush, and squeeze her tighter to me.

"Mandy was the mommy who had me in her tummy."

Oh, Ava.

A tight smile edges on my face as the teacher becomes slightly wide-eyed. I'm not sure if she knows the full story, but it's not the first time I've received that look. Many people assume Lydia and I are a couple, and we don't correct them anymore. People will think what they want to. Most are strangers and their opinions don't matter. It has become a running joke. And Lydia thinks it's funny when she tells me her brother, Owen, is next on my list. I cringe, I really do, but I love her sense of humour.

But I don't have time to explain to her teacher what our situation is. Lydia is at home and she needs me.

"I should get going."

She closes her mouth, glances at the name on the identification, and hands it back to me.

"No problem. I'll see you tomorrow, Ava."

"Bye." She waves as I take her hand and lead her to the car.

"Okay, young lady. Before you get in, I need to fix your hair. It's a health hazard."

She grunts and relaxes her shoulders, so her bag falls to the floor. I braid her hair quickly. Once she's home, I'll bath her and braid it properly. It'll stay in place for a few days, so Lydia won't have to worry about doing it.

On the way home, Ava fills me in on all her news from school. She doesn't ask why I collected her, and she almost bounces off the roof when I tell her we're getting ice-cream.

I don't know which one Lydia likes, so I buy one in each flavour, because you can never have enough ice-cream.

When we get to the house, Lydia calls out to say she's upstairs. I unpack the groceries and get Ava settled with a movie while I make sure Lydia is okay.

"Mama is a little tired today. You okay here for a few minutes while I do something, and when I come down, I'll fix us some dinner?"

She's already engrossed in the opening credits. "Uh, huh."

Upstairs, Lydia's room has the distinct smell of sickness. It's dark, the blinds are closed, and I can smell vomit somewhere.

Why didn't she call me sooner?

"Ava's downstairs watching a movie," I answer before she can ask. "Were you going to lie here all day, and not tell anybody? How long have you been like this?"

She rolls her eyes and wipes a bony hand over her lips.

"You can't give out to me. I'm sick."

It's good to still see humour dancing in her eyes. She sighs but I hardly notice, because she doesn't have the energy for a full one.

"I started feeling bad on the walk home from the school this morning. I thought it was the medication, but this shit is nasty."

Lydia doesn't curse. I've never heard her utter one bad word.

This must be bad.

Time to make her comfortable because she's bent like a pretzel in the bed. And she's lost so much weight, she's hidden under the covers.

"Are you strong enough to sit up in the chair for ten minutes? I can get new bed sheets on."

"You don't have to."

"I know, but I want to."

She tries to smile, I think. "You're a star. I might take a shower."

That's a good sign.

While I help Lydia into her seat in the shower, I get to work tidying the room. I sweep and wash the floors, open the windows, change the bedsheets, and lay out clean pajamas. She looks marginally better when she comes back into the room.

I glance at her shoulders but quickly avert my eyes. I knew she'd lost weight, but oh my word. Her collarbone is jutting out almost painfully, and when she turns to get dressed, I can see each of her vertebrae.

"I'll be back in a few minutes. I'll make some soup." She's about to object when I raise my palm and stop her. "You can't take your medication on an empty stomach. You'll make yourself worse, and it'll stop me from nagging if you do it."

Her nose scrunches and she grunts just like Ava does. "Anything to stop you from nagging," she mutters.

"Hey, I heard that."

She laughs, and it warms my soul.

Later that evening, after dinner, I bathe Ava, braid her hair, and get her ready for bed. I tidy downstairs while Lydia reads her a bedtime story, and I make sure Ava's homework is packed away. When I go back upstairs with a hot water bottle for Lydia, Ava is already snoring. I kiss her head and ask any god who will listen to keep her safe and give her strength over the months to come. At least when I lost Nick, I was old enough to understand it.

"You okay with me staying tonight?"

Lydia is trying to hold up a book when I go back into her bedroom.

"Of course." Now, I know things are bad. The Lydia I know, would never give in and admit she needs help. "Want to climb in here and watch a movie with me?" She pulls back the covers and smirks.

"You know people are already talking about us, and now you want to share a bed with me. Got something you want to say?"

"If I were to fall in love with a woman, it would be you, Mandy Parker." She winks and laughs hoarsely as I press the hot water bottle to her back.

I take one of her million cushions from her walk-in wardrobe. "Things are about to get so kinky." She looks almost scared. Her back has been aching all day. "This may help. My mom's back sometimes spasms, and it helps when she lies on her side with a cushion between her knees. It will take the pressure off your hips."

She doesn't argue when I position her on her right side and lift her knee to place the cushion there. I put another cushion at her back and sandwich the hot water bottle between it.

"You should have been a doctor. This feels amazing."

"I know, right!" I delicately squeeze her forearm. "We can watch a movie another night. You should get some sleep."

Her eyes are already closing, and she can't deny it when a yawn takes over her face.

She grabs my hand before I walk away. "I wanted to talk to you for a minute."

Oh, no.

This is the talk.

The one I could sense coming, and no amount of time will prepare me for this moment.

"Sure." I shrug, trying to hide the fear I'm feeling.

She pats the bed, beckoning me to sit. I do as she asks.

"You look petrified, Mandy," she states, arching an eyebrow. I hate being this easy to read. "Relax."

I smile, but it quickly falters, and we both inhale a shaky breath.

"Thank you," she says quietly, clasping her fingers with mine.

My eyes bulge. I shake my head. "For what?"

"For being more than I hoped for. For being a friend. For being patient with Alex and his stubborn ways. But most of all, for being an amazing mother to Ava."

Licking my lips, I swallow the lump lodged in my throat. Tears fall anyway because I know this is what I feared it was going to be.

This is goodbye.

"I should thank you, Lydia. Ava is all you and she's beautiful for it."

She shrugs but a prideful smile pulls at her lips and her eyes sparkle. "I suppose we could go around in circles thanking each other. I'm just happy she has you in her life."

"She always will," I assure her.

She nods, patting the top of my hand. "I know that." She rests both our hands at her side, adjusting herself back on her pillows. "I want to tell you when the time comes, Ava will go to Alex."

I can't help but smile. Ava will be happy with him, and he treats her like a little princess.

"But I want you to continue what you're doing together. Alex won't get in the way of that. I wanted to assure you when I'm not here, it doesn't mean Ava is taken away too."

I swipe at the tears flowing down my cheeks, but a strained sob erupts deep in my chest. I stand and gently wrap my arms around her narrow shoulders. She hugs me back as tightly as she can.

"Thank you, Lydia. I can never thank you enough for this."

Pulling away, she takes my face in her hands, and I find myself staring into very familiar blue eyes, and it makes my chest crack wide open.

"He's hurt and confused, but the day he stops loving you will be the day hell freezes over."

It's nice of her to say, but Alex has made his decision and I'm okay with that.

Scratch that, I'm not. I hate it, but I understand, and I don't have any other choice.

"A love like yours doesn't come around every day. I should know." She smiles and her eyes aren't sad. She's accepted it.

I know what she's trying to say: *Don't give up.*

***

When I wake, I'm in pitch black, enveloped in blankets, and I no longer have the book I was reading. I rub my eyes, hoping they'll adjust to the dark. I'm in the guest bedroom.

How?

I fell asleep on the chair in Lydia's room, reading a book. I vaguely remember my head pressed against something hard, but I thought I was dreaming.

How the hell did I get in here?

Like alarm bells, my mind races.

Alex.

My stomach does a somersault, and I remind myself to take a breath.

Unless I was sleepwalking, there's no other way I could have come in here.

I pull back the covers and shiver as the cool night air creeps across my skin. It's 5.30 a.m., and when I open the bedroom door, the moonlight is filtering through the windows into the hall. I briefly check on Lydia. No one is in there but her, and Ava is sleeping like a starfish, but alone.

Downstairs, I tiptoe to avoid the creak of the wooden floors. I distinctly remember turning off all the lights down here, so when I see the glow from overhead the stove illuminating the kitchen, my pulse races, and I'm suddenly wide awake.

Approaching the doorway, I see him. His strong, broad structure hunches over, staring at his laptop, biceps strained and the sight swirls low in my belly.

As if sensing me, he sits up straight and glances over his shoulder. I can't remember the last time he looked at me for more than a few seconds, but there's no denying how his eyes rake over me, and my fingers dig into the door frame for support.

Then it's gone. Not his stare, but the warmth in his depths. He closes his laptop and stands up.

"Thank you, Mandy." I think my heart has stopped, or I've spiralled into shock. "For being here today for Ava and Lydia. I'm sorry I couldn't get here sooner." His voice is low, raspy, and does something to my nervous system because goosebumps play out on my skin. I'm glad it's still dark so he can't see the blush on my skin.

"Lydia's my friend, and I'll always be here for Ava."

His gaze locks with mine for a long second, and he nods. He has accepted that much.

Clearing his throat, he shifts his weight from one foot to another. He's nervous, or scared, or both. "Lydia isn't getting any better. I don't want Ava around too much at the end. She's young but old enough to remember."

I know what he's about to ask, and he doesn't need to.

"I'll be here, Alex. Anytime. You don't even need to call. Drop her off or I can come to get her."

He nods again and runs a hand over his stubble.

Silence.

Nothing to fill the space between us and my insides tighten.

"Did you carry me to bed?" I blurt, unable to stop myself.

I swear, I see a shadow on a smirk on his lips, but it's gone before I can tell for certain. "You looked uncomfortable on the chair."

"You didn't have-"

"It wouldn't be the first time I carried you to bed, Mandy."

251

Oh, sweet divine.

My blood has turned to lava, and everything in me is burning. When Alex carried me to bed, it was rarely for sleep. I stutter, trying my best to untangle my tongue and cool myself of the vicious flush sweeping over me.

I swallow, building enough courage to ask, "Can we talk?"

"No," he responds as fast, and I don't feel so hot anymore. Here comes the ice wall of Alex.

"Alex?"

"Go home, Mandy."

I bite my lip.

Don't cry.

This is stupid. I purse my lips together hard before sucking in what air I can to stop myself from crying. "We can't go on like this forever."

My entire body stiffens as he stands tall and strides towards me. He stops inches away from my face, and I feel his warm breath rush over me. I almost close my eyes and moan. And when his hand comes up and tucks my hair behind my ear and off my shoulder, I can't hold back the heavy breath that escapes me.

"You need to go home, Mandy."

One quick brush of his thumb across my lips and he's gone.

THIRTY-TWO

Church bells.

Rain.

The sound of distant sobs.

Bleakness.

A familiar feeling of emptiness.

It was like every other funeral.

But it wasn't.

Lydia wasn't religious, but her mother was, so she wanted a typical Catholic burial.

Four days.

It took four days after I joked with her and tucked her into bed with a hot water bottle for her to succumb to the illness that was eating her from the inside out.

Those four days were filled with laughter echoing around the walls of her home, cuddles and watching movies with her daughter, and saying goodbye to her family.

We thought she was being dramatic. She was happy and had more energy than usual.

Surely, she had a little while longer?

But Lydia knew something we didn't. She knew when she was tired, and she knew when it was her time.

She asked if Ava could stay with me. Alex made her comfortable, said goodnight, and went to sleep in the guest bedroom.

She never woke up.

At the church, I tried to sneak in at the back, but in Alex's arms, Ava's big eyes spotted me as they took their seats in the front pew. Tony waved me forward as I battled with the lump bobbing in my throat. The music Lydia chose and the way the singer was singing punched me right in the gut.

I offered a brief salute and tried to take my seat with Garry, Claire, and Sally. Alex turned with Ava's small hands still resting on his shoulders, and tilted his chin, beckoning me to come to him.

"I'll be back in a sec," I whispered to my friends before scurrying up the aisle to see why I was needed.

I rubbed my hand down Ava's back. "Hey, sweetheart. Are you doing okay?"

She nodded, clutching her bear a little tighter.

Tony gestured to the seats in the pew. "You'll sit with us, Mandy."

I swear my entire face went on fire.

"That's okay," I stuttered, almost stumbling backward. "This is for family. I can take Ava if it's too much for her?"

He squeezed my forearm. "You are family, love." And with that, they took their places in the front row.

My eyes stung with the will to cry, but I wouldn't let myself. Instead, a tight smile curled on my lips. It didn't feel right, though. I couldn't do it to Alex. He didn't need to feel uncomfortable at his sister's funeral.

I ignored the curious glares from strangers, kissed Ava's hand, and whispered, "It's okay. I'm going to…"

Words stopped falling out of my mouth when I felt heat on the small of my back, and his hand pressed gently through the fabric of my blouse. As if reading my thoughts, he said, "Lydia would have wanted you here for Ava." He blinked slowly. And again. "We all want you here."

No more words were necessary. I shook my head and sat down. Alex followed, and with the side of his body against mine, he rested Ava on his knee.

Midway through, she shuffled onto my lap and rested her head against my chest. All the while, she kept a tight grip on Alex's hand. She fell asleep there, even through the singing and the booming voice of the priest. I stayed still, with my face buried in her hair, even as people stood and kneeled. Nothing was going to move me or make me disturb little sleeping beauty.

Selfishly, I was glad she slept through it. She didn't need to remember this part. She said her goodbyes to her mama when it mattered. That was enough.

After the mass, when people gathered outside the church before going to the burial, the rain stopped, and the sun broke through the clouds. I like to think it was Lydia. Though, with her sense of humour, she would have rained down on us all.

But not Ava.

Not her pride and joy.

Ava woke as we were leaving the church and she clung to Alex's black coat like she could keep him planted on the ground. When he swooped her up in his arms and spun her around, she giggled. Everyone laughed, and my heart became a little lighter.

"How are you holding up?" Claire asked as we stood together in our small huddle.

What could I say? I wasn't sick. I wasn't dying. I was here, but my little girl was only feet away, hurting like no child should, and I couldn't take the pain away.

I shrugged. "I'll be fine." It was all I could say. "Thanks for coming today."

Her eyes became a little wider, and her head tilted forward: her signal someone was coming this way. I felt a firm squeeze of my shoulder, and when I spun around, something trapped me in familiar blue eyes. I forgot how tall he was when he stood so close.

Even then, in the middle of a funeral, my heart pounded against my chest.

I needed to get a grip.

He swallowed. Hard. I didn't know if being around me was that difficult or if I made him want to puke. Ava's arms were still wrapped around his neck for dear life, and she was already falling back to sleep.

"Can you take Ava home with you? It's going to rain again, and I don't want her getting sick. It's best if she goes home and gets some rest."

"Of course." Whatever she needed.

I reminded myself to breathe and took a sidestep around him to check her. Flushed cheeks, bear in one hand, the other gripping Alex's jacket, closed lids and even breathing. She was out for the count. Poor thing.

"Here." Garry shuffled forward, reaching out his arms. "I'll take her, Alex."

She slid out of Alex's arms without a peep.

"We'll get her into the car."

Claire gave me a reassuring one-arm hug before walking away with Garry and Sally.

"Tell your family I'm thinking of them." It was pathetic, but it's all I could give them. "You should get going, and I better get to Ava before she wakes again."

A dip of his chin and, "Thank you, Mandy," set my skin on fire, but only with the need to comfort him.

Inside his massive strong chest, there was a heart breaking. No tears, but I could tell all the same. He'd lost his sister; one of the most important people in his life. He became Ava's sole guardian overnight. The latter, I knew he'd be great at, but it's different when you have someone guiding you.

My fingers twitched, and without thinking, or having the time to stop myself, I threw my arms around his neck. When he didn't push me away, I sank into him and fought with the knot in my chest when both his hands went to my back, pressing me closer.

My Alex.

Only he wasn't.

Not anymore.

Though it only lasted the briefest of moments, I hoped it brought him some relief from what must have been agony.

His eyes glanced over my shoulder, toward my car. "I'll come and get her later."

"You know where I am."

Shoulders tensed, and with the tightest of smiles, he turned and walked away, like all the times before.

That was two months ago, and Ava has continued to stay with me a few nights a week. It's heartbreaking to watch her deal with the unbearable loss of her mama. She gets upset, lashes out, becomes frustrated. Then she giggles and acts totally normal. But behind her coffee-coloured eyes, there are moments of such overwhelming pain, and no matter what I do, I can't make her feel better. I hug her, comfort her, play with her. I do whatever she wants, but it's not enough.

Yes, I'm her mother, but I'm not the woman who held her since the day she was born.

I'm still learning.

She doesn't like her hair stroked when she's upset. I don't always know what cuddly toy she prefers to go to bed with because it changes every night, depending on her mood. What I know: I'm determined to find out. I want to know everything about her. I need to prove to her I'm not going anywhere.

"Mommy Mandy." I hear her small voice before I see her standing in the doorway of my bedroom. My room is dark, so I only see her silhouette. Her curls stick out in crazy angles and she clutches at her cuddly elephant—the good mood toy. "Can I sleep with you?" She yawns, already crawling under the blankets.

"Of course." I pull back the duvet and she cuddles into my side.

"I had a nightmare that I fell out of a rollercoaster."

I bite the inside of my cheek to smother the laugh.

She had a party for her birthday, but it was too soon after Lydia died, and her absence was felt more that day than any other. A happy day filled with sadness, and we couldn't escape it. So, she's leaving for a trip tomorrow with Owen, Charlotte, and their two boys. They're going to a theme park. It will be good for her to spend time with kids her own age.

"You will not fall out of the rollercoaster, Ava. And you don't have to go on if you don't want to. You know that." I rub her arm.

"And... And." The tiniest of sobs bubbles in her chest.

I sit up frantically, pulling her onto my lap. "Oh, Ava. What is it, sweetheart?"

"I miss... I miss..."

I'm holding my breath and mentally preparing how I'll comfort her through this.

"I miss Alex. I didn't call him today."

I close my eyes and a single tear leaks from the corner of my eye. I expected her to say she misses her mama. But she's right. We didn't call Alex today, because she was up with nightmares again last night, and she fell asleep early on the couch before I carried her to bed.

Alex is picking her up tomorrow before she goes on her trip, but if speaking to him makes her feel better, so be it.

"I'll text him and see if he's still awake."

"Okay," she trails off into a hiccup.

257

I sit up, switch on the bedside lamp, and Ava rests her head on my chest

Me: Hey. Are you awake? Ava's having a tough time sleeping and wants to say goodnight.

I don't receive a reply. Instead, my phone buzzes with an incoming video message, and like an idiot, I run my fingers through my hair.

He's not calling for me.

Idiot.

Ava's face lights up as bright as the screen. "You know what to do, little lady."

She squirms with excitement and grabs the phone. "Alex," she sings, swaying side to side. "I miss you."

"Hey, princess. I miss you too."

"Can you come over?"

"Ava," I exclaim, more than a little shocked. It's out of my mouth before I have a chance to think about it. I try to collect myself. "It's late. Alex is tired."

"He's awake. Look." She turns the phone so I'm staring straight at him, and it takes all my effort not to slide down under the covers. I'm suddenly all too aware of my strappy top, and how my hair is a messy knot on top of my head.

"Hi," I breathe, hating how hot my face has gotten.

"Hi. I'm coming over."

My mouth goes dry, and my voice gets lost somewhere.

He's doing what?

Alex has succeeded in never being in my presence for longer than five minutes. Other than discussing arrangements for Ava, he doesn't stay around. And mostly, someone else picks her up because he's working. We've spoken words, but we've hardly talked to each other in months. I mean, properly talked to each other. And now he wants to walk into my house and do what, exactly?

But when I look down at thick batting eyelashes and a bottom lip jutting out more than it should, I know I've already lost this battle. It's no wonder Alex caved so easily.

He must see the resigned look on my face because a slow smirk pulls on his lips. "Take it from me. Don't argue with her. She always wins. See you in thirty minutes."

By the time the doorbell rings, Ava is bouncing on my bed with anticipation. So much for sleep. She's wired to the moon.

I don't know why I'm shaking when I open the door, or why my pulse becomes erratic. Maybe it's the sight of him at my door in his white t-shirt and grey sweatpants. God, I hate how this man can pull off everything.

"I had to bring this guy." He opens his palms and points to the furball circling around my legs.

At the sight of his panting tongue, I can't contain my excitement. "Bandit. I missed you." I crouch down and kiss his head, but he's already running away from me in search of Ava's voice.

Her scream is ear piercing. I stand back from the door and look up at Alex. I forgot what it was like to see that amused grin on his face.

"Come in. I think someone is looking forward to seeing you."

When he steps inside, a familiar zing echoes in my chest and his presence fills my home. Head towards his shoulders to look down at me, the same smug smirk plays on his face. "Nice robe."

My entire face is burning.

Is he being playful with me?

Either way, I grab onto it.

"I decided after the last time you showed up, I needed to invest in something with less risk of exposing myself." I giggle nervously, something knotting below my ribcage.

"I liked the other one." And he walks away.

What was that?

Mentally chastising myself and coming out of momentary shock, I close my mouth and follow him.

Ava bounces from the bed and into his arms, and at the sight of him, she becomes lighter. Her face is bright. There's no more sadness in her eyes.

Ava has houses with me and Alex, but he's her home. I see it every time they're together.

"It's past your bedtime, young lady."

"Can we watch a movie to fall asleep to?" she asks quietly. She's doing it again. Fluttering eyelashes, and an exaggerated pout. I swear she has magic powers.

He's apprehensive when he looks at me, seeking permission without asking.

I shrug. "If it helps her sleep," I agree, but inside, everything is

259

twisting. Having him here like this is too much. But this is what I wanted, isn't it? Normal. For us to get on with things.

Then why is the sight of him still making my throat burn?

As if reading my mind, he puts Ava back on the bed, tucks her under the blanket, and kisses her head. He glances at me, his features pained, and I think it's the look he used to give when he wanted to fix me. But maybe I'm grasping at something that isn't there. "I'm leaving once you're asleep. You know that, right?"

She wiggles under the duvet. "I know."

As he grabs the remote, he gets comfortable with Ava tucked under his arm, resting her head on his chest. The sight pulls at everything good, and I catch a single tear before it falls.

It's beautiful.

I back away. "Enjoy the movie, sweetheart. I'll be outside if you need me."

Outside frantically thinking about how the man I can't stop loving is here.

"No, you don't." His demanding voice stops me in my tracks, tingling over every inch of me. "You're not leaving your own bedroom, Mandy."

Jesus, why can't he see it? Why can't he see it's killing me from the inside out?

"Alex, I can't," I choke on the words, clearing my throat quickly.

I can't do this with him.

Not yet.

"Please," I beg in a desperate whisper.

Please see it, Alex.

See that I'm too in love with you to drag my heart through hope.

I don't get to hope with him.

And as if it all hits him at once, his face drops, as do his eyes, along my body, all the way to the floor and back to mine again. Surely, he didn't think I'd forgotten what we had, or it was easy for me to give up. In my head, I know better. My heart is having a harder time.

I don't need him looking at me like this. He needs to look at me like he has for months. Cold. Closed off. No hope.

I need it because if I see something different, it will crush everything.

"Mandy." My name is warm and desperate from his lips.

No.

I shake my head, tears of frustration making my vision blurry.

My silent pleading must work because with a clenched jaw, those familiar blue eyes glaze over with ice and his chest becomes tense. It hurts, but not as much as the alternative.

"I'll be out of here once she's asleep," he clips, turning away to turn on the movie.

My body relaxes with a relieved sigh.

He gets it now.

He continues to get it, even while he leaves without saying a word, and when he comes back the next day to pick up Ava, there's no hint of the warmth or amusement he briefly showed me last night. The same frosty look is in his eyes. He only tolerates looking at me, and when we talk, it's back to revolving around Ava.

His distance with me I can deal with.

Simple.

Clean cut.

It makes it hard to breathe, but I can live with it.

The memories of him are a little harder to accept.

THIRTY-THREE

I'm startled awake, feeling flustered, confused, and wondering where the loud banging is coming from. The harsh sound erupts through my bedroom, and my heart pounds against my chest. As I sit up, my phone buzzes on my bedside locker, and my throat closes when I see Alex's name.

Hesitantly, I answer. "Hello?"

"Open the door."

"Alex?"

Nothing.

"Is Ava okay?" She left for her trip yesterday, but when she called me tonight, she was happy.

"She's fine. Open the goddamn door, Mandy." It's an order now, his voice becoming louder and more frantic.

I get out of bed, my hands trembling, and the only light filtering through my windows is from the moon.

Through the glass, I see him standing there, leaning towards the door, his arms resting on either side.

Slowly, I open it, instinctively taking a step back, afraid of what I will see. He raises his head, his once blue eyes becoming dark, and his hands still gripping the door frame. If he holds it any tighter, he will break it. His knuckles have turned white.

Neither of us says anything. His glare is boring a hole through me, and I don't know why, but my eyes fill with salty moisture.

I swallow, trying to find my voice. "Alex?" It is a bare whisper.

"Fuck it," he says gruffly as he storms through the door, slamming it so hard the picture frames rattle on the wall. He doesn't break his stride, coming towards me like he's on a mission, and my feet slowly take backward steps.

I don't want to, but I need to separate myself from his wildness. But even in his crazed state, my body feels drawn to him. And it doesn't matter how far I back away because in two paces he has caught up with me, putting his hands on either side of my head and crushing his mouth over mine. His mouth is hot and fast, skilled and steady, and not once pulling away. My lips part in a gasp, but he sees his opportunity, and with a flick of his tongue against mine, I moan into him.

I can hardly breathe, but I don't care, and my hands reach for his shirt, pulling him closer because no matter how hard he is kissing me, I need more. I need to fix whatever I have broken in him. Because I have broken him. And I continue to break him every time he must look at me.

Gone is *My Alex*, that once kissed me like I would be the one to break. His tenderness has disappeared and was replaced with a shattered hardness. I have fractured the purest parts of him. The part that loved with heat rather than the coldness he is holding me with.

I need to mend him.

I have to try.

"You didn't break me, Mandy. Nobody has ever broken me," he murmurs against my lips, like he can read my mind. He leaves one hand in my hair as he places the other on my lower back, moving me with him until my back reaches the wall, supporting my unsteady legs. He doesn't stop kissing me. Each movement of his mouth is harsher than the last. He kisses me so much my lips hurt. "You"—his lips move across my jaw and down my neck and I gasp as his hand brushes across my breast—"You shattered me."

My head falls back against the wall as a single tear slides down my cheek.

No, Alex, I shattered both of us.

With shaky hands, I reach up and press my palms firm against his hard chest. I need so much right now, but I need him to stop.

"Alex," I shout, surprised I have words. I push against him, granting

263

us both some space, and my head falls between my shoulders.

I watch as tears drop from my eyes and splash at my feet.

His palms go back to either side of my head, and gently, he moves my face until I'm looking up at him. He's softer now, and behind the coldness flickers a brief moment of warmth. He steps closer, and his body presses against mine. His fingers move the wild strands of hair away from my face. I shut my eyes as I feel his thumb move from my hair to wipe my tears from my cheeks.

"Tell me to leave, Mandy. Tell me you don't want this, and I will walk out the door right now."

It isn't fair, and he knows it. He knows I can't tell him to leave because I need him as much as he needs me right now.

With my eyes still closed, I shake my head, knowing I can't stand to watch him walk away again.

And then his hands are everywhere. All over my body, moving so fast and feverishly, I don't know which parts are burning from his touch. His mouth feels like it is kissing every inch of visible skin.

Before I catch another breath, we are moving again into my bedroom. Our clothes are quickly discarded and thrown aside, removing the only barrier between us.

And when I stand there naked, he steps back, his eyes wildly wandering over my body. He can look. Any shyness I once felt left when he walked through my door. I have nothing to hide anymore. There are no more secrets.

But I know it's already too late. The damage is done.

When he lays me on the bed with his hand behind my head, he does so gently, and with a total contrast to the look in his eyes.

He stills over me, granting himself a moment to look, and the growl that comes from the back of his throat is tainted with regret and mistakes we both wish were never made.

This isn't the way we were. This is pain and confusion. One of us is begging for forgiveness. The other is fighting to accept what he can't.

I see it. He's fighting to forgive me while fighting to let go. He's fighting to love me.

And when at first, he moves slowly, my hips motion with his, and like a switch, there he is.

My Alex.

The warmth, heat, and passion come pouring out of him with every kiss he places on my skin, over my lips, across my breasts, and down my body. He nips, sucks, teases, and brands every inch of me until I buck against him.

But somewhere along the way, I lose him, and he loses in the fight to forgive me.

He laces his fingers in mine, raises my hand above my head, and holds me there while he tucks his other hand under my knee, raising it higher, angling himself deeper and my leg wraps around his bicep. His hips push faster, harder, relentless, and unforgiving until my back arches beneath him.

"Alex," I cry out in a tortured gasp, and I'm unsure how much longer my body can hold on.

He releases his grip on my leg, lifting his head to look down at me, and the moment our eyes lock, I know neither of us can take any more. My body quivers violently as his shoulders tense. His muscles are taut and like stone.

"Fuck. Mandy," he groans against my lips.

And as our bodies tense together, my fingers digging into the muscles of his back, I realize something.

This isn't mending.

This isn't about fixing fractured pieces of each other.

This isn't love.

This is the end.

This is goodbye.

THIRTY-FOUR

I'm staring at my phone on Monday morning when it buzzes in my hand. I take a second to realize it's ringing because my body is numb. Alex left last night without a word, and as I laid on the bed, in the same position he left me in, I could feel his body on mine long after he was gone. When I heard the front door slam shut, something inside me froze over so much it shattered into a thousand tiny pieces, each of them sharp shards slicing through me from the inside out. I'm not sure if I was grasping at tiny rays of hope before last night, but they're not there anymore. I'm reaching out and coming back empty.

Alex is gone. And he made sure I knew it last night.

I can't remember what it felt like to have him inside me when he loved me because last night was so powerful, and very little of what he gave me was love.

I called in sick to work because I hadn't slept, and my eyes are wandering around in search of something that isn't there.

My attention averts back to the vibrating annoyance in my hand. I sigh and push away the uneaten toast on the table.

"Hello."

"Hello, is this Mandy Parker?" a female voice that is far too cheerful chimes.

I roll my eyes because if this is a telemarketer, I could do with the place to vent my anger.

"Yes," I say through clenched teeth.

"I am calling on behalf of solicitor Ryan Hanley. He would like to know if you can make an appointment to come and see him?"

Why the hell is a solicitor calling me?

"For what reason?"

"Mr. Hanley is the family solicitor acting on behalf of Alex Hale."

My mouth goes dry, and I can hear my breathing escape in heavy pants.

"Okay," I trail off because that tells me nothing.

"Can you come in today and Mr. Hanley will go over all the details with you?"

My mind races, but I come up empty. "Sure," I say when all other words fail me. I'm pretty sure this lady won't be able to share much with me anyway.

"How does 2 p.m. sound?"

That's four hours away. I'm going to go out of my mind.

"Have you got anything earlier?" I ask.

"Mr. Hale said he can come in at 11 a.m. or 2 p.m."

Alex is going to be there. Now I think I'm having a panic attack.

"Miss Parker, are you okay?"

I shake my head and take a gulp from my glass of water. My hands are shaking.

"I can be there for eleven."

She makes the appointment and hangs up. Saliva pools in my mouth and bile rises to my throat.

"Shit," I groan, dashing to the bathroom to stick my head in the toilet. When I've stopped heaving, I pat my clammy forehead, switch on the shower, and undress. The hot water does little to relax my tense muscles, and my back is so tight I think it might spasm.

I hate not knowing what's going on, and I thought I would have more time to process last night before running into Alex again. I assumed he would pass the dropping off of Ava over the next few weeks to his father or brother.

I dress quickly into a pinstripe wrap dress, black tights, and boots. My hair dries into its natural waves as I apply my makeup. Not too much because I'm going to sweat it off. I can't calm my pulse, and now I'm pacing in the kitchen. I've never dressed so fast.

I search for the address of the solicitor's office, slip my arms into my coat, and grab my bag before rushing to the car. I'll be early but I can't handle staying in the house any longer.

My phone rings over the Bluetooth speaker of the car, and the caller ID shows me it's Garry.

"Hey," I answer with a shaky breath.

"Everything okay? I noticed there's a substitute in your class today."

"Shit. I don't know Garry. I'll tell you why I'm not in. I promise. I just don't have the time right now. I'm on my way to meet Alex at a solicitor's office."

I say it because he might be my friend, but he's also Alex's, and I hold on to small hope he might know something.

"What?" he blurts.

Well, that theory goes up in smoke. I should know better. Garry would never keep something from me.

"I'm as clueless as you are. I got the call thirty minutes ago."

"Sorry you're going through this. Let me know how it goes," he finishes before we say goodbye.

I don't remember the drive to the swanky offices on Main Street. I don't remember parking the car, and how I got to the fourth floor. But I'm here now, standing in front of a glass panel desk with my clammy palms. I wipe them along my coat and look for somewhere I can get water. Don't these places always have water dispensers?

"Can I help you?" A young woman with jet black hair sleeked back in a bun moves her eyes away from her computer screen.

"Give me a sec." I wave my hand at her when my eyes see the water. I fill a plastic cup and gulp it back. I go back to her, fidgeting with the business cards on the counter. I fix them. "Mandy Parker," I tell her and try my best at a smile, but I look like a need to vomit because I do.

"You're early." I think she is about to tell me to take a seat, but she doesn't. Instead, she says, "They're in there now. I will bring you in."

They are in there.

Sweet baby Jesus, I am going to die.

I slip off my coat, throw it over my arm, and smooth down the imaginary wrinkles on my dress. The young woman smiles at me sympathetically, and I regret not asking her what this is about because she looks like she knows.

She opens the large door and into a spacious office. Everything is mahogany and brown leather, and Alex.

Not any Alex.

It's Alex in a suit.

And my body is having a reaction to him I don't want to have because even when I walk on the plush carpet of the office, he doesn't turn to look at me.

"Mandy." The tall man gets up from his desk to greet me. Dark hair greying at the temples, and a broad smile. "Ryan Hanley. It's nice to meet you." He holds out his hand and I take it.

"Mandy Parker," I stutter. I'm an idiot. He already knows my name. "Nice to meet you too."

"Please, take a seat." He gestures to the brown leather chair in front of his desk.

To my surprise, Alex pulls it out from the desk so I can sit, and I hate when my stomach does a somersault. He sits in the chair next to me.

My gaze darts between the two men. Ryan is tossing through papers on his desk, and Alex is lost in thought somewhere.

Hello, I am dying here.

I can't help it when I open my mouth and blurt, "Can someone tell me what's going on?"

Ryan's head bobs up from his papers, and his brows narrow almost painfully. He looks at Alex and back at me again. He appears confused, like I should already know the answer to my question. He shakes off his expression and plasters a smile on his mouth.

"Apologies Mandy. I'll get started." He finds the sheets he is looking for. "You are here today because Lydia Hale mentioned you in her will."

My mouth gapes open, and I gasp, making my already dry tongue feel like sandpaper.

"Excuse me?"

"I will just read what I have here."

Poor guy looks awkward as hell. I'm obviously not the only one who can feel the tension between me and Alex.

He pushes his glasses onto the bridge of his nose and begins, "I, Lydia Hale, grant full guardianship of my daughter, Ava Hale, to my brother Alex Hale."

No surprise. She told me this.

Ryan looks up at me again and his eyes go all soft. "Mandy, Lydia put a clause in her will." He goes back to the piece of paper. "Should my brother agree and grant permission to the following terms, I wish for Mandy Parker, birth mother of my daughter, to share guardianship with my brother." He arches an eyebrow with a grin when his eyes meet mine again. "Mr. Hale has agreed to these terms."

The world has begun to move in slow motion, and the rest of what Ryan says goes by in a blur. Moisture stings at my eyes, and it's only when I'm finding it difficult to catch my breath, I realize I'm sobbing with my hand pressed against my mouth.

Every emotion I've felt for over seven years comes pouring out of me and fills the entire office. The emptiness I'm harbouring, the regrets that have nested themselves in my brain, and the longing that has occupied my heart, collide together and explode out of my body with every sob and shudder of my shoulders. But most of all, waves of relief and joy wash over me in their place.

"Miss Parker." Ryan pulls my attention back to him and I wipe at my wet face. "There are some legal documents I will need you to sign. Mr. Hale has already signed what he needs to."

I nod because if he said I had to walk through fire at this second, I would do it.

"Ryan, can you give us a minute?" It's the first time I've heard Alex speak.

"Of course." Ryan gathers his papers, filing them away in his large folder, and leaves the office.

When we're alone, Alex reaches over for a box of tissues and offers them to me. I pull at the paper and wipe the mascara-soaked tears from my cheeks.

"Thank you," I whisper through a broken voice.

He leans back, throwing his ankle across his other thigh. He looks relaxed, but his posture tells me a different story, and when he runs a finger roughly across his chin, I know he's trying to keep it together long enough so he doesn't explode. And I can't tell which emotion will win in his battle. His walls are up, and I'm shut out by impenetrable barriers.

"Do you have to go back to work?" he asks gruffly.

I shake my head. I'm too embarrassed to admit I took the day off because of last night.

"We need to talk through some things." I can feel his eyes burning through the side of my face. "About Ava," he quickly corrects because God forbid, I would grasp on to one shred of hope for us. "Can you come to my house after we leave?"

I meet his gaze now because I'm shocked he has asked. I'm petrified of walking through the doors of his beach house and what emotions it will conjure up. But he's right. We need to go through arrangements for Ava.

This is what we are now. We are scheduled meetings, drop-offs, and collections.

It's agonizing. But I can't dwell on anything else when I've been given the most amazing gift. Not even when he's two feet away and making the hair on the back of my neck stand with anticipation.

Exactly what I'm anticipating, I don't know.

"I can meet you there," I agree, sitting up so straight I think my back might crack.

He stands, buttoning his suit jacket at his waist like he has finished a business deal.

I'm business now.

Something to negotiate with.

I'm pretty sure I'm disoriented from shock, and I'm sure I imagine it when he wipes a tear away from my cheek with his thumb before he leaves.

I always had an active imagination when grasping at hope.

THIRTY-FIVE

"Alex?"

His front door is open, so I knock and call out, not wanting to waltz in. I'm no longer a familiar guest in his home and I haven't been for some time. Bandit greets me, wagging his tail until I pet him.

"I'm in the kitchen."

My chest tightens as I step inside.

His smell. His presence. Everything here is him.

Except it isn't just him anymore, and I can see how Ava has already made her stamp on the place. They've packed the smaller room to my left with toys, and a pink hairbrush and hair clips are on the table in the hallway. I tried to show him once how to do her hair. He's getting better at it.

I lean against the kitchen door frame and cross my arms over my chest as if it can protect me somehow. I know we need to have this conversation, but I'm not prepared for what he will say.

The large window gives me a view of the ocean and washes over my nerves like a warm blanket. I inhale a breath to calm my erratic pulse.

When he turns around, he doesn't raise his eyes to look at me. I'm used to it.

He feels as tense as I do. His back is rigid against his white shirt. He has rid himself of the tie and rolled the sleeves up to his elbows. And dammit, if it doesn't make heat go all the way to my toes. He places the coffee cups on the table and pulls out a chair for me before sitting on the other side of the table.

"Sit down, Mandy." He still hasn't looked at me, but I sit anyway.

I take a minute to look around, trying to focus my eyes on something other than him. But memories I don't want come flooding back. All the times I pottered around barefoot in this kitchen with nothing but his t-shirt. Or the time we couldn't make it to the bedroom, so he sat me on the counter and took me there. When he made me dinner and set this exact table with candles and filled the room with low music. When I fell asleep on the sofa after we stayed up most of the night talking, and I woke in his arms as he carried me to bed. This house isn't just Alex and Ava. I'm here too. Or at least I was. Those memories evaporate in a cloud of smoke the moment I remember them.

I don't want to look at him because I'm afraid of what I'll see when he looks back. I don't want to see what was in his eyes when he came to my house last night. It killed me once. I don't think I can do it again.

But when I finally find the courage to look his way, he is staring at me. And although I can see the coldness that has become part of how he looks at me now, something else flickers across his face. Something raw and tormented. He rubs his hand roughly over the stubble across his jaw, his shoulders slouching as he lets out a long breath.

I want to reach out and ease the tension across his chest. I want to soothe him. But I think better of it. That part of him said what he needed to when he took me to bed last night.

"I think it's best if we give Ava some structure," he starts. "Half of the week with me, and half with you. But I also don't want to force her into anything she isn't ready for. In the beginning, until she gets used to the arrangement, we let her stay with you like she always does, for a night or two, and if she wants to stay longer, she can. I can come and get her from your house in the mornings for school because I know you need to get to work too."

I can't argue with that. It's whatever Ava is comfortable with. "Of course. That sounds good," I say before taking a sip of coffee.

That was easier than I expected.

I still can't believe I'm sitting here discussing living arrangements for my daughter. I have yet to process I have her back in my life in this way.

I tuck my hair behind my ears and muster up the nerve to ask, "Why didn't you tell me about Lydia's will?" I wrap my hands around the coffee cup, trying my best to get heat from somewhere because he is showing only ice.

"I wasn't sure if I wanted to agree to it," he answers honestly, and as much as it hurts, I'm grateful for it. "But it's what's best for Ava, and she's the only one who matters."

I nod my head in agreement.

"Thank you," I whisper. It isn't enough, but words will never describe how grateful I am.

"I'm not doing it for you."

"I know."

His hand balls in a fist before releasing again and running his fingers through his hair.

"What happened last night," he begins, shaking his head. My entire body clams up. "It shouldn't have. It won't happen again."

I close my eyes, fighting the tears that are coming. I know it can never happen again. I don't want it like that. But here he is, finishing the parts last night didn't, and closing his heart to me completely.

"I know," I say again, allowing myself a breath.

"Jesus Christ, Mandy," he yells through clenched teeth, pushing his chair back and going to the counter. He leans against it, his head falling between his shoulders. "I need more. I need you to say something else other than 'I know'."

"But I don't know what to say to you, Alex. I know this is finished. I know it can't happen again. I know we need to have this conversation to put a close to things because we can't end it with whatever that fucked up goodbye was last night."

He flinches, but I need to say it. We both need to accept we will be part of each other's lives forever, just not in the way we both expected a year ago.

"I know." Now he is the one to say it, and the irony isn't lost on me. He stands straight, his eyes becoming softer with each steady breath. "Why didn't you just say something, Mandy?"

"Does it matter? Would it have mattered then? Eventually, we were going to realize something. And what then? Would we not be here anyway, if I told you sooner? But Ava needs us. Both of us. She needs simple. Not us fighting with feelings and bitterness because of what could have been. We need to do it for her because God knows the little girl has suffered enough."

His eyes widen. "Don't you know you have something to do with that? Because my sister stepped in and became the mother you never were."

I know he wants to hurt me. He wants me to feel what he is feeling. But he doesn't realize, I've already hurt more than he will ever know. I have over seven years of hurt. But his words seem to cut somewhere I wasn't hurt before, and that part of me just started bleeding out.

I want to scream at him. I want to hit him. I want to roll up in a ball and hide. I want to do all of that. But most of all, I want to go back in time and stop him from saying what he said.

"Alex, every day since the morning I allowed someone to take her from my arms, I've known. She was mine until she wasn't anymore. I will never replace Lydia in Ava's life. She was her mother." I put my cup down and swallow to steady my voice. "I knew coming back into her life would reopen wounds for everyone. As much as I would have given my life to set eyes on her. Just once. I never expected to see her again." I throw my arms out wide. "But here I am. Whatever I did to have her back, I don't know, but I'm beyond grateful. I know your sister was her mother, but so am I. So, whatever you want to throw at me to hurt me, be my guest. But I'm not leaving her again. And I don't need you reminding me of what I've caused because I've lived with it every day." Standing, I wipe away the moisture that has fallen onto my cheeks.

I can't hold back any longer. He may be angry, but I am too. I'm angry at him for walking away and not asking these questions before.

I'm angry because he gave up.

"So, fuck you, Alex. Fuck you and the way you look at me now."

His head jolts up, shocked I'm the one getting angry with him.

"I didn't give her up out of lack of love. I gave her up because I loved her with every part of me. Have I regretted it every day since? You know I have. Giving her up broke something in me not even you could put back together. She's my everything, Alex. She always has been."

He says nothing. He stares through with a blazing power in his eyes.

I can't stand to see him look at me like this anymore. I need to walk away from him and get the hell out of here.

I turn away, but something stops me before I can leave the kitchen. Maybe I want him to punish me more, or maybe I can't live with not knowing the answers.

"Will you ever forgive me, Alex? Will there be a day when I look at you and don't see hate?"

His face drops, his mouth setting into a hard line. Something ruptures in him then, because I jump as his palm comes down hard on the countertop.

"Hate you? You think I hate you?" he snaps. His eyes roam around, and he inhales so harshly, his nostrils flare with irritation. "I hate that I'm still in love with you. I hate that I can think of nobody else. What I really hate Mandy, is I must spend a life looking at you when I can't touch you. Because you have no idea how much I want to. But I can't. You don't deserve what happened last night. I won't do that to you again."

I wish I hadn't asked. I want him to hate me. Somehow, it's easier than knowing he still loves me.

"As for forgiving you. I forgave you a long time ago. You may not realize this, but you didn't just come into my life that day in the storm. You've been in my life for seven years. I looked at Ava every day and thanked the amazing woman who was selfless enough to give her up. But then you came into my life like a fucking hurricane, and you changed everything I thought I already knew."

Rounding the counter, he stalks towards me. He towers over me, but I put my hand out, placing it on his chest to stop him. If he comes any closer, I won't be able to resist touching him more, and I need to resist him.

With eyes rimmed red, his shoulders vibrate with each hard breath.

But he doesn't care what I want or what I'm fighting against because regardless of my efforts, he reaches his hands up to cup either side of my face. And with his touch, my sobs erupt. Uncontrollable and raw. Because I know, as long as I live, he will be the only one to touch me and cause such an effect.

"I'm sorry for the way I've treated you. But I don't know how to act with you anymore. I can't kiss you when I want. I can't pick you up and bring you to bed like I want. I can't call you mine. And you were *mine*, Mandy."

I'm still yours, Alex. I always will be.

Lowering his head, he leans his forehead against mine, and his thumb strokes over my lips. We're standing here in silence, and we're both shattering each other with every shared breath.

276

His lips are right there, and if I move slightly, I can press mine against them.

He strokes the skin under my eyes, catching the tears as they fall. "I'm angry because I can't have you. But if we fuck up again, it's not just our hearts we'll break."

And there it is.

He doesn't have to say another word because, at that moment, I understand everything. It isn't about us anymore, and he's right.

"Alex," I cry, leaning into the warmth of his hand.

"You need to leave, Mandy, because I want to do a lot more than kiss you, and I've already promised I wouldn't do that again. But I can't let you go, so you need to be the one to leave."

This isn't goodbye. I'll see him again. But this is the end of what we were to each other.

I take a shaky breath before blowing it out again.

This isn't about us, I remind myself.

This is for Ava and everything else I've already failed her in.

I look up under eyes filled with endless tears, knowing once I do this, my heart will never mend the same. I place my lips gently against his cheek as a single tear falls from the corner of his eye.

"Goodbye, Alex."

THIRTY-SIX

When I pull up outside my childhood home, I take a deep breath to calm my spiralling nerves. This should have been the first home Ava came to when she was born. It should have been where she spent the first years of her life. But she's here now, and that's all that matters. I can't change the past. I know that.

It's been three months since we agreed to joint custody, and Ava was the first to bring up meeting my family.

Our family.

As much as I wanted to show my daughter to the world, I didn't want to pressure her. Ava suffered enough loss and pain in her young life without crowding her with strangers. But I've come to learn: the little girl sitting in the back seat is the strongest person I've ever met. We're getting to know each other still, but the comfortable relationship of a mother and daughter is settling, natural, instinctually always present, and every day our bond molds deeper and deeper.

I discussed it with Alex when I dropped her off last week. I wanted to make sure he was comfortable with the arrangement of Ava coming to stay with me in my family's home for a few days. He agreed, as he always does when it's something Ava wants.

We're civil with each other, understanding we both want what is best for Ava, and she needs it. She deserves it.

She deserves so much more, but that is all we can give her.

I still ache every time I drive away and leave them both. My house seems too cold and lonely without the giggling of my little girl to fill the space or the warmth Alex naturally brings every time he steps inside to collect her. My heart bleeds when he looks at me and can't see anything else but the secrets I failed to tell him. I love him with everything. I always will. He has become embedded in me. Nothing will remove him. But I can't expect him to love me back in the same way. Not now. We've said too much, either with our words and more so with our actions.

I called ahead, warning my mother for the umpteenth time not to overdo it. Ava will be overwhelmed enough without having a welcoming party and a house full of people. My mother agreed to everything, promising it would just be my parents and Matt.

I'm sure they're feeling as nervous as I am. Finally, after years of wishing, but knowing, they would never set eyes on her again.

"And try not to cry too much, Mom," I warned, but she couldn't promise that.

"I will leave the door unlocked. We'll wait in the back garden so we're not crowding her." My mother's voice was bubbling with excitement, and I appreciated the amount of thought she was putting into this meeting.

"My tummy feels funny." Ava reaches for my hand as we get out of the car. "But I think it's because I'm excited," she says, smiling.

"My tummy feels funny too." I hug her closer, leaning down to kiss the top of her head. "This way." I guide her through the front door and down the hallway. I hear hushed chatter in the garden through the open back doors.

Ava squeezes my hand a little tighter.

"We're here," I call out, not wanting to surprise them too much.

My mother squeals and my heart begins pounding viciously. If I'm like this, I can't imagine how Ava is feeling.

As we round the door, hesitantly stepping out into the garden, they've lined up, and I'm sure no one is breathing. My mother's hand shoots over her mouth as Ava steps out from behind me.

But no tears.

Not yet anyway.

She's fighting hard with herself.

Half of Ava's body is hiding behind me, as if using me as her shield.

I will always be her shield.

"Guys," I say, tears coming to me now. I never thought I would see this day. "This is Ava."

Ava's smile widens as she steps out in front of me, her body swaying from side to side. I admire her confidence and promise I'll always do my best to protect it.

Afraid to speak, together they take a step closer.

"Ava, this is my mom and dad. And this is my brother Matt."

"Hi." Her voice pipes up and she flashes them that breathtaking smile of hers.

"Hey Ava," they all say in unison.

My mother kneels, allowing some space between them.

"Hey, precious girl." Her eyes well up, but I don't mind. She can feel this. My mother can embrace this moment, and I don't blame her if she blubbers until she can't speak. But she doesn't. Somehow, she controls her tears before they fall. Instead, it's my father's eyes that have become red, and he coughs through a sob.

"Hey, Grandma."

My mother's gasp tears my heart to shreds. Neither of us expected that. This little girl embraces all the love given to her.

"Oh yes, I'm your grandma, sweetheart."

"I've never had a grandma before. And Grandad." Ava's eyes look up at my father. She's controlling this situation completely, and I'm in complete awe of her. She doesn't need my help. I wish Alex was here to see it. "You have grey hair like my other grandad. I like it." She giggles, her cheeks blushing a soft pink.

My father's tears are endless, slipping down his face.

"Thank you, little lady." His voice sounds tight, and he places his hand over his mouth.

Then my eyes move to Matt. And I wish I could reach out and hug him because he looks petrified. Proud but petrified.

So, I do. I walk to his side, slipping under his arm to hug him. He smiles down at me, and his shoulders visibly relax.

"She's amazing," he breathes.

"I know. And you'll have this with your baby soon." Any day, Suzie is due to give birth.

"You're Mommy's brother," Ava states, very matter of fact. "That means you're my uncle, right?"

He leaves my side and kneels next to our mother.

"That's right. I'm Uncle Matt, and I'm the one that's going to get you in trouble." He winks, beaming at her.

Ava laughs loudly, and suddenly, I see how much her mischievous eyes resemble Matt's.

"I got you something," he says. "Would you like to see it?"

"Yes, please," she squeals, and when Matt guides her to the table at the bottom of the garden, she reaches up and takes his hand. His smile disappears and his eyes almost pop out of his head. When he looks back at me, I know exactly what he's feeling. I had it too the first time Ava reached for my hand.

He covers the top of her hand with his other one, both his palms wrapped around her fingers in a silent appreciation for such a simple gesture. And I know from the look in his eyes, Ava has already wrapped him around one of those little fingers, and that is where she will always keep him.

My parents come to my side, putting their arms around my waist as we watch Matt and Ava walking hand in hand. There's sorrow that comes with watching the scene unfold. This shouldn't be the first time they are doing this. But the joy overpowers any sadness because no matter what my regrets are, they are doing it now, and that is hope coming to fruition.

Matt flips a switch on a small white machine and bubbles fly out, floating around Ava and covering the air around us.

Her eyes become bigger, and a giggling scream escapes her.

"Mom," she gasps, breathless. "Uncle Matt got me a bubble machine."

We laugh at her excitement.

She makes everyone happy.

Ava makes everyone whole again.

And in the space of a minute, Ava becomes the centre of their entire universe, as she is mine. My heart feels so swollen, I think it might burst.

Later, when Matt hesitates about Ava painting his nails, she looks up at him with those enormous eyes of hers and says, "But Uncle Alex always lets me paint his nails." Not to be outdone by Alex, he happily agrees. After all, he's competing for the title of *World's Best Uncle* here. And although I won't ruin his hopes by saying Alex would win every time, by also being a father to Ava, I happily watch anyway as they bond over pink nail polish.

When it's time for Ava to go to bed, she goes to each of them, hugging them tightly, her little arms spreading so much love and mending broken hearts. They all embrace her a little longer, holding onto the feeling of having her back in their lives.

I tuck her into bed, handing her the grey bunny to cuddle, and lay down beside her.

"You must be tired. You had a big day today." I brush her hair away from her face.

"It was so much fun." She smiles, her lips breaking into a yawn at the same time.

"Can I meet my dad's family soon too?"

My heart twists. How I would have loved for Nick to set eyes on her. God, he would have adored her.

"If you'd like to. I can arrange it for the next time we visit. I'm sure they would love to meet you."

Ava nods. "I'd like to," she simply answers.

I hate it will take so long for them to meet her, but all of this had to be on Ava's terms. There are so many situations that happened in her life she didn't have a voice in. I'm determined to give her control of this one.

"I have a big family now." Her eyes roam around the room as her nose scrunches up. Somewhere in her mind, she's processing something. "I like it." She nods again, coming to a decision.

And those words alone make me feel okay about all of this. Everything is where it is meant to be. My world has fallen back on its axis.

Ava cuddles into me, laying her head on my chest.

"Goodnight, sweetheart," I whisper, kissing the top of her head.

"Goodnight, Mom."

I don't intend to, but the comfort of sleep comes to me too, with my little girl still wrapped in my arms.

***

"Hey, you."

I draw my eyes to him, standing over me with a wide smile and soft eyes. "Where have you been?"

"Around." He shrugs.

282

"Are you not going to sit with me?"

His eyes narrow as his chest fills with a breath. "I'm afraid we don't have much time today, love. Walk with me?" He reaches out his hand to help me stand up from the sand.

As we walk with a space between us, I slip my hands into my pockets. He does the same while turning to look at me.

"At least you don't sit like you used to."

What was he talking about?

"You used to sit in a ball, holding yourself together. You're at ease now," he explains, because he knows me so well, he answers before I can ask. He looks happy and content. Peaceful. "I'm guessing it has something to do with our daughter?"

My grin spreads across my face, and I'm embraced by a sense of pride.

"She fills in the hole you had in your heart."

I nod, allowing a tear to creep down my cheek. "She is my heart, Nick."

"I know."

As we stroll along the edge of the water, watching the sunrise over the ocean, nothing but the sound of waves between us, I begin to feel distant.

"You're leaving now?" I ask, my voice wobbly, and I swallow back the lump threatening to choke me.

"My job here is done. You don't need me anymore. Our little girl came back to you."

I know it's time. I've wanted to say goodbye to him for a while, but I could never muster the courage. Now I understand. I needed him. I held onto him until there were no other reasons to hold on.

We stop walking, turning to face each other, his black hair blowing into his face. It's the same face that resembled our daughter so much. He leans forward, gracing my cheek with a simple kiss.

"Give her that from me."

"And many more," I agree.

Before he leaves, he spins back on his heels. "Don't you want to know what I forgot to tell you?"

I don't know why, but his question brings me peace.

I shake my head firmly, knowing what should have always been my answer.

"No," I say, shrugging my shoulders. "It doesn't matter anymore.

All the things we never said are insignificant. We said what was most important."

"There's my girl." His smile is wide, and he dips his chin, something about the shake of his head becoming final. "Goodbye, love."

I close my eyes, the sound of the ocean disappearing around me. And I let go.

***

The next morning, I wake to an empty bed. My eyes scan the room but no sign of Ava, just tousled sheets by my side. As I leave my room and make my way downstairs, the sound of a familiar giggle eases the tension stiffening my back.

My dad is leaning against the back door, drinking in the scene playing out in the garden.

"Morning." I yawn, looking over his shoulder to see Ava helping my mother plant some flowers.

"Hello, sweetheart." He kisses the top of my head.

"She didn't wake me."

He smiles down at me, eager to tell me something. "I was up early this morning and when I heard movement in your room, I thought I would see you both. But her little sleepy head came wondering in here with a 'Morning Grandad'. Like she's been doing it every morning for seven years." His face swells with pride. "And just like that, she made herself at home. I made her some breakfast, and we sat together and had a chat. I was getting to know my granddaughter." The look in his eyes makes tears dust in mine. "I'll tell you, Mandy," he says, excited. "She's awful bright." It's been less than twenty-four hours and this man already thinks Ava is his sun, moon, and stars. "Your mother thought she'd show her how to plant some flowers. But the big child…" He dips his head towards Matt. "He's been trying to get her attention for ages."

That makes me laugh. He's a child at heart, too.

"She's still in her pajamas."

"Nobody can see her in the garden. She's fine. She's happy."

He's right, as he mostly always is.

She is happy.

284

I feel a sudden lump form in my throat, so I hug my father from the side, resting my ear against his chest.

"You're doing amazing, sweetheart." He kisses the top of my head.

"Thank you. She misses her mama every day, but I think she's adjusting."

"She will always miss her mama. But can you imagine how much harder her life would be if she had none."

I let out a small laugh.

"You always make sense, Dad."

"That's what I'm here for. At least you listen to me." He throws his eyes towards Matt again. He rubs his hand up and down my arm, squeezing supportively. "How are things going with Alex? Co-parenting, I mean," he drawls, knowing the subject of Alex is still very raw.

I shrug, taking a long breath. "He's amazing with Ava. We get on with it, for Ava's sake. She leads us and calls the shots. It's working. She comes with me for half the week and back to Alex for the other half."

"And how are you?"

I know he isn't asking how I am. Not really. He's asking how I am after Alex.

"I miss him every day."

He holds me closer, in a way only a father can with his daughter. The same way I've seen Alex hold Ava.

"Life didn't throw that many coincidences at you both and mean for nothing to come of it. Sometimes it's simply fate. And a man doesn't look at a woman the way Alex looked at you and not feel anything. Give it time. Time is the greatest healer."

Despite knowing the truth, I offer him a small smile, but I say nothing.

I don't need to.

Words won't explain how I feel, and no amount of time will heal what is broken. Only one person can do that.

THIRTY-SEVEN

"Ava? Sweetie? It's time to wake up. We're here." I stretch my arm to the back seat, gently shaking her leg.

Her cheeks flush with the heat of sleep, and she yawns before her eyes flutter open. Her small body stretches out on the seat, becoming rigid for a moment, and her lips curve up into a sweet smile. She's had a crazy two days, becoming acquainted with a whole new family and it was a two-hour drive back, so I understand why she is exhausted.

Her hair clip clings to a few strands of her black hair, swinging in front of her face as she gets her bearings.

"His car isn't here," Ava says, looking around.

I hadn't noticed, but she's right, and the house looks dark. It isn't like Alex to be late, especially for Ava. I check my phone. I've missed a text.

Alex: Sorry. Running a few minutes late. Be there soon.

I don't mind. I welcome the opportunity for more time with the little girl in the back seat.

I reply, telling him we are at the house, but there isn't any rush.

"Uncle Alex is on his way. Want to take a walk on the beach while we wait?"

Her petite face lights up, her eyes becoming wide, and she nods her head ecstatically with approval.

When I've helped her out of the car, I fix her hair clip, removing the strands of hair back from her face. Her face is far too pretty to be hidden behind so much hair.

Ava reaches up to take my hand, totally oblivious it makes my heart inflate every time she does it.

It's summer, but a chill lingers in the air, and the grey sky threatens a storm.

Just a few minutes on the beach before the rain comes.

"Can we see everyone again soon?" Ava asks, looking up for answers.

"Of course we can." I swing both of our hands as we step onto the sand. "Somehow, I think they may come to see you before we have a chance to see them." I know my family won't be able to stay away.

"I don't want you to go." Ava lowers her head, saying it mostly to herself.

Before we approach the water, I kneel, taking Ava's face in my hands. Her eyes seem too young for so much longing.

"You will see me in a few days. And I'll always be here for you. When I'm not with you, you can call me."

She seems content with the answer.

In my best attempts to lighten the mood, I dip my fingers in the water that's coming up to meet our feet and splash the drops on her arm. She squeals and jumps back, her shock only lasting a moment before she breaks into a heart-warming laugh. A laugh that comes from deep within her belly, and her shoulders shake.

I love her laugh.

I never want her to stop.

So, I splash her again.

For a second, Ava doesn't move, and then she swings her foot under the water and kicks it towards me, soaking my hair and sweater.

The cold water causes my breath to catch in my throat, but Ava laughs so hard, her knees are buckling.

"Hey," I shriek, standing up, breaking into a giggle of my own.

I sweep her up in my arms, swinging her around in circles before we both fall down. Now we're both destroyed in sand, wet, and happy.

When I look at her, I don't see myself, or Nick, or any trace of her biology. All I see at this moment is Alex. This happy, charismatic, laughing little girl; Alex taught her that. He taught her playfulness. Her nature—good, pure, and thoughtful—is all Alex. And my chest clamps up.

"You're the best." Ava wraps her arms around my neck, squeezing me tight.

"No, you're the best." I kiss her warm cheek.

"Uncle Alex," she shouts, kissing me quickly before rushing from my arms.

I stand, shaking off the sand from my jeans, and when I look up, there he is. Standing at the top of the beach, hands in his pockets, watching the scene unfold. I'm not sure how long he's been standing there, but I can tell, even from this distance, he's smiling.

I reach him after Ava. He scoops her up with ease, and she somehow looks smaller in his arms.

"I came home, and I was wondering who those two beautiful girls on the beach were." He rustles Ava's hair with his palm.

He glances towards me briefly, a smile curling at the corner of his mouth.

"It's going to rain, kid. You should say goodbye to your mom and get inside." He sets her back on her feet. "I will get your things from the car."

"I'll pick you up after school on Wednesday, okay?" I tell her as I cuddle her close and try to hold on to the feeling of having my baby in my arms. I always feel empty when she leaves. "I love you."

"I love you too," Ava says before skipping inside the house.

And now we're alone, and there suddenly isn't enough air on this beach. I don't know if the sound I'm hearing is from the crashing of the waves or my heart beating madly.

"I could watch you two together forever." He dips his chin, putting a hand back in his pocket while running the other through his hair.

"She's a blessing." Unexpectedly, my eyes well up, and it may have something to do with how much I love my daughter or how close Alex is standing.

With that, a heavy raindrop falls on my cheek. I crane my neck to look up at the angry sky and know it's going to pour soon.

When I lower my head again, he's staring at me. I know that look. Aching, wanting, and painful.

Hesitantly, he stretches out his hand and wipes away the raindrop from my cheek with his thumb. I don't breathe as he strokes me because I've forgotten how to, and his finger gently presses against the

288

corner of my lips.

"We should get the stuff from the car before you get soaked." He drops his hand and gestures for me to go with him.

As we walk, his fingers sweep against mine in a fleeting brush of his knuckles, and my skin feels so hot, he could have been branding the very spot he is touching. He's as nervous as I am. I can tell from how his chest is rising and falling, his shoulders rounding forward, and breathing heavy.

As we get to the car, the heavens open. No warning with a brief shower, just an instant heavy downpour and a rumble of thunder in the distance.

I fumble to open the trunk with wet hands. I give him Ava's backpack, and when I do, I spot the large black umbrella hiding in the back, blending in with the carpet of the trunk. I grab it and take a step back to open it. When I lift it over us both, my body becomes acutely aware of how close he is. His warmth is a total contrast to the cold drops falling around me.

"Take this," I offer, holding out my hand to give him the umbrella. "It's yours, anyway."

His eyelids open wide, and I can see the cogs turning in his head. He realizes the significance.

It's *his* umbrella.

The same one he covered me with the first day we met. It's been in my trunk for over a year, hiding, as if it would only show itself at the right moment.

"Go. Get inside before it gets worse." I avert my gaze to my shoes, hoping he will walk away for both of our sakes, but not wanting him to.

I can't bear having him so close without being able to reach up and touch him or press my lips to his.

His eyes close briefly, and then he doesn't say a word before he turns and walks away. I want to grab his arm and tell him not to go. I want to beg him to forgive me. I want him to make everything right, the way it used to be.

I don't want to watch him walk away again, so I busy myself with closing the trunk, not caring that the rain is saturating through my clothes.

"I can't." My heart skips a beat when I hear him, his voice loud and firm.

He turns back to look at me, his frantic breathing in sync with mine because we even share our crazy.

"I can't let you drive away again because damn it, I will never stop loving you."

He throws the backpack and umbrella to the ground and in three large strides, my face is in his hands and his lips crush against mine. His hunger makes my legs shake and my arms collapse to my side.

There isn't any need to say what we are feeling. This kiss says it all.

He misses me, too.

He wants me.

He needs me.

He loves me as much as I love him.

His hands grip my hips, pulling me closer when his kiss becomes softer. My hands are in his hair, as if making up for every touch we've missed out on.

When he pulls away, I keep my eyes closed because if he regrets that kiss, I don't want to see it. I don't want to look into his eyes and see how that kiss was a mistake. Because to me, it wasn't a mistake.

It was everything.

I can't regret it because if only for a minute, I was whole again.

"Mandy," he whispers and nuzzles his head in the crook of my neck.

I'm not sure if the moisture on my face is from tears or the raindrops.

Probably both.

"Look at me, Mandy," he pleads.

Time to face the truth.

But when I open my eyes, his face doesn't say regret. It doesn't say the kiss was a mistake.

All I see is *My Alex*. Some wounds and bruises are buried behind his eyes, but he's mine.

All tension leaves my shoulders with a long exhale, and it's like with that breath I let go of all the months of pain and longing. None of it matters now as we stand here, staring at each other, breathing frantically, and absolutely soaked through.

None of it matters.

He matters.

Ava matters.

We matter together.

"Come inside." It isn't a question.

I can't find the words yet, so I nod and try to smile through my endless sobs.

"You kissed my mom." Ava appears on the porch, squealing as her legs stomp with excitement. And without a care in the world, she runs down the steps and straight into Alex's arms. She pushes her wet hair back from her face. Her mouth turns down and she shivers. "It was gross."

When I look at Alex, we both throw our heads back with laughter. She doesn't mince her words.

"Get used to it, kid. That's what people do when they're in love." His lips edge up in an amused smirk and when he winks at me like he used to, I melt all the way to my feet.

There he is.

He kisses Ava's forehead and then the top of my head before moving aside.

"You take the lead, remember?"

No, it's not the rain. I'm definitely crying.

I reach up, placing my palm on his chest while my other hand intertwines with his.

"This time," I say, "We do it together."

EPILOGUE

One year later.

I'm somewhere between consciousness and living out the remnants of whatever dream I was having. It's that place where everything is peaceful. Where there is no past or future, only a comfortable present.

No knowledge of regrets.

No guilt.

No longing.

No burn in my chest.

Everything is right in the world.

I search around in my head for the nightmares, but there aren't any.

No nightmares.

Not in over a year.

The light around me filters through my struggling lids, and wetness and soft pressure invade the skin of my face.

I blink, my eyes fluttering open to black curls, warm chocolate eyes, and pouting pink lips smothering me with kisses.

Now the burning in my chest isn't from pain. It's from love, and all is still right in the world.

"Morning, baby girl." I yawn, kissing her head. I pull back the covers and tap the sheets next to me. She jumps in, giggling as she stretches her arms out towards me. In her hands is pink paper folded into a card.

It's the most beautiful card I've ever seen.

"Happy birthday, Mommy," she chimes with pride.

"You made this?" I smile, taking the card from her hand. The picture is full of rainbows, sparkles, glitter, and everything Ava. "Thank you, sweetheart. It's the best card ever."

She continues to name the people she's drawn. "This is me, and you, and Uncle Alex. And this," she points to two suns she's coloured in either corner, smiley faces in each, "this is Mama, and this is Nick."

My heart twists and I hug her close. Her smile doesn't falter, though, and it's exactly as she always is. The loss in her life doesn't get her down. She has her moments, of course, but she has an emotional maturity far beyond her years, and I can't help but wish she didn't have to. I tell her stories about Nick all the time, and she talks about her mama. She's not afraid. I'm sure she feels the loss, but it doesn't appear like she fears the loss of love, because Alex and I make up for it every day.

"And who is this?" I point to her drawing of a person laying down holding balloons, and he appears to be wrapped up in bandages. I already know who it is. She's eight and has an unhealthy obsession with everything pink, Monster Trucks, my makeup bag, and Tutankhamun. She's as random as she is adorable.

"It's a mummy," she answers like it is the most natural thing in the world to have on a birthday card. But it's hers and I love it even more for that reason. Who knows, maybe Tutankhamun and I share a birthday.

My phone vibrates on the bedside locker, forcing me tear my eyes away from the card.

"It's Nana," I inform Ava, and she bounces with excitement. "Hey, Kate," I answer, smiling. She calls every year.

"Happy birthday, love. From all of us." I know she always calls because Nick can't.

"Thank you. Hold on. I'll put you on speaker. Ava's here."

Her throaty laugh is pure joy. Since meeting Nick's family, Ava did what she naturally does. She burrowed her way through their hearts. And she's all they have left of their son. She's cherished. As she should be.

"That's why I'm calling. I wanted to ask you if it's okay for her to spend the weekend with us next week?"

I don't get the chance to answer before Ava's body climbs over mine to get closer to the phone.

"Nana, I want to," she almost screams. "I love going to yours and Grandpa's house."

I half laugh, half grimace. "She can hear you just fine Ava. And so can the rest of the town."

She sneers at me with an attitude no eight-year-old should have.

"Excellent. We can have a girl's day. We can get our nails done."

Ava screeches. "I want yellow this time."

"Whatever you want."

I don't think Ava has ever heard the word 'No' from any of her grandparents.

After Ava finishes her weekly catch-up with Kate, a familiar prickle crawls up my spine.

"Got room in there for me?" Alex appears at the door, holding a tray and a smirk I feel all the way to my fingertips. "I brought breakfast."

"Well, in that case, get in here." I throw the covers from the other side of the bed. Ava bounces in the middle, then settles as Alex lays the tray down.

"Pancakes," both me and Ava squeal.

It's Saturday morning. We always have pancakes on Saturday mornings.

Alex tilts his head, narrowing his eyes at us as he shakes the thoughts away.

"God, I'm in trouble when you get older, kid." He kisses Ava's forehead as he puts a plate of pancakes on her lap. "You are becoming more and more like your mom. Beautiful."

And God help the first person who comes to the door to bring her on a date.

I blush because I haven't learned how to stop doing it yet. He winks at me, and I think I become one with the mattress.

It turns out I never got used to the effect he has on me. I've become more comfortable with it and eased into it because the time we spent apart, I realized: that feeling brings me back to being me—wholly and unapologetically. We fit back together, like two halves of a magnet that had been forced to separate, and even on our bad days, we don't switch sides and repel against each other. We just fit. Sticking by each other and supporting.

After the day in the storm, we promised to take things slow, but we couldn't rewind time, and we fell back into *us*. We tended to the wounds we caused in each other. Though forgiveness was never our issue, we still needed time to heal and mend, both for each other and ourselves. Put Ava in our mix, and the little lady would mend even the most shattered of hearts. And everything just—I don't know—settled. We molded into what we are now.

A family.

We're crazy. Dysfunctional. Fun. Far from normal. And totally and utterly in love with each other.

Our days are filled with school activities, after-school dance classes, homework, some tantrums, and laughter. Sprinkled on top is some mayhem and a lot of mundanities. And I love every minute.

I'm not perfect, but I've held onto the title of *'mother'* with the tightest grip, and I won't let go now. Every day, I learn something I didn't know yesterday. Every day, I struggle to keep up. Every day, I fight with the regrets of all I missed. But every day I am grateful for who I have in my life and the new memories we create—together.

Because together, we are perfectly imperfect.

And when our day is over, and Ava is tucked up in bed, I get to curl up in the arms of the man who still makes my skin tingle with anticipation, and the hairs on the back of my neck stand with awareness when he enters a room. He brought the warmth back into my life and ignited a flame I will forever protect. And with the three of us together, I know I never have to fear the cold again.

He comes to my side of the bed, hands me a cup of coffee, and crouches down so he is looking straight at me.

"May the fourth be with you." He chuckles deeply, and I grin so wide it makes my face hurt.

"And also with you," I manage to say through another wave of laughter.

Happy memories.

He cups one side of my face with his hand. "Happy birthday, baby." He leans in and presses his mouth against mine. It's long, deep, motionless, but it still causes my stomach to flip. We could be frozen in time. And I would happily stay this way, in this room with Ava and Alex.

"Disgusting." Ava sneers, heaving mockingly.

We both roll our eyes before he goes to the other side of the bed, throws his arm around Ava while intertwining his fingers with mine.

"We should go for a stroll on the beach later. What do you think, Ava?" He pins his eyes to her, and she giggles, her eyebrows motioning up and down. She does that when she's being mischievous.

I throw my head back against the headboard. "Don't tell me you're going to throw me in again?" I moan, remembering the last time they had a sneaky plan. It started with Alex throwing me over his shoulder, Ava giggling her delight behind us, and me screaming so much my throat hurt. Before I knew it, Alex and Ava were laughing so hard they had tears running down their face, and I was spluttering on seawater while dripping wet. Sweet heavens, those two were dangerous. But heat rushes to my cheeks when I remember how the evening ended. Alex put Ava to bed and joined me in the shower, making sure the hot water wasn't the only thing to heat my skin.

"Don't worry, Mom. We're only going for a walk."

I swear to God—they winked at each other.

I need to be on high alert with these two.

When we finish our breakfast, we get up to dress. I'm on my own in the bedroom because Ava batted her lashes and convinced Alex to do her hair.

"He does it better, Mom," she whined. "Please, Alex." She popped her bottom lip over her top, and I think I saw him go to mush.

He doesn't do her hair better. He's still brutal at it and gets his fingers tangled in her elastics. He's so scared he'll hurt her, he skims over her hair and hardly gets the knots out of her curls. It usually results in me having to fix it, and Ava screaming bloody murder.

I can hear them whispering in her bedroom down the hall. I can't make out actual sentences, but those two are definitely up to something.

"I can hear you." I poke my head around our bedroom door and bellow down the hall.

Alex grunts and Ava hushes him. "Baby, no you can't. Stop eavesdropping," he shouts back at me.

More giggling.

In the battle of nature versus nurture. Nurture has won. Biologically, Ava is not Alex's daughter. But here's the thing—she is. When she gets mad, her brows furrow in the same deep-set scowl as his. Their eyes are different, but they flare with the same warmth and depth. When they laugh, it comes from the deepest part of their belly, and it makes my heart so full, I always think it will burst. I've learned to never let them get hungry at the same time because it's a war zone in this house. When they love, they love with every cell in their body. And when they look at each other, it's the same look I share with my dad.

No, Alex and Ava don't share DNA, but it doesn't matter because she is his and he is hers, and he would move heaven and earth to make sure she knows it.

"Get your butt moving, kid," he echoes before coming into our bedroom.

And my chest does it again—it fills with so much heat, I might combust. An amused smirk plays at the corner of his mouth, and his eyes roam over me. My entire body sings and my spine stiffens.

"She good?" I ask, trying to distract him while tying my hair back.

But when he looks at me the way he is, nothing will distract him.

"Yep," he clips, and in one stride his lips are pressing along my neck, across my jaw, until his mouth is over mine, but he doesn't kiss me. He lingers there and my breath hitches. His thumb brushes across my lower lip, and my tongue slips out to lick along where he has touched.

"Don't start something you can't finish, Mr. Hale." I look up at him, my voice breathy, and my eyes glossy.

He tugs at my bottom lip. "Don't worry. I'm going to finish. Tonight, I am going to put my tongue over every part of your body."

I can't help my quiet moan and with that, the pressure of his mouth is on me, his tongue tangling in mine and his hands cup my ass.

"Well, this doesn't feel any older." He laughs quietly against my mouth when I slap his arm.

"Quiet, old man. Let's get moving. If you are going to throw me in, I want to get it over with."

***

As the waves lap up at our feet and splash onto our legs, Ava runs ahead, kicking the water as she goes. Alex wraps a strong arm around my shoulder, and I hug his waist as we stroll.

"She's happy." He tilts his head towards Ava, his eyes soft, and a hint of a smile on the corner of his mouth. I know he worries for her, but seeing her so playful, so at ease with her life, and downright joyful, seems to lessen his concerns.

Like me, Alex wonders if he's making his sister proud, and I know he is.

"You're amazing." I rub my palm along his chest before stretching up, kissing him to answer the question he didn't ask.

He puts his fingers under my chin, keeping my face up. "How did I get so lucky, huh?"

I breathe into a sigh, relaxing into him. "We both got lucky, Alex."

Fate.

Coincidence.

Luck.

Whatever you want to call it. It happened. And we are exactly where we are supposed to be.

His eyes bore through to the deepest parts of my soul, and I'm lost again, in bright blue spools with flecks of hot amber as they search every inch of my face.

"Mandy-"

"Mom, look what I found." Ava's roar breaks our gaze, and I leave his side to run to hers. I kneel to see a new shell in her hand and she's brushing off the sand with her fingers.

"Another one for your collection. Good girl." I kiss her cheek before standing again and wiping the sand from my knees.

I turn back to go to Alex and halt mid-stride.

He isn't where I left him.

He's right there in front of me.

Except I'm not looking up at him anymore.

I'm looking down.

I'm looking down at Alex on one knee.

Ava is doing her happy dance and clapping her hands, but I hardly hear it. The crash of the waves rushes through my ears, and then everything is quiet.

I gasp, throwing my hand over my mouth, and feel tears I didn't know were flowing until they wet my hand.

"Have you found a shell too?" I ask. My eyes are so wide, I think they might pop out.

He laughs, but his eyes remain stoic.

He's gazing up at me with all heat, passion, and love.

My eyes dart to a black velvet box in his hand.

Oh shit, this is actually happening.

"Marry me?"

And in the second I take to answer, every moment leading up to this, flashes in front of me.

Nick.

Turning off those machines.

Handing Ava over to someone else.

A gorgeous man with an umbrella.

Finding Ava.

Saying goodbye.

The heartache.

The pain.

But most of all, the love.

"I think I like birthdays now," I cry, and he smiles because he remembers too.

My heart takes over, moving my legs until I run into his arms.

I kiss every part of his face because I can.

Ava's laugh fills the entire beach as she runs into his arms too, and he holds us both.

He laughs through my feverish kisses. "Can I take that as a yes?"

I place my forehead against his.

"Yes."

We love hearing your thoughts.
If you enjoyed Losing Love, please consider leaving a review on
Amazon or Goodreads.

What Will Be Book Series

GET IN TOUCH

You can reach me on my website. I would love to see you there.
www.lauraashleygallagher.com

You will also find me on Facebook, Instagram, and Tiktok.

ACKNOWLEDGMENTS

Losing Love was the story that drew blood, sweat, and a lot of tears from me. But I'm hoping I brought the sensitivity and care to Mandy, Alex, and Ava's story that it deserves. I fell madly in love with these characters, and I hope you have too.

Shane... the most amazing husband. There's not much that I can say that will ever be enough. Thank you for always being there with encouragement when I needed it, and listening without complaining when I'd rant and get frustrated about the number of times I rewrote this book. When I'm freaking out, you always have the right words for me. So, for future freak-outs, I'm sorry. But thank you in advance because I'll know you'll be there. I love you.

To my son, Liam. Thank you for being mommy's best salesman. There isn't a person you don't meet without mentioning that your mom has written a book. Thank you for keeping everyday fun. And by the way, I love you more.

Mam... the woman this book is dedicated to – thank you. I hope people can see in this book, the many amazing relationships between mother and daughter because without ours, I don't think I could have written them with so much love. Since I was a little girl, you have encouraged me to follow my dreams and always told me I could do it, and for that, I will never be able to thank you enough.

Dad... for the same reason as above. Mandy has a relationship with her father that I mirrored on ours. It's filled with love, encouragement, and advice that always makes sense. I love you.

Liz... my sister, my best friend, my biggest supporter, and my partner in crime. You were the first to read this and I can't tell you how nervous I was, but your encouragement always keeps me excited to keep writing. You have the biggest heart of anyone I know. Please don't get sick of my writing because I have too many story ideas and I need your mind (you know what I mean).

My amazing beta readers: Caryn Walsh, Allison Harraden, Danielle Hennessy, Emily Scallan, Bernadette Hayes, Ashley L. Castillo, and Lisa Powell. Thank you for your invaluable advice, feedback, and support. I am eternally grateful to each one of you.

Thank you to the amazing Booktok community. I have received so much advice and gained amazing friends. I never thought when I signed up to Tiktok that it would become so much more than just marketing.

To my incredible ARC team, thank you for giving this book a chance. You are all amazing. I hope you enjoyed Losing Love.

And to my wonderful readers, I hope you fall in love with these characters as I have. None of this would be possible without you. It means everything.